D1453095

THE
SLOT

The Slot

John

Clagett

AN AUTHORS GUILD BACKINPRINT.COM EDITION

The Slot

All Rights Reserved © 1958, 2000 by John Clagett

AN AUTHORS GUILD BACKINPRINT.COM EDITION

Published by iUniverse.com, Inc.

For information address:
iUniverse.com, Inc.
620 North 48th Street, Suite 201
Lincoln, NE 68504-3467
www.iuniverse.com

Originally published by Crown Publishers, Inc.

ISBN: 0-595-00395-8

Printed in the United States of America

For all the men who rode the boats; and especially for the men of the PT 111; and most especially for those of her crew who will remain forever young.

Masters, there is many a man to cry "War, War!" who yet knows but little the meaning of it. War, in the beginning, has so high an entrance, and so wide, that every man may enter when he pleases, and may find war easily. But Truly, what the end of war shall be is not so easy to know.

—GEOFFREY CHAUCER

A lane of clear water began between Cape Esperance, on Guadalcanal, and Savo Island. It ran to the northwest, bordered by more islands: the Russells, New Georgia, where a Japanese base was building, Choiseul, and at the end, three hundred miles from Guadalcanal, Shortland Island. A strong enemy base lay on Shortland; just beyond was Bougainville. All the strength of the Japanese Southern Pacific Fleet could be funneled down this lane.

You could say it was a bowling alley, hemmed in by islands, with American forces the pins.

You could say it was the rails down which ran the Tokyo Express to supply the Japanese troops on Guadalcanal.

Or, you could just say it was The Slot. Which says it all.

In November of 1942 the weight of the Pacific war rested on Guadalcanal. We had taken the part of the island that held Henderson Field; now we had to keep it.

The waters around Guadalcanal were too hot for big naval vessels to remain there. Destroyers, cruisers—even battleships —of both sides came to the island during times of crisis and fought it out in the darkness of Ironbottomed Bay. But when the major battles were over, the big ships went away. The PTs stayed there all the time.

In the intervals between battles, the U.S. planes from Henderson Field kept the enemy away during daylight; but when darkness crept down the sides of Guadalcanal's mountains, making the flashes of mortar bursts look from the sea like white fireworks, Japanese destroyer forces prowled down The Slot, carrying soldiers, guns, ammunition, and food, to reinforce their positions on Guadalcanal. Night after night they came; night after night the PTs went out to stop them.

The PTs were the only force that could try to stop them. The PTs were all we had.

1

UNDER THE BLUE and white sky of the May morning, Brooklyn Navy Yard was ugly as a steel mill. Lieutenant (jg) Charles Noble walked along track-scarred roads, through cinder areas and around drydocks, to the accompaniment of the near and far hammering of rivet guns. The air smelled of hot steel and smoke. Pier H was a long way from the gate. The chatter of the rivet guns faded behind Noble, and water glinted ahead, with the Manhattan skyline visible in the distance; now he heard a many-voiced roaring which reminded him of the *Lexington's* flight deck with planes warming up. He walked around a shack and found himself at the head of a slip; a short distance down one of the 400-foot piers that bordered it a dingy concrete barge with a high superstructure was tied up. Outboard of this barge were six motor torpedo boats.

A slight breeze carried metallic, high-octane exhaust to Noble, but he barely noticed it as he studied the boats. Foreshortened, with their sterns toward him, they seemed broad and squat with gear-cluttered decks. Disappointment touched Noble's elation; he shrugged and walked toward the barge until its high sides deadened the direct motor roar. He walked across the gangplank and into the cavernous interior of the concrete barge, where sailors were busy over torpedoes, engines, toolboxes and mess tables: a confused combination of classroom and machine shop all permeated with the smell of cooking. As Noble looked about him, a man, bare to his greasy dungaree pants and wearing an oil-soaked CPO cap, stepped off the inboard PT.

"Oh, Chief," Noble said, lifting a hand.

"Aye, sir?"

"Where can I find the squadron commander's office?"

"Up yonder." The chief flicked a thumb toward the Yard. "His office is up at Building 109. You a new squadron officer, Lieutenant?" His eyes flicked briefly to the heavy Academy ring on Noble's left hand.

"That's right. Noble's my name."

The chief offered his hand and Noble took it, glad of his one and a half stripes. CPOs rarely shook hands with an ensign.

"I'm McLeod, Mister Noble, chief motor mac. Welcome aboard. I got to get out of sight. Old man'll be coming down any minute, and he'd have my ass if he saw me out of uniform like this. He's a hard man, Lieutenant. You better hurry if you want to see him; the boats will be going out soon."

McLeod's grizzled chest vanished and Noble walked across the barge for a better look at the boats. From this angle the PTs were beautiful, like the new destroyers, which seemed to move forward even when sitting still. The PTs were about eighty feet long and were painted Navy grey. Noble's eyes swept over the canopy and forward turret to the cockpit, aft of which was a long, low deck house and another turret, this one on the port side. Two torpedo tubes were located on each side, and the decks were spaced with hatches, ventilators, and guns. The boats were low in the water; they looked ready to fly.

"Hey, Charlie!" somebody shouted from a cockpit. Noble saw a hand waving from the outer boat. He stared and with a rush of gladness recognized Pat Bunch, his roommate at the Naval Academy. Right then he knew that this was going to be good duty. He started across the boats to his friend, then

3

remembered McLeod's warning. Better report first. He waved and turned away toward the building the chief had indicated.

He climbed the wooden stairs of the yard building and came out on a barn-like upper deck. A door marked MTB RONS led into an office in which a yeoman pounded a typewriter, while another fussed with a Silex. Two officers sat at a desk; the one behind it glanced at Noble through horn-rimmed spectacles. He had a crew haircut, black with a little frost, and his eyes behind the glasses looked like grey marbles.

"Well?"

"Lieutenant (jg) Noble reporting for duty, sir."

"Well, made it, did you? Fine, fine. This is Lieutenant Wakefield, commanding officer of a squadron down at Norfolk. Ollie, Noble here is one of our new officers."

"Hi," Wakefield, a stocky, brown-faced officer, said, as he held out his hand. "I remember you. I dusted your tail with a broom once."

"Good old Academy," said the squadron commander, Lieutenant Morton Daggs according to the name plate on his desk. "I got many happy memories of the place—they damned near killed me." He laughed thunderously as Noble looked again at the plate. USNR all right. "Sit down, Noble," Daggs went on. "I'll be through with Ollie here in a minute."

"I'm just going." Wakefield stood up. "Betty's waiting at the hotel for a last spree in New York."

"Ollie's bunch is shoving off," Daggs said as they shook hands. "Christ! I wish it was us. I'm hungry to get a whack at the yellow bastards. I'm gonna bring back some ears. Right, Ollie?"

"I'll be happy to keep my own, Mort. See you in Tokyo. Good luck to you, Charlie."

"Let's go in the other office," Daggs said, standing up. His six feet put him three inches above Noble. "I'll fill you in."

The next room was so small that the one desk and few chairs crowded it. Daggs sat down.

"Haul up a chair, Charlie," he boomed. "Well, now. I haven't

4

much to say except that this outfit here has only one job, and that's to kill Japs. Understand?"

"Yes, sir."

"That's the boy. By God, Charlie, I like the cut of your jib. Just between you and me, most of these reserves we got ain't worth the powder to blow 'em to hell, as we say down in Texas. Nothin' like the old Academy to make a man. That right?"

"Yes, sir." Noble sounded the junior officer's chant, but he wondered about that USNR on Daggs' desk. Moreover, he himself had served with some mighty good reserve officers.

"I didn't quite make it all the way," Daggs went on. "I got tired of taking it, and I quit. Wangled me a reserve commission, though, and here I am. A businessman, by God, *and* a naval officer. Best combination in the world, I'll tell you."

"Guess you're right, sir."

"Hope to tell you I'm right. Look: you Regulars have been riding soft and easy on Uncle Sam, been doing it for years. Ah, you're not just sitting around, I know that, but you haven't had the cutthroat competition a man runs into in business. I been in the oil field supply game down in Texas, and if any Jap is meaner than old Leatherhead Atwood—you've heard of L. H. Atwood, big Texas oil man—I'll eat him. The Jap, not Leatherhead. Business, that's where you learn to step in and hit first. Why, do you think a good businessman would have let the goddamn Japs crap on us at Pearl Harbor? Hell, no. By God, a businessman learns to protect his investment. Why, if old Leatherhead had been running Pearl Harbor, he'd have caught the Japs before they were even out of home port."

"I hadn't thought about it that way." Noble wondered how long this would go on. Daggs removed his glasses, wiped them and his face with a handkerchief, and smiled at his new officer.

"Of course not. You're a Regular. You ain't been out in the hard world, son. Say, you call me Mort, eh, Charlie?"

"Why, sure, Mort. Thanks."

"I can judge a man quick. Down Texas way you got to be

5

able to size up a stranger before a cat can dig the necessary hole." He roared with laughter, his eyes nearly hidden by bunched-up cheeks, his small mouth wide open. Noble wondered what Daggs' Academy nickname had been; Bullethead would have been a likely one.

The squadron commander stopped laughing and looked stern. "Now, look here," he said. "There's one thing about me; when I holler froggy, everybody jumps! I'm an easy man to get along with, anybody'll tell you that, but by God I demand obedience and speed, and carrying out orders to the last goddamn syllable!" He pounded the desk, and Noble thought that the roaring could be heard down at the dock. "Got it? All right, by God. I just hope we'll be in business soon, killing them stinking Japs. And I just pray and hope that we'll get sent to a good hot spot. Son, there ain't but three things in the world worthwhile: money, fighting, and a woman. You'll see. And this outfit is gonna do plenty of fighting, plenty of killing, and, if the boys are like me, plenty of loving. Right?"

"Sure." Noble knew from his own experience that men who'd been shot at didn't talk this way.

"Guess that's it," Daggs said, looking at his watch. "I'll be shoving off with the boats now; we'll be late getting back—that will make lunch late. Let's see—you come back up at fifteen hundred and we'll talk. Glad to have you aboard. Just remember what I said, and you and me'll get along all right."

The typewriter was still clacking in the outer office, and a chief yeoman in neat blues was looking over a stack of service records. He stood up when Noble entered, a long, lean man whose face had the sorrowful, meditative look of a hound dog. The new officer introduced himself, and they shook hands.

"Chief Yeoman Manson," the chief said. "If you got your orders, I can take care of them now."

"Thanks. Here they are."

"How are your ear drums, Mister Noble?" Manson asked.

"Bruised." Their eyes met and Manson almost smiled. "By

the way, how long was the squadron commander at the Academy?"

Manson rubbed his long nose and a twinkle showed deep in his mournful eyes.

"Entered in July, 1932, and left in November, 1932."

"That was quick."

"Yes, sir."

"So was his Texas residence," drawled the yeoman at the typewriter. "Two years; then he went back to where he came from—Iowa."

2

WHEN THE BOATS got back from the morning run, Charlie Noble and Pat Bunch took up their old relationship as if the two years since they had seen each other had never been. Having Pat in the same outfit gave Noble a warm feeling. At lunch, which was eaten at an ordinary crew's mess table and served by mess cooks grumbling at the lateness of the hour, Noble met a dozen officers. Mighty young-looking in general, they were just names to him now, but he knew that would change quickly enough. The lunch itself drove such thoughts from his mind with shrimp cocktail, steak, three vegetables, salad, hot rolls, apple pie, cheese, milk and coffee.

"Love that cook," Pat said with his mouth full.

"Amen, brother," agreed a tall officer named Jim Print.

Noble looked at Pat over his coffee cup. He was the same Pat Bunch, tall and darkly tanned, with a few lines in his face; he was more mature perhaps, but his constant gaiety was still about him. Noble knew that this gaiety only increased as circumstances worsened. It was this faculty that made life around him so pleasant.

"Say, Patsy boy," Noble said, putting down his cup. "I've got twenty minutes before I report to the commander. How about showing me over your boat?"

"Come along, C. Noble, you damned old galley smokepipe."

Noble followed Pat from the barge to his boat, the Ninety-One, which was outside in the nest. They had to pass over two others, and the boats moved beneath them, so light that they responded even to the shifting weight of two men. As Bunch stepped aboard the Ninety-One, a seaman built like a wrestler and naked to the waist stood up from behind a torpedo tube, wrench in hand.

"Hi, Skipper," he drawled, a flashing grin making his hard face pleasant.

"Judas Priest, Raven!" Bunch exclaimed. "You know the old man said to wear shirts when alongside a Navy Yard dock. Are you trying to get my tail in a sling?"

"No, sir, Skipper, I ain't. I figured the commander couldn't see me working on that crank gear, and the sun feels mighty good."

"Raven, he can see around corners and through six inches of concrete, you know that. Put on your shirt, and if I catch you without it again I'll paint you dungaree-blue from the belly button up in self defense."

"Okay," said Raven, grinning affectionately at Bunch. He picked up his shirt. "Anything *you* say, Skipper."

"Different from the fleet," Noble said as they walked forward.

"Damn right. I really like this, just because of the way you can treat the men. You know how it is on the carriers. An officer and an enlisted man can like each other, but there's always a hell of a wall between them. When you're on a ship with about three thousand men I guess it's necessary, but in these boats that wall is gone. About a third, maybe half of our men are old Navy; they're tin-can men, cream of the fleet. They won't take advantage of you. You go to bat for them, and they'd die before they'd let you down. I mean it. And the old hands keep the new ones in line. All nine of my men are friends of mine. Hell, we like being together on this little old peanut shell."

9

"Looks like good duty, pal."

"The best."

They went into the cockpit—armored with a sheet of three-sixteenths-inch steel, enough to turn a twenty-five caliber rifle bullet—by squeezing forward through a narrow, shielded opening until they were standing in the eight- by six-foot space that was the control station of the PT. The wheel was to the left with three throttles beside it, each marked for ahead, neutral, and reverse. In addition to the three tachometers, one for each engine, Noble identified three manifold pressure gauges. A compass, a buzzer button, and, on the starboard, four torpedo firing keys and a hand microphone completed the simple control equipment.

"We carry three thousand gallons of hundred-octane gasoline, don't we, Pat?"

"That's right."

"Self-sealing tanks?"

"What do you think this is? Ya wanna live forever?"

"Hell, yes. I'd rather have that armor plate between the seat of my pants and the gas tanks."

"I'll refer your request to Buships."

Noble followed Pat through the narrow hatch that led from the cockpit into the charthouse, two steps down. This was about ten by twelve feet, with a big chart table and four rectangular ports for visibility forward and to either side. A radio set was mounted to the left of the hatchway, with a blue-leather cushioned chair in front of it.

"Hey, Cooky!" Bunch yelled. "Two cups of joe; we got a distinguished guest."

"Christ, Cap, ain't you just et?" came an aggrieved voice from below.

"Who the hell's captain of this here United States warship? Two cups, Cooky."

"Okay, Cap. Two cups joe."

Bunch led the way down a vertical ladder to a narrow passageway. To the right was a complete electric galley, with a big refrigerator. Just aft of the galley was a booth with table and blue leather-cushioned benches.

"Wardroom," Pat said. "I only eat there when I'm mad at these apes. At least here there's always a girl's leg to pinch."

"As if you hadn't had girls there." The cook put the coffee on the wardroom table. "Lieutenant, the Cap here near drives us nuts sometimes, the good-lookin' babes he brings aboard. 'Show her the boat,' he says. Huh. Seems like mostly he shows 'em the captain's room." He grinned at Bunch with the same affection and pride that Raven had shown.

"I quit!" Pat said. "I've got the lowest-minded, most suspicious bunch of bums on this boat I ever saw." He pointed forward. "There's the crew's quarters." Noble looked into a large, well-lighted, blue and white compartment which had plenty of room for nine bunks, a mess table, and nine lockers. "Crew's head's up in the forepeak." Bunch led the way aft to the crew's dayroom, a large cheerful place with a blue-cushioned transom against either bulkhead, ports on each side, and a ladder leading up to an overhead hatchway. Bunch undogged an oval hatch in the after bulkhead and Noble looked through into the engine room. Three huge, shining engines stood among a bewildering network of instruments, gear shifts, gauges, piping, and generators. Everything, even the white paint, was spotless, and the metal shone like silver.

"Man!" Noble said, looking over the three great engines.

"Aren't they beautiful?" Pat exclaimed. "Thirteen hundred and fifty horses in each one of them."

"That's a lot of power. Your boys keep the place well, too. Where are the officers' quarters?"

"Typical. I show you the best engine room in the squadron and all you wanna know is where you sack out. Okay."

They went forward again and Pat opened a door just opposite the wardroom.

"Well, damn me!" Noble exclaimed. "I'm a yachtsman at last."

The little room was white-walled and carpeted in blue. The

wide bunk was covered with blue leather, and, in addition, there was a small mahogany desk with a cushioned chair, a bureau, and a wardrobe. The connecting washroom led to the exec's room, which was just like Pat's except for its slightly smaller size.

"That's the quick tour, buddy," Bunch said proudly. "Isn't she a honey? I wouldn't swap her for the *Saratoga*."

"I don't blame you. Say," he said, looking at his watch, "I'm late! Be seeing you. And thanks."

Daggs was at his desk in the main office when Noble entered, panting after his hurried dash from the boats. The squadron commander looked up from some papers.

"Goddammit, Charlie, I said fifteen hundred. You bear a tit when I holler."

"Yes, sir." Why the devil did he always have to talk so loud?

"See you don't forget it. Well, now. You're senior to Bunch, aren't you?"

"Yes, sir. About eleven numbers."

"Okay, then you're squadron executive officer; you'll be senior watch officer too. Also you're gunnery and torpedo officer, and commander, Division Three. Your boat, the Ninety-Seven, will be delivered tomorrow."

"Yes, *sir!*"

"Now, one thing more, Charlie," Daggs went on more affably. "My wife and sister are arriving at sixteen hundred on the train from Washington, Penn Station. I got business here and I want you to meet them. How about it?"

"Why, sure, glad to."

"Fine. Take the station wagon outside. I've got rooms at the St. George. Okay? Then shove off, son. You haven't got too much time."

Noble saluted and walked down the stairs to a tan Plymouth station wagon with a sailor in the driver's seat. To the devil with how Daggs talked; Noble was a division commander, the squadron exec, and head of a department; best of all, his own

12

boat would be delivered the next day. His own command; small, but who cared?

Noble enjoyed the pull through the yard. The guard saluted as they drove out onto Sand Street, odorous and dingy with its uniform shops, junk shops, small restaurants, and clanging streetcars clashing like aimless beetles. Salvation Army Cafeteria—"Eat as the Lord's guest and pay what you can." Like all men on earth, he thought—the Lord's guests in a dwelling place unimaginably perfect, in which man took and ate and lived, paying what he could. Well, man had eaten, right enough; maybe this war was the check. How now, brown C. Noble, aren't you getting philosophical.

"I'll park in the government spaces in front of the Post Office," the driver said, when they pulled up before the grimy pillars at Pennsylvania Station.

"Good. If I notice a slight smell of beer when I get back I won't sniff too hard."

"Aye, aye. You're picking up PT ways fast, Mister Noble."

Jostled by hurrying crowds, he went through the entrance, down wide steps, into the vast, echoing concourse and stopped at last before a closed gateway labeled, "Washington Express, Due to arrive 4 P. M.: 20 minutes late." Twenty minutes. Not enough time for a drink or a look at Thirty-Fourth Street.

"Goddamn Pennsy," a soldier grumbled. "I only got until eight in the morning, and my girl's train is late."

"You'll be wore out long before eight," his companion offered.

A girl's vibrant voice sounded: "He's tall, Mom, and black-haired, and he's got those chevrons on his sleeve. Oh, I hope you like him, Mom, I know you will!"

"Hmph. Looks as if I'll have to like him."

The gate was opening at last. People came hurrying out carrying two-suiters and duffle bags. Excitement mounted among those waiting. Daggs had said to Noble with a grin, "When you see a blonde who makes you whistle, that'll be Delilah. Just pick the prettiest girl who gets off the train. The

13

old lady'll be with her." Already Noble had seen two or three whistle-worthy girls, but none were blondes and . . .

"Goddlemighty!" Noble stared at the purple eyes, the golden hair under a tiny hat, short skirt, silken legs, the smart black suit, and the leopard coat. She was carrying a dressing case and a bag. The woman with her must be the commander's wife, Noble thought. Tough duty, boy.

"Miss Daggs?" he said courteously to the blonde, saluting like an RAF movie hero.

"Why, yes," she said, then smiled at him approvingly. "Don't tell me that Mort . . . "

"Lieutenant Daggs was detained on duty, ma'am. He gave me the pleasure of taking care of you—and Mrs. Daggs." He made himself turn away from Delilah and smile at her companion.

"Mrs. Daggs?" he said, saluting again but feeling silly this time. "I'm Lieutenant Noble. Welcome to New York, ma'am."

Looking surprisingly young to be Daggs' wife, she stood by Delilah with an eager, searching expression. "The old lady," Daggs had said with something like a sneer. She wore flat heels, and her eyes were four inches below Noble's. Seeming thin to him at first, her face on second look took on beauty of lips, eyes, and a faint concavity of cheeks. Except for a little lipstick she wore no makeup, which made her seem pale in the cavernous light, and her hazel-grey eyes very large. She wore a grey-blue suit that minimized rather than accentuated the curves of her body. Noble approved of her, and at the same same time sympathized with her for having to stand beside Delilah, who could outshine any woman. Mrs. Daggs offered her hand; Noble took it, but deserted it quickly for Delilah's soft fingers.

"This is uncommonly nice of you," Mrs. Daggs said pleasantly, enunciating clearly and well. She rounded o's and e's in a manner that reminded Noble of Charleston, South Carolina. "I hope we haven't caused too much trouble. Is the hotel near?"

14

"Not very, but I have a station wagon waiting. Here, let me take these things."

Mrs. Daggs gave Noble her suitcase gratefully; Delilah added hers to his load, but retained the dressing case.

"I won't let this out of my sight," she smiled. "I've got plans for New York."

In the station wagon, Noble felt an excitement whenever he touched Delilah. Mrs. Daggs said little, but her lips were parted slightly as she watched crowds, buildings, the bridge, and the beginnings of Brooklyn. Noble saw the driver's face in the rear-view mirror; he was studying Delilah with hopeless hunger. He caught the lieutenant's eye and grinned wryly, shaking his head. Noble knew just how he felt.

Entering the St. George hotel, Noble guided the women across the immense lobby to the desk, where he deposited the suitcases and unwillingly said good-by.

"Why, you're not leaving us!" said Delilah. "Come on up and have a drink."

"Oh, Di!" Mrs. Daggs stopped, bit her lip, and smiled at the lieutenant apologetically. "Of course, Mister Noble," and he wondered if his disappointment had shown that plainly. "A drink is small payment for your kindness. Di is right. I insist."

"But you must be tired."

"Nothing like a drink for that tired feeling," Delilah said. She smiled at Noble.

He went with them into the elevator, which was haunted by the hotel smell of plush carpets and old cigars. A bellboy showed them into one of two adjoining rooms, and Mrs. Daggs tipped him so promptly that Noble hadn't even gotten his hand into his pocket.

Noble reached for the phone but Di beat him to that too. She grinned and ordered highballs. Noble could have sworn that a waiter was at the door before he could turn around. Mrs. Daggs stood at the window, which framed a view of the bridge, the river, and the jagged skyline of Manhattan.

"It makes one feel so Lilliputian," she murmured. "It's hardly fair; I'm small enough already. Doesn't it make you feel small, Mister Noble?"

"Yes. This town gives me an ant complex, as if something enormous were going to squash me at any moment."

Delilah stretched, straining her blouse. "I don't feel like an ant," she said. "More like a water-filled balloon. I gotta go."

She went into the adjoining room. Mrs. Daggs smiled, but she seemed a little confused.

"Delilah is very direct, Mister Noble. Honest, perhaps; at any rate it doesn't seem offensive in her."

"It certainly doesn't," Noble agreed warmly. Offensive? Delilah? Nothing about her could be offensive to him.

Delilah returned, picked up one of the drinks, and seated herself on Mrs. Daggs' chair arm. Noble pulled up another chair and for a moment they gazed out on the view, not speaking. Noble took advantage of the women's concentration to study Delilah.

The thigh and hip made a splendid sweep under the black material, and the breasts were a sharp silhouette; her face had high, though not prominent, cheekbones, a small, delicate nose, and sensuously bowed lips. Her brows were of dark bronze, and her skin creamy white. She shook her head, bending it back, baring the white throat.

"What's the matter, Lieutenant Noble . . . No; I'm going to call you Charlie."

"Please do."

"Okay. What's the matter, Charlie?"

"Why, nothing. Nothing at all. Except maybe . . . May I call you Delilah?"

"Delilah! Makes me think of barber shops. Make it Di. That's Kathleen over there. Right, Kathleen? She likes you, Charlie. I can tell."

"Really, Di, you might let us make our own rapprochement. But of course it is all right . . . Charles. After all, you are our first friend in New York, and one of Morton's shipmates."

"Thank you." Di, for delight. Noble liked that better than

Delilah. But unlike Delilah, she would never need to clip a man's hair to weaken him. She had Noble feeling like jelly all over.

He sat with them a few minutes longer, but Daggs didn't arrive. Kathleen glanced repeatedly at the door and bit her lips, while her part in the conversation diminished. Six o'clock. They'd want to bathe and dress before dinner.

"I must be going," he said finally. "I apologize for hanging around, but it has been such a pleasure."

"You must come up again," Kathleen answered, smiling at him in a way that made him think she really meant what she said. "I imagine we'll be seeing a good deal of you; I want to meet and get to know all of Morton's friends."

"I'll look forward to it."

"So will I," Delilah said. "I don't know a soul here but you. Don't fail me, Charlie."

Fail her? Noble thought fast. Tonight they were tired; tomorrow night Daggs would no doubt take them out on the town. He could weasel in on that, but somehow he didn't want to have Daggs present on his first date with Delilah.

"Would you have dinner with me the day after tomorrow, Di?"

"I'd love to. Can we go to a night club? Wonderful! Even if I did have to fish for the invitation."

"Di! You're hopeless," said Mrs. Daggs.

"It didn't take much fishing," Noble said, smiling at Delilah. Not with that bait, he added silently.

17

3

NOBLE WAS WATCHING a new and glossy PT coming into the slip, with the Elco pennant flying from her mast. He rubbed his palms against his khaki pants, for this was his boat. Look out, you ape! Do you want to knock a hole in her? Easy! Ah, made it. The engines shut off as the lines were secured. Noble stood looking at the Disney mosquito and torpedo emblem and at the 97 painted in white on the canopy. He shook hands with the wizened man in the yachting cap, after being introduced by Daggs as the new boat's commanding officer, and signed a receipt. Someone pulled down the Elco pennant, and Noble planted the short-staffed American ensign in the socket on the fantail.

"Congratulations, Charlie, she's all yours," Daggs boomed. "Cap'n, how about a drink up at the club?"

"Thanks, but I've got to get back. Come on, you men."

Charles Noble hardly saw them climb into the waiting motor cruiser and pull away, for he was looking over his boat and feeling her move slightly in the cruiser's wake. He went into the steel box of the cockpit and touched the wheel. It was solid and polished, swinging readily to his hand, the nerve-ending controlling, at his will, a man-made and powerful extension of his body.

"Hi, Skipper. Permission to come aboard?"

At Noble's nod, Jim Print came into the cockpit, his eyes shining. "Here come the men," Print added.

"Good." Noble looked at Print, his executive officer; up to now they had met only casually. One hell of a lot was going to depend on the quality of this brown-faced, brown-haired, wiry boy from Split Rock, Wyoming.

"Boy, she's pretty!" Print said. "I found out what a PT was like when I saw one in a newsreel at Landers, back in Wyoming, and right then I decided that was how I was going to fight the war. Now I've got one roped and tied, ready for the old Split T brand."

"Split T?"

"My Dad's brand. Split T Ranch, best spread in Wyoming." Jim grinned. "Jeff Mason, he's the foreman, told me that it stood for Split Tail Ranch, and Dad fired him for a week; then on my eighteenth birthday Dad gave me my first drink of whiskey—first one he knew about anyway—and told me Jeff was right."

"Sounds like my kind of ranch."

"You come visit it someday, Skipper. My mother died when I was two years old, and it has sort of been a man's place. During some hard years Dad and Jeff did a good deal of duding, and I guess some of those eastern girls . . . That was when Dad changed the brand to a Split T."

Looking beyond his exec, Noble saw a group of seamen coming out across the other boats.

"All right, men," he called. "Come aboard."

The dangareed sailors stepped onto the Ninety-Seven with their sea bags, and Noble carefully watched the way each man looked about him as he did so. One face, with dark hair and skin, was half sneering. Another, belonging to a tall and wiry sailor, was as expressionless as an Indianhead nickel. Nobel watched mature faces that were stamped with dependability; young and cocky faces; and two boys' faces, smooth and unlined, with excitement hardly contained under make-believe sailors' swagger. He looked down at his list as the last man came aboard. Sterns, torpedoman, first class, was the senior right-arm rate.

"Sterns!"

"Sterns here, sir."

That he was an old Navy man was as plain from his voice and manner as it was from his record. He was big, with light blue eyes, sandy hair, and an ugly, stubborn face. He needed a shave; he probably always needed a shave, Noble thought; and solid assurance was written all over him.

"You're senior petty officer," Noble said crisply. "Take charge. Lay the men below and drop the gear, then come up and muster on the foredeck."

"Aye, aye, sir. Down below, men."

The half-sneer Noble had seen had widened now, and he caught the dark man's eyes on his class ring. The man following was out of place, with his dark hair, grey at the temples, and his look of poise and breeding. Noble saw that his hands were well-kept and immaculate.

"They're a good bunch," Print said. "I've been going through their records. Did you know that Everard, the radioman, has a Ph.D.?"

"A Ph.D.?"

"Take a look. Here's his service record."

"What the devil is he doing here?"

"That's beyond me. We've got four old Navy men, though, all of them off destroyers."

That's good, Noble thought. That's fine. He rubbed the smooth plywood of the instrument panel and touched the wheel. He stood on the step to look fore and aft along the boat's glistening length. He wondered why a weapon was nearly always beautiful; maybe it was because men were completely functional in designing them. He breathed deeply. The PT had been his for twenty minutes already, and he hadn't even been below yet; but that would have to wait, for the crew was coming back topside. Noble went out onto the foredeck as the men formed two rough ranks. Sterns took the muster list.

"Warder."

"Hyo."

Noble studied Warder, motor machinist's mate, first class. He was forty or so, stocky and sun-bronzed, with brown-grey hair and grey eyes. Noble liked his slow smile. He noted that Warder had the blunt, expressive hands of the practicing mechanic, and he was sure he was fortunate in his chief engineer.

"Welton."

"Yere."

Radleigh Welton, ship's cook, first class. A little wrinkled, sound apple of a man, forty-one by the record. He had faded blue eyes and evidently false teeth. Noble liked him.

"Everard."

"Here, sir."

The doctor of philosophy had a sensitive, intelligent face; he was of medium height, slenderly built, and yet strong and wiry-looking. Squash and tennis, no doubt, Noble thought; probably some skiing, and plenty of swimming. Got his degree from Yale University according to the record. Navy going swank. Noble was impressed by Everard. What's the man doing as a radioman, second class, on a motor torpedo boat? he wondered.

"Radelewski."

The sneer was pronounced, and Noble could read the man's mind. He was probably thinking: The goddamn trade school monkey, holding quarters like this was a lousy battleship. The skipper looked down at the service record. Radelewski came from New York City and had been a garage mechanic. This was his first duty. Five ten, about; weighing maybe one sixty. A tough guy, but probably a good practical mechanic.

"Yeah," Radelewski answered at last. Sterns looked at him steadily, and Noble saw a muscle in the torpedoman's cheek move, then relax.

"Hill."

21

"Heeyah."

Hill, quartermaster, second class, was a solid man, ruddy-cheeked and light-haired; six feet tall, with a good weight for his inches. Vermont, first hitch, some previous PT experience. Good.

"Johnson."

"Heah."

That sounded familiar. Record? Well, what do you know—Greenville, Kentucky. Mean old boys they grew up there in Greenville, and Johnson looked the part. He was long and lean, with the dirt farmer's big hands and deceiving stringiness. Plenty of trouble in his record. Busted twice—insolence and insubordination, drunkenness and AOL. Typical Greenville boy. He had long arms, a skinny neck, and a big Adam's apple; probably strong as a mule. Gunner's mate, and no doubt a good one. Himself a Kentuckian, Noble recognized the type—Daniel Boone, the long hunters—out of place in the twentieth century. Hard, cantankerous, proud, but well worth winning over.

"Floyd."

"Here—sir."

One of the kids. Shaved once a week, maybe. Smooth, untroubled face, and one that by rights should stay that way for years yet. Damn the war anyway, Noble thought. Floyd was a good-looking boy, well-built, with good, steady brown eyes. He came from North Haven, Connecticut. Noble resolved to try to take good care of the two kids.

"Benton."

"Yes, sir."

The other youngster was fresh-faced and big-eyed, with a tough façade. He looked scared but excited, and he seemed to be a nice, big boy. Noble knew that these kids often turned out to be mighty good sailors.

"All present or accounted for, sir," Sterns said, wheeling to deliver his salute.

"Very well." Noble faced the crew, looking into a question they felt, and feeling his own question keenly. Was he going to be a bastard? That was theirs. Was he going to have to be a bastard? That was his. They were waiting for him to say something.

"Men," Noble began, looking full into Radelewski's sneer. "We're all in the same boat. We'll make it a good one. When you're dismissed, go below and stow your gear, then get the inventory lists and go over all of your departmental equipment. Glad to have you with me. All right, Sterns. Dismiss them."

The two lines dissolved as the men started down to their sea bags and lockers. Noble saw Floyd and Benton looking at him cautiously, and grinned at them, glad that he was in PTs where he could be friends with his men.

"I'm going below and open the log," he told Jim, patting the grey-green book.

"First entry, MTB Ninety-Seven," Print said. "It must be quite a feeling."

The captain's quarters smelled wonderfully new and exciting, tinged with oiled metal, leather, fabric, paint, but it seemed empty in spite of the furniture. Never mind, it would soon be home. Even traveling in a pair of suitcases you carried bits of yourself: a picture or two, perhaps an ash tray, old pipes, shaving gear—and thoughts. These things would change the feel of the room. The chair was comfortable. Noble opened the book and started to write: "21 May, 1942. USS PT Ninety-Seven accepted and in service. Lt. (jg) Charles Noble, USN, Commanding Officer. Aboard as Executive Officer and crew are . . ."

Finished with the log entry, Noble was sitting relaxed, soaking in the smell and feel of his boat, when a knock sounded at the door.

"Sir, Mister Daggs would like to see you in the office. Right away, sir," the office messenger said.

"Okay. Thanks."

As he walked to the office, Noble wondered what the old boy wanted now. Another sister, maybe. He grinned at this thought. One's plenty, bud.

"Good morning, sir."

"Oh, yeah, Charlie. Say, I want to thank you for taking care of the little woman and Di yesterday. You made quite a hit there."

"That was a pleasure, Mort. Just call on me any time at all."

"I can see that Di's already got your tongue hanging out, eh, Charlie? You're not the only one. She's driven more men crazy than . . . She's so damned beautiful; ain't she a peach, a real, honest-to-God peach? But I tell you, she's a good girl." Daggs turned solemn. "She's friendly, and easy in her talk, but she's saving herself for a man who can give her all the things a woman wants, and who's a real man too. It's not as common a combination as you might think."

"No," Noble said shortly. Was he being warned off, or just prepared against eventual disappointment? He hoped he was a man, but as for the other requirement, well, he was going to sleep on his boat because he couldn't afford hotel life ashore.

"Don't take me wrong, son; I'll be mighty proud to have you show Di the town. She likes you, Charlie, same as I do."

"Thanks, Mort."

"Now, right after lunch the first division is going down into the lower bay and try making a smoke screen. You fill your smoke generator; better get one of the other boat captains to ride with you this first time, and you come along. Take the Ninety-One's place. Okay?"

"You bet! I'll get at it right away, and . . . "

"Now, look, son, we're off personal matters now. I like being friendly, but when I give an order I expect a Navy answer, not some half-assed thing like 'you bet.' 'You bet,' for God's sake."

"Aye, aye, sir."

"That's better. I'll see you, son."

Other boats were starting their motors, and Noble fidgeted nervously behind the wheel of the Ninety-Seven. He looked sideways at Pat standing in a cockpit corner, grinning like the Cheshire cat. Well, how about it? Noble thought. He checked the throttles to see that they were in neutral and looked around at his expectant crew.

"Okay, Warder," he said. "Wind 'em up."

"Aye, aye, sir." Warder went aft eagerly with Radelewski and Floyd. Noble kicked over the low steering platform under the wheel and stepped up on it.

"Johnson, lift number two."

Johnson lifted the amidships line, flaking it down on the deck in the proper flat coil.

"Hill, keep an eye on the chart and don't let me get lost. Somebody's got to know where the hell we're going."

"Aye, aye, sir." Noble liked his quartermaster's alert look and quiet smile.

"Benton, you'll handle the stern line. Sterns, take the bow line. Welton, stand by with a fender forward. I'm going to twist her."

Benton tore aft as if he thought the line would get away from him, while Welton and Sterns went to their posts with deliberate purposefulness.

"How about me, Skipper?" Jim asked plaintively. "What am I supposed to do?"

"Stand here, look handsome, hold my hand, and be ready to take over if I faint."

"Suppose I faint first?"

"You can't; you're junior to me. What the hell are they doing back there—playing tiddledy winks?"

In answer, a starter whined shrilly and a tach needle wavered; then came an explosion, another, then a roar, with the needle darting to the right, while a cloud of grey smoke arose with the breeze-born stink of exhaust. The motor settled to a steady roar as another starter whined. In another moment all three tachometer needles were hovering around 600. Noble

25

wiped his hand on his pants and brought the rudder amid-ships. Christ. Suppose he hit a piling? That could hole the boat. Ran into driftwood and ruined a propeller? This baby wasn't like a motor launch; the slightest roughness in a landing could knock a hole in her paper-thin sides. Well, the engines should be warm enough now.

"Want me to take her out for you?" Pat asked.

"Nope. I might as well learn now."

"You'll have to twist her. Remember what I told you?"

"Sure, sure."

"Okay. You look kind of pale, that's all."

"Nerts to you, P. Bunch."

"Independent type, eh? Here comes Zeus down the deck. Stand by."

"Who?" Noble asked, puzzled.

"Zeus. Wasn't he in charge of the Olympus thunder department? Just call me Mort, son. I like the cut of your jib!"

"So the first-name treatment is standard procedure, huh?"

"Until he gets mad at you," Pat said.

Daggs came striding along, chest out.

"Take 'em away!" he roared.

"Bring in the stern line," Noble shouted. A wind was forcing the boat against the next one in the nest, and she was still heading in, stern toward the opening, as the Elco boys had left her. "Check with the bow line," Sterns stood solidly, with one turn of his line around the cleat, while Welton dangled a cork fender between the rubstrakes of the two boats. Noble spun the wheel hard right, pressed the buzzer, and moved the starboard throttle to ahead. The deck moved slightly, the boat vibrated, and the line Sterns held grew taut; Noble watched the two boats grind together with all the pressure concentrated against Welton's fender. He buzzed again, and moved the port throttle astern. The boat quivered more, the forward motion stopped, and the stern swung out against the wind. Noble held her so until the fantail was well out, buzzed, and moved both throttles to neutral.

"Take in the bow line," he ordered.

The line was slack and the boat motionless; Sterns stepped to the neighboring boat, took the loop from the cleat, and came back aboard the Ninety-Seven. Noble moved the port throttle astern and the boat inched steadily away from the nest.

"Nice going so far, Charlie," Pat said.

Noble didn't answer, for the stern was swinging in toward the pier again. He spun the wheel to starboard and moved the starboard throttle ahead. Movement slowed, then the boat commenced turning around on her heel. Noble held his breath, but she went on swinging around until the bow was heading for the opening of the slip. Noble sighed with relief and shifted the wing throttles to ahead, noting that his crew was busy bringing in the fenders and flaking down lines; Hill had taken in the flag astern and had the under-way colors flying from the tripod mast. Noble warmed to his men. This was a good crew.

As the bow moved out of the slip, Noble blew a long blast on the air horn; little use, for when the Ninety-Seven emerged into the river, a tugboat was bearing down on her from fifty yards away, with white water piled high before its bows. Noble hit the buzzer and shoved both throttles well ahead. Power surged beneath him, and the Ninety-Seven shot forward like a cat and cleared the tugboat by twenty yards. The tug's captain leaned out of his wheelhouse and raucously yelled something that Noble didn't catch.

"Crap on you too!" Sterns bellowed. "You blind sonofabitch!"

"Hey, Sterns," Noble called. "You're communications officer from now on." Most of the crew were around the cockpit now, and they laughed and looked pleased.

"Them blanking tugboat skippers," Sterns said. "They got the worst goddamn sea manners of anybody afloat."

Out in the river, Noble came to port and headed downstream. He glowed with the feel of his boat, skimming along, charged with vitality and maneuverability. As she slid along the wake-ridged, greasy water, the sun was bright, the air fresh, and light sparkled even from the ridgetops of those dirty ripples.

"She handles like a Ford V-8," Noble told Jim.

"Is it a stiff wheel?"

"No; bless the man who designed these balanced rudders. Why, you can turn the wheel with two fingers."

Noble kept a wary eye on a passing ferry, ready to change course if necessary. He looked about him briefly at the water ridged with innumerable wakes, scummed with dirt and oil, specked with flotsam.

"Plenty of East River trout," Pat Bunch grinned. "I thank the Lord we've got strainers over the water system intakes."

"We don't pump that water into the engines, do we?"

"No. There's a sealed cooling system in the engine jacket, using distilled water—if you can get it—and you transfer the heat from that water into what you pump in from overside."

Noble cut in the third engine. The bow stayed down and the boat slid along at twelve knots, the tachs hovering at 900. A big wake swung out from bow and fantail. Noble looked astern. A boat was dropping in behind him. All of his crew, except for the two senior engineers, were on deck in the warm sunshine, most of them clustered about the cockpit.

"On frequency, Everard?"

"Right on, sir. No one is saying anything."

When she passed under Brooklyn Bridge, hollowly resounding to traffic and the echoed roar of her engines, the Ninety-Seven led in a column of three PTs.

"Here comes Daggs." Pat grimaced astern where a fourth PT was racing toward them with white spray at its bows. A tug with four barges in tow tooted angrily. "The commander gives us hell for doing that," Pat said.

"Why?"

"The tugboat captains claim the wake breaks tow lines, cracks towing posts, all sorts of things."

The exec's boat flashed past the Ninety-Seven and sheered into line, leaning inward as it turned, then dropped speed from thirty knots to ten in a heartbeat, as the broad flat forehull sagged down. The spreading wake made the Ninety-Seven pitch and roll as it slapped hollowly against her thin sides. Almost at once Noble found his boat dropping behind; he increased speed to 1000 RPM, about fifteen knots.

"Everard, Hill," Noble said. "Come into the cockpit. This will be your under-way stations. As long as it's not too crowded, anybody else who wants to can join us."

After the four PTs had run through Buttermilk Channel, between Governor's Island and Brooklyn, and emerged into the upper bay, Noble beckoned to Print.

"Here, Jim, you take her awhile."

"Jesus," Jim said, getting his hands on the wheel. The boat wavered for a moment and he overcompensated, causing as bad a swing in the other direction. Then the Ninety-Seven settled down and swept smoothly along again.

"Just like driving a car," Print marveled. "Sure is an easy wheel."

"Pat, will you take charge up here, please? I want to look around a little."

Noble, knowing that a ship under way is a creature different from the same vessel alongside the dock, wanted to examine his command with the engines running, away from land and superior officers. She was a world in her own, right now; small, maybe, but nonetheless real. He went first to the lazarette, which contained a warning smell of fumes. He lifted the deck plates and was pleased to find the bilges dry. The engine room was hot and ear-splitting, but Warder grinned contentedly at him from the tractor seat above the center engine. Radelewski, fussing with a valve on the cooling water-intake, with his eyes intent on a gauge, didn't see Noble. He looked happy and excited.

"How are they doing?" Noble shouted to Warder.

29

"Four-oh, Skipper. A little warm, maybe, but they've only had a few hours' running time. Good engines, sir."

Noble crouched down by Radelewski, who gave him an annoyed look and started to stand up.

"Never mind," Noble bellowed above the noise. "I'm just snooping. Carry on."

He went forward into the dayroom, and through the ports he saw the superstructure of a merchant ship sliding past. In his cabin, the pictures on the desk were capsized from vibration and the slight movement over the channel wakes. The ventilators were humming and the roar of the engines had a hollow sound. Crew's quarters was silent and deserted, and the deck pitched up and down beneath him; he balanced to it with one foot advanced. He went up through the forward hatch and walked all the way aft to where Sterns crouched over the smoke generator. He grinned up at Noble, his craggy face showing full confidence, and a steady, settled good nature.

Now the PTs had passed through the Narrows, and Noble felt the deck jerk forward beneath him as the boat increased speed. Returning to the cockpit, he walked slightly uphill, the wind ruffling his pants and shirt and pulling at his cap with insistent fingers. Just as he reached the cockpit, the Ninety-Seven passed close to a crowded ferry. Noble looked up at the masses of white faces at upper and lower rails; many of the passengers waved at him, and suddenly he was very glad that he was on the PT instead of aboard the ferry, traveling the rutted way of a routine life. He waved with something close to pity as the ferry flung back the PT's roar from its tiered sides. Meeting a straggling procession of ships, the column moved down the lower bay.

"Pat, take her now if you don't mind," Noble said. "We'll be getting high-speed maneuvering soon."

"Right. Actually the high-speed work is easy enough, but you've really got to watch the other boats."

As the Ninety-Seven passed Sandy Hook, a man stood up on the canopy of the exec's boat and pumped a closed fist up and down. Pat inched the throttles forward and the roaring multiplied under his fingers. The fantail dropped, and the bow lifted, with sheets of spray soaring to either side. The boat moved faster, faster, and laden with a feeling of increasing momentum, the inner protest of his body, Noble rocked back on his heels, seized the grab rail, and threw his cap down into the chart room, so that he could peer into the stinging wind. He felt a fine and joyous exultation, and when he looked at Pat, he saw that his eyes were glowing as the Ninety-Seven flashed smoothly along the flat path of the leading boat's screw-wash, riding between the spreading, rolling V-waves of her wake, with the square, muffler-ridged stern barely fifty feet in front of Noble's bow.

Close work, damned close, Noble thought, noticing how Pat's narrowed eyes never for a moment left the boat ahead. It flipped suddenly to one side—the Ninety-Seven following, heeling in toward the turn—then straightened out as a floating plank flashed by. The tachometers hovered at 2500 RPM.

"How fast?" Noble yelled at Bunch.

"About forty-five knots, maybe forty-seven."

Forty-seven knots equalled about fifty-three miles an hour on land. Man, oh man! Noble exulted. The radio speaker rasped as someone blew across a waiting microphone, and all eyes went to the square black box on the cockpit wall.

"Prep Tare Div One from Comdiv One. Form line of bearing, one three five relative; execute to follow. Over." Unmistakably it was Daggs' voice.

"He doesn't really need the radio," Noble muttered. At his nod Everard picked up the small round microphone.

"From Prep Tare Ninety-Seven, roger, wilco. Over."

The other boats answered in turn, and a long minute of waiting followed.

"Execute!"

The Ninety-Seven swung sharply to starboard as Pat turned the wheel. The deck slid beneath Noble; the bow rose endlessly, up and up, on and up on the wake of Daggs' boat. Up yet further, a poising, then a roller-coaster down-swooping that left his belly clawing in empty air. CRASH! Up again as gear clattered and fell below decks, then the spine-quivering down plunge. CRASH! Sheets of water flew; Noble was deluged, his eyes blinded by salt water; then the Ninety-Seven was through the wake and straightening up, coming back to her old course. Now each boat was forty-five degrees to starboard of the boat ahead of it, and all were on the same course. Noble's knees felt weak, and his belly was only now bracing up and steadying.

"Wow!" he exclaimed weakly.

"That's nothing," Pat grinned. "Wait until you get outside on a rough day at high speed. It goes on for hours like the worst of that back there. Always have at least one handhold at high speed, or you'll get hurt for sure."

"I can believe it."

Again the squawk box breathed raspingly.

"Make smoke—execute to follow!"

Noble leaped onto the step and looked aft to where Sterns knelt by the smoke generator valve; the skipper held one hand high, holding on with the other and balancing with the boat's vibrating pitch.

"Execute!"

His arm came down and Stern's face turned from him to the machine under his own hands. Whiteness hissed from the water behind the boat, billowing, rising, tangible as whipped cream or cotton, expanding, making a wall, an increasing fog bank that grew from the stream of black gunk spurting from the generator to the water with which it combined. Each of the four boats seemingly towed behind it now a long funnel dragged by its spout. The four long trails of whiteness blended together into a wall of smoke, an end to visibility, a thing behind which a ship could take refuge.

The division stopped making smoke after two minutes and came back into column, the Ninety-Seven sliding, stern whipping around, rolling sharply as it hit the wake sideways, then falling into the flat white water of the exec's boat. Daggs swung hard left, the Ninety-Seven following, skimming and banking, with the inboard engine changing tone as its propeller tipped more deeply under the surface. The PTs made an incredibly small turning circle, and the division reversed course within seconds. All hands looked to port as they raced along close by the soaring fog bank that had sprung to life in two minutes on this clear blue day.

"Guess it works," Pat said.

"Lord, yes."

"Damned handy if you're being shot at."

"It may stink," the Ninety-Seven's skipper agreed, "but I love that black stuff now."

"Back to the barn!" Daggs ordered, over the T.B.S., and the division went home.

On the dock, Noble felt strangely weak; his ears roared and buzzed still and his face smarted from wind burn. But he was happy clear through, and he could hardly wait to get out on his boat again.

4

NOBLE HAD ARRANGED to meet Delilah in the bar of the St. George. For this first evening, he wanted Di to himself. He showered and shaved on the barge, and went back to his boat to shift into blues. He knotted his tie, put on his coat and cap, and swung up into the cockpit. Dusk had come and the Yard was a blaze of lights. Looped strings of brilliance marked the great bridges, and Manhattan was a jagged sparkle against a dark blue sky rapidly turning black. Noble took a deep breath of anticipation and started for the gate.

When Delilah came into the bar, smart and correct in a black dress, small hat, cloth coat, and some striking silver Mexican jewelry, male eyes snapped to her, and reluctantly away as Noble stood up to greet her.

"Di," he said, taking her hand. "You're lovely."

"That's nice, Charlie; I'm glad you think so. Where are we going?"

"Over to Manhattan?"

"Oh, yes, let's!"

"Di, I, uh . . ." Damn the Navy and Navy paymasters and late travel vouchers and pay. Was Delilah enough of a Navy girl to understand? "Do you mind riding the subway over? I'm, oh, hell, you know what the Navy's like."

"Of course I know, and I don't mind the subway a bit. I

can think of much better ways to spend money than on taxicabs."

Noble escorted her to the clanging elevator, along passageways that she lit up with her radiance, and onto the drafty, odorous platform. Noble was glad that an approaching roar and rattle came soon; this was a hell of a place to bring *her*. Then followed the bullet-like rush through darkness to Forty-Second Street and the shuttle, still riding those two nickels; uptown to Fifty-First, and out again into the night.

"Just a couple of blocks to walk," Noble said. Di grinned cheerfully at him. Lord, she's a good sport, he thought happily.

"Where are you taking me?"

"I'm afraid not the Stork Club, even though it is close by. We're heading for the Isle de Paris." One of the PT officers who knew Manhattan as Noble had known the *Lexington* had suggested the place.

"The Stork Club! Oh, Charlie!"

"I'm sorry," he said gently.

They walked along in silence for a moment, through the hurrying streets and past canopied apartment houses where expensive-looking people strolled in and out, and doormen eyed Noble with casual contempt. To hell with all of them, he thought; still it would be fun to live like that. He guessed Di was pretty disappointed.

"Charlie!" Suppressed excitement lay in her voice. "You won't get mad?"

"Mad? Me?" He'd been afraid that she was the one who was angry.

"I know the stingy old Navy and what they pay you, but I've got some money. Let me help out and let's go to the Stork Club! Please?"

"No," Noble said. "You're my guest and you're not going to pay for anything."

"Oh, men are so foolish."

"I guess so. I'm sorry I can't take you where you want to go."

"Now you're mad, and you promised you wouldn't be."

35

Noble had done nothing of the sort, but he certainly wasn't angry—not with her, anyway. They walked along in silence until he saw the Isle de Paris just ahead.

"Here we are," he said cheerfully, and Di smiled at him. They got a good table, the cocktails were excellent, and the food good; and at 9:30 the dinner ensemble began to play dance music.

"Why, Charlie," Di exclaimed happily. "This is marvelous. I'm having such fun."

So was Noble. He realized that half the men in the place were watching Di. After a rapid assessment of resources he ordered champagne—New York State. Delilah danced beautifully, and they spent most of the time on the floor. Noble asked nothing more than to go on holding her in his arms forever, and it was three o'clock when they reached the street again. Noble flagged a cruising cab.

"I really wouldn't mind the subway again."

"You're an angel, but I can afford a taxi now; really I can. The St. George, driver."

The cab swung away into the streets that were relatively deserted at this hour. Noble settled back onto the lumpy leather seat, close beside Di. Toward the last hour they'd been holding hands discreetly under the cloth, and now her hand curled warmly about his. He put his arm across her shoulders and she settled comfortably against him.

"I feel as if I'd known you for years," she murmured drowsily. "My, isn't that breeze wonderful? Whups!" The cab lurched around a corner and they slid together on the slick seat. "I can feel the champagne when he does that," Di said. "I've had such a good time."

"I'm glad."

Noble reached up slowly and gently placed his fingertips against her cheek. She turned her face toward him and he kissed her. Lord! Noble relinquished her lips unwillingly; looking forward, he saw the driver's eyes in the rear-view mirror.

"Why, that driver!" Di said indignantly. "He's watching us." She drew away from Noble and he cursed the hackie silently. Di was taking off her black hat; Noble put his hand in her hair and tried to kiss her again, without success. "Not with him watching," she said grimly. "Wait; I'll fix him." She leaned forward across the seat and hung the black hat over the rear-view mirror.

"Say, what the hell, lady!" the driver blurted.

"I was afraid you might have a wreck," Di said sweetly.

"Yeah, but now how'm I going to see behind me? S'posin' a cop spots that?"

"You've got an outside mirror," Noble pointed out, grinning at Di.

"Well, hell, buddy, can't say as I blame you. Lady, I've had a lot of things done to me in a hack, but that's a new one. You kids have fun."

Delilah came to Noble, her arms going around his shoulders. Ah, the wonderful feeling of a girl in your arms in a dark cab, the bumping at intersections, the lights flowing through, then dark; kissing and kissing, feeling her lips open under yours and the tongue tip, and the warm pressure of her body against yours. Perfume and silky hair, soft lips, warmth.

Brooklyn Bridge passed unnoticed, and the driver's voice seemed to come to Noble from another country, bringing to him the realization that the cab had stopped near bright lights.

"Here we are, Mac. Hotel St. George. Want your hat now, lady?"

"My God!" Di exclaimed. "We can't get out like this!"

"Drive around the block," Noble ordered hastily, seeing the doorman approaching. The cab pulled away into the quiet street, and he used a handkerchief while Di straightened herself out with the sound of sliding fabric.

"That champagne is dangerous!" Di laughed breathlessly.

"It's the bubbles," Noble said. "They affect me that way too."

"Here we are again," the driver said. "Or do you want I should drive around the block some more? You can put your hat on the mirror if you want to, lady; what the hell, you're only young once."

"No, thank you," Di said demurely. "I've got him hooked now."

Noble gave a good tip to the hackie, who winked at him and glanced over at Di under the canopy. He shook his head.

"You sure can pick 'em, Mac," he said warmly. Noble took Di's arm and they went with dignity into the hotel. He hesitated at the elevator, holding his breath. Delilah's eyes were big and her face was flushed.

"I'll take you up," Noble offered hopefully, and Delilah nodded. Upstairs, they stopped before her door. She opened her purse.

"Di?" Noble said, taking her in his arms.

She moved her head back and forth, avoiding his mouth, but she said nothing. Noble stepped back and she found the key.

"Why, look," she said—was it with relief? "There's a light in Mort and Kathleen's room. You can just see the glimmer around that trick transom."

Hell!

"Let's have a nightcap with them. All right, Charlie?"

"Of course, Di." Nothing else for it. If of herself she will not love, nothing will make her, the devil take her. But Noble didn't want the devil to take Delilah; he wanted to do that himself. Now Di was rapping on her brother's door. There was a pause.

"Maybe they're asleep," Noble suggested hopefully.

"No, I hear somebody."

"Who is it?" Kathleen's voice was low, yet distinct even through the door.

"It's me," Di said. "Open up, Kathleen. Oh, Charlie's with me, so if you're not decent holler Kings X."

"Look, Di," Noble began in embarrassment, but then the door opened, showing Mrs. Daggs outlined against soft light. She was smiling at them.

"Do come in," she said, sounding as if she meant it. "I'm so glad you came by; I'm rather lonesome."

"Lonesome?" Di asked. Noble saw a book and knitting on the seat of an easy chair by a lamp. The radio was playing dance music. "Where's Mort?"

"He phoned at seven and said he had to take one of his PT boats out on some night exercises. Apparently they were rather unexpected."

"Oh," said Di.

Noble held his smile of greeting, hiding his surprise. He was pretty sure that no boats had gone out; none of the squadron had been placed on ready status. Well. None of his business. They all sat down.

He wondered how he had thought Kathleen plain when he first saw her. Grey-blue eyes, soft brown hair that looked just right, a blue sweater that hinted at a fine bosom. She had a sweet roundness, somehow; a freshness that alongside Di's exotic beauty was like a rose beside an orchid, cool morning after perfumed night. Daggs was lucky to have a wife like her, Noble decided, one hell of a lot luckier than he deserved if Noble's ideas about the night exercises were correct.

"Wouldn't you two like a nightcap?" Kathleen inquired. She glanced gravely at Noble, but there was a sparkle of humor in her eyes. "You look as if you'd been having a pleasant time."

"We do, eh?" Di said. "Well, we did have a pleasant time; at least I did, a lovely time." She stood up. "Charlie, I'm tired. Would you excuse me? I think I'll say good night."

"Why, of course, Di. It is late." He stood up as well.

"Oh, don't bother," Delilah said, yawning. "I'll use the connecting door. You stay and keep Kathleen company. Thanks for a wonderful evening."

What the bloody, blue-blazing hell? Noble fumed, as she left.

"You musn't mind Delilah," Kathleen said evenly, but he noticed that her cheeks were pink. "She just acts like this at

39

times. I suppose great beauty sometimes makes one rather arrogant."

"You're not arrogant," he said swiftly. She stopped, then stared at him. She smiled.

"That was nice of you. A woman loves compliments, even untrue ones. But you haven't said whether you want that nightcap."

"No, thank you. I really think I must be going. It's quite late."

"Perhaps so. It has been nice seeing you again."

Her voice was sad, and Noble looked at her sharply. Her shoulders were sagging slightly as she gazed down at the knitting in her lap. He felt sorry for her.

"I'll run along. Good night. No, don't get up."

She disregarded this and escorted him to the door, her walk poised and graceful.

"Good night, Charles," she said, standing in the door. Noble could hear the sadness again, a tinge of hopeless despair. He knew that she realized, or at least suspected, what her husband was doing. Damned shame, he thought, cursing Daggs silently. She held out her hand. He took it, and acting on impulse, leaned over and kissed her cheek lightly. Ghost of soap, cleanness, lavender. She looked surprised, then smiled levelly at him.

"You're a nice boy," she said, touching his cheek gently. "Good night."

5

"Who was the heavy date last night, son?" inquired Pat Bunch, standing in the door of Noble's stateroom.

"The squadron commander's sister," Noble said shortly.

"Ho, ho! Charlie's took to ear-banging; no use; flattery will get you nowhere with Mort. He's a judge of human nature—he says so himself."

"Just wait until you see Delilah, pal," Noble said, grinning.

"Hah. Now if you want to meet a really good-looking girl, why don't you come along with me tonight? She even has a roommate."

It would be fun going out with Pat. "Sure, why not?" he said, yawning ostentatiously. "Anything for a friend."

After Pat had gone, Noble looked around him contentedly. He was settled; any naval vessel was home to him as soon as he was unpacked. He sighed comfortably, and got up to start a day of swinging for compass deviation and making RPM speed checks. The day passed rapidly, and in the evening Noble picked up Pat on the Ninety-One. As Bunch was shrugging into his jacket, Bertram Pollock, the cook of the Ninety-One, stuck his head through the door.

"Hey, Cap," he drawled, "you gettin' any lately? I know a guy who sells Spanish Fly. Want I should get you some?"

"Where the hell's my forty-five?" Pat said. "Gad, Charlie, did you ever hear anything like it?"

"Not exactly." Noble grinned.

"Look, Cap, start her on gin, then switch to rum and gin mixed. That'll do it every time. Why, I had an uncle once, ugliest old bastard—so don't you feel discouraged—and he gave it to the purtiest girl in town, told her it was a rum collins, and the next thing you know . . . What are you doing with that forty-five, Cap? That thing might be loaded!"

"It is," Pat said evenly. "You're going to have some real lead in your ass if you don't get out of here."

"Okay, Cap, I'm going. You can't tell some people nothing."

Gerry was nearly as beautiful as Delilah, but in a more subtle way. Her roommate Janet was all right too, a competent, poised, and attractive brunette. After dinner and a show, courtesy of the Officers' Service Committee, the quartet stopped in at an obscure and reasonable little night club. Janet was a good dancer; Gerry was a superlative one. Dancing with her, Noble wondered what the relationship was between this girl and Pat. They made few overt demonstrations of affection—not even the almost automatic touching of bodies and handclaspings that make others feel like fifth wheels—but once or twice Noble had seen them looking at each other with an almost despairing intensity.

"Pat's quite a lad," Noble casually said to Gerry as they danced.

"You're his best friend, aren't you?"

"I hope he considers me that. We were roommates at the Academy. You couldn't have a better man to live with."

"Does he ever lose that amazing cheerfulness of his? Oh, I know he can get mad; I've seen him. But I mean the way he takes, well, unpleasant things in such a way that you enjoy going through them with him."

"I know. I've never seen him when he couldn't make you feel better; no matter what. Even at Pearl Harbor, he . . . well, never mind."

42

"His men love him, don't they?"

"I guess they do."

"So do I."

"Why, Gerry, that's wonderful. I guess that makes us kind of kin. Kissing cousins, maybe?"

"Maybe so. You know it's funny. I always thought I'd fall for some handsome giant with a million dollars in his kick, and look at me."

"Pat's mighty lucky." Lucky! Noble thought. Why, the old bastard. Wait'll I get him alone.

Toward midnight it was decided that they should go to the girls' apartment for coffee. In the elevator a fellow passenger, a broad, well-padded lady, dropped her purse and stooped for it before Pat or Noble could make the gesture; doing so she pointed a round vastness at Gerry. No one spoke.

When they got in the apartment, Gerry turned to Pat with an anxious look. "Pat darling," she said. "Do I look anything like that when I stoop over?"

Pat grinned. "Gerry, with some women I want to stick a pin in it; with others I feel a wild desire to kick it; but when you, my little bird, assume the angle, I just want to pat it."

Gerry looked relieved. "You know where the makings are. Fix us all a drink, will you, dear? I want to have a little talk with Janet."

"Sure. Have a good talk. I'll put on the coffee, too."

Pat maintained an unusual silence as he mixed highballs in the little kitchen. He lit the gas, filled a coffee pot, and spooned coffee into the container, still not saying anything.

He lifted his glass and drank. "Damn everything," he said listlessly.

"What's this? Pat Bunch morose?"

"Why not. Look at Pagliacci."

"Gerry?"

"Does it stick out that badly? Of course, it's Gerry. She won't marry me; she's determined to have a career, and me, I'm stuck with the blue suit and the brass buttons. God,

Charlie, she's a girl! I've thought I was in love before, but this time I'm sunk. Damn it, when you find a girl like Gerry you'd better grab her."

"I couldn't agree more."

They picked up two trays and went into the living room. Gerry was crying. Setting down his tray, Pat hurried over to her.

"Here, what's the matter?"

"Nothing," she said, snuffling. "I just . . . Oh, damn you, Bunch, *damn* you."

"Hey," Pat said.

"Pat, what did you say you want to do when I lean over like the lady in the elevator?"

"Why, I said I want to pat it."

"Is that all you want?"

Noble watched Pat's face, seeing first bewilderment, then a growing excitement not unmixed with despair.

"I don't understand," Pat said.

"Do you love me?"

"I love you, Gerry."

"You asked me to marry you; I said I couldn't, but . . . Pat, now I will."

"*Gerry!*" Color came back into Pat's face, bringing happiness with it. He reached for her.

"I mean now, Pat," she said.

"Now? Tomorrow? To*night?*"

"I've got a car. We can drive to Maryland and be back by lunch tomorrow."

"All right," Pat said, dazedly. "All *right!* We'll get married tonight, this minute, but dammit, woman, hold still; I want to kiss you."

They kissed tenderly and gently. Noble, watching, was speechless with a strange sorrow and a wild envy. Pat turned Gerry loose and flung both arms in the air.

"I forgot," he howled. "I've got to be back aboard at eight in the morning."

"No you don't," Noble assured him. "I'm the executive officer, and I've just given you a twenty-four-hour emergency leave. Let's drink a toast to your happiness, and then you shove off, boy."

They all drank. Noble took a deep draught, and put his glass on the table. He shook hands with Janet and Pat, kissed Gerry on the cheek, and went alone into the night.

For the next few days Noble went through the process of turning his boat into a functioning weapon. His crew worked in well together, and Jim Print was an ideal man to handle them, seeming to establish firm rapport without noticeable effort. Noble hoped to do as well eventually, but as commanding officer he was unable to use certain informal short cuts that Jim took advantage of. Noble was the man who might have to get all or some of them killed someday; that he would share their fate was of some help, but still that fact stood between them.

He saw little of Pat Bunch during these busy days, except when they met for lunch on the barge. Outwardly, Bunch looked much the same, though he was quieter than before. The wry, puckish look was gone from his face and in its place Noble thought he saw deep contentment.

"You know what my crew did?" he told Charlie on Tuesday. "They bought a pair of percale sheets with rosebuds on 'em —Lord knows where they found them these days—and a pair of matching pillow cases marked His and Hers, and they sent them up to Gerry with an orchid and a congratulations card. How the hell they knew about it I can't figure."

"Probably took one look at your face when you staggered aboard the other morning. It's written all over it."

"What is?"

"Happiness, you wart hog, happiness."

"I guess you're right. Charlie, I never knew what it meant to be happy. I always had plenty of fun before, but I was just existing. Now I go through this filthy town and I feel

45

sorry for every sonofabitch I see because he hasn't got Gerry. I go home and she has drinks ready, and she comes running in an apron—she cooks dinner nearly every night—and kisses me. Charlie, I just can't believe it."

"You're lucky, Pat."

"Yes, I am. You know, it all seems so right to me, I wonder why we waited so long. The best thing is, Gerry feels the same way."

Friday morning dawned clear and gentle, and Noble had permission to spend the day on Long Island Sound, training his crew at piloting. When the Ninety-Seven nosed out of the slip into the East River her skipper was completely happy. He had a date with Delilah on Saturday night, he had been paid, and now he had all day to play with his boat. Tugs had no terrors for him now; he knew the speed and agility of his command and he defied any tugboat captain to hit him. Up the greasy, flowing river, past Blackwell's Island, and into the roiled, powerful tides of Hell Gate the PT went. Once through the Gate, she headed for North Brother Light, to the left of Riker's Island, then steered 092 degrees True to clear Hunt's Point, roared past Throgs Neck, and entered the open Sound.

Long Island Sound was blue and sparkling, with only a few high clouds floating in the sky. The crew clustered around the cockpit, laughing and joking. Noble put Radelewski at the wheel, while he and Print erected a cardboard screen before the helmsman, so he couldn't see ahead, and ordered him to steer 123 degrees, Compass.

"I can't see!" Radelewski protested. "What is this?"

"This is fog," Noble told him gravely. "You steer the course, and if you don't run right into Execution Rock Light I'll cut your grog ration."

"Huh," Radelewski grunted. The swinging compass face soon had him sweating, and he missed the light by a good deal. But it was pretty fair steering at that, Noble knew. For some time he ran back and forth from buoy to buoy, giving himself, Print, and each member of the crew practice in steering by compass. The PT was off Sea Cliff when Johnson came on deck with his guitar. Ding Hau Welton, the cook, brought out a harmonica, and the crew clustered around them. Noble climbed to his under-way seat high in the after starboard corner of the cockpit, propped his feet on the grab rail, and lit a cigar. He looked happily around over his boat. Jim, at the wheel, had the motors turning up 1900 RPM for a speed of a little better than thirty-five knots; Warder's smile, and the sustained, nearly hypnotic roar told the skipper that the engines were performing well. The waves in the Sound were slight and regular, and the Ninety-Seven swooped over, down the other slope, and up again, with just enough motion to make the swift rush exhilarating. Rainbows vibrated in the leaping white wake, and the salt wind whipped and burned, giving perfect balance to the warmth of the sun. God, it was good. Johnson played a few familiar chords and broke into high, somewhat nasal song.

"She was a-coming down the mountain, making ninety
    miles an hour."

The crew joined in. Noble slipped down from his perch and got his finger on the air-horn button, singing with the rest.

"When her whistle broke into a scream," the song continued, and Noble pressed the button twice; "Blawt, blawt!" shrieked the air horn. The men looked around at their captain with wide, pleased grins, then sang on.

"He was found in the wreck with his hand on the throttle,
    and scalded to death by the steam."

Everyone aboard was singing now.

"Now ladies fair, from my story take warning, and listen
    to its dire turn,
Never speak harsh words to your true-loving husband,
    he may leave you and never return."

"That's it, you know!" Noble exclaimed. "The Old Ninety-Seven. What do you say, boys?"

"Why, hell yes, Skipper!" Ike Sterns shouted. "Old Ninety-Seven. That's our boat."

"When you were bringing the torpedo alcohol aboard didn't I notice a can with a loose top?"

"Skipper, I do believe you're right." Sterns' face was one broad grin.

"Ding Hau, have we got any powdered lemonade? Good. Make a pitcher and then turn your back while Sterns does his duty— Good grief, Jim, you're fifteen degrees off course."

Print laughed, swinging the wheel.

They all had one drink apiece to the Old Ninety-Seven, christening her properly. Everard took the last glass of loaded lemonade, went forward, and sloshed it against the boat's glistening bow.

"I christen thee Old Ninety-Seven," he intoned. "Long may you wave."

"Amen," said Noble.

The sun was setting when the Old Ninety-Seven's lines went ashore at the Navy Yard dock. Noble was tired, his face was caked with salt and burned by sun and wind, but he felt good. His men reflected the same feeling. Noble couldn't explain it but he knew that boat and crew had come alive. They were a unit; boat, officers, and men were one. Nothing could happen to one without affecting all. They were a boat crew. From here on in, whatever fate held would be met by this crew not as individuals, but as the Ninety-Seven boat, craft and men spoken of as one.

"Okay, boys," Noble said. "I'm going up to report. Sterns, when I get back we'll have just one more round of torpedo juice, and then you put that top back on tight. Understand?"

"We'll wait for you, Skipper."

Print went below and Everard stood alone in the cockpit, watching the captain walk away through the dusk to the barge. He liked the captain. Everard found in him no arrogance, nor yet any lack of firmness and resolution. Noble so fully believed that his position of authority had been earned by accomplishment at the Naval Academy and at sea that he, Everard, unconsciously felt the same. And Noble is right, Everard mused. Democracy demands leaders; the requisite demand is that the path to leadership be open to all. Instead of having gone to the Naval Academy, Everard had had four wonderful years at Yale, followed by graduate school, the Ph.D., and an instructorship at Yale. Before him had stretched the prospect of a comfortable, leisurely life in a fulfilling and worthwhile career. His and Noble's worlds never would have intersected had it not been for the war. And the other men aboard? . . .

"Hey, Sparks!" Radelewski shouted from below. "Come on down and get a shot." Radelewski walked back to the mess table as Everard came below. He wanted that creep Everard in on it too; Johnson and the two kids already had their glasses full. Warder was back checking the engines, and Sterns had gone somewhere after bringing out the juice. Those two would bang ears with the captain, and Radelewski wanted to find out who had the guts not to. He especially wanted to find out about the radioman—radio girls they called them in the fleet, he remembered hearing, and he thought this bird sure fitted that name with his quiet, superior talk.

"Have a drink," Radelewski said, handing Everard a glass of the lemonade and alcohol.

"I think the captain wants us to wait," the radioman answered, just as Radelewski had expected.

"Ah, come on," the motor machinist's mate said.

Jim Print, sitting on his bunk rolling a cigarette as Jeff Mason had taught him to do, had the door open a crack, and he could hear the men. He didn't like eavesdropping, but he was wondering if maybe Charlie wasn't giving them too much rope. He'd found out on the ranch that you couldn't let a hand go too far. Just as he thought; they were getting ready to have a couple before Charlie got back. He sat tight.

Coming into the quarters, Ike Sterns saw Radelewski lifting his glass. Those stupid bastards; they don't want a happy ship. He didn't blame the kids, they'd follow anybody; Johnson would always be bad news as far as discipline went, and Everard didn't know his tail from the hawsehole yet, though he would. But that cocky Radelewski! He was the one Sterns would have to kick into line; once he knew the score, this would be a good crew.

"Put down that glass," Sterns said.

"Ah, knock it off. You ain't no blanking officer."

Radelewski looked mean, but Sterns knew it was a bluff—though he hoped it wasn't. Still, it wouldn't have been a fair fight; he had forty pounds on Radelewski and he'd boxed in the Fleet and been in barroom brawls from Shanghai to Caimanera.

"Put it down," he said again. "All you guys, pour that stuff back into the pitcher. Pour it back. Johnson. You hear me?"

"Brown nose," Radelewski said, tipping his untasted glass into the pitcher.

"When we get liberty I'll be at the Sand Street Oasis," Sterns told him steadily. "Come there and call me a brown nose."

"Maybe I will." But everyone knew the motor machinist's mate wouldn't do it. Sterns relaxed, and in that moment they heard somebody coming down the ladder.

It was Noble, and as he came into the crew's quarters he noted that Sterns' face was red and that tension was perceptible in the air. The pitcher was still full, and the captain could guess that his senior petty officer had come through as he had expected him to. Print came out of his room and Noble filled all the glasses.

"Here's to the Old Ninety-Seven," he said. They all drank, and Noble added, "And here's to some new shiny gold braid."

"What's that?" Jim exclaimed.

"Gold braid, boy. The Alnav came in today. It's Lieutenant Commander Daggs, USNR, now. And I, my boys, am a full-fledged, honest-to-God senior lieutenant. You'd better treat me respectfully from now on."

"Congratulations, Charlie," Print said warmly, seconded by

most of the crew. Noble smiled in thanks; the pleasure in Jim's voice, and in those of the men, added immensely to his own.

"And I'm glad Mister Daggs got promoted," Benton said happily. "I was cleaning up the office the other day, and he asked me my name; said he liked the cut of my jib."

"Yeah," Sterns said, a glint in his eye.

Well, Noble thought wryly, tomorrow was another day, and it was just possible that Daggs might improve with his new rank. And tomorrow night there would be Delilah.

6

THE HOTEL PHONE smelled of cigar smoke as Noble rang Delilah's room; with male egotism, he was remembering the taxi, not the rejection in the hotel corridor.

"Hello, Di.'" he said eagerly. "This is Charlie. Are you ready?"

"Not quite, but please come on up. I promised Mort and Kathleen we'd go with them. Is that all right?"

"That's fine," Noble said, grimacing at the blank wall.

"Come up to Mort's room then; Kathleen and I are using mine."

Daggs opened the door, booming, "Come in, Charlie; throw your cap over there and let's us have a snort. This is a day to celebrate. Got to wet down our stripes. Say when."

"When, whoa!"

"Yes, sir, Mister Exec. By God, Charlie, it's me and you, boy. I run the show and you see that it runs the way I want it. Right?"

"Yes, sir."

"Bung ho, son. Well, I see Kathleen won the race."

Turning, Noble realized that Mrs. Daggs was truly beautiful. Her full skirt was of a pink that matched her cheeks and it was touched with silver thread; she wore a white blouse that revealed just a hint of her breasts, and her eyes were joyous and gay. The skirt swelled out from a waist that looked unbelievably slender.

"Charlie," she said with a warm smile. "How nice of you to be willing to go with us."

Their eyes met for a moment and the enchantment he saw in hers made his next words completely sincere.

"I'm awfully pleased, Kathleen. We'll have fun."

Then Delilah came through the door. She wore a black low-cut dress, and a velvet strand around her neck accentuated the swelling ivory between dress and lovely throat. With earrings of silver, hair of gold, bright eyes, scarlet lips, the slim waist, and the sweep of long, arrogant legs through the black skirt, she looked stunning.

"Quit slobbering, son!" Daggs roared. "By God, ain't she a pip, though?"

"Hi, Charlie," she said, noting his confusion. "How are the taxis lately?"

In the squadron station wagon downstairs, Daggs at the wheel, the party drove to the Officers' Club. Workmen had left a strip of mud in front of the entrance, and Daggs lifted Delilah over it. Noble caught Kathleen's eye; she came to him and he lifted her across the wet clay, acutely conscious of her light warmth in his arms.

"Thank you, Charles."

"I couldn't let those silver slippers be ruined. And, say, you called me Charlie a little while ago."

"All right. Thank you, Charlie." She laughed.

The large main room of the club was decorated with clusters of boarding axes and cutlasses, fragments of anchor cable from old frigates, shields, scrolls, and all the symbolism of sea power. A waiter led Daggs' party into the room, and as he passed a table occupied by six or seven of the PT squadron officers, Noble saw Jim Print's face actually pale as he sighted Delilah. Noble smiled and winked at his exec, who barely managed to wink back, for at the moment the lovely blonde girl's black-sheathed hip swished by him.

The commander's party was seated at the table and ordered dinner. After the meal, when the liqueurs were served, Noble took Delilah out on the dance floor.

She danced closely, her lips so near to his cheek that he caught the faint sweetness of Cointreau on her warm breath. He was vividly conscious of her breasts, and her bare back was soft and alive under his hand. Looking past the gold of her hair he saw Jim Print approaching. Hell! But Jim hung back until he caught his skipper's eye, then lifted one eyebrow inquiringly. Noble smiled and shrugged. Instantly Jim stood beside them.

"Di," Noble said lightly, "I'd like to present the only man here I'd trust with you—my exec, Jim Print. Jim, Miss Daggs."

"I'm proud," Jim said. "Only one minor correction: Charlie can't trust me around you, me nor any other man. Thanks, old fellow. You can go home now."

Noble heard Di's laugh as Jim whirled her away. He stood for a moment remembering how her eyes had lit up at the sight of Jim. Well, no wonder. Jim was a fine-looking bird— the tall, whipcord type, with wavy hair and even teeth, and the assurance and grace of background. He returned soberly to the table.

Kathleen's expression showed both sympathy and eagerness. Daggs had made no move to dance with her. "Well, Charlie, got thrown pretty quick there, didn't you?" he said, looking around for the waiter.

"I planned it that way. Now that Di's taken care of I can do what I've wanted to all along. Kathleen, may I have this dance?"

"Oh, yes!" she said, smiling up at him.

Her back wasn't so soft as Di's, and it felt cool through the thin cloth of the blouse. She was graceful and erect in Noble's arms.

"We dance well together," he said, pleased.

"We certainly do."

He wondered why the hell Daggs preferred drinking alone

to dancing with Kathleen. There was a pleasant warmth about her that was spiritual rather than physical. Noble felt that she liked him, and he was flattered. Afterward, when Daggs finally danced with her, Noble sat alone at the table, watching Delilah whirl from one pair of arms to the other, flushed and happy. He went out and touched her partner's shoulder.

"Remember me?" he asked.

"Sure. Why, I never forget a face. Ferdinand Grenoble, isn't it?"

"Having fun?"

"Oh, wonderful. My, you and Mort have some nice men in your squadron. Jim, for instance. What's he like? Where's he from?"

"Wyoming, by way of Stanford."

"Really? I *thought* he talked like a cowboy."

"Well, I understand his father's ranch is about the size of Connecticut."

"Mmm! Money?"

"Jim doesn't say, of course, but I do notice that he gets his khaki pants from Brooks Brothers."

Just then another member of the squadron bore down; Delilah shrugged helplessly, happily, and Noble went back to the table. Kathleen was there alone.

"Where's Mort?" he inquired, sitting down.

"Dancing with some incredibly beautiful starlet in gold lamé and red hair, and with a pair of rather formidable-looking objects on her chest."

"Why, Kathleen!"

"Well, one can hardly ignore them."

The music had stopped, and when Daggs and his partner stepped apart Noble could understand Kathleen's remark. The red-haired girl's breasts stood outward and upward, sharply pointed, like a Petty girl's standard equipment. All she needed was the telephone.

"Nice structural material there," Noble said. "Steel maybe?"

"Oh, Charles, you are a comfort."

"Will you dance this one with me?"

"Of course I will."

They danced, and Noble no longer minded Delilah's absence so much. He saw her with Jim in the shadows behind the bandstand. They were dancing as if they were one body. As he moved by with Kathleen he saw Delilah kiss Jim's cheek. Jim was rapt and unseeing.

"I'm sorry," Kathleen said gently.

Noble considered this, somewhat surprised to find that he wasn't particularly unhappy. He had merely been the first to meet Di; he had known from the beginning, deep down, that he hadn't the charm, the glamour, for so exceptional a beauty. Once she had met Jim he had been out of it. Noble had a pang of memory, but it went away.

"It's all right," he said. "It really is."

"I'm so glad."

At eleven o'clock the dance floor was cleared to let two Hollywood starlets perform. Jim Print stood close to Delilah, watching the scene. Daggs escorted the red-haired girl to the platform where she sang a couple of songs. Everyone applauded. The other starlet recited something and sang a risqué ditty Jim had heard before. He could identify Daggs' laughter over all the noise. Seeing Charlie sitting at a table with Mrs. Daggs bothered Print; after all, the skipper had brought Delilah here, and he had seemed pretty well gone on her. Then, as the dancing began again, he felt Di's warm hand twine around his and, smothering conscience without an effort, he led Di back on the floor. But Print could barely finish a sentence to the girl; one of the PT officers would cut in after ten steps.

"Hell," he said to Delilah at last. "I can't get anywhere this way."

"Then let's do something about it."

"What?"

"Let's find another place to dance."

"But you came with Charlie," he said with surprise.

"I won't ask you again, Jim."

"Why . . ." Print began just as an officer cut in. Di caught Print's eye as she danced away, and he nodded at her. He stood for a moment looking after her, then went to find Charlie Noble.

He discovered his skipper alone at the table. Good. Print was feeling pretty shaky. This was a mean thing to do, but maybe talking frankly to Charlie about it would help. Print liked his skipper; if Charlie objects, he thought, I'm damned if I do it. I won't mess up the Old Ninety-Seven for any woman.

"Charlie," Print said bluntly. "Di wants me to take her out dancing, somewhere else." I guess there might have been better ways to say it, he thought, but he respected Charlie, and knew he had seen him and Di dancing behind the bandstand. At the skipper's friendly smile Jim knew everything would be all right.

"Go ahead, bub," Noble said tolerantly. "But I'll demand all the gory details Monday morning."

"Really, Charlie—and I mean the hell out of this—you say no, and I'll lay off."

"I know that, Jim. Look, any man gets excited at the sight of a girl like Di, but she's not for me, you crap-head; she's made that plenty clear. I had my chance. Have fun, son."

"Charlie . . ."

"It really is all right. I don't know why; two hours ago I'd have slugged you with that water pitcher. Go on, and good luck."

Noble meant it, rather to his surprise. It would have been different, perhaps, had he thought he had any chance with her. A man burns with longing at sight of a girl like Di. Healing comes with the realization that she is out of his reach. When she'd avoided his kisses outside her room that night—that was when he'd known.

Five minutes later Noble saw them leave the club. Kathleen, who was with him at the table, looked at him questioningly.

57

"I said 'blessings, my children,'" he told her.

"Charlie, some damned girl is going to be luckier than she deserves some day."

"Is she?" Noble muttered, suddenly cold.

Her soft voice speaking with certainty of a future in which Noble could not believe touched a contact in his mind: Pearl Harbor, the *Oklahoma*, classmates he'd known and liked fried on steel decks, blown apart, drowned in fuel oil. Some of them had been trapped from December 7 until after Christmas, marking the days on the bulkhead paint until they died. Temporary duty on the *Lexington*, the old Lex; he had received his orders to PTs barely in time to leave her before she weighed anchor on a mission that led to the Coral Sea. Christ! he thought now, feeling his palms wet with sweat. *That* was the only future he could believe in: the war, waiting for him beyond this. And woman's world of sympathy, softness, love—this was only a respite.

With an effort he brought himself back and said, laughing, "Poor girl. I feel sorry for her, whoever she is."

Just before midnight Daggs found Noble alone.

"Charlie," the commander said, swaying slightly, "I've gotta go to Washington. Tonight."

"What's up?"

"Nothin', really; you know how those bastards are: what kinda toilet paper we're usin', maybe. Just routine." He winked at Noble. "Look, Charlie, you take care Kathleen, huh? Take her home with you'n Di; say, where's she at anyway? Anyway, you take Kathleen home. Here's a key to the station wagon. An old friend of mine from Public Relations is gonna take me to the airport. He's gotta take the two Hollywood broads there anyway. See?" He winked again.

"Sure," Noble said. "I see." He winked back.

"You rallright, Charlie. I talked to the old lady. You see she gets home. I'll be back sometime Sun'ay."

"Sure. Have a good trip—Mort."

"You bet I will. So long, Charlie."

58

"Yes, sir," Noble said, feeling sad and angry. How the hell could a man prefer a brassy red-headed bitch, with six-inch tits at an elevation of three oh double oh, to a woman like Kathleen?

When Noble returned to the table, the warm color was gone from Kathleen's cheeks.

"I'm in luck," he said as he sat down, avoiding her eyes.

"Then Morton went through with it?"

"Why, of course. After all, when an officer gets orders from Washington he has to obey them."

"Will you take me home now? I'm sorry, but I don't think I'd be much fun."

"I don't agree about that, but of course I'll take you home."

She slumped spiritlessly in his arms as he lifted her over the mud again. Somehow the sight of the little silver shoes angered him anew. Poor thing, he thought savagely. Kathleen was silent as Noble drove along the park and stopped by the side entrance of the hotel. He escorted her across the vast lobby and into the smoky elevator, then down the corridor. In her once-gay pink and silver and white she unlocked the door to her room, looking forlorn. Noble saw that her lips were quivering and that her hazel-grey eyes were moist with unshed tears. He took her hand.

"Good night," he said. "Thank you for everything."

He turned away.

"Charles!" she exclaimed.

Noble whirled. Kathleen's arms were outstretched and her face, flushed again, was almost pleading. He went into her arms, and they kissed passionately; and then he was holding her, rocking her in the smoke- and perfume-smelling corridor. She clutched him furiously, her body close against his. His heart was pounding hard as they drew apart, and it seemed to him that her eyes were like first-water diamonds. She looked behind her into the room with disgust, then back at Noble.

"Charles?" she said pleadingly. The question, unexpressed,

was in her eyes; he answered it by pulling her out of the doorway as, hand in hand like children, they ran down the corridor toward the elevators.

At midnight Jim Print and Delilah were in the Stork Club with the waiter bringing the second bottle of champagne. Even among these beautiful and expensive women Delilah stood out like Diamond Butte at sunset. Jim loved the way she moved, with the same dainty, sure gracefulness as a thoroughbred mare. The admiring looks of the men around them made Print realize even more how lucky he was.

"Jim!" Delilah whispered, squeezing his arm fiercely. "Look! There's Cary Grant!"

Noble had ordered Scotch and the orchestra was playing quiet dance music, so he didn't care how smoky and crowded the place was. A brown-haired girl sang "I've Told Every Little Star" as he danced with Kathleen.

"Hi," Noble said, seeing her faraway look, and growing sad. She squeezed his hand and sang along with the song. She had a sweet, low voice, and Noble held her silently, dancing, until the number was over.

"I've never had such a good time. You're so nice."

"Nonsense," he said. "I'm just luring you on."

Another Scotch, then they were in the station wagon. It drove itself across the 59th Street Bridge and onto Queens Boulevard. They went on through a night that was magic, stopped again to dance, then drove on. She was sitting close to him and the touch of her body brought him comfort and serenity, yet also a conflictingly sad realization that he had no right to her, nor any hope of her. Most of all, however, he felt tenderness, and a hope that she was experiencing the same bitter-sweet happiness he knew.

At three in the morning the station wagon found a park

with pools of blackness under the trees and the elevated train track that bordered it. Slowly, Noble drove through the park, turned the station wagon, and stopped in the shadow of the elevated. He waited a moment for any protest. None came. He switched off the engine, threw his cap to the back seat, and turned to her. She came sweetly and eagerly into his arms, and they kissed. Her lips were warm and tender.

"Charles."

He hushed her murmur with kisses. His left hand went to her breasts and her body moved slightly. Her breasts were small, round, and perfect. He kissed them, tasting her and smelling a faint sweet perfume. Kathleen sighed and slumped down into the seat, turning to him, turning her back against the door, going soft and wonderfully sweet. Noble felt her slim leg through the crinkly, metal-threaded material of the pink and silver skirt; he reached down and took the hem, pulling it upward. Her legs in the pale light, were lovely, straight and wonderful. . . .

They loved each other there in the front seat of the station wagon, and afterwards Noble felt relaxed, calm and happy; he felt no uncleanness, no remorse, no distaste. He realized he was in love, the real love that finds its greatest expression when physical passion is for the moment quiescent.

Kathleen's eyes were shut, and her quietness frightened him. He kissed her cheek.

"You're not sorry?"

She smiled. "How could I be? I'm happy now, for tonight. Don't you know what you have given me?"

"I was taking, not giving."

Her eyes opened. "You couldn't be more wrong. I know what giving is. Perhaps because I've encountered so little of it."

"You were giving too."

"Of course. That's why it was so good."

"I know."

She smiled again. "I knew I was going to do this, Charles,

61

when Morton went away. I knew all along, but I'd be damned if I'd misbehave in Morton's bed. I'm rather pleased somehow, now, that this is his station wagon. Woman is an unpredictable thing, eh?" Noble kissed her.

"So strong and young."

"Young?" Noble said in mock indignation.

"How old are you, Charlie?"

"Twenty-five."

"Why, you're a year older than I am."

"Yes, my child."

They were silent with wonder, gratitude, and love. From far off came the faint sounds of the sleeping city, the desert of people; from the park, leaves stirred and whispered, grass spread its fragrance over the warm night.

"Darling, there's a car coming."

"I wish this could last forever."

She kissed him, gently now, after the warmth and sweetness of loving. He sat up and reached for his cap and started the engine. With one last reluctant look about the park and at Kathleen's quietly smiling face, he drove off.

Jim Print didn't ask Delilah to go to his apartment; they just went there. He turned on the light and closed the door. Delilah's lipstick was blurred from their kisses in the taxi, and the pupils of her violet eyes were large. She swayed toward him and they kissed for a long, long time. Then she pushed him away.

"Hold up, cowboy; I've got some repairing to do." She opened her gold purse and took out a mirror. "Holy Christopher! I'm a mess. How about that drink, Jim?"

"I haven't any champagne."

"Whiskey'll do fine."

When he brought the drinks the repair work was finished, though her purse was still open on the coffee table. He put the tray down by her gold lipstick.

"What's this, Jim?" Delilah asked, holding up a long, slim object that she found on the mantel.

"A branding iron."

"The kind you use on your ranch?"

"That's right. Jeff Mason gave it to me when I left home; he told me to put the old Split T brand on a Jap."

"Are you going to?"

"Don't be silly. In the first place I'm not going to get that close to one of those gents, not if I can help it. In the second place, you only put your brand on a critter that belongs to you, and I haven't lost any Japs."

Di's eyes were shining. "Jim!" she said.

"What is it?" God, she was beautiful.

"Brand *me!*"

"You're crazy! Hurt you? Oh, Delilah."

Her eyes swept to the coffee table, and her open purse.

"We can use lipstick on it. Jim, I want to belong to you."

Whiskey on top of the champagne made this proposition seem fine to Print. His head whirled at a thought: to brand, even in lipstick, bare skin was necessary.

"All right," he said.

Delilah smeared the face of the branding iron thickly with her lipstick. "There," she said breathlessly. "That will do it."

She stood up and Print could see her breasts lift. The dress made a smooth, wonderful curve over her hips and legs.

"Where do you brand?" she asked, her husky voice filling him with a wild impatience.

"Here," he said, touching the side of her left buttock.

"That high? Okay, pardner."

She reached down and lifted the dress on that side, revealing that she wore no stockings; her perfect leg was like pale marble, as was the rounded thigh. When the dress was up to her waist her flank was bare.

"Go ahead," she said.

Print's hands were shaking. He took the iron, held his breath, and pressed the head against white flesh. Di gasped as the iron touched her, flinching as if it burned. He moved the branding iron away, revealing the red Split T.

"You . . . you ought to be branded on the other side too," Print managed to say.

"Yes, yes, everywhere, anywhere." She started to lift the other side of the dress.

"We'll get lipstick on it."

She looked at him and her fingers went to a zipper. She lifted the dress over her head and her white body flared into radiance in the room. She flung the dress on the couch and stood before Jim naked except for high-heeled gold shoes, silver earrings, and the strand of black velvet around her throat. Something hammered inside Jim.

"Go ahead, Jim," Di said in a queer, high-pitched voice.

He branded her again and again. She cried out and swayed, a picture of red and white and gold. Print caught her and carried her to the bedroom. He ripped down the coverlet and put her on the white sheet; she held up her arms to him and he dropped to his knees and kissed her a hundred times. Then he went into her arms . . .

He stood by the bed looking down at the girl, feeling strangely weak, unbound, like a crazy man come sane again to find the world still mad. Everything had been wonderful, but love. She hadn't felt it at all. Poor girl, he thought; she tried so hard not to let him know. But she had been unable to conceal that deep-cored, cold stillness in her body, the shudder of revulsion, not passion. She was crying, the tears running down her cheeks.

"Jim," she moaned. "I thought I could this time; I liked you so much; I thought you were . . . Oh, Jim, what am I ever going to do?"

He knelt beside her, stroking her cheek, feeling sorry for her, and terribly sad that so lovely a woman lacked the one essential trait of love, without which all the gorgeous beauty became a mockery.

"It's all right, Di," he murmured again and again.

Noble placed his hand gently on Kathleen's as they sat in the car, eating the hamburgers and coffee they had ordered at the drive-in. Suspense was consuming him. He had to know. "Darling, when can we be together again?"

"I've been sitting here terrified that you'd ask me that—and then terrified that you wouldn't. I don't know, darling; I can't share two men's beds." Suddenly she was crying, with half a hamburger incongruously in her hand.

"I love you," Noble said.

"That too?" she wailed softly. "I was afraid both ways there too. I don't know, I don't know. I don't think I can do this— Oh, Charlie, don't ask me anything now. Please!"

"All right, darling." He touched her hand and it clutched around his. They sat in silence, feeling the last of their night slipping away. Dawn would come soon.

"I'll always remember this night," she said sadly. "I just don't know what I'll do if you're not around. Darling, we must go home."

As they drove away, Noble felt empty and dragged out; happy still, but with the knowledge that only minutes remained.

He kissed her good night at her hotel entrance. Then he went away, leaving her standing there looking after him; that was the way she wanted the good night to be. He stopped at the street corner and gazed back. Slim and fulfilled, in white and silver and pink, she stood smiling at him with the soft, wise, happy smile she had worn since they left the Officers' Club. She raised her hand and threw him a kiss. He returned it, then lunged around the corner, not wanting to go, but feeling drawn already by the pull of his boat, rocking gently in the grey ripples down by the cinder-grimed pier.

7

SHORTLY AFTER NOON on Sunday, Noble received a despatch for the squadron from the Yard communications office. The heavy twenty-millimeter gun mounts were to be replaced by much lighter tripod stands, the despatch said, the work to be done by local contractors. That meant Archer's Yacht Yard out on Long Island Sound. Noble knew that as soon as the last boats were delivered from Elco, the squadron was to make a training and shakedown cruise to Newport, Rhode Island. This despatch would be of immediate interest to the squadron commander. He went to the phone, and then stopped. The last thing he wanted to do this afternoon was to talk to Daggs.

Previously, mornings-after had been remorseful affairs with flag half-masted, for the puritanical tradition was not yet stamped from his blood. But this time he'd waked up smiling and feeling good. Here, he thought, I've made love to my commanding officer's wife, one step worse than adultery for a naval officer, but I love her; that's why everything feels so right. He remembered what Pat Bunch had said. It felt as if he had done the things he was supposed to do. Well. There it was. Besides, after last night she couldn't love the commander, she loved him. Thus reassured, he dialed the number; sure enough, Daggs answered.

"Commander Daggs speaking. What d'you want?"

He sounded sour and hung over. The despatch had come uncoded, so Noble relayed it over the phone.

"Okay, Charlie," Daggs growled. "Take your boat to Archer's tomorrow and arrange for the gun-mount modifications. Work to start as soon as we get back from Newport."

"Aye, aye, sir."

"Another thing. I've sublet an apartment. I'll give you the address and phone number; have Manson put them in the office records. See you tomorrow, Charlie."

Back on the Ninety-Seven Noble sat in the wardroom, remembering the conversation, surprised that he had felt so little strain talking to Kathleen's husband and his own commanding officer. Sure *must* be love; never before had he made love to a married woman. He stretched, and then heard someone coming aboard. Steps clattered down the ladder and John Everard walked past the tiny booth.

"Hello, Everard," Noble said. "You're back early."

"Yes, sir. It was either this or taking a train from New Haven at four in the morning, and I wanted to spare my wife that."

"Well, glad to have you aboard. I've been wanting a talk with you anyway. Will you have a cup of coffee with me?"

Coffee sounded good to Everard, as did the opportunity of talking with his commanding officer. "Thank you, sir," he said. "I'd like that."

"Bring it back here."

"In the wardroom?" Everard asked, somewhat sardonically. He had difficulty in taking these military games seriously.

"Sure," Noble grinned. "Nobody's around to witness the desecration."

Everard sat down across from the skipper, studying him as he sipped the coffee. Noble's face was more serene than the radioman had ever seen it; it was as if a shadow that Everard had not hitherto realized existed had passed from his eyes. Noble's features were regular enough, and the skipper was blessed with good teeth. He had blue eyes and plain brown

67

hair. It was an intelligent and kindly face, Everard thought; and now, with the lines that had seemed so strange in so young a man washed away, it was a happy one. Noble's build was as average as his face; five feet nine, perhaps, slender, erect, and well muscled. But somehow the captain was no longer average to Everard.

"Everard," Noble began, rather hesitantly. "This is none of my business, but what is a man with your qualifications doing sitting down with me in this undergrown booth only by my permission? Hell, you ought to be outranking me. Do you mind my asking?"

"Not at all, except that when I tell you you'll consider me a fool, and properly so."

"Try me," Noble said with a smile.

"Well, all my life," Everard said slowly," things have been made easy for me. My parents were well off, I've had good health, and I've been able to get along with people—an ability gained, I suppose, from a happy childhood with plenty of security and affection."

"That's the best inheritance anybody can have."

"Yes. After grammar school I went to a good prep school and then on to Yale. My performance wasn't sensational, but I was a Whiffenpoof—I'm proud of that; and I was tapped for Skull and Bones."

"A good all-around Yale man, eh?"

"I suppose so, sir. After that there was Yale Graduate School. During my second year as a graduate student I married Martha Belham, a Smith girl. Money was no problem for us and we had a fine life. I was appointed to the Yale Faculty and I've been there ever since. I was an assistant professor; I have two wonderful children and a lovely wife. My marriage has been successful. Never an emergency—except when the children were born, and even then Martha had an easy time."

"And you chucked all that away?"

"Temporarily, anyway. I warned you, sir. But see here. I was thirty-six years old and what had I done? What had I undergone? One of my professors in graduate school said something that took root in a rather curious manner in my mind, and I guess the war brought it to the surface."

"What was it?"

"Well, in his welcome to the students, he commended us for having embarked on a difficult road. 'You have abandoned the life of action,' he said, 'for the life of the mind.' Abandoned the life of action? I'd never *known* it."

"I think I understand how that might bother you."

"Then you are one of the very few, sir. At any rate, the war came along. Of course I would do something about it; that ran in the tradition: for God, for Country, and for Yale. Not a bad motto at that. I investigated. Either service would have commissioned me, and then given me a desk job somewhere— historical section, writing; teaching in some of the special programs; public relations; or psychological warfare. No hope at all for active service away from a desk. I chose the Navy because I like to sail; I used my connections in Washington to ensure that after I enlisted I would be ordered to PTs. They have intrigued me since I first heard of them. So here I am."

"What does your wife think, if you don't mind my asking."

"Martha was furious at first, then hurt because she thought it was caused by some lack on her part. She has ended by accepting the situation. I suppose she realizes that this is my big spree, so to speak. We were married quite young."

"Then you're here for the one great adventure of your life."

"It sounds utterly ridiculous now, doesn't it? But yes, that was my idea, though less sharply formulated."

"Regret your decision?"

"Most of the time—yes. But at occasional flashes, when we're under way, for instance, I'd change places with no one on earth."

"I know. Everard, it's not too late. I could help you get the officers' training course, perhaps up at Quonset."

"That's very good of you." Here was the decision to be made again, Everard thought. He looked at Noble, and realized that his captain was quite serious. Everard drew a deep breath. "No, sir," he said at last. "I want to stick to my fool impulse, thereby proving it not foolish, perhaps. Anyway, I want to stay with this boat."

"Good."

"After we've had some duty overseas, especially if this crew is broken up, I might very well accept your offer, sir."

"Okay. I'll do everything I can."

"I appreciate it, sir."

"No thanks necessary. I'm on the side of anybody in my crew any time, anywhere."

And he was, Noble realized, as the Ninety-Seven roared through the choppy waters of the Sound on its way to Archer's. Last night's hung-over crew (Jim Print looked worst of all) had metamorphosed into a smoothly-functioning organism this morning; and as the PT swept past Throgs Neck, Noble knew that he would do as much for any of them as he had offered to do for Everard.

Noble found it a pleasure to work with Donald Archer and his gang of white-mustached Scotch workmen. Archer simply nodded when Noble told him what was needed for the squadron; he got his foremen on the blueprints and his men taking measurements on the boat without delay. In the afternoon the Ninety-Seven's skipper took his exec for a walk up along the curving beach. From the shore, a low bluff mounted up above the Sound, its tall green trees seeded with beach cottages.

"What do you think of the crew now, Jim?" Noble asked, wondering what could bring the usual smile back to Jim's face.

"The crew?" Print repeated, looking startled. He picked up a rock and threw it at a sign that said "Cottage for Rent," missing it by feet. "The crew's all right," he said at last.

"Yes, I think we made out pretty well. Johnson is something of a foul ball, but I notice he practically sleeps with the guns. Radelewski now. I don't know. He bothers me a little."

"Ski's pretty cocky, but he loves the engines. Warder says he's a good mechanic and doesn't mind work."

"Fine. If he helps keep the engines running right I don't give a damn how cocky he is." Noble looked over at Print again and hesitated. He scowled down at his feet. "Look, it's none of my business, but is everything all right? You act worried. Tell me to go to hell if you want to."

His exec grinned for the first time.

"Hell, it's just a hangover. I'll be all right tomorrow."

"Good!" Noble said heartily. For a moment he thought his exec was going to say something more, but the words died and he stayed silent. They walked back to Archer's without speaking, and finding that the yard force was through with the boat, collected the crew and headed back to the Navy Yard.

But the next day Jim felt even more haggard, and he wondered if he could ever forget Saturday night . . .

The brands on the lovely white body were blurred, and the sheets were smeared with lipstick as Print lay propped up on an elbow beside Delilah, who was crying soundlessly. She had tried, he knew that, wanting terribly to know love, but the physical act hadn't touched her. Worse, he now suspected that these preliminary passages that had so enflamed him had been meaningless to her—that she had been trying even then, acting, attempting to kindle in herself the missing fire.

"I'm sorry, Di," Print told her.

"I'm licked," she said in a monotone of hopeless despair. "Jim, you hit me so hard when I first saw you that I thought you'd be the one who could . . . "

Print swore to himself.

"I was married, Jim; it only lasted a year. It was . . . this same thing. I couldn't keep on acting. I guess I can't blame him."

"Have you seen a doctor?"

"Yes. He said there was nothing physical. Look, it's not . . . oh, hell, I don't like other women, it's not that."

"Of course not!"

"Jim . . . Could you marry me? I think you could save me."

It caught Print unprepared. Marry her? A woman who

71

couldn't love? Maybe there were men who didn't need response, men for whom her superlative surface beauty would be enough, but he wasn't one of those; he had to have a whole woman. She was watching him closely, and before he could think of anything to say she spoke again.

"I see, Jim. I'm going to dress now. Will you please take my things to the bathroom. I'll wash this stuff off." Then she added with a sudden bitterness: "Maybe I *should* have made you burn it on."

He took her home and tried vainly to sleep when he returned. He went out at noon on Sunday and started drinking, knowing he had to do something to drown out those memories. When he got drunk he only wanted her again, realizing that he had never seen anything so beautiful—white and gold and red. Once in a dreary bar he found himself crying silently over the knowledge that she was fruit of wax, lovelier than life outside, but hollow within. God, he felt sorry for her. . . .

As the days passed, he was still sorry for her. Only now other things worried him as well. Charlie Noble had said he thought Daggs would improve with the responsibility of command, but he had been wrong. It seemed that the commander got meaner every day. He was always chewing somebody out, and always within hearing distance of as many people as possible. One day, Print had encountered Delilah in Daggs' office, and she had looked at him as if she couldn't quite remember who he was. He knew that she was in a position to make things mighty uncomfortable for him. But surely she wouldn't tell Daggs—or would she? Print knew she had been angry that night, and that the humiliation she must have felt, after seeing his reaction to her proposal of marriage, might well have turned to hate by this time. What with one thing and another, Print was mighty glad when everyone got aboard the PTs one morning, and the twelve-boat squadron went roaring up Long Island Sound to Newport.

8

JULY WAS HALF over and the squadron had been at Newport for two weeks, based at the Melville Net and Fuel Depot. Charles Noble stood in the cockpit of the Ninety-Seven, looking out over the silky blueness of Narragansett Bay. On either side, the other boats of the squadron were spread out in a line abreast, muttering along at a steady twenty knots. Daggs' boat was next to the Ninety-Seven, about two hundred yards away.

"It's nuts," Jim Print said. "Absolutely screwy."

"Come, come, Jim. Just because we were out on patrol all last night and now we're combing the Bay when we ought to be sleeping—so what? Doncha know they's a wah on?"

"Eleven submarines on the surface, in column, heading for Narragansett Bay. I'll bet that Army airedale was drunk. Why the hell didn't he attack them?"

"It was a transport plane," Noble said patiently. "Nothing to attack with."

"Come on now, Charlie. Do you really think they'll try to force the nets here?"

"No, and neither does the admiral, but with that twenty-ship convoy due tonight, he can't take any chances. Twenty loaded merchant ships would be quite a prize—Jim!"

Noble's voice cracked with excitement as he fumbled for

his binoculars. A black round object with a glint of metal was poking from the water ahead of the commander's boat. Periscope!

"What bit *you?*"

"There!" Noble shouted. He got the glasses to his eyes, hearing a buzzer sound sharply from over water, then shouts, and the mounting roar of goosed engines. He had the glass on the object and saw, distinctly, a vertical, floating tree limb with a tin can over the end. Then the commander's boat flashed into his field of vision and across the thing.

"Oh, hell," Noble said, dropping the glasses to their straps and laughing with embarrassment. "I thought that damned piece of wood was a periscope. A fine naval officer I am, thinking I see a periscope in thirty feet or so of water."

"You scared hell out of me." Print grinned. "I . . . "

"Skipper!" Sterns shouted. "The commander has just dropped two depth charges!"

"What's that? Depth charges! Why, he too must have thought that limb was a periscope!" A horrible thought struck him. "Ike! The charges are set for forty feet, aren't they?"

"Yes, sir."

"Oh, God!" Noble exclaimed, remembering the chart soundings. He stared, frozen, waiting for explosions that already were overdue. None came.

"Hill," Noble asked with mounting uneasiness, "what's the depth and bottom where those charges were dropped?"

Within a minute Hill was back from the chart room.

"Thirty-eight feet, sir," he said. "Soft mud bottom."

"Holy cats!"

"This area is marked for convoy anchorage on the chart, too, sir."

Ike Sterns whistled. "Well," he declared, "they won't use it for ammunition ships, not now."

"But it's got to be used!" Noble cried. "The convoy is due to anchor here tonight." But he knew Sterns was right, and that put the cap on it; the admiral would have to be advised, with major plans and orders changed. Daggs would be on a hot spot indeed for dropping depth charges in anchorage water too shallow to explode them.

"The admiral better pick him another anchorage," Sterns answered steadily. "With the soft mud bottom there's no way of telling when them damned ash cans will sink that extra two feet, and then—blooey!"

"Oh, Lord," Noble said. He saw that Daggs' boat had lost way, was stopping, and he brought his own throttles to neutral.

"Prep Ninety-Seven from Prep Ninety!" Daggs' voice came stormily from the radio speaker. "Report alongside me immediately; all other boats lie to."

"Now what?" Noble muttered. "Okay, Jim; take her alongside."

The Ninety-Seven closed on the Ninety. Daggs was standing by the after torpedo tube, looking extremely angry and red in the face.

"Noble!" Daggs shouted. "You're gunnery and torpedo officer of this squadron, aren't you?"

"Yes, sir."

"Then maybe you'll explain to me why when I dropped two goddamn depth charges in the goddamn water they didn't go off! Hey?"

"The water isn't deep enough, Commander," Noble said angrily. Holy hell, hadn't he even looked at the chart?

"Don't give me that crap, Noble. Stop the blanking gundecking!"

"They are set for forty feet, sir," Noble said, trying to keep the anger out of his voice. "There's only thirty-eight feet of water where you dropped the charges." Daggs glared, not saying anything. "That's a soft mud bottom, Commander," Noble continued. "They might explode any time in the next twenty-four hours, and a convoy is due to anchor here tonight."

"My goddamn depth charges were set for thirty-five feet,"

Daggs half screamed. "Hell, they're all supposed to be set for thirty-five feet! They're defective, not set right. Noble, you're responsible! Hear me?"

"Yes, sir." Noble felt hot and cold all over.

"You've got shallow-water diving gear aboard?"

"Yes, sir."

"All right. I've got bearings on where I dropped the charges. You send your torpedoman down and have him put the safety forks on them. Then drag 'em out. I'll take the rest of the squadron back to base, and I'll have a word with you when you get in."

Noble was too angry to say anything.

"Did you hear me?" Daggs bellowed.

"Aye, aye, sir."

"All right. You got your tail in a sling; now try and get it out."

Noble was shaking as the rest of the squadron got under way, Daggs' boat in the lead. God Almighty. Send Sterns down? The bastard!

Ike Sterns thought: Christ, I'm glad I'm not an officer and have to take that crap. He knew Daggs' ash cans had been set for forty feet, like all the rest in the squadron; moreover the commander knew it too. Noble's face was red as he looked over at Sterns.

"You heard the commander, Sterns," he said. "Get the shallow-water diving gear ready."

"Aye, aye, sir," Sterns said blankly.

"Johnson, you and Benton get the anchor line out of the forepeak and lay it out on deck. Floyd, get the coil of one-inch out of the lazarette. Bear a hand, you guys. We've got a job to do."

Radelewski helped Sterns get out the helmet, hose and pump. "Hey, Sterns," the motor mac sneered, "how do you know them depth charges won't go off while you're trying to put the safety forks on?"

"I don't."

76

"No," Radelewski said. "You don't. Get your ass blowed off just because an officer pulls a bull."

Sterns found nothing to say to this, for at heart he agreed. Crap! he thought. A guy don't mind taking his chances, but to fumble around a sinking depth charge that might go off any second and shove enough sea water up his gut to blow him apart like a gutted fish! God damn Daggs anyway! He finished connecting the hose to the pump and the helmet air-intake.

"Okay, Sterns," Noble said, coming up to him. "Get the spare safety forks. I want to practice putting forks on our depth charges with my eyes shut before I make the dive." Only after Noble had spoken did Sterns realize that the skipper was in swimming trunks.

"What's that?" Sterns demanded, seeing Radelewski's mouth drop. "You're going down, sir?"

"Of course," Noble snapped. "What the hell did you think?"

Radelewski looked up at the sun. It was still pretty high, so the skipper should have light enough down there. He was tending the hose, Ike Sterns had the line, and the two kids were pumping. The bubbles came up like a beer bottle running over, and he could see the hose and lines for five or six feet down. He was sweating. If the depth charges went off under the Ninety-Seven they would blow the goddamn boat all apart—his engines too! Gertie's knees, but it would be a wallop! Then Radelewski thought of Noble down there feeling around for the ash can in the mud. He kept watching the bubbles. It seemed like the skipper had been down a blanking long time.

Print was sure of one thing: if Charlie got killed, he'd see Daggs court-martialed. Everard was on the hand alidade checking that the bearings held steady. Print had his hand on the throttles. The engines were running, but out of gear. A cloud was coming close to the sun; without sunlight the bottom down there would be darker than ever for Charlie. Oh, Lord! Print prayed, please don't let these depth charges explode!

After wandering around in the mud and murk for what seemed forever, Noble found the first depth charge by barking his shin on it. He squatted down in the brown-green shadow as he stared through the square glass windows of his helmet. Thank God the exploder end was up! At the third try he got the fork on and breathed again, finding himself dizzy with suspense, and so damned scared that he was afraid he'd lose his guts. He jerked the line once; immediately a second line with a hook and strap on it came down. He managed to dig it around and under the ash can, then pulled on it. The depth charge pulled loose, stirring up the mud, then went on up and out of sight.

At first Floyd had been thinking what a swell story this would be to tell the guys back home; then he suddenly realized what could happen and he was too scared to think any more. He and Benton kept the air pump hopping. Ike Sterns shouted suddenly and grabbed the other line, the one with the hook, and dropped it overboard. After a while he pulled on it again.

"All right, you guys!" he shouted. "I got it coming up; come on and bear a hand!" Everybody else went and grabbed the line and hauled the muddy black depth charge on deck and tied it to the 20-mm. mount.

"Holy Mary!" Ski exclaimed. "Look at the mud line. That thing had sunk a foot. I hope the other one didn't land in a softer place."

Mister Print moved the boat along slowly, with Mister Noble walking along on the bottom, to the place where the second charge had been dropped. It was only a little way.

Everard realized that he had never before known what suspense was like. It was a freezing cold in the intestines, a shaking in the backbone, a slickness in the hands. At times he could hardly keep the bearings accurate. He had felt a little

78

like this when Martha had had their first child, but somehow then he had been quite confident that all would be well. Now he didn't know; the only thing that made him feel better was the memory of Sterns' face when Mr. Noble said that he was going to do the diving. Everard wondered if the captain knew how much he had given back to Sterns when he did that. But Sterns hadn't been afraid, Everard reflected. He was sure that the torpedoman's offer to dive, after he had learned that it was, genuinely, for him a voluntary affair, had been perfectly sincere.

"God, he can't find it!" Print gasped. "Are those bearings right on, Everard?"

"Right on, sir."

Just then Sterns whooped again.

"He's got it; the skipper did it, boys. All safe now! Get that blanking line over, Warder; hurry up."

Everard was glad to get his hands on the line again, and soon the two depth charges, now as inert and safe as the ash cans for which they were named, were tied tightly against the gun mount. The captain came bobbing up to the surface. He looked exhausted when Everard and Sterns helped him aboard, and he sat down on the ammunition chest and put his head in his hands for several minutes. Everard had never heard a man swear the way Ike Sterns did.

By the time the boat got back to the Melville depot, Noble was feeling himself again. I'm a hell of a naval officer, he thought; I almost fainted when I felt that nice warm deck under my feet again.

"What are you going to do with the depth charges?" Print asked.

"I know what I'd like to do with them," Noble answered, grinning at his exec.

"Take the safety forks off first, Skipper," Ike Sterns put in.

Noble hadn't realized that the torpedoman had been stand-

ing beside him. Damn it all; he'd not meant to have an enlisted man hear him criticize his commanding officer, even
by implication.

"That's enough, Sterns," he said sharply. "Get a crew together and transfer these charges back to the commander's
boat."

"Aye, aye, sir."

"Well?" Daggs demanded, glowering, after Noble had
knocked on his office door and walked in. His small eyes
had a red tinge to them and his face was the same color.

"You told me you wanted to see me when I got back,
sir."

"The charges, the charges, how about the goddamn depth
charges?"

"Oh, they're safe now. I'm having them put back aboard
your boat. I'll have the firing mechanisms checked right
away, sir."

"Well, that's fine, Charlie, that's fine," Daggs said, a changed
man instantly. "That was good work. By God, you made a
mistake, but you fixed it up. I don't ever hold a grudge against
a man who does that. I reckon I won't need to chew you
out this time, son, but don't you let it happen again."

"Commander," Noble said, looking at him, "I'd like a
seventy-two hour leave this weekend." Daggs blinked; he
realized Noble knew the policy had been against overnight
leave for anyone in the squadron.

"Why, sure, Charlie," he said affably. "You go right ahead."

Noble walked out of the office into the warm dusk. He
was going to use that seventy-two for a trip to New York.
He was going to see Kathleen.

80

9

On Saturday morning Noble sat in a slick leather chair in the lobby of the New Yorker; after the third puff he ground out his cigarette in an ashtray, never taking his eyes from the clock above the stairs leading from the subway. Kathleen was to meet him under the clock for lunch, and it was nearly twelve.

He looked down at the florist's box in his hands. Kathleen liked gardenias. Automatically he looked at his watch. Twelve o'clock. The big clock on the wall agreed. A slender girl in light blue hurried up the stairs and he half rose—no, not Kathleen. My God, Noble thought. I haven't been this excited about meeting someone since . . . There she was!

She was wearing a simple grey summer dress, loosely cut. Noble rose; her lips were parted as she looked around; then she saw him coming toward her. Her quick smile went through Noble; something other than gladness lay behind her smile, though. Sadness? Fear?

"Kathleen," he said, taking her hand.

"Why, Charles, you're thinner, and you look tired. Brown as an Indian too. What have you been doing?"

"Patrolling and escorting, mostly. But you look wonderful, darling. I have something for you."

"How nice. Gardenias! They're beautiful."

She was radiant as she pinned them on. Her cheeks were softly pink, and her lips had the same curve as the petals. The scent of the blossoms surrounded her like magic. She gave Noble both hands and they smiled joyfully at each other.

"I'm so happy now," she said. "But do you know, I was terrified in the subway. A married woman meeting a man, morning sober, but I don't feel guilty or frightened any more. I'm glad I'm here."

"I love you, Kathleen."

The smile went away, but it returned. "I won't even say you mustn't. I won't say no to anything now."

Noble supposed it was a good lunch that came after the martinis, but he never really knew. He was too busy looking at her across the table.

"Gosh," he said. "I hate to budge, but I've got tickets to a matinee. After the show comes dinner, and then . . . What's the matter?"

"I can't have dinner with you."

"Why not?"

"I just can't."

His face fell with disappointment.

"Darling, listen. If we had dinner and a few drinks, as we would, and went dancing, as we would, and I was in your arms—Charlie, I'm too fond of you—why, I'd end up in your bed. Oh, I keep remembering our night and I'll never regret it; but I told you I wouldn't be wife to two men. I'd feel dirty, and cheap, don't you see? If I behaved like that, you know what you would think me. And it wouldn't be fair."

"I guess not," Noble said dully.

"Poor Charles," she said, touching his hand. "Have I disappointed you dreadfully?"

"Yes," he said, and then, ashamed of himself, he smiled at her. "But here's to the afternoon, anyway."

"You're so damn sweet," she said, her eyes brimming. "If you had gone on looking like that, I would simply have had to go to your room with you now. I couldn't have helped myself."

"You would!" Noble said. "Just wait a minute, I'll get it back. Like this?"

"No."

"This?" By this time she was laughing. But then she became serious again.

"I'll go up with you, Charles, if you say so; but I don't want to, and it wouldn't be the same. I think perhaps we might never be happy together again if I did. Darling, do understand."

Noble, with an effort, beat down temptation. "I understand," he said. "It's all right. You see, I love you. I want to marry you. Can't we ever be together again?"

"I'm another man's wife."

"What do I care for that?" he half shouted. "I want to marry you!"

"Shh, people will hear you. There's so little you know about me."

"I know I don't want any other woman but you."

"If I could only be alone, live by myself in a quiet place for a few weeks and think things out. I have a little money of my own, but I don't know where to go. I'm thinking of leaving Morton, Charles."

"You mean, really leaving him?"

"Yes; but I'm just not sure. I've got to get away from everybody."

Noble suddenly remembered Jim Print throwing a rock at a sign that read: "Cottage for Rent."

"Kathleen," he said excitedly, "I know the place."

He told her of the neat little bungalows, the wooded bluff, and the blue and green quiet of the Sound, with the gulls crying on the shore. Her face brightened so he had to warn her. "That was weeks ago, dear; it might be rented."

83

"Oh, no. It can't be. Let's go and see!"

"How about our show?"

"Can't we see the house instead? It sounds just heavenly. I can write Morton that I've gone back to his mother's and he'll never know the difference, not until I've had the time I want, anyway."

"We'll go," Noble said.

"Darling. Listen. This is to get away, to have time to think and decide. This isn't a love nest we're arranging. You know that, don't you?"

"I know it, Kathleen. Let's go right away. We'll have a picnic supper on the beach. How about it?"

"That's a wonderful idea!"

At the top of a wooded bluff stood the cottages. All during the train trip to Darien, followed by a short hop by bus, Noble and Kathleen had grown more excited. Now Noble pointed to a long wooden stairway. "The sign was at the foot of this," he said.

"Let's see if the cabin's still available," said Kathleen breathlessly, and they hurried over to a small, neat cottage at the head of the stairs. The door opened after Noble's second knock to reveal a gaunt woman with a forbidding face.

"Yes?"

"Good afternoon, ma'am. A sign down on the beach said a cottage was for rent."

"This is it. I'm Mrs. Powers. Are you interested?"

Noble paused, but Kathleen didn't speak up. "My friend here, Mrs. Daggs, wanted a quiet place to spend a few weeks, and I thought this might be what she wanted."

The woman's eyes moved to Kathleen, who stood tensely.

Mrs. Powers' eyes softened. "I see," she said. Noble wondered if she did. "Come in; I'll show you around."

The cottage was quite ordinary, but pin-neat and spotless;

also there was a wonderful view of the blue and white Sound through the windows of the living room and bedroom.

"It's very nice," Kathleen said.

"Well, now, I'm not sure I'll rent. I've got that cottage down on the beach, and this one is a little large for me. Thought I might move down there and rent this one; wouldn't do it, except that this war has made summer renters scarce."

"I know," Kathleen said thoughtfully.

"Think you'll want it?"

"Well, I'm not quite sure. Oh, it *is* nice; please don't think I don't like it, Mrs. Powers."

For the first time Mrs. Powers smiled. "I can see you do, and you can call me Annie." Her sharp eyes turned on Noble. "Young man, I'm glad to see you in uniform. Have you done any fighting, or are you just one of these smart young men from 90 Church Street?"

"I've done some fighting, Annie." Noble grinned.

"Ah, if you knew what a man's voice saying that name does to me. Stick to this boy, Mrs. Daggs; he has a tongue in his mouth and an eye in his head. It's nearly four. Would you like a cup of tea with me?"

"That's good of you," Noble said after a glance at Kathleen, "but we have a picnic supper with us to eat on the beach. If it's all right?"

"And why shouldn't it be? The beach is public. Just go down the steps there; a nice place to eat is beyond the pavilion about a hundred feet. The trees grow close enough to the sand to give shade. Have a good picnic. But remember, you two, if other folks decide on the cottage before you do and plunk down the money—they get it."

"We understand."

Annie glared at them and went inside, slamming the door.

"Charles," Kathleen said. "You're wonderful."

"You heard her. She likes uniforms."

"Silly, let's eat."

The picnic was a great success until a woman came along

the beach with a little girl, perhaps four years old, wearing a yellow dress.

"Mummy," the girl said as they came by. "What are those two people doing? Why are they sitting so close together?"

"Hush, Francey." They passed on and Noble smiled at Kathleen, only to be shocked to see her silent tears.

"Hey! What's this?"

"I don't think I can go through with it."

"What?"

"Leave Morton. I'll never be able to do it."

"It can't be this bad."

"Oh, Charlie, there are things you just don't know."

"Then tell me."

"I can't. Oh, God!"

Noble, sobered by her distress, and bewildered that it should have been set off by a child's thoughtless remark, hesitated, then put his arm around her shoulder and drew her sob-shaken body against him. She started to pull away.

"No," he said firmly. "To hell with bed, to hell with anything. You're in trouble, that's all I need to know. The least I can do is try to comfort you. You don't have to tell me anything."

He stroked her hair gently. She shivered and broke into a renewed storm of weeping, burrowing her head against his chest. They sat for a long time. At last the sobs died down, and, spent, she half lay against him. He smelled faint perfume, clean hair. She lifted her pale face to him, her eyes showing the effect of the tears.

"Do you hate me, Charlie?"

"Hate you?"

"I'd better go home; we'll tell Annie. But I do want you to know what a comfortable, good person you are."

"Flattery will get you nowhere, woman," Noble said, trying to hide the bleak desolation he felt. "And, don't worry; you don't have to make a decision now. Think it over and if you decide to take this place, let me know."

"How can I? Someone might notice my letter."

"Write me at General Delivery, Newport."

"All right. I'll try."

"May I write you, darling?"

"But . . ."

"How far are you in the city from a branch Post Office?"

"Why, not far. It's the Clinton branch office."

"I'll write you there, General Delivery?"

"Why, yes. I'd like to hear from you."

"Good." He felt better; at least she wouldn't be entirely out of his reach.

10

CHARLES NOBLE was sitting at his desk aboard the Ninety-Seven, scowling at the bulkhead. He was feeling sick and let down. Even Sterns! Sterns on top of everything else.

His hand was clenched on the desk; he uncurled the fingers, brought them back to a fist. Two weeks since he had left Kathleen, and not a word from her. He had written ten times, and now the General Delivery clerk at the Newport Post Office would shake his head even before Noble could ask if he had a letter. To hell with it.

Each time he had been so sure the letter would be there, and when it wasn't he was sharply tempted to go out and get drunk. But the memory of Kathleen's sorrow restrained him. She had problems he knew nothing about. Well, he wasn't having any picnic himself. Patrols every other night, training runs every day; Daggs getting more arrogant and harder to please; worst of all, the Ninety-Seven's crew going sour.

Now Sterns. Noble had just finished bawling hell out of the torpedoman; number two torpedo's air pressure had dropped 300 pounds. Sheer incompetence, Noble repeated to himself. Hell, when Johnson and Radelewski and the kids fouled up, he didn't think so much of it, but Ike . . .

Jim Print knocked and came in at Noble's word. He didn't look happy.

"Damn it, Jim," Noble said peevishly. "What the hell is wrong with this crew? Nobody does anything right any more."

Print hesitated, then blurted, "Go look in the mirror, Charlie."

"What?"

"You're the one who's off."

"You mean . . ."

"I mean you're harder to please than Daggs these days. I heard Ike tell you two days ago that that torpedo needed air, and you didn't pay any attention to him."

"Well, I will be damned!" Noble stared at Jim, saying nothing more. The generator was running aft, and someone laughed on deck. Noble stood up, his face red.

"Sorry," Print said.

"Sorry? For God's sake, thanks, Jim. I'll stop acting like a kid that's lost its candy. I see it now. Why the hell didn't you kick my tail?"

"Mutiny, Charlie, mutiny."

"Horse manure. Come on up with me while I eat some crow."

Noble hoped he would never have to feel like that again. He was angry at himself as he went up the ladder, angry clear through. He found the men sitting on the foredeck, still laughing, and it hurt when they stiffened up and became quiet as he walked up to them. Sterns looked away.

"Sterns," Noble said carefully. "Mr. Print has reminded me that you gave me the dope on that torpedo two days ago. He's right. I'm sorry. I'm sorry as hell."

The torpedoman looked at Noble in embarrassment, then his craggy face split with one of his grins.

"Hell, that's all right, Skipper. A little chewin' out never hurt nobody."

"It may not hurt the guy on the receiving end if he doesn't deserve it, but it raises hell with the guy doing the chewing. Sit down, Sterns. You too, Warder. Mind if I join you? The sun feels good, doesn't it?"

89

"Sure does, Skipper," Sterns said. "Ding Hau was telling us some China Station stories. Say, Ding, where'd you get that name anyway?"

Ding Hau stretched out on the deck and gave his audience a grin. He was relaxing now, so he wasn't wearing his false teeth. He also took them out and put them on a shelf over the stove when he was cooking. The men called them Ding Hau's saltshakers.

"It was in Shanghai," the cook said. "A bunch of us dropped in on a whore house. You never saw so many women, so many kinds of women, in one place. Well, the boys had told me that old one about the Chinese women being laid out thwartship. Anyway, I was bound to see for myself, so I picked a Chinese girl. She says, 'Too small—no good. You pay me double price—okay?' Well, the guys was laughing like hell, and I was embarrassed, but I did want to see how they worked it, so I said okay too. Well." Ding stopped and smiled reminiscently.

"Well, what?" Noble demanded. "Don't leave us dangling."

"About two hours later she brought me back to where the other guys were. She says, 'He little man, but he Ding Hau.' Ding Hau means 'Okay.' 'One-half price to you, big boy. You Ding Hau.' It stuck, and that's sort of been my name ever since."

"I reckon you're too old now, Ding," Radelewski chortled. "Reckon I'll call you Was Ding Hau from now on."

"You ask Fanny or her girls," Sterns put in. "She feeds old Ding free beer whenever he comes up to the Oasis. You young punks got the wrong idea about when a man gets old."

"Mister Noble," Warder said, "don't you reckon we'll be going out pretty soon?"

"You mean really out? Yes, I think so."

"Reckon there's any chance we'll go by way of Dago?"

"Afraid not. We'll probably go west from the Panama Canal. Why?"

"I've got a family in San Diego," Warder said. "My wife and me, we decided the kids ought to go to one school more than six months at a time, so we bought a house out there. I was kind of hoping to see them."

"That's tough, Warder. I'll try to get leave for you if you want."

"I can't afford the trip, Skipper, but thanks a lot."

To Print it was wonderful to see how tickled the crew was to have Charlie himself again; well, so was he. He hoped the trouble wasn't Di, for he'd already decided he was going to try her again when the squadron went back to New York.

"Liberty tonight for all hands but the duty section," Noble announced. "Overnight if you want it. Jim, let's go to town together."

"Pardner, you're speaking my language."

When they got to Newport that evening, Noble's first stop was the Post Office, and this time Print went in with him. "Anything for Charles Noble?" he heard the skipper ask at the General Delivery window.

The man looked through a rank of pigeon holes.

"Nope, Mac," he said. "Say, are you sure that letter's coming?"

"No," Charlie said clearly. "I'm not sure at all."

Very well, Noble thought resignedly as they left the Post Office. I guess that does it. He didn't blame Kathleen; if she couldn't make the break, she couldn't. Who the hell was he to make her leave her husband? But she might have written him and told him her decision. Well, that's the way it goes. He was sad, and a little tired, but at least there were no more holds on him. Ding Hau's story had made him think of women, and Warder's question, reminding him that the squadron would be pointing for war soon, put the cap on it. In the Skaal Room, they sat down next to a table with two girls.

"Ah," Print said, "what do you make of this task force to starboard?"

Noble looked over at the table. The girls seemed all right. One was watching him; he returned the compliment and lifted his glass to her. She had a good, pleasant face and not too much makeup; her eyes were nice; and the superstructure that showed above the table looked worthy of closer inspection.

"Bums away," he said, getting up. He walked over to the girls' table, followed by Print.

"May I have this dance?" he asked the girl with the nice eyes.

"Surely," she said, smiling.

Mary was her name. Her hull was okay, Noble decided; a little more blister than usual, maybe, but that went with her turrets—a six-inch cruiser if ever he saw one—and the whole effect was quite lush. She laughed well, too. Lighthearted was the word for her. She spoke well, danced well, did everything well, and with an unquenchable gaiety. Mary had a car, and after a few more drinks the foursome adjourned to the Stonebridge Inn, some miles away, where Jim and Noble were joined by some other PT officers. There the enlarged party danced some more, swapping around. Apparently there was a telephone operators' convention at the Inn, and the PT officers were quite swallowed up. Noble saw Jim in a booth with girls on each side. In contrast, Mary and Noble were relatively alone at one corner of the bar.

"It's stuffy in here," he said.

"Yassuh, Mistuh Bones, it sho is. What's the old end man supposed to say next?"

"Why, fresh air, of course. Outside."

"Okay, but I'll take this drink with me."

"Naturally."

A moon was shining, romantically enough, and the smell of salt marsh drifted over the land. The jukebox rolled the barrel out through the Inn windows, and in parked cars Noble saw the glow of cigarettes.

"Let's sit in my car," Mary said.

92

Noble helped her in, sat beside her, and took a gulp of his drink. She had a nice perfume. There was something sane and healthy about this girl, he decided; her amusement wasn't cynical or bitter.

"I'm pretty lucky," he said, drinking.

"No lines, Charlie." Mary drank too. "Sweet words sound fine to me when a lad means them, but not as step one of Whortlebottom's guaranteed easy method."

"Okay, no line. Still I'm lucky. I wanted to find a girl tonight."

"Really? Well, pal, I wasn't at the Skaal Room just to breathe the secondhand air."

"I'd like to kiss you, but I'm afraid I'll spill your drink."

"Listen to the man. If you make me spill a drink with a kiss I'll figure it's worth it. Come on."

Noble grinned to himself. He put his glass on the floor and kissed her, softly, not pushingly or demandingly, trying to ask a question with it. The meeting was a gentle one, but it grew in fervor and lasted some time. He drew away finally and picked up his drink. She tossed hers out of the window.

"I don't need to drink any more," she said.

Noble awoke in the brass double bed of the tourist room in the grey dawn, awake as always at the time he set for himself, a result of two years of watch-standing. Six o'clock. Mary was still asleep, short hair tousled above her relaxed and serene face, and one breast exposed above the covers. Noble felt soft and surfeited; the sharp pain that had gnawed at him for the past two weeks was gone.

When he leaned over and kissed her she awoke at once and smiled. She sat up partially and leaned on an elbow, heedless of the covers fallen to her waist.

"Good morning," she said, smiling. She flopped down again, stretching both arms above her head, breasts moving nicely with the tautened muscles. "I must say, Reluctant Dragon, that for a slow starter you run a *very* good race once you've hit the track."

"Mary, thanks for everything."

"I believe you mean that. Thank you too, Charlie. Women get lonely too, you know. They also get hungry. Let's have breakfast and I'll drive you back to your station."

"I can catch a bus."

"Don't be silly." She got out of bed and wandered nude around the room, collecting scattered clothing. She seemed puzzled, while Noble lay back and watched her mature, compact body. "Ah! there they are," she said, bringing a pair of filmy pants from under an antimacassar. "Now how the devil did they get there?"

"I guess we had a rather tempestuous entrance," Noble said lazily.

"You nearly had an ignominious exit," she answered. He reached out and slapped her behind resoundingly. "Just bashful, that's all," he told her.

They had breakfast at a diner and afterward she drove him back to Melville. Noble felt clearheaded, comfortable, and almost happy. Mary made no attempt to kiss him at the gate.

"Here's my phone number," she said, smiling almost shyly. "Thirty miles isn't so far. If you want to, call me. It was fun."

"It was grand. Good-by, Mary."

When Noble went aboard the Ninety-Seven, Jim Print, who obviously had a hangover, stared at him in amazement.

"Where the hell did you go last night?" he demanded. "You look like you'd just spent a week at a rest cure."

"I did."

Noble wrote Kathleen that day, realizing that this letter was different from the others. He didn't feel differently about her; the change lay in the fact that he was healed, well again, free of self-pity. He wondered uneasily if the other letters had whined like a spoiled pup. He knew he wrote well now, saying what he meant easily and clearly. He wrote that he loved her, then sat looking at the word. Did he? Could he have loved her and still gone with Mary? It seemed odd, but yes, there was no doubt in his mind: Mary was balm but Kathleen was peace. Noble sent the letter, and duty sent the Ninety-Seven on patrol; he and his crew were one again, the boat was once more the happy home of men. Twice he called Mary. They stayed at a house in the country where leaves rustled outside their window, and great trucks rumbling by on the road beneath became part of the soothing and sleepy sounds of night. The lady of the house served clear, hot coffee, dishes of scrambled eggs, and crisp bacon. It all was good and Noble grew content again. They spoke of love sometimes, but as an abstraction only; false words of love did not come between them.

At the end of ten days a letter came:

. . . I still don't know, Charles. I rather doubt that I can ever leave him. Don't think bitterly of me. It may be that we'll never meet again, but you have been wonderful to me, and you have given me confidence and hope.

I know from your last letter that you have found a girl. Is she good to you? I hope she is not as good for you as I am. . . . There, I've said it. I'm such a fool. It is what I wanted to happen, but now that it has, I'm actually jealous. Is she a good lover? Don't mistake me, my dear; I don't blame you, and I do want to see you again, but still—I don't know. Aren't women fools?

                                        Warmly,
                                                Kathleen.

He was shaken with happiness over this letter, yet frightened as well, for she sounded so serious about the possibility that they might not meet again.

It was with mixed emotions, therefore, that Noble received the news, early in August, that the squadron was ordered back to New York. Just before the boats shoved off, Commander Daggs came on board the Ninety-Seven.

"Got a burr under your tail, Charlie?" he roared. "Well, I reckon Di will be glad to see you. She says she's getting pretty lonesome down there, especially since the old lady left for my folks'."

Charlie started at that, Print noticed, and when he spoke his voice sounded rather strange.

"Mrs. Daggs has gone home then?"

"Yep. Left a few days ago. I guess the big city was a little too much for her. I hope we won't be there too goddamn long ourselves. I want to get after them blanking Japs."

"You bet," Noble said, and his voice sounded normal now.

"You're a fighting man too, Charlie, just like me," Daggs said. "Knew it first time I laid eyes on you. All right, men!" he shouted suddenly. "Let's go to New York; there's a hell of a lot more women down there than up here in this hole."

The trip south was undistinguished except for a spell of bad weather which made Print doubly glad to get back to New York, with its sheltered water—and Di. He had meant to see her that night, but she was out when he called; and on the next morning Daggs sent the Ninety-Seven to Archer's. The boat was to be there two or three weeks, since the commander wanted Noble to supervise the installation of the new 20-mm. mounts on all the PTs. The other boats would come up in turn as needed. Print was, of course, disappointed, although he'd still be able to come in at night by train. But Charlie looked happy as a bug at the orders.

Indeed, Noble could nearly have kissed Daggs when he received them. The commander's report might have meant just what he said—Kathleen had gone home—or it might mean the excuse they had decided on if she went to the cottage. . . . He managed to hide his delight from Daggs, but Jim, who was pretty glum, was curious about his captain's reaction to three weeks in the sticks. Noble told his exec that he liked fresh air. Jim threw up his hands.

The crew of the Ninety-Seven greeted Donald Archer and quickly got settled alongside his dock; water hoses and power leads were brought aboard. It was late afternoon by then, and Jim Print started at once for New York, accompanied by several of the men. Noble could hardly contain himself as he went out of the yacht-yard gate. He took the road that ran above the bluff, for it would be quicker than the beach. The last half mile seemed endlessly long, but finally he reached the head of the steps and the cottage, so close now, where Kathleen might be. He wasn't too hopeful, not after the letter, but still any hope at all made his blood pound. Oh God! he thought. I hope she comes to the door!

He knocked, then knocked again. He heard a bird singing. Then footsteps. They were too heavy. Noble froze; he knew Kathleen's light step on a floor.

This door opened, and a door of hope closed as Annie Powers peered questioningly at Noble through her glasses.

"Why," she said, "it's the young man."

"Yes," Noble said, dashed hope making his voice thick and bitter in his mouth.

So it was really ended, and he had lost her. Standing in the door with his hat in his hand, Noble's memory went back to the station wagon and whispered words, and he tried to face the reality that he would be one of those who go through life with only memories of the one love lost. Lucky the man who grasps it and holds on, he thought. But what was the woman saying?

"I know someone who is going to be very glad to see you," she exclaimed, smiling warmly at him.

"What?"

"Kathleen rented the beach cottage; it's the smaller of the two so we decided it would be better for her. You hurry down there, young man, and mind you treat her right."

Without knowing what he said to Annie, Noble was stumbling down the long wooden stairs. But even as he did so, he cautioned himself to control his eagerness. He remembered he had nearly lost Kathleen once through pressing too hard; not again. If he couldn't have her body, he would not forfeit the pleasure of being with her. The last few steps led to a light-colored wooden door, set in a brown shingled wall. In front of the door was a small wooden platform; tall trees hung over the low roof of the hillside cottage. He noted that the door paint was somewhat faded; he hunted for a bell, then knocked, his heart bumping.

The door framed Kathleen, in simple brown skirt and sweater, like a full-length portrait. Eyes and lips parted with happiness and pleasure, and her face turned radiant at the sight of him.

"Charles! Is it really you?"

She started to come forward, then dropped back, wanting Noble to come inside. He was through the door, dropping his cap, only vaguely seeing the light carpet, the double bed by the door, and the blue Sound beyond the windows of a glassed-in front porch. Kathleen's arms were open, and he was in them. How he had dreamed, so many times, of clasping her slenderness, being with her. Now he felt it all in reality: her breasts, her body against him, her arms around him. He kissed her gently and tenderly; she returned his kiss. Remember, Noble. He stepped back, her arms trailing softly across his shoulders, her palms going to his cheeks. She held his face between her hands and looked at him.

"Oh, Charles, it's so good to see you. I owe this house to you. I've been happy here."

"I'm glad, darling," he said. Kisses and kisses; can a man tell a kiss of gratitude from one of love or passion? He thought so; and there had been only innocence, friendship, comradeliness in her embrace.

"Now for the grand tour," Kathleen laughed. "It is such a dear, homey little place. I love it."

Noble wondered if she realized what the sight of her bed,

so redolent of her, did to him. Toward the Sound, the floor dropped a step to a glassed-in porch, with a few chairs and a sewing table. Down the steps was another porch equipped with wicker chairs and chaise longue; to the right was the kitchen, and an outside door led to a small, hedged-in terrace. There was another door opening on steps going down to the road and the beach beyond.

"It's wonderful, simply wonderful," Noble said.

"Don't you dare sneer at our house. Just for that out you go—to the beach."

"I didn't bring my trunks, damn it all."

"That's a shame. And I haven't any men's trunks here; the stingy dogs always take them on home when they go. Well, at least we can walk on the beach."

Noble loved the feel of sand under his feet, and the sights and sounds of salt water. A few late bathers still were there, mostly mothers with small children, casting an eye at the low sun; soon the fathers, hot from work, joined their families. Charles and Kathleen watched them silently. He was happy just to be with her, and it seemed to him she was contented too. The children worried Noble at first, for he remembered how the sight of one had led to a storm of crying, but Kathleen was smiling gently. Noble watched the family groups; almost as if by ritual, shortly after the father joined them, women began going back up to the cottages, leading reluctant children, while the men lay on the sand and relaxed, or chased through the gentle waves into the water.

"There they go, chained to their domestic rounds, poor creatures," he said, indicating the retreating housewives.

"Poor? I have envied them ever since I've been here. Now that I've got a man to cook for, I'll go fix our supper." She said it proudly.

"We can eat at a restaurant."

"So, you don't trust my cooking, eh? You'll eat it and like it, Charles Noble."

"Aye, aye."

She cooked well, even though she apologized more than once as they ate; through the lower porch windows they watched the soft dusk come in over the Sound. She hadn't expected him, she explained; if she had she would have had steak, or chicken if the meat points failed; and the biscuits hadn't turned out well, and she never had been able to cook cauliflower properly.

"Don't be so damned modest, woman," Noble said, chewing happily. "If you were any good in bed and had a million dollars I'd marry you."

Later, when Noble wanted to help with the dishes, she told him to sit out in the porch rocker. "That way I can look up now and then and see you," she said. "You're in the hands of a dangerous type of woman, Lieutenant senior grade Noble— the domestic type."

Noble obediently smoked and rocked, watching her through the kitchen door. She kept up a flow of light talk as she put things on shelves and wiped cutlery. He marveled at her; her usual sadness was gone; she seemed content, fulfilled, without a care. Noble was so damned glad. And he wasn't going to take a chance of bringing the sadness back; he hoped to love her—Lord how he hoped to love her—but she would have to give the signal. So far she had not done so.

After she was finished, he went into the kitchen and made drinks, carrying them out to the porch where she was busy over sewing. The small radio was playing music, and she smiled up at him in the lamplight.

"Thank you, dear. Now pull that chair close and tell me all about the girl in Newport. What was she like?"

"Who?"

"Why, the girl in Newport."

"My strength is as the strength of ten because my heart is pure."

"Hmm. I've heard your other motto, I believe: Never refrain, never complain, never explain. Come on, now, was she a blonde?"

"Who?"

"I'll hurl this glass at you in a moment."

"There's an old Academy cheer," Noble said with dignity. "It goes thusly, and I quote, 'Rooti ti toot, rooti ti toot; we are the boys of the Institute. We don't smoke and we don't chew, and we don't go with girls who do! Our class won the Bib-ull.' "

"All right, Charles. Tell me, what is the Academy like?"

"A four-year ordeal that somehow turns out to be the most fulfilling and happy years of your life. It's a funny damned thing. You curse the place while you're there, except that every now and then, when by some fluke you have ten seconds to spare, you realize you're happy. Comradeship, pride of belonging; something like that, I guess."

Comradeship, friendship. The painful thought of Bulldog Ed and Eric crossed his mind. They were dead now, and the memory was more poignant because of his present happiness.

"Charlie, what is it?"

"Oh, nothing."

"You looked so sad."

"Indigestion, no doubt. Those dreadful biscuits."

"Is that why you ate six of them?"

"Braggart. It was four."

With the memory gone, Noble was happy again. To realize that he was alone with Kathleen above the sleepy murmur of salt water on a beach was like waking up from a dream to find it no dream. For a moment he hoped for the signal, but comradeship was all there was. At eleven o'clock he stood up and held out his hand.

"I'll have a busy day tomorrow. I'll be going now."

She looked surprised before smiling warmly and pleasantly at him. They walked hand in hand to the door.

"Good night," Noble said, leaning over to kiss her cheek, fighting down the wild desire to enfold her whole body. "I had a wonderful time." She wasn't smiling now. Did she look frightened?

101

"Charles," she said, softly, urgently. "Aren't you coming back again?"

Was her voice trembling? Was he coming back? God, didn't she realize that he was only going now because he couldn't hold back from her any longer; not sitting there and seeing her, being with her?

"Of course I'm coming back," he said. "May I come tomorrow at five?"

"Oh, yes."

"If you'll have me I'll be here every day for the next three weeks. You'll get tired of me."

"No, I won't! I'm so glad you can come again. Three weeks! That will be wonderful."

She stood on the threshold, smiling at him. He waved. The peepers were calling in the woods and the wash of small waves came up from the beach.

11

AT THE END of the dock beyond the Ninety-Seven's mooring place a light hung over the water, and a constant stir of life concentrated beneath it at night. Buck Johnson was squatting on his haunches on the dock and watching the little fish playing around under the light. He was thinking about nights on the river at home, running trot-lines and such. It would be still as all get-out except for frogs whooping from the bank and water dripping from the paddles. Every now and then Frank would take a nip out of the bottle and pass it back to Buck. Sometimes they'd find a bush that one of the lines was tied to shaking up and down, and Frank would say, "We got one, by God, Buck."

If Johnson was paddling he'd come in slow against the current to the limb, and Frank would reach down and take the line. He'd pull the boat along the line, and Buck would keep it pointed upstream so the hooks wouldn't drag along the length of the boat and maybe catch one of them in the leg. After a while old Frank would say, "Here it is, Buck; this is the one; easy now." And Buck would see the line heading straight down in the water and circling around, and the white side of a fish would shine up through the water in the lantern light. Then Frank would have him aboard, flapping and slithering in the bottom of the boat. If it was a buffalo or a catfish, or sometimes even a big trout, they'd feel pretty good; if it was only a goddamn gar or a turtle, Frank would cuss to curl a man's hair.

When the water was clear and the moon right, they'd do some gigging, and when the river was up and muddy they'd put out traps, just to show them goddamn townboys that all the fish didn't belong to them. Them and their game wardens.

"Hello, Johnson."

Johnson jumped, then turned to see Noble standing beside him. Goddammit, he thought, can't a man even set by hisself at night and think about things without one of them officers pokin' along? Johnson didn't like officers. His pa had said to him, "Buck, don't you never say sir to nobody but God. Us Johnsons ain't got much but this old wore-out farm and our independence, and we aim to keep both. You hear me, Buck?" Johnson started to stand up, not saying anything.

"Sit down," Noble said. "Mind if I join you?"

Johnson said he didn't, and the skipper sat down and gave him a cigarette. Johnson lit it, thinking Noble wasn't so bad as some. He hadn't had much trouble with the skipper, and most of those times he reckoned it was his fault. If the man hadn't been his boss, put over him, Johnson might have liked him, a little.

"I see you're from Greenville, Kentucky," Noble murmured after a while.

"Reckon I am," Johnson said, wondering what the skipper was prying around for.

"I'm from Kenton," Noble said.

Johnson looked up. "You are?"

"Yeah. I am." Noble flicked his match into the water. "How'd you come to join the Navy, Johnson? You were in before the draft started."

"Ah, Frank, he's my oldest brother, he went and got married up, and Pap gave him the farm, and I reckon I was plum tard of wrastlin' a mule over them fields. Then me and an old boy was in town one Saturday, drinking a lot of beer in the poolroom and having a good time, and he says, 'I'm goin' down to the Post Office to get me some mail,' and I told him he didn't have no mail—hell, nobody he knew could write. He cussed me and went, and I went along, and there was a man there in a blue suit. He got me and Ted into a room and says join the Navy and see the world, and it seemed like a good idear to me, so I did it."

"It's as good a way as any," Noble said. He didn't laugh. Johnson got kind of comfortable. It seemed mighty strange, but it looked to the gunner's mate as if the skipper was just being friendly. "I'll say one thing about that county of yours," Noble went on. "It's got the slipperiest damn roads I ever saw. Quail hunting up there once I parked my car carefully at the side of the road. I had the brakes on and rocks under the wheels. I came back and it was in the ditch. It just happened there was one of you Greenville boys close by with a team of mules. 'How did it happen?' I asked him. He said, 'I don't know, Mister. Just rolled, I guess. Pull you out for five dollars.' He did, and I haven't quail-hunted up there since."

Johnson grinned to himself, remembering how him and Frank used to pull that stunt every quail season. He especially remembered the faces of the townboys when they came back tired from hunting to find their cars in the ditch. Once one of them got mad and wanted to fight; him and Frank really laid that one out.

"That there clay is mighty slick," he said.

"Yes," Noble said, grinning. He threw his cigarette into the water and got up. "I think I'll turn in, Johnson. Good night."

"Good night, sir," Johnson said, and then sat in silent surprise. Like his Pa said, he didn't call anybody sir, unless he had to. He sure had done it this time though, and without any club hanging over him either.

Larry Floyd, fireman first class, felt pretty good driving up to the gate at Archer's, and he hoped that some of his buddies would see him. Nobody was there, though. Jane stopped the Ford and smiled at him. "Remember, Larry," she said, "you're having dinner with me tomorrow night. Thank you so much for fixing the car, and I enjoyed the movie a lot."

"It was pretty corny," Floyd said. "And anybody could have fixed your car; a condenser isn't hard to put in."

"Well, it was very clever and very nice of you to do it."

She wasn't so pretty, except when she smiled like that, but she was small and her figure was like one of the girls back home. He bet she'd look good in an evening dress even if she was pretty old—thirty maybe. For a minute Floyd thought he'd kiss her, but then he remembered one of his buddies had told him to take it easy the first time—he'd get farther that way.

"Good night," he said, holding out his hand.

"I'll pick you up tomorrow at five o'clock," she said, squeezing it. "If you'd like to bring one of your friends, it will be all right."

Floyd said good-by and went through the gate. He noticed that she didn't drive away until he was nearly to the boat.

The boat, war—everything was gone from Noble's mind as he took the long stairs two at a time, waving at Annie as he passed her house. The door of the little cottage opened before he reached it, and Kathleen stood there smiling eagerly at him. He leaped down the last few steps.

"Right on the tick," Kathleen said as he entered the house.

"That's a pretty dress," he said. It was white and rather low-necked, with bright colors embroidered around the neckline, and bright figures on the hem. It showed off her figure well. "I brought you something."

"I thank you. Hmm. Gurgles nicely, doesn't it? Charlie, I'm so happy!" She twirled on the carpet, laughing, as the skirt

106

flowed outward and upward, giving him a flash of slim, round legs. "Let's go dancing tonight. There's a little place up over the hill; I've had a drink there and it's not expensive."

"Fine. Dinner too?"

"Oh, no. We'll swim, then we'll eat here, and sample your present before going dancing."

Noble was glad he had the cool water to plunge into when he saw Kathleen on the beach. Her suit was a modest, one-piece affair, but, Lord, she had an exquisite figure. He couldn't help watching her.

"What's the matter? Don't you like my suit?"

"My only complaint is that it ain't transparent."

"Why, Charlie Noble!"

After an invigorating dip, they lay together on the sand. The gull cries seemed to become more poignant, even softer. Shadow passed over the beach, and Kathleen sat up. She threw her head back, smoothing her hair with her hands in the wonderful feminine gesture. Noble watched, marveling at her. Every line of leg, arm, breast, throat and face was dear to him. She looked down at him tenderly.

"God, you're beautiful!" he said.

"That's my cue to prove I can cook, too. Come along soon."

"Okay." He rolled over on his stomach and lit a cigarette, watching her walk away. She looked back twice over her shoulder before she reached the road. He loved the way she walked. He lay there for a while, then he could stand being away from her no longer. He took one more plunge, and went up in his dripping trunks to the cottage where he shivered under the outdoor shower before going in.

Dinner—chicken and damned good chicken, Noble decided—and then they had two Scotch and sodas apiece and went dancing. The tavern was nearly empty; a tall, thin man stoked the jukebox regularly, and they took advantage of his music and danced.

"You dance as well as I remembered, Kathleen."

"It's easy to dance with you," she said simply.

They were alone with themselves as they finished a drink and continued to dance; for Noble nothing else existed but the girl in his arms, and each dance she was warmer, yet cool and sweet. Noble was beginning to feel something other than comradeship between them: an intimation that the wall of laughing friendship was melting away. They no longer laughed and joked; they danced silently, lost in each other.

At last the nickel man put on a song they had danced to before—"Stage Door Canteen." Noble sang softly to her with the music. He could feel the current of her giving.

The music ended. They stopped dancing. Noble pressed her close; she trembled slightly, and for the first time since the song had started, looked up at him. Her eyes were bright and her lips quivering; she seemed almost frightened.

"Kathleen," he said. "I love you."

"I love you, Charles," she whispered. She squeezed his hand and then stepped away.

They walked back to the cottage in the moonlight, through the smells and sounds of a summer night. The Sound was pulsing sleepily below; Kathleen said nothing all the way. When they went into the house, she stopped just inside the door and gave him a long, sweetly grave look.

"Coward!" she said, smiling suddenly. "You look scared to death."

"I am."

"Goop," she said laughing, then saw his face. "You are! Oh, my dear, don't you want me? What are you afraid of?"

"Of hurting you," he said soberly.

"You'll never hurt me," she said softly. "Come into our house, my love."

"These officers are crazy bastards," Radelewski said to the civilian who was buying the drinks.

"How do you mean?"

"Well, you take this morning. I was carrying a cup of joe

down to the engine room, and I had got as far as the cockpit when Noble come back aboard—he's the skipper. He jumped onto the boat from the dock, stomped his foot, and sang out: 'My gallant crew, good morning.'

"Now what the hell kind of way is that for a man to act? I can tell you just what he said because I had Sparks—that's Everard—write the words down for me later. Anyway, Everard was foolin' with the radio; he dropped his tools, hopped up, and damned if he didn't sing too! 'Sir, good morning!'

"Noble he bowed and warbled: 'I trust you are all quite well?' This time the kid, Benton, joined in with Everard. 'Quite well, and you, sir?'

"I never heard the like. By this time Print, the exec, is sticking his head out of the charthouse hatch, his hair standing up ever whichaways.

" 'Christ,' says Print, 'It's too early in the morning for him to be drunk so I reckon she put out.'

" 'You do us proud, sir.' That was Benton, Everard, and Print. I seen two or three workmen come out of the machine shop, a girl stuck her head out of the office window, and Archer comes around the corner, grinning like hell.

" 'I am the Captain of the Pinafore!' Pinafore, for Christ's sake. He went on like that with that crazy Archer coming in on it too. It was a kind of good tune, at that, and like I said, afterward I made Benton and Everard learn it to me. I like Johnson and his guitar-blues songs better, though. Anyway, that Noble was one real happy sonofabitch."

Sterns was enjoying the morning, a nice cool time of day, cheerful with the risen sun but not yet hot. Some pretty good woods lay to one side of Archer's. Sterns decided he would drop over there one morning with his twenty-two and try for a few squirrels. The woods were part of some rich man's estate, and Sterns knew the owner would be plenty peed off, but he didn't mind that. He never killed game out of season, but to have ground posted just added sauce to hunting for him. He was smacking his lips at the thought of a squirrel stew when he saw a Ford coupé pull up at the gate, and damned if Floyd didn't get out of it. Sterns went up to meet him.

Floyd was red as a channel buoy but proud as a sonofabitch. There was a smudge of lipstick on his collar. Sterns had once had a redhead in Long Beach who used to send him back aboard that same way.

"Ah, Chief, you're just jealous because you're too damned old," Floyd said, in answer to Sterns' teasing. He seemed to have gained new confidence.

"I could lay there with my hand on it, anyways," Sterns said. "I reckon I'll go ashore tonight."

Sterns liked it at Archer's; the workmen were good men who did an honest job, totally different from the bastardly Navy Yard workers. The PT men took it pretty easy at Archer's, for there was nothing much to be done other than boat maintenance. Sterns remembered that particular day a long time, because of something that happened in midmorning. The whole crew took a swim off the dock, and when they came back aboard Everard's portable radio was giving out a news broadcast.

"Listen!" Noble said tensely. "Listen to that."

"We repeat the bulletin," the announcer said excitedly. "A special Navy Department communiqué has just announced that the U.S. Marines have invaded the islands of Guadalcanal and Tulagi in the South Pacific. A beachhead has been secured on Guadalcanal after light fighting, but heavy resistance has been encountered on Tulagi. This station will broadcast additional bulletins as received."

"Guadalcanal?" Radelewski said. "Where the hell is that?"

Everard knew, or at least he had heard of the place from Jack London. Of course the Solomon Islands must have changed since his day; at any rate he certainly hoped they had. Noble caught his eye.

"The inevitable white man," the skipper said ponderously. "Snider rifles cracking in the bush, smoke signals on Malaita, sharks' teeth and fever, and head-hunters curing their game back in the dripping jungles. Eh, Everard?"

"Yes indeed." Everard smiled at Noble, thinking that there was nothing like a book shared between men.

"Jungle?" said Radelewski. "Head-hunters?"

"Cannibals too," Noble said. "Filed teeth gnawing your shinbones."

"Aw, crap," Ski said, grinning unwillingly.

"Hill, go break out a chart of the Pacific," Noble said. "Let's see exactly where this place is." Soon they were all gathered around the chart spread out on the clean deck boards.

"Way out there!" Sterns said. "Jesus."

"You can see why," Noble explained. "The Japs can't attack Australia and New Zealand if we can grab Guadalcanal and hold it. I think they've started an airfield there; seems like I read that."

"I wonder what it's like," Ski said, sounding less cocky than Everard had ever heard him.

"You will probably find out," Noble said.

"You mean we'll go there?" Print asked excitedly.

"It's ideal PT territory; look at all the islands up that chain. Restricted waters, reefs, narrow passages. Don't think the Japs will let go easily. They'll fight it out. We're nearly ready to be shipped out. Head-hunters, here we come."

"Are we the only squadron ready to go?" Radelewski asked uneasily.

"No. There are a couple down in Panama. They're probably on their way now."

"Damned Gook islands," Stern grumbled. "Gooney birds and jungle rot."

The crew was thoughtful that day, and everyone who didn't have the duty went ashore at five. Noble picked up his suitcase and went off whistling. No doubt about it, Everard thought; he was whistling the wedding march.

The Ninety-Seven stayed on at Archer's for three weeks after her crew heard about Guadalcanal. Warder wouldn't have minded spending the rest of the war there. It was only a little yacht-yard, the water was clean, and it was quiet and peaceful. He only wished he had Clara and the kids in one of the little houses over on the bluff. He never talked much about his family to the boys on the boat; he reckoned they might have found it hard to believe that a man married to a woman for sixteen years could miss her so much. The boys were half the time talking about women, bragging. Hell, he knew, he'd been there; but there's no love-making like that between a man and woman who know each other, trust each other, and have taken it thick and thin—and an enlisted man's wife hits some pretty thin times, he knew—until both of them realize that they're not whole any more by themselves. It gets so that every time you touch your wife there's a thousand other times under that, and memories, and the children, and fights maybe, pretty quick healed up, and good times aplenty. All these things can go into a settled man's loving, giving it layers of meaning that the tomcatting young bachelors never imagined existed.

He sure would have liked to have Clara come East before he shipped out, but the house in San Diego took all of his pay. He rolled cigarettes, and he didn't go ashore much or drink any to speak of. In six months more his twenty years would be up; well, with this blanking war on there wouldn't be any more twenty-year retirements for a while, but it would end someday. Then he and Clara would be sitting pretty.

For Jim Print, it was not so serene a period. There came a time when Delilah wouldn't see him any more, and he knew she had given up. He nearly went crazy for a while; finally he asked her to marry him, but she wouldn't do it.

It was right about then that he noticed her new diamond-and-ruby wristwatch.

Noble wanted these weeks to last forever. Every time the phone rang at Archer's he felt sick, expecting to be ordered back to Brooklyn. Each day, at five o'clock, he knew he'd had one more reprieve. He kept storing pictures in his memory. One was of the evening Kathleen called him into the bathroom. She was stretched out in the tub, which was half full of water topped with suds. Her hair was pinned on top of her head, and she smiled up at him, her breasts making little islands in the foam.

"Will you wash my back? What's the good of having a man around if you can't have your back washed, I always say."

"I sure will," Noble said, grabbing the cloth.

"Come on in; it's much nicer that way."

Everything in the cottage—scratched doors, worn woodwork, the maltreated furniture, windows, stairs—became a picture inexpressibly dear to him; for this was the home of his happiness. The night in the station wagon had been a fluke, he now knew, a hurried glimpse of heaven snatched under an El. Here in this cottage the completeness of love had opened for him.

Another picture was the evening Annie Powers came down to see them. Noble poured drinks, and the three of them sat on the little porch, talking, drinking slowly, and watching the rose afterglow of sunset change to blue, star-shot sky over the rippling Sound.

"So peaceful," Kathleen said.

"Yes," Annie agreed harshly. "Peaceful here, but the men are dying just the same."

"Now Annie," Noble put in. "Men always die."

"Yes, and they do, but in the natural order of things. These days it is the young strong ones, the brave ones who die. It is a black sin and a shameful waste."

"Yes," Kathleen said, looking stricken.

Annie blew her nose.

"Never mind me," she said. "It's just that . . . Mr. Powers was killed in France. We had been married six months when he left me, and my daughter has never seen her father's face, except in a picture."

"Oh, Annie!" Kathleen said with quick compassion.

"Now, don't you cry at me; I'm over it. It's just the waste of it all. Live your life while you can, I say. Young man, get me another drink."

"Coming right up, Annie."

Along about ten Noble was getting a bit embarrassed. Annie knew they weren't married; whether she realized they were lovers he didn't know. He was on the point of speaking about returning to the boat when Annie stood up.

"Thank you for a nice evening," she said. "I'll be getting along home. You two will be wanting to get to bed."

"Why, Annie," Noble said; he saw that Kathleen was suddenly pale.

"Now, children," Annie said, "I knew what was up the first time I saw you two. But keep in mind, I've taken nearly as much pleasure from your loving as you have. It's just what I said: love while you can. To look down on this roof and to know that a young man about to go to war is under it with his sweet woman makes me feel good."

"Annie, you're wonderful!" Noble leaned over and kissed her cheek. Kathleen, crying, fell into Annie's arms. After a while Annie went home. Then Noble and Kathleen turned out the lights and went to bed in the summer night.

12

NOBLE MARKED THE days by the arriving boats; each required about forty-eight hours for the alterations, but one by one the list approached the end.

Pat Bunch: "Where do I get a train to town?"

"You can't wait, eh?" Noble was sympathetic; he knew exactly how his friend felt.

"Time is getting short. We're on official standby now."

"The Solomons?"

"I see you're guessing the way I am. Daggs too, I judge. He's quieted down some lately."

"How's Gerry?"

Pat Bunch shook his head, indicating inexpressible emotion. "What a wonderful girl," he said quietly.

"You're very lucky, Pat." If only things were so serene for Kathleen and him.

"But I've got to leave her, Charlie. Sometimes I almost think I shouldn't have met her."

"I understand," Noble said. Not so serene after all. Poor Pat; to be married to Gerry and then have to turn away.

"Do you?" Pat asked. "If I get killed—okay. I'll have had the best of everything. But suppose I come back without legs, or eyes, maybe. She'd stick with me the rest of my life, I know she would. Hell." He grinned, for a moment the old carefree Pat. "I might even get my pecker shot off; think of coming back to Gerry, as her husband, in that shape. I'd shoot myself for sure."

"It's going to be a long war."

"Don't I know it?"

As for Noble, he was happy as long as he could keep his thoughts from the future. Evenings with the sound of small waves and crickets crying; the smells of the summer nights; Kathleen in the lamplight; Kathleen in bed, always lighted for love, two-toned: gardenia-white at breasts and loins, light gold everywhere else.

The last boat came and left, and the Ninety-Seven must return as well.

"Charles, you're coming back, aren't you? Oh, my dear, it isn't over?" Kathleen clung to Noble, shaking. Deeply touched, he patted her hair.

"I'm not even taking my toothbrush. I'll take the train and be back for dinner."

"For certain?"

"Yes. If the New Haven Railroad operates, I'll be here."

His confidence was mostly pretense, Noble realized sadly as he went through the early summer morning toward Archer's. He'd be back, sure; but for how long? No matter, he'd had heaven, the closest a man living can arrive to it, anyway. He was no longer the seeking individual of all his previous days; he had found himself. He'd always be thankful for the three weeks, take any more time allowed him, and go to the war grateful.

For eighteen days Noble rode the New Haven railroad to Darien, then took the bus to the shady street down which Annie smiled at him from a window of her cottage. She was at that window as regularly now as Kathleen was at the open door. On the nineteenth day, in midafternoon, the orders came.

"Mister Noble," the messenger said breathlessly. "The commander wants to see you right away."

Noble knew in that moment, and men who had heard the message looked at him and at each other; only a few of them smiled. Daggs was alone in his office, and Noble stepped in and saluted, conscious now of how little he had seen of Daggs for the past weeks, wrapped up as he had been in the little house and Kathleen. Kathleen! Quite abruptly the fact struck him hard: this man was Kathleen's husband; he knew her body as Noble knew it; he was a man Noble had deeply wronged.

"Yes, sir?" he said.

The commander's face was expressionless as he turned from a despatch he held in his hand to Noble.

"Well, Charlie, here we are."

"Orders out?"

"Yes, we're gonna get at them Japs at last. A Saturday afternoon too; wouldn't you know it?"

"We're pretty well ready, sir."

"Of course we are; I've seen to that. Now. Your division will get under way for Norfolk Monday morning. Two tankers are waiting for you. Norfolk will put you aboard them and you'll shove off right away." Daggs leaned across the desk and lowered his voice. "Guadalcanal, Charlie."

"I thought so," Noble said.

"Did, hey? Well, keep it to yourself until you sail from Norfolk. The other divisions will come down as soon as tankers are ready for them."

"Which division will you be with, sir?"

"None of 'em, by God. I'm taking the base force by train to Frisco next week. We'll go aboard a PT tender there and shove off for Nouméa, New Caledonia. I'll be waiting for you there when you arrive."

"That's fine, sir. A tender. I'd been wondering how we'd handle maintenance."

"Well, that's about it. Look, you know Archer pretty well;

117

you take your boat out there right away and load on all the muffler spares he can let you have. Okay?"

"Yes, sir!"

"All right, son. Collect your crew and get going."

It seemed to Everard that even before Noble got back from the commander's office everyone knew the first division was to leave New York on Monday. Everard put down a box of crystals and gazed at the radio set. Rumor also said there was to be no more liberty. How, in that case, was he going to see Martha? And the children? He looked around him, half dazed, at the blue and white charthouse, the riot guns, rifles, and submachine guns on the bulkheads, the spotless deck, the chart table.

"Oh, boy!" Benton exclaimed. "We're getting started!"

"Wonder where we're going?" Floyd asked excitedly.

"Ah, nowhere much. You'll see," Radelewski growled.

Just then Noble jumped aboard and came down into the charthouse.

"We're going out to Archer's again," he announced, grinning happily. "We'll pick up some spares there and come back tomorrow morning." He caught the radioman's eye. "Everard, get your bag packed and onto the dock. I can hand out a few overnight leaves for men with families they can reach. Be back here before eight hundred, Monday."

"Yes, sir," Everard exclaimed, flooded with relief.

"Anybody else in reach of a wife or family?" Noble asked. "Jim, how about you?"

"Nope," Print said. "I'll come along with the boat."

"Radelewski? You're a New Yorker."

"I ain't married."

"How about your folks?"

"Well, I would kind of like to say good-by to the old lady."

"Okay. Forty-eight for you. Warder, wind 'em up. You two guys get ashore fast."

Never had the trip seemed longer to Noble. Only with difficulty did he maintain the customary low speed in restricted waters; once in the open Sound, he pushed the throttles forward and ran for Kathleen at forty-five knots. Archer welcomed the crew heartily.

"I can let you have whatever you want," he said when Charlie told him his needs. "Matter of fact, I could have the spares aboard in time for you to go back tonight, if you like."

"Tomorrow is soon enough," Noble said hastily, then reddened at Archer's grin. A good commanding officer would stay on hand until business was finished, Charlie told himself; still Jim had said he wasn't going in to the city. Jim could take care of it. Within ten minutes, Noble was on his way to the cottage.

An hour later Jim was sitting on deck, half reading, half drowsing, when Archer came up the dock.

"Has the skipper gone ashore?"

"Why, yes," Jim said. "Some time ago. Something wrong?"

"Well, not exactly wrong, dammit, but I'm going to town tonight, and I'd like to take the signed requisitions with me and drop them at 90 Church in the morning. And look, does Charlie want spare control rods too? Also he ought to take more flaps than he has on this list; the exhaust acid and salt water corrode them mighty fast." Jim thought Archer looked a little annoyed. Well, he didn't blame him too much.

"Maybe I can help," he said slowly. Charlie had told him where he could be found in emergencies. "I'll go get Charlie," Print offered. He knew it might be embarrassing, but this was something only the skipper could handle.

Archer brightened. "That's fine. I'll be leaving at about five."

"I'll have him here before then," Jim promised.

As he came up to the cottage, Jim took off his cap and scratched his head. He felt some suspense, and a good deal of distaste. Of course all the crew knew the skipper was living with a girl ashore, but it hurt him to think of old Charlie shacked up with some slut.

"Dammit," he growled. "What would Emily Post say? I hope they're taking ten."

Then he became conscious of the sound of a running shower, and he heard Charlie whistling. He felt better; the skipper must be washing off salt water outdoors; he could grab him and maybe never see the girl. He went quietly around the corner of the house.

High shrubbery enclosed the shower from passersby, and Charlie was standing naked in the spray, singing now. A slender, tanned girl wearing only a large beach towel was removing her swimming cap; head back, she passed her hands through her short hair. Jim made a noise; she jumped, eyes enormous in her shocked face.

"Jesus Christ!" Jim exclaimed aloud. "It's Mrs. Daggs!"

Instantly he cursed himself and the shock that had made him speak. The girl cried something inarticulate and ran wildly into the house.

Print and Noble faced each other. The skipper wrapped a towel around his waist with shaking hands. The moment grew endlessly as Jim fumbled for words to apologize.

Charlie Noble felt numb. Discovered! And he had assured Kathleen that they were safe here. Anger rose in him, then the sight of Jim's misery smothered it. Jim. After all, Jim. What real harm? He knew that Jim would never tell. Of all the people in the world, here was the one he would have been most willing to take into his secret. But this was Kathleen's secret too.

"God, Charlie, I'm sorry. Archer wants you, wants some dope on flaps and rods, he's going to New York and wants the papers signed. You said I could . . ."

"Sure, sure. You did right. It's okay. I guess I don't have to tell you to . . ."

"To keep my trap shut? Hell no, what do you think I am? Well, I'll be going. Archer's leaving at five o'clock."

"Jim, wait."

Noble knew this was serious. This could wreck their last night together—he hadn't told her yet this was their last night. He had seen the shame on Kathleen's face as she ran by him.

"There's one thing I want you to know, Jim. I love Kathleen. This is for keeps, if I can make it that way."

"Sure. Of course you do. You know anything you do is all right with me."

"I've got to make this right with Kathleen. Will you stay for dinner?"

"Hey, now wait!"

"No, I mean it. You know about us now, and I want you to know it all. I want you to understand."

"Well, anything you say, Skipper."

"You wait here, will you?"

It seemed a long wait to Print. He fidgeted and took his cap off. He put it on. "Big-mouthed bastard," he muttered. "Are you ever going to learn to keep your big mouth shut?" He polished his shoes on his trouser-legs. He looked at his watch. At last the door opened.

"Come in, Jim," Charlie said. He was dressed now.

Kathleen was waiting on the porch. Her face was pale at first, then pink. She looked into Print's eyes gravely and without any sign of embarrassment other than her heightened color.

"Kathleen," Charlie said. "You know Jim."

Print never knew what he said, but she couldn't have been more poised and cool if she and Charlie had been married for years.

"It's nice of you to stay for dinner, Jim," she said, holding out her hand. "I know you're Charles' friend. You're very welcome here."

They shook hands. She seemed younger than when he'd last seen her at that Officers' Club dance; she had blossomed.

They insisted on showing Print the house. He thought it was a pretty scarred-up little place, but he'd be roped and tied if they didn't seem to think it was the equal of the

Waldorf. Then Charlie poured Jim a drink and got his cap to go back to the boats.

"I'll make it fast," Noble said. "I'll be back in an hour."

"Just what I was hoping for," Print said with a leer. "Kathleen, we have a whole hour together. Alone!"

"Marvelous," she said, trying to smile.

"Damn it," Noble complained. "You don't have to act so pleased."

He left them with a lighthearted good-by kiss from Kathleen.

Jim watched the door close behind him, then looked uneasily at the floor. He had thought he possessed an urbanity equal to any situation, but now . . . He searched wildly for a flippant remark, found none, considered silence. For an hour? Judas, somebody's got to say something, he thought. Maybe I should do my old vanishing coin trick. What the hell, she had sense. Why not just tell her what he was thinking? He raised his eyes and found her looking at him. She appeared half pitying, half amused at his confusion.

"I hope I haven't spoiled everything," he said.

"You haven't," she said quietly. "Although, when you first showed up, I wasn't so sure."

Print squirmed. "How about now?" he asked.

She smiled suddenly at him.

"Now I'm fine. You're just an old friend of the family coming to call."

"That's it." Compassion filled Jim. "That's really it. An old friend. A kind of big-mouthed friend," he added. Their eyes met, and he felt a great relief. But then he saw the question in her eyes. He tried to forestall it. "Now that I'm an old friend, why don't we go for a swim, huh?"

"Oh, no, not that easily. You know what I want to ask. You have orders to leave, haven't you?"

"Yes." He couldn't put her off.

"When?"

"Monday."

"And this is Saturday." Print could see her lips quiver, but she didn't give way for a moment. He thought he'd leave it to Charlie to tell her that there'd be no more liberty after tonight.

"I knew, of course," she said, low-voiced. "I knew it would end soon, but now . . . Oh, God!"

She was crying quietly. Print shifted from one foot to the other. In a moment or two she shook her head hard, rubbed her hands across her face, and smiled at him through tears.

"Sorry, Jim. I'm a fine hostess. You haven't seen the terrace yet. I'll show you that."

"Here." Print handed her a handkerchief. She used it and smiled at him. Hell fire! he thought; everybody in the squadron knew about the commander's week ends; bedamned if he'd blame her for falling in love with a guy like Charlie.

"Terrace?" he said scornfully. "Has this dump got a terrace?"

"Dump? Why, I'll slaughter you, calling this dump a dump. It's got . . ." Here she hesitated, blushed, and then grinned like a kid. "It's got the prettiest ceilings in the world."

Right then Print began admiring her.

"Here, where's the damned terrace!" he said. "I don't believe there is one."

She led him through a door beside the kitchen, and sure enough there was a small, flagstoned area with shoulder-high shrubbery around it and a tall sycamore above. It was nice there in the shade. Kathleen was looking at a wooden bench and Print saw tears start again.

"Come on," he said roughly. "Knock it off, now."

Then she was in his arms, not crying much, just a tear trickling down each cheek while she tried to smile up at him. He patted her back, suddenly envious to hell and gone of Charlie. He knew damned well that this wasn't a woman who got no exaltation from love.

"You're nice, Jim," she said. "I see why Charlie likes you so much."

Print felt rather funny holding her. A group of people were going down the wooden stairs by the terrace, and two fat women looked at them with shocked expressions. A little fat man with a bald head was right behind them, winding a camera. As Print watched he stopped and took a picture of the Sound.

"Look," Kathleen said, "let's go up on the road where there's more privacy." Print saw the people disappearing, still sneaking looks back at the terrace.

"Why, those nosey bastards! Let's shock 'em good," Jim suggested. "Gimme a real kiss!"

He kissed her soundly and swung her up in his arms; then he gave a Tarzan, bull-ape victory cry and ran into the house with her. She was laughing when he put her down.

"Thank you, Jim. I won't feel sorry for myself any more."

"I wish I could say that," he said, suddenly serious.

"Delilah?"

"Yes. Do you know?"

"Yes. She thought you were the one. I've never felt so sorry for anyone in my life when she found out that even you couldn't . . ."

"I asked her to marry me."

"I admire her that she wouldn't. Morton and Delilah's parents are responsible for a good deal of her trouble. They thought sex nasty and dirty. They drummed into the defenseless little boy and girl that sex was wrong. No woman could enjoy it; no man should be anything but ashamed and guilty if he enjoyed it."

"That may have caused it, then."

"I think so too, but who am I to say what's right or wrong? I'm married to Morton, but I love Charles . . . Oh, Jim, this is our last day, our last night, isn't it? I know it, even if you didn't say so. Then I can't put it off any longer."

"Put what off?"

"Nothing, Jim. Now how about pouring both of us a drink?"

Kathleen was lighthearted and cheerful when Charlie came

back, but Print knew from the way Noble looked at her that the skipper realized she had been crying. Print left after dinner, though Noble tried to get him to stay longer.

"Don't be a jerk," Jim told him. He kissed Kathleen at the door.

"Good-by, Jim," she said.

Kathleen told Noble at once that she knew when he was leaving, and he was glad Jim had spared him that job. She came into Noble's arms then, kissing him with a passion rare even for her, and the night, with both of them knowing the end was so near, was one of wild abandon. Dawn was grey when love, by exhaustion, at last ceased. The night had been one to remember forever.

They had breakfast together with the world fresh in earliness. Noble had a swim first, but the bacon, eggs, toast and coffee were brassy with the taste of grief. He ate without pleasure; now, at seven o'clock on this morning, it was finished. Then he wondered why so early; he still had an hour. He finished breakfast, looking all the while at the girl across from him in a cheerful summer print dress.

"You're done, Charles?"

"Yes, darling. I've forty minutes yet. Why are we so early?"

"I had to be sure there would be time. I must talk to you."

Noble felt sudden fear.

"Then listen, my darling. I love you. We have had six weeks as lovers. If I live to be ninety my life will still be six weeks long."

"What do you mean?"

"I'm going back to Morton."

"No! You can't!"

"Do you remember the day we saw this place together and I cried at the sight of a little girl?"

"Yes," he whispered.

"I have a daughter, Charles. She is four years old."

"God almighty!"

"I can't live without her."

125

He couldn't grasp it. Kathleen a mother! Kathleen and a daughter, who perhaps looked like her, smiled like her, was as sweet . . . "Why"—of course; and a sudden happiness welled up inside him—"I'll love her, darling. Let her be my daughter too!"

"Dearest, you don't understand. These six weeks have made my life worthwhile. But I can't have love all my life; I must be grateful for what I do have."

"What are you trying to say?"

"I married Morton five years ago. I thought I loved him, and perhaps then I did. But soon I found . . . I found that he was ashamed of love. He rarely kissed me on the lips. He felt guilty about sex. I wanted to love him, Charles!—really I did!"

"You poor kid."

"A friend of Mort's came along. He was gay and sophisticated; I gave in to him. For the first time in years I enjoyed being loved. Then Morton discovered us, and since then I have been trapped. He threatened that if I ever divorced him, he'd tell the story to the court; they'd declare me an unfit mother and give him the child. I must go back to him, Charles, because that is the only way I can go back to Ellen. She is living with Morton's mother now; we couldn't bring her to New York and hotels."

"Kathleen . . . "

He couldn't grasp it. This was his Kathleen, sitting across the table, telling him that their life together was over, forever.

"Ellen needs me; I can't desert her. I know; I tried. After I was unfaithful to Morton, we separated for a time, but I couldn't live without her. I went back to him, begging. He agreed to give me another chance. That was just before he came up here to New York. When I joined him, it was for a second attempt, one that I meant to do my honest best to make successful. But you know what happened. He went out with other women openly, slept with me only when he was drunk."

"He should be . . . "

126

"Then you came along. I guess I knew all along that I couldn't leave Morton, for that would mean giving up Ellen, this time forever. But I did think we could have a little while together. I took advantage of you. It wasn't fair to you—but I do love you, and I think I've made you happy too."

"You have, Kathleen, you have."

"You don't hate me for using you?"

"Hate you? I love you, Kathleen, I'll always love you."

"Oh, Charles!" she said, and began crying softly.

He pushed the breakfast table aside and took her in his arms.

"You'll never go back to him, Kathleen. Never!"

Noble was drained of hope. Nothing shook her determination, nothing cracked that sad, serene inflexibility. She stroked his hair tenderly, resignedly. Noble looked at his watch. It was time to go.

He dressed again. With Kathleen lying on the bed, he wandered about the little house. The bathroom, where he opened the medicine cabinet from which his toothbrush and shaving gear had been removed; the smell of lavender and soap was the smell of Kathleen, dear to him now above all others. The porches; the kitchen; the stairs to the beach; the terrace and the bench where, one starry night, they had made love with dawn a faint streak in the sky.

He came back into the living room where she still lay on the bed. She smiled at him shakily, then she got up and hid her body in a robe and her naked feet in slippers. They went through the door together and stood for a last time together on its threshold.

"Good-by, my love," she said proudly, sadly. "Kiss me quickly and go. I can't hold on much longer. Charles, I love you so!"

She was crying now, as he climbed up the long steps, but she smiled up at him contortedly. Farther, farther, she was vanishing from him. Their eyes met. She shook her head, gestured in a movement that was only the beginning of a waved farewell; then she was gone. The house had taken her. Noble was alone and forlorn at the top of the long stair.

The crew of the Old Ninety-Seven was quiet during that morning's trip back to the Navy Yard. Print had the wheel, and Noble, perched numbly on his under-way seat, knew that every man was thinking that this was the last day. For Noble, time had already run out, and he was ready to sail.

Pier H was like a disturbed ants' nest; and the Ninety-Seven's crew was busied at once unloading the muffler spares and bringing aboard a hundred different things, all of which had to be secured for sea. Propellers, drive shafts, fifty-caliber ammunition, Joe's reverse gears, impulse charges, shotgun shells, canned hash, canned chili. A final set of items consisted of a forty-five automatic and a new type of helmet for each man.

"Well," Noble said at last. "I guess we're finished loading; now we'll go take on fuel up at Newton Creek. Warder! Wind 'em up."

And in the morning we'll be off for the South Pacific, Print thought. Then he wondered if he had been eating locoweed, for he really wasn't sorry; seemed to him that it was time he took a hand in this war.

Noble stood on the deck of the Ninety-Seven, looking over the dark but light-spangled Yard. A tug blew from the river. Small waves rocked the PT beneath him. From far off came the sound of a train's whistle, charged for him with sorrow. He might once have ridden that very train out to the cottage.

"Well, boy," he murmured to himself. "The dream's over. You've been lucky as hell, really lucky. You've had six weeks. Now you're in the Navy again."

He loved the Navy, too. It folded around him in the low voices of his men preparing for sleep below, in the smell of paint, salt water, oil, weapons. He looked up at the stars and down at the grey shapes of the other boats. Lights on the barge made zig-zag movements on the rippled water. He touched the wheel of his boat, feeling that she knew he was back again.

The train whistled again somewhere. The breeze was growing a little stronger. Noble made a motion in the moving air with his hand, waving in the direction of the bluff and the cottage. Then he went below.

It was over.

13

Noble led the seven other officers of his division through the doors of the Officers' Club of the Naval Operating Base, Norfolk. The PT officers, Prep Tares as they were beginning to call themselves, were about to perform a solemn ritual—that of having the last drink ashore. The four boats already were secured in their cradles to the foredecks of two Navy tankers, the *Drake* and the *Gasper*. It was 1700; in two hours they were to sail for the South Pacific. The club bar had opened at four, and already the place was doing a good business. The *Gasper* would be just about under way, Noble reflected soberly, when these desk jockeys had finished dinner. As the eight Prep Tares took a table, Noble heard a girl behind them say to her companion, "Look at the tan on those officers who just came in. What do you think they do?"

"Golf," her companion said in a bored tone. "Probably got a gravy train."

"*Son of a bitch!*" Howard Warren of the Ninety-Eight said with great slowness. He rose to his feet. "I shall smite him hip and thigh."

Noble grinned and pulled him down, although looking around the luxurious club with gay officers eagerly talking to pretty girls in light summer frocks, he, too, felt a slight irritation at

130

these shorebirds. But then, they were only following orders, he knew, just as his orders had been to take his squadron down to Norfolk. He recalled the run south now with excitement. He could still feel his pride as he had looked over the two nests of two boats each that made up his division; they were low in the water, but they were ready. And then the eyes of the men had turned upon him as he called out: "All hands, second division, go aboard. Wind 'em up; we're getting under way." He recalled the parting with Pat Bunch, who had walked up as the first motor came alive. "I suppose it reveals a poverty in human resources," Noble had said, taking Pat's proffered hand, "but damned if I'm not sorry to leave you." And Pat's simple reply: "See you out there." Then the elation as the four PTs had moved into column, each boat a little on the quarter of the one ahead to avoid the wake. . . . Looking around at his officers now, Noble relaxed. He would not change places with anyone at the club.

All the same, though—didn't the girls look wonderful? He saw the same thought on the faces of the other Prep Tares. Noble watched a lovely, tanned, blonde girl in her bright dress, and sadness welled up in him. He was going to a different world than this; a world of men, with none of the softness of woman in it. And he knew his foreknowledge of that world's existence gave this time, this place—girls' voices laughing, deeper voices of the men, the smell of good food, good liquor, and the overhanging tang of beer—a flavor that shorebirds would never taste.

"Well, boys," Noble said. "Just time for one more."

"God," Print murmured, "already?"

They sipped slowly, looking at each other from time to time. All the dramatic toasts—here's to a safe voyage and a good landfall; here's to luck; here's to this land, may we see it again —were unspoken. Eyes went back to the girls, tenderly. Then, the drinks finished, the Prep Tares stood up slowly, reluctantly, and walked out of the club.

Noble led the way from the *Gasper*'s quarter-deck up a

ladder to the thwartship, sheltered deck that lay beneath the bridge. He paused there to look down at the Ninety-Seven and Ninety-Eight, Jim Print waiting with him. The cradles were welded to the tanker deck, and steel-wire rope with gooseneck shackles held the boats fast to the cradles. The goosenecks would allow the PTs to cut loose fast if the tanker got sunk. The boats were canopied with camouflage netting, but the cockpits and all guns were clear.

Johnson was in the forward turret of the Ninety-Seven, oiling the fifties. Noble heard music dimly. Followed by Print, he climbed a series of ladders until he reached the deck of the Ninety-Seven. Johnson grinned at him as he went below. In the charthouse Hill was sitting on the chart table with the windup phonograph Noble had bought, playing the Mills Brothers' "Paper Doll." Noble liked the tune. Most of his crew were in the charthouse, and the smell of coffee drifted up from the galley below.

"Buying this machine was a good idea, Skipper," Hill said.

"Yes, sir," Benton added. "We pitched in and got a lot of good records."

"Fine," Noble said, starting on down to his cabin.

"Wait a minute, Skipper," Sterns said. "Go on, Everard; what're you waiting for?"

Everard came forward with a small oblong package. "This is for you, sir, from the crew," he said. "Our best wishes, Captain."

"For me?" Noble said, with originality.

As he opened the package Sterns said gravely, "We thought you oughta have something to take the place of that babe out in Connecticut."

"Hmm," Noble said. "I see what you mean." He held up the six-inch-long ceramic South Seas girl. Lying supine, hands behind her head, she was coffee-colored and naked except for a lei: breasts scarlet-tipped, black eyes languorous. "Why, you bastards," Noble said, laughing. "Well-turned ankle, by Jove. Thanks, boys."

They grinned self-consciously, and Noble was glad to see Radelewski joining with the rest of them.

"I'll keep her forever," he said. He wondered if his crew knew how much this gesture meant to him.

Chow call, and the PT officers went into the wardroom together to find the *Gasper's* people just unfolding their napkins. The Prep Tares took their places meekly, still a little awed—after the PT barge in Brooklyn—by the white linen and gleaming silver. The exec, a stocky, brown-faced officer who had once put Noble on the report back at the Academy, smiled at them.

"Welcome, little sheep," he said. "We can use some more material for our poker games. Look out for the chief engineer, there: he's got a version he calls high-diddle-diddled. Appropriate name too, especially the diddled part."

The chief, a lean man with a mahogany complexion, flashed his brilliant false teeth at the newcomers. He was an ex-merchant marine officer, as was the navigator.

"Don't scare 'em off, Ed," he said.

"This is going to be one long payday." Print's eyes gleamed. "The only thing that worries me is what am I going to do with all the money."

"I wouldn't worry about that if I was you," said the navigator kindly.

"By the way, Charlie," the exec said as Noble started on his soup. "We're short of qualified watch standers. Do you mind taking a watch? It'll be one in three for a while."

Noble smiled to himself; "Do you mind?" was typical of the atmosphere of this ship, a happy one he already knew.

"Why, no, not at all," he said.

"Good." The exec grinned. "Take the eight-to-twelve tonight, then. The captain wants an experienced officer of the deck for this first night in convoy."

"Pat 'em on the back while you kick 'em in the ass," the chief drawled.

"Just psychology," the exec said.

Talk turned to the war, and Noble noticed how the table sobered when Guadalcanal was brought up. He felt his own stomach tighten. There could be no doubt that Guadalcanal was now a major battlefield, a turning point. America was paying for that air strip! Four cruisers sunk the first night; then the *Saratoga* smacked, but good; destroyers downed right and left. News had just been received of the sinking of the *Wasp*. It was touch and go in the South Pacific.

"Never mind, you toy-boat skippers," the navigator said kindly. "You probably won't make it there anyway."

"How come?" Print asked.

"Torpedo junction, son. The subs will let us by on the trip down while we're riding high—you can't sink an empty tanker anyway. But when we load up with that hundred octane and Grade C in Aruba, we'll be for it."

"God damn you, Navigator," the exec said. "You trying to scare me?"

"I've seen tankers burning," the navigator went on calmly, "from close enough to hear the men screaming, see 'em jumping overboard with their clothes burning, see them try to swim until that damned burning gas catches up with them."

Noble was relieved that just then the public address system crackled, then rasped, "Now stations all special sea details. Stations all special sea details."

"Heigh-ho," said the exec. "Coffee on the bridge."

Noble and Print found the crew below on the Ninety-Seven. "Well, boys," Noble said, "better come topside; this is the last of the United States you'll see for some time."

As the Old Ninety-Seven's crew grouped companionably in the cockpit, a faint pulse from the tanker's deck announced that the propeller was turning over. The lines already were singled up; now they came in. The tide was setting the tanker off, and as the last line splashed from the shore, the strip of water between the ship's side and the dock widened rapidly. Deck vibration increased, and the *Gasper* was under way.

Two days out of Norfolk.

Larry Floyd just couldn't believe this Gulf Stream. The water was so blue it was almost purple, and it had little patches of golden seaweed floating on it. Every now and then flying fish would jump out of the water and go fluttering along with just their tails wet, using their fins like wings. Floyd was happy; this sure beat working in that filling station. He had one small worry; he'd have to miss Mass for a long time. But the Father back in Norfolk had patted him on the shoulder and said he was a soldier of God, and that he could worship in his heart. Floyd had answered that he wasn't any soldier, he was a sailor. The Father had just smiled and patted his shoulder again.

Six days out of Norfolk.

Aruba. Oil, goats, cactus, and whores. The two tankers filled with high-octane gasoline and fuel oil. They left at dawn of the fourth day; as the *Gasper* and *Drake* pulled away from the dock, a subchaser was unloading the burned and dying remnants of the crews of two tankers that had put to sea just three hours earlier.

Ten days out of Norfolk.

It was dark and Noble had the deck. The convoy was making its usual speed of ten knots. The bridge was very quiet, just wind and water sounds; and a faint glow from the binnacle was the only light. It all felt and tasted and smelled good to Noble; this was the Navy, this bridge knew calm and resolution. Calm and resolution were needed, for submarines swarmed along Torpedo Junction. A torpedo might hit the *Gasper* at any moment.

Rain was falling when Noble was relieved at a quarter to twelve. The *Gasper* had been zigzagging with the convoy, and the Ninety-Seven's skipper detested a zigzag plan. He was tired and his room looked good to him as he undressed and went to bed. The tanker was rolling far over, slowly and with grace. The motion was soothing to Noble. Lying there in utter darkness thinking of Kathleen, he found himself remembering a poem:

> Oh, Western wind, when will you blow,
> That the small rain down can rain?
> Christ, that my love were in my arms
> And I in my bed again!

The bunk swung slowly beneath him. Rain pattered on the planking overhead. He went to sleep.

Twelve days out of Norfolk.
The Panama Canal. The tankers went through without delay. Benton had never dreamed of anything like that canal. After passing through the first locks, some of them as high as a ten-story building, the *Gasper* went steaming through what looked like a long, narrow lake. Jungle grew down on each side, and that excited Benton. He could see strange birds flying around, the shore was so close. After the lake, the tanker went into a cut where the sides slanted up like the knobs around Lick River. The water was muddy-looking and full of alligators. Toward dusk it started raining, and everything got dismal and depressing. The *Gasper* went through more locks in the rain and tied up at about midnight with a million lights visible through the rain.

Two hours out of Panama.
After forty-eight hours in Panama, Sterns was almost glad to see the blue mountains turn grey, merge with clouds, and fade away, leaving the group of ships alone on the Pacific: two tankers, four minesweepers, and one lonely, ridiculously

small subchaser, all rising and falling over the long, deliberate swells. A few sea gulls swooped and wheeled around the vessels, sending them on with harsh, mournful cries. The Pacific swells were high but far apart, and as regular as a vastly slowed metronome. Their long crests reached for miles on either hand, suggesting the vast spaces, empty even of islands, across which they had gathered strength. Over all was the deep sky, the heat of the sun, and the wild and lonely wind.

Fourteen days out of Panama.

Land, home, and his old accustomed life already were becoming a fading past to John Everard. It was almost an effort to recall the last night with Martha. The two of them had been in bed, the love-making and the weeping over; Martha had been asleep. One gets to know a woman's breathing, he had thought. For a time she had been feigning sleep so that he might sleep, but she pretended too well. He had seen it happen with his children more than once. Martha's hand had been soft and relaxed in his; Everard remembered he had had to fight down a sudden fear that he might never hold it again.

Lying awake there in the dark, he had gone over it all once again: John Everard, Ph.D., professor, husband and father. Why had he done it? Why had he traded that for radioman, second class, J. Everard, USNR, of the PT Ninety-Seven? A cog whose home would be a narrow leather bunk and a square locker hemmed in by TNT and hundred-octane gasoline.

He had groaned softly. How about Noble and his offer to recommend him for Officers' Training? That had once been a way out. But thinking in the night, Everard had known that if he quit, living with himself would have been impossible. Courage, he had thought; why does a man feel that, somewhere, he must exhibit courage? It was enough to know

137

it had to be done, he'd realized; it was enough to know he must be brave. So he would go away from these things he loved.

The alarm clock had buzzed, steadily, unpleasantly, and he had heard Martha begin to stretch luxuriously as he had seen her do so many times, catlike, her slender body lithe and beautiful. Then he'd heard the gasp of her indrawn breath as full awakening hit her. He had leaned over to caress her face and kiss her gently.

"Oh, John!" she had said. "Let's hide!"

God knew he wanted to, but he had kissed her again and moved from her arms out of bed.

Hardest of all had been when he'd gone upstairs to see his children. They were still young enough to occupy the same room. He had looked at golden hair and brown hair, the first short and curly, the second long and very fine; and at their infinitely innocent and beautiful faces; and at their half-curled rosy fists. Deepest sorrow and pain had filled him as he knelt between the beds and kissed the children gently.

And then it had been out to the car—parked for the night on the street so the garage door opening wouldn't wake the children—down narrow streets empty at this hour, past the fortified tower of Sterling Library, where he had spent so much of his adult life, and finally the squat ugliness of the railroad station.

"Well," Martha had said. "Well . . ." And then she had begun crying again. Everard, the sailor, had embraced his sobbing wife on the dirty sidewalk, oblivious of the watching cop. They had been still murmuring in each other's arms when he'd heard the public address system call his train.

"John," Martha had said, sniffling. "John, take care of yourself."

"I will, dear, I'll be back; it won't be long. Remember that."

"Good-by . . . my sailor husband."

That had been her acceptance, her forgiveness. He had

138

kissed her, mumbled broken phrases of love, and fled through the swinging doors into the station.

The memories, so sharp at the time, so unforgettable he had thought, were already becoming vague in this dreamy eternity in which the only reality was the ships, and the Pacific heaving and swinging in its sleepy swell. At night pale-green fire danced and surged at the bow, liquid light climbed the sides of the ship and streamed away in veils; changing constellations glittered on the wave slopes, and the occasional whitecaps were crowned with light. Standing in the *Gasper's* bow, watching this display, Everard could think of death without much fear; in those hours, the old lure of action and adventure returned and he was almost happy.

Twenty-four days out of Panama.

Jim Print stood with many others on the afterdeck of the *Gasper*, hearing the roar of surf getting closer and closer ahead. He looked back with regret at the scene they were leaving.

"Prettiest place I ever saw," he said, feeling sad. The mountain went up 3,000 feet, grey bare rock above the last clinging green. White-beach arms spread to either side beneath the mountain, covered with trees and flowers. Green-yellow grass houses were dotted beneath the palms, the water was alive with outrigger canoes loaded with golden people, waving good-by. An incredibly sweet smell of flowers, earth, green things, fruit, and woodsmoke hung over all.

"It's a dream," Everard said slowly. "Islands of the blest."

"Didja see that babe Hill brought down to the dock?" Radelewski cackled. "Man, was she stacked! Where'd you find that one, Jos*iah*?"

Hill smiled slowly.

"You mean Tetua? I was swimming in one of those cricks, and she came in too."

Print looked at Hill. The quartermaster was half smiling,

139

but he looked sad too, and he ignored Ski's continued needling. Now the surf of the entrance to Bora Bora boiled close on either hand; the roar died, and they were in the open sea. "I'm coming back here someday," Hill said.

Three days out of Bora Bora.
Charlie Noble came whistling into the crew's quarters of the Ninety-Seven to find Radelewski drunk.

There was no mistaking it. The motor machinist's mate was swaying slightly, a silly grin on his face. He looked straight at Noble and drank from the plastic glass he held in his hand; the skipper became conscious of the faint odor of torpedo alcohol. It was a shock, turning Noble cold and still. He had just been boasting to the exec about how dependable and loyal his crew was. Anger filled him.

"Here's the boss," Radelewski said loudly. "How about a drink? C'mon, you guys, let's all have a little drink."

Dead silence filled the room. The rest of the men were waiting, deferring, Noble knew, to Sterns, who stood waiting for orders. The proper course was clear. Noble knew that an officer never, except in serious emergency, personally attempts to handle a drunk enlisted man; dignity is too precious and too easily lost. He need but give the word, and Sterns and the others would hustle Radelewski back to the dayroom. But Noble's anger was fanned by the realization that a PT was not a battleship; in small craft an officer's position could not be maintained by the book alone. He advanced on Radelewski.

"Hand me that glass," he said, the coldness of his voice surprising him.

Radelewski stared at him, not moving.

"I thought," Noble said, more coldly still, "that we had men in this crew. Guess I was wrong. Sterns, see that the alcohol is locked up, and bring me the key."

"Aye, aye, sir."

"Well, Radelewski?" Noble demanded. The man still didn't

move. Anger flared into rage; Noble stepped forward and knocked the glass clattering from the motor mac's hand. Radelewski, his face filled with hate, dropped into a half crouch, glaring at Noble.

"Now I guess you'll put me on the report, huh?" he said loudly.

Noble looked at him, coldly, impersonally. The man was about ready to attack him. All right, let him try it; he'd get a lesson he'd never forget.

"Easy to talk from behind them bars on your collar," Radelewski said tightly. "You'd love to throw me into Portsmouth for twenty years, wouldn't you?"

"No," Noble said quietly. "I wouldn't throw you into Portsmouth."

The resolution in Noble's voice shook Radelewski; he stared at his captain, not recognizing the pale, burning-eyed man before him. Suddenly he was sober. He looked about at the other enlisted men. They were staring at him in intense anger; he realized they were all against him. Suddenly his isolation, the knowledge of what he had almost done, frightened him.

"I . . ." he started to talk. He swallowed. "I'm sorry, Cap'n," he said. He realized he *was* sorry.

Noble relaxed slowly, passing his hand over his face.

"Very well, Radelewski," he said quietly. "We'll forget the whole thing. Clean up that mess. Sterns, lock up the alcohol and bring me the keys." He turned and left the compartment.

Radelewski stared after him. "Well, whaddaya know," he murmured. "He was practically inviting me to take a swing at him."

"Damned good thing you didn't take him up on it," Sterns said. "He'd have beat hell out of you, not that you didn't have it coming. The skipper fought welterweight under Spike Webb for four years at the Naval Academy."

"Well, I'm a sonofabitch," Radelewski said weakly. He got a rag and cleaned up the spilled drink without another word.

Fifty days out of Norfolk.

The *Gasper's* jackstaff was lined up with a slim white tower rising from the sea; beyond the tower were high-piled land clouds. A hovering swarm of sea gulls convoyed the tankers along the channel, whose entrance through the barrier reefs was marked by the tower. This was November 11, and Nouméa, New Caledonia, lay just ahead. The voyage was nearly over. Jim Print stood beside Noble on the tanker's flying bridge.

"Are we ready to hit the water?" Noble asked.

"I've double-checked your list."

"Good. Jim, do you feel like I do?"

"If you mean you want to turn around and go on home, pardner, then we're the Gold Dust Twins for sure."

"That's just what I mean."

In an hour, New Caledonia was in plain sight, with its hills blue with trees, and its unending lagoon flecked with little wooded islands. Here and there the water changed through the blue-green spectrum to near-white, marking where a reef came nearly to the surface. For another two hours the *Gasper* threaded her way through the narrow channel; then she passed the submarine nets and dropped her hook in the immense harbor of Nouméa. Noble whistled as he looked over the shipping in the great bay.

Within an hour, a fifty-ton crane was alongside. Two hours more, and all the PTs were in the water, with their tanks filled with gasoline from the *Gasper* and the *Drake*. Then it was noon, and the Prep Tares went back aboard the ships for a last meal.

The wardroom of the *Gasper* had spread itself: chicken and dressing, fruit salad, hot rolls, asparagus, and canned corn on the cob. Even the Captain was there, grinning sardonically from the head of the table while the chief, his false teeth twinkling and his faded blue eyes alight, kept everyone laughing with his filthiest stories. It was an occasion. The navigator recommended to the chief that he retire to Tasmania

142

where, according to that undoubtedly trustworthy master mariner, there existed the delightful ratio of seven women for every man. The chief took out his false teeth, polished them with his napkin, put them back carefully, and emitted a long wolf howl.

When the gathering had broken up and good-bys had been said, the Prep Tares climbed from the tanker's low foredeck to the boats. The Ninety-Seven danced and shifted beneath Noble like an impatient horse. The crew piled aboard, looking back and exchanging insulting good-bys with the *Gasper's* men, who lined the rails to see the PTs shove off.

"Wind 'em up," Noble said, trying to hide the excitement in his voice.

The starters whined, the deck quivered, and the engines coughed grey smoke astern and settled down to a steady, ear-filling roar. Noble gestured, and Johnson took in the bow line, allowing the bow to drift away from the Ninety-Eight.

"Cast off astern."

Noble rang once on the buzzer and shifted the port throttle to ahead. He felt power beneath his hand as the boat moved slowly away from the tanker. Noble looked up to the bridge and saw the exec leaning on his elbows, chin in hands, brooding down on the PTs.

"All clear aft, Skipper," Jim reported.

Noble cut in the center and starboard throttles and the boat surged forward. Back on the *Gasper,* the exec and the chief held their hands high. The buzzer rang three times in the cockpit. The engines were warm. Noble scanned the several miles of open water that lay ahead; he wanted to test top speed and burn out any carbon that might have accumulated in the cylinders. He turned the wheel loose and grasped the throttles with both hands, moving them ahead slowly and carefully. Acceleration pushed him back on his heels. The bow rose, the stern settled, and the snowy rooster's tail formed astern. Shirt sleeves and the slacks of pants legs snapped as the wind began to howl, the flag on the mast whipped and cracked. Faster and faster the PT skimmed through the water, hurling her wake high into the air and far out to either side.

"Hang on!" Noble yelled, and spun the wheel. The Ninety-Seven skidded and banked inward like a fighter plane, with the other three boats following her. Noble gripped the wheel and stared ahead to where ships were rushing toward him and the hills were becoming clear and close. The wind screamed, whipping his hair. A surge of exultation swept through him. This was the beginning!

14

THE PTs WERE safely anchored in a landlocked cove when the *Gasper's* whaleboat came by to take Noble in to report. All the way to the beach he searched for the PT tender, which he knew to be a large converted yacht, but she was not in sight. However, Commander Morton Daggs was waiting at the dock. Noble's insides curled at sight of him.

The bell jangled, the whaleboat engine surged into astern, and the bowhook went over with the line. Noble stepped onto the float, walked up the ramp, and saluted Daggs.

"Hello, Commander," he said.

"I see you made it, Noble," Daggs said briefly. The lieutenant noticed the use of his last name; a constraint hung between them. Noble studied the commander. His face was less round than before, his cheeks less ruddy, his eyes less hard and bright; when they shook hands, Daggs no longer tried to crush Noble's fingers as had been his habit. The Ninety-Seven's skipper sensed his commanding officer's agitation, and sought to end the silence.

"No ears yet, Commander?"

"Ears? Oh, yeah; nope, no ears yet; just give me time." For a moment the old bluster returned. "How we gonna win the war if they keep holding a man back?" It faded. "Come on; I've got me an office. We'll talk there."

Tension continued to grow in Noble during the short jeep ride through the colorful streets of Nouméa, shaded by umbrella-shaped flamboyant trees, and filled with jostling crowds—made up of soldiers, sailors, civilians, and natives, among them an occasional native trooper in shorts, red fez, and orange-dyed hair—all of whom ignored the jeep's constant horn. The destination was one of a half-dozen Quonset huts in the yard of a large house. Daggs led the way into a dusty cubicle and closed the door. In spite of a small open window and humming electric fan, the place was oven-hot. Noble could feel his shirt sticking to his shoulders under his khaki jacket.

"You can throw that damned coat away," Daggs said, offering a cigarette. "You won't need such out here."

Noble produced matches and they lit up, smoking in silence. Something lay hard upon Daggs, but Noble felt it wasn't Kathleen. Something closer, more immediate, was putting that quiver in his hand. Noble had a thousand questions, but he hesitated to ask them. Daggs sighed suddenly.

"Look," he said. "There's a lot to do. The *Marlboro,* our tender, went on up to Guadalcanal two weeks ago. Jake Hughes and Ollie Wakefield have got some boats up there. They been doing a great job."

"I heard they had sunk some ships," Noble said, remembering a news broadcast that he had listened to with excitement on the *Gasper.*

"They've done a lot. Pretty hot up there, son." Daggs hesitated. "You'll draw paint from supply depot; get the boats painted green."

"Green?"

"That's it. You'll operate at night and stay tied up in the bushes during the day. They say those Jap Zeros are thicker'n bees up there."

Sunk ships . . . bushes . . . Zeros. Noble's hands grew moist. He was nearly there; it was a real war he was going to again.

"They need your boats bad, Noble. Soon as you get them

painted, come alongside the supply dock and load stores. We'll get you off in a day or two."

"Aren't you going with us, Commander?" Noble asked.

Daggs didn't meet Noble's eyes, and in a flash Noble knew what the barrier had been between them: Daggs wasn't going. Jap-hating, bloodthirsty, action-craving Daggs was going to stick in Nouméa.

"We need a base here," Daggs said. "I got to stay and get things ready." A base in Nouméa—twelve hundred miles from the action zone? "You'll operate as part of Wakefield's squadron," Daggs went on. "By God!" There was a shade of bluster now, although rather hollow. "I sure would like to be going along, but you know how it is. Save some for me, son."

"I'll be sure and do that," Noble said. "Tough luck, sir. Can't argue with orders though."

"Orders? By God, that's right, Charlie. Orders are orders. A guy has got to do like he's told in the Navy."

Noble was admitted to see a staff operations officer after an hour's wait. At first he was irritated by the staff officer's manner, for his attention was elsewhere and half the time he didn't seem to know what Noble was saying. But when he was told that a major engagement was making up at Guadalcanal, Noble understood not only this commander but the feeling of tension and strain over the whole headquarters.

"It'll be a big one," the commander said tersely. "Heavy stuff on both sides. If we lose this one, Noble, your boats may be operating right here, or maybe from Espiritu Santo."

"Is it that bad, sir?" he asked worriedly.

"Yes," the commander said.

Noble would have stayed on in the operations room longer, but when rear-admiral's stripes started appearing, he knew it was no place for a senior grade lieutenant, and got out. Noble drew paint and made a futile visit to the Fleet Post Office for mail; toward sunset rain started to fall, and by the time he found a boat and headed back to his division it was pitch dark. Noble huddled cold and wet on the thwart of the whaleboat. He didn't blame Daggs. He was scared too. This was a hell of a way from home, an alien place where he didn't belong; and suppose that fight up north went sour? The wind had increased and whitecaps were slopping over the bow, blowing back in scuds of spray, when the whaleboat rounded a point and entered the calmer waters of the little cove. Noble saw a dark shape looming ahead. He stood up on the thwart and yelled through cupped hands, "Ninety-Seven, ahoy!" At once he heard an answering shout, "Over here, sir."

As the boat came alongside, guided by two flashlight beams, Noble realized how hungry, cold, tired, and discouraged he was. Jim and Everard reached down and helped him onto the deck, while the coxswain passed up the paint buckets. Then, as the whaleboat pitched away into the rainy darkness, Noble groped into the cockpit. He swung down into the dry chart-house, and from there into the warm, brightly lit quarters below. Steaks were sizzling on the stove, and Ding Hau was chopping lettuce while keeping an eye on the bubbling Silexes. The phonograph was singing softly and lazily. Already Noble felt better, and by the time he had shifted into dry khakis and drunk a preliminary cup of coffee, he felt like a new man.

The morning broke sunny, and all day all hands painted ship. There was no gleam to this paint; it was flat, dark, light-absorbent. A fighting color. By night the four boats of the division were a uniform dull green. The next morning Noble took the boats to the dock and they loaded stores. Daggs came down to the dock after lunch and took Noble ashore with him. The commander looked strange, Noble thought, breathing hard; one minute red in the face, the next pale. Daggs led the way to another dock and aboard the *Covey*, an old four-pipe destroyer that had been cut down to two stacks and converted to mine-sweeping. Daggs introduced Noble to her captain, a haggard senior lieutenant.

"Captain Jensen, this is Lieutenant Noble," Daggs said. "He'll be in command of the four PTs going up with you."

"Glad to meet you, Noble." As they shook hands Noble studied Jensen. He was a thin young man with deep welts under his eyes. He smoked one cigarette after another.

"What d'you think of the news from up north?" Jensen said.

"I hadn't heard, sir," said Noble. "What happened?"

"We came out on top," Jensen said quietly, "but we took a hell of a shellacking doing it. Pretty confused, but we lost some destroyers and had four cruisers smacked to hell and gone."

"Judas." Noble let out his breath. "I'm glad we licked them."

"It's not over yet. That was just a preliminary; the main bout is coming up. This was bad enough. *Portland, San Francisco, Juneau* smashed up. *Atlanta* sunk. Five destroyers sunk. No telling what else by now."

Into that, Noble was taking four little wooden boats. He swallowed hard. "Well," he said, "I guess I'd better get my PT boat up there to take the *Atlanta's* place."

Jensen looked at him grimly and nodded.

"That's about the size of it. We'll be leaving here the day after tomorrow. I'm escorting some landing craft as far as Buttons, and . . ."

"Excuse me, sir?"

"Don't you know the code names for the bases between here and Guadalcanal? Nouméa is White Poppy, Efate is Roses, Espiritu is Buttons."

"White Poppy!" Daggs snorted. "Roses!"

"What's Guadalcanal?"

"Cactus. You'll see the connection when you get there. Now, I suggest that you proceed independently to Buttons. You can run up the chain of islands. Stop over a day at Efate; it's a damned nice spot and you can rest up there and refuel. I'll meet you at Espiritu. Okay?"

"Yes sir."

"Fine. I'll load gas in drums onto my decks, and we'll pull in at Star Harbor on San Cristobal—that's the southernmost of the Solomons—and refuel you before dark. That lets us make the last leg at night, and you want to get to Cactus with plenty of gas in your tanks; you can't tell what you'll be dodging. And after daylight there are sure to be enemy planes tooling around."

This guy's scaring hell out of me, thought Noble. Daggs didn't say a word.

"It's touch and go up there," Jensen said wearily. "I had to shoot it out with a cruiser at night, running like hell. If he hadn't been hunting transports he'd have got me for sure. I've been strafed, bombed, shelled and machine-gunned; I've had torpedoes run under this old bucket, and I've made high-speed runs through uncharted reefs." He shook his head. "It's building up again, too. That's why they're in a hurry to get you up there."

"Let's go ashore and knock back a few," Daggs said when they left the *Covey* at three o'clock. "You'll be all set after you get fueled, won't you?"

"Yes, sir, except for a few rabbits' feet."

"You scared, Noble?" Daggs said roughly.

"Frankly, hell, yes, sir."

Daggs looked at Noble strangely. What the hell does he expect? Noble wondered. The first drink tasted and felt good to Noble, who was ready for some Dutch courage—so did the second and third. Then he slowed down, but Daggs, already ahead of him, kept going steadily.

"It's a hell of a world, Charlie," Daggs said mournfully as he ordered his sixth, or maybe seventh. It was dim and cool in the bar; the rolled bamboo curtains sheltered it from the heat, while allowing any breeze to filter through.

"Some parts of it are all right."

"Yeah, some. Long's you ain't married. You ain't married, are you, Charlie? That's right; 'course you're not. Never get married, son, screw 'em and scram, that's the way. Wish I had stuck to it."

Noble was uncomfortable and tried to change the subject.

150

In vain; Daggs kept returning to it. Something was really bothering the man, Noble decided. Daggs was sweating freely, his shirt a dark brown mass clinging to his heavy body.

"Take a look at that," the commander said, handing Noble an envelope originally addressed to Daggs at New York, with a printed return address from the "Alland Detective Agency, Chicago, Illinois."

"Jus' came this mornin'. Been all the way to Tulagi and back. Hell a thing for a man fighting for his country to get, him ten thousand miles from home."

"Is that so?" Noble controlled his voice and handed the envelope back to Daggs, who fumbled with it.

"All our mail is goin' to Tulagi, 'cause that's where the boats are. The mail clerk here says lots mail up north, maybe. Listen, Charlie, you look over that mail up there, and when you see a letter like *that*, from those people, you get it on a plane, on plane, by God, and you get it down here? Understan'? I'm askin' you to do this, and I'm orderin' you to do this too. Understan'?"

"Yes, sir," Noble said, a premonition of new danger adding to the tension he already felt.

"You know my wife? You know Kathleen? Sure, you know Kathleen. You know she said she was goin' home? Didja know that? Well, she didn't."

"Commander," Noble said desperately, stone sober, "I've got to be getting back to the boats."

"You wait," Daggs said. "You wait right here. Wanna tell you . . . wanna tell you whatta bish—bitch!—m'wife is. She didn't go home. I thought she was home with my folks in Iowa, but my folks wrote askin' 'bout her. So I wrote this detective agency. And this letter here they wrote day I left N'York for San Francisco. I only got it this mornin'."

"That's too bad."

"Sure is. Specially since the letter says m'wife not home, m'wife livin' with naval officer somewhere. Don' say where,

151

says brief phomed—phoned—report all they had; full report supposed to follow. Only I ain't got it, see? 'N when I get it I'll know where, and I'll know who, goddam him, *who*."

"They don't know who it is?' Noble said, his voice strangely calm.

"No. Say they got a picture . . ."

"A picture?"

"Yeah, a picture. Say send it unner seprate cover, nex' day. But it hasn't got here. 'N when it does get here, I'll know who he is. I'll fix 'im! I'll kill him! Livin' with my wife."

Daggs put his head on his hands, rolling it from side to side. Noble was sick with a kind of pity, but no longer with fear. This was what all the beauty, all the high excitement and tenderness had led to, then: a fat man crying in his sweat in a dark bar. Noble came close; for a moment he almost told Daggs that he, Noble, had been Kathleen's lover. But something stopped him. What good would it do? Daggs would probably try to kill him. Well, Noble was going to an area where every man knew he might be dead before the next day. If Noble was to die anyway, then why not spare both Daggs and himself torment?

"I'm sorry, sir," Noble said.

"It's all right, Charlie. You sen' me that letter, hear? You sen' it to me, Charlie. Promise?"

"I promise." Noble said. "I'll send it down by air when it comes." He would do it too; he would not open or destroy or delay the letter. He owed this man that much.

Two days later at dawn the voyage recommenced, but now the four PTs were alone. Through the nets, then down the endless lagoon until late morning, then through Queen Charlotte Pass to the waiting breakers. From that time until the boats pulled into Vila Harbor, Efate, the next morning, no man could turn loose a safe handhold for a moment, even in fitful sleep in bed. Twenty-four hours at Efate—a Christmas cake of an island set in a blue-green sea—then on to Espiritu Santo. As the boats neared Santo, rain clouds piled high, and PTs came into Segond Channel under grey, cold rain, fitting accompaniment to the sights that awaited them at the naval base.

"Jesus Christ!" Sterns said in awe. They were passing a mass of torn, smoke-stained wreckage—all that remained of a destroyer. Noble looked around at his silent crew, who grew even more silent as the Ninety-Seven passed ship after ship: destroyers, cruisers, even, to Noble's blank astonishment, the tremendous bulk of a battleship. The cruisers were shattered wrecks—bows gone, masts down, sterns riddled, superstructures pocked and jagged. The battleship's upper works were scarred and torn, the exposed steel already rusting in the corrosive climate.

"Who did you say won this battle, Skipper?" Ding Hau's usually merry face was solemn in the grey, streaming rain.

"We did."

"Makes you wonder what the other fellow looks like."

"Mister Noble," Benton's voice was strained. "Where did all this, all these things here, where did they happen?"

"Right where we're going. Guadalcanal."

"When?"

"A few nights ago."

"Holy Mary!" Radelewski had lost his cockiness, and who could blame him? Noble thought. These men had not known before the unimaginable ferocity of high-explosive havoc; now, looking at the heavy, mangled steel, they could realize what might happen to the tender bodies of men. Jim turned a pale face toward Noble and tried to smile. The skipper couldn't answer it. Of this crew, only he and Warder had been at Pearl Harbor, and so knew already what the others were finding out; but the sight of the mangled ships brought back to Noble that knowledge, bitter and deforming in memory.

153

"Okay," the skipper said with relief. "There's the tanker ahead. Stand by to fuel."

The division got under way at three in the morning, with the *Covey* in the lead, and ran all day under a grey and rain-filled sky. Print noticed there was no joking among the crew that day, nor did he feel like joking himself. The seas were short and mean, and he could barely stay in his bunk below; topside he got wet and miserable. Everything was a mess—grey day, grey ocean, dirty-green old destroyer, pitching and rolling up ahead fit to tie a guy's guts in knots just to look at it. Worse than the weather and the rough water was the knowledge that ahead were no more pretty islands, no more comfortable bases—only Guadalcanal, Cactus, seeming now to Print like an ominous monster that engulfed men by thousands and mangled ships.

The boat kept at twenty-seven knots all day, and Print thanked God that the engines didn't conk out. At sunset the division pulled into Star Harbor, San Cristobal, tied up alongside the *Covey*, and started fueling from the drums on her decks. Nothing was in sight but the round bay with thick, dark-looking jungle coming down on all sides. The clouds broke up in the west and the whole sky turned red, so that the converted destroyer and the four PTs seemed to be lying in a pool of red ink. The Ninety-Seven fueled first, and with pleasure, since the *Covey* passed over a cold can of beer for each man. Fueling had barely started when narrow canoes came sidling out of the jungle, careful at first about coming close, but directly alongside before many minutes had passed. The three or four men sitting in each canoe were black as a dark night, but considerably shinier. They seemed nervous but friendly, smiling a good deal, not saying much among themselves, just sitting there looking at the PTs. Print noticed that their paddles, ornamented with inlaid mother-of-pearl, had spear points on the upper ends.

"Hey, Radelewski," Print said. "Did you notice their teeth?"

"Yeah. Black as hell, ain't they?"

"That's from chewing betel nut, but look closer—there's one smiling. Look at his teeth."

"Holy hell!" Radelewski said uneasily. "They come down to sharp points."

"That's right. Filed down. These lads are cannibals."

Ski smiled weakly.

After fueling, the Ninety-Seven patrolled the narrow entrance to discourage submarines. As the boat ran back and forth, the last red faded from sky and water, and the Ninety-Seven was in complete, rolling blackness. Rain commenced again and Print felt a million miles from home.

In this black squall with rain roaring down, the division started the last leg. The blacked-out *Covey* hit twenty-seven knots, and in five minutes the PTs had lost her. She finally had to slow down and show a light for five minutes, with Jensen swearing over the radio fit to scorch his soul. Noble didn't blame him. The Ninety-Seven's engines conked twice and the Ninety-Eight's once. Noble wasn't seasick, but his body was so tired from the heavy pounding that when Ding Hau brought up a liverwurst sandwich, he had to throw it overboard. The boats should have reached Tulagi during the night, but when daylight came they still were twenty miles out, with the Ninety-Eight being towed by the *Covey*. Twenty miles to port lay a long, Paris-green island with high, jagged peaks topped by clouds. Noble couldn't take his eyes off it.

"Skipper, what island is that?" Benton asked.

Noble could see the tenseness in the stubbled, drawn faces of his crew as he answered quietly, "Guadalcanal."

15

A LANE of clear water began between Cape Esperance, on Guadalcanal, and Savo Island. It ran to the northwest, bordered on north and south by more islands: the Russells, New Georgia, where an enemy base was building, Choiseul, and at the end, three hundred miles from Guadalcanal, Shortland Island. A strong enemy base lay on Shortland; just beyond was Bougainville. All the strength of the Japanese Southern Pacific Fleet could be funneled down this lane.

You could say it was a bowling alley, hemmed in by islands, with American forces the pins.

You could say it was the rails down which ran the Tokyo Express to supply the Japanese troops on Guadalcanal.

Or you could just say it was The Slot. Which says it all.

In that November the weight of the Pacific war rested on Guadalcanal. We had taken the part of the island that held Henderson Field; now we had to keep it.

The Japanese Army still occupied much of the island, including Cape Esperance; the Japanese Navy struggled to supply and reinforce the Army by way of Esperance Beach.

The waters around Guadalcanal were too hot for big naval vessels to remain there. Destroyers, cruisers—even battleships —of both sides came to the islands during times of crisis and fought it out in the darkness of Ironbottomed Bay. When the major battles were over, the big ships went away. The PTs stayed there all the time.

In the intervals between battles, the U.S. planes from Henderson Field kept the enemy away during daylight; but when darkness crept down the sides of the mountains of Guadalcanal, making the flashes of mortar bursts look from the sea like white fireworks, Japanese destroyer forces prowled down The Slot, carrying soldiers, guns, ammunition, and food, to reinforce their positions on Guadalcanal. Night after night they came; night after night the PTs went out to stop them. The PTs were the only force that could try to stop them. The PTs were all we had.

Why didn't larger American vessels, destroyers at least, turn the Express back? The answer was simple: we had nearly run out of Navy. Such destroyers as remained had to stay with the surviving pair of carriers, or the two new battleships, or the handful of light and heavy cruisers, to make up task forces strong enough to stop major enemy punches.

So at night, the PTs went out on Ironbottomed Bay and fought Japanese destroyers at our end of The Slot. How long would it go on? Until Guadalcanal was secure, or until the Japanese Navy gave up. In that November, neither of these looked very imminent.

16

PRINT FINISHED DRAPING the mosquito net over his cot and looked around at Charlie, who was examining the row of four cots, the thick thatched roof that came down to within four feet of the neatly-woven bamboo floor, and the A-shaped door through which was visible the creek, shining blue in the sun, and the bending palm trees. Beyond the creek was a high cliff of jungle across which drifted a flock of cockatoos, white specks against the green.

"Home sweet home," Noble said. "God, I feel a million miles from nowhere."

"Me, too." The two mahogany bureaus from the boat, with the oil lanterns on their polished tops, looked funny against the roof posts, Print thought. They had really stripped ship; every movable article not required for combat had been brought ashore on Florida Island.

"You want your boat as light as you can get it," Commander Wakefield had told the newcomers. "Those Jap destroyers are fast, I mean *fast*, and you need every damned bit of speed you can get when they chase you."

"Chase us?"

"Hell, yes, Charlie. You'll have one of them behind you before long, you laying smoke and shooting at her searchlight, and her throwing shells at you. If she hangs on too long," Wakefield said, "you drop a depth charge. That bothers them."

"Jesus," Noble had muttered.

"You'll live ashore in the village," Wakefield said. "The boats are too hot. We keep them tied up in the bushes with two men aboard."

Now Print loaded his pipe. "Since you're going out to-night, Charlie, you'd better take a nap. You didn't get any sleep last night."

"A good idea. Wake me at four, huh?"

Print nodded and stepped out of the hut. A funny, moldy smell hung over the place; he guessed it came from the rim of exposed mud that made a brown fringe to the grass, and from the huts themselves; but mostly it just came from the dank moistness of everything. His face had been wet with sweat ever since they'd pulled up alongside the dock that morning. A breeze blew in onto the village from Tulagi Harbor across the bay, but even the breeze was hot. Print walked down the rough wooden steps to the ground four feet below. The village was a pretty place: a green, grassy point with water on two sides and a little brook coming down from the jungle to cut the area in two. Scattered through it, shading the huts, were tall, graceful palms, which rustled and moved in the wind. Not far from the hut the Ninety-Seven's men had pitched their two pyramid tents. Print went over and looked into one of them.

"Ho, Benton. It looks like you boys are mighty well fixed up."

"Yes, sir," Benton said. He had just been thinking that they had things in good shape. Benton was pleased with the big tent, canvas hot in the sun. It smelled like camping trips at home. Now he looked proudly around at the cots under mosquito bars, the boxes to sit on, the lanterns, and the lockers from the boat. "This is nice."

"Ditch her deep. It rains plenty out here."

159

"We have," Ike Sterns assured Print. "I hear the skipper is going out on patrol tonight."

"That's right. We'll all go out tomorrow night; he's just learning the landmarks this time. They don't expect anything much down."

"How about our squadron?" Ski demanded.

"All boats are thrown in together. The base force has enough trouble keeping half of them operating at one time. Then the crews take turns, one night in, the next out."

"You mean we may have to take out another boat?"

"We might."

"Hell with that. Don't let 'em screw us thataway, Mr. Print."

Print laughed. "You like the Old Ninety-Seven, do you, boys?"

"Damn right," Ike said, and the others noisily agreed.

When Jim woke him up at 1600, Noble was as wet as if he'd been in a bath, and his mouth tasted foul with daytime sleep. He sat up dizzily under the net, and then pulled on his shorts and shoes, took soap and towel, and went with Jim to find the swimming place. They discovered it a hundred yards up the brook: a place of unearthly beauty. It was a round pool, perhaps forty feet across, backed up against high, mossy rocks that were covered with ferns, vines, and flowers. Water fell fifty feet from the rocks into the pool. The close shore was of white sand.

"I'll be damned," Print said. "Where's Dorothy Lamour?"

The cool soft water made Noble feel like a human being again. After a while the two officers reluctantly got out of the pool and went back to the hut. Noble dressed in khakis, put two cigars in his shirt pocket, belted on forty-five, canteen, and shark knife, thrust his arm through the chin strap of the steel helmet, and went down to the pier with Jim. The pier was made of steel runway-matting laid over cement-filled steel drums that were upended on the coral. They waited together a few minutes, looking across the mouth of the creek toward the bay, and to Tulagi Island beyond it, sheltering Tulagi Harbor from the open sea. Tulagi was high and ragged looking across the sun-dazzled waters of the bay. Noble could make out the gaunt structures of the two floating drydocks at the base at Sesapi, and he could hear the roar of motors being tested. After a while a Higgins boat came up the creek and Noble climbed in, leaving Jim behind; he would come up later with the crew for late chow. The creek narrowed to a 100-yard-wide strip of water runing through dense jungle, then widened into a round pool some 300 yards in diameter. The *Marlboro*, the PT tender, lay against the west shore of this pool, covered with camouflage netting studded with palm branches. The patrol officers climbed aboard.

Of the dozen officers assembled in the wardroom, Noble knew Ollie Wakefield, Jake Hughes, and Dick Bareling, all three Academy men. Jake was skipper of Ron Three, Ollie of Two. Noble had met some of the other officers; now other names were given and he shook hands around. They all looked much alike to him—tired, thin, hollow-eyed, and with the greenish tinge all white men seemed to get in the Solomons. Little joking took place around the wardroom table. These were the officers with patrol duty that night. Noble didn't say very much, knowing that these strangers would very soon be friends, and that this newness soon would change to accustomed ease. Noble talked mostly to Ollie and Jake Hughes.

As a matter of fact, Noble hadn't much to say. Though he knew that nothing big was expected down, he still was apprehensive about the night that lay ahead, with the dark waters, the unfriendly coast, squalls, and perhaps planes or barges. Thank God for the three-quarter moon that would be up soon; with its light flooding the sea, the Japs wouldn't send down their ships.

After dinner, officers and men climbed down from the tender onto two of the boats which had just finished fueling. The sun was setting as Noble went down the Jacob's ladder and stepped onto the inboard boat. When it passed the village, Noble saw Jim and the crew of the Ninety-Seven standing on the dock. He lifted a hand and they all waved back, Print holding up one hand with the thumb and forefinger circled for good luck.

The PT base on Tulagi was three long, rough piers, stretching out from a shelf of flat ground at the foot of a steep hill, whose vertical pitch made it difficult for a plane to bomb the base. The shelf of ground was covered with board huts, grass shacks, and the thickly crowded tents of the PT base force; other tents were placed up the sides of the hill wherever a flat space could be found. Two crippled destroyers and a shot-up cruiser were at anchor in the bay, camouflaged; in the gathering dusk the bright-blue arcs of welding and cutting torches could be seen aboard.

The boat captains filed into the radio shack, where they would wait for the courier boat from Guadalcanal. This shack, the PT command post, was a large thatched hut with half a dozen radio sets beneath the eaves, a few desks, some chairs, and a table or two. Warren Manson, the squadron's chief yeoman, got up to shake hands.

"Glad to see you again, Mister Noble," he said. His face was mournful as ever, but his dark eyes were pleased. "I got a lot of paper work for you to go over tomorrow."

"Right. Good to see you too, Manson. You've been here about two weeks now, haven't you?"

"Two weeks," the chief yeoman said. He reflected a moment. "Two goddamned weeks. I been thinking they was months."

When the courier boat arrived, nothing new or big was reported; and as night fell, Wakefield's boat pulled away from the dock with Noble in the cockpit. Light still hung down on the water, and already a glow above the jungled hills told of the rising moon.

"Nothing to this one," Wakefield murmured as the PT

162

moved down the harbor past the government buildings, such as they were.

"I'm damned glad to hear it," Noble told him honestly. Wakefield laughed. The boat lined up on the two dim-purple range lights and threaded her way through the entrance. Out of the channel, the world cooled with the sea wind, and the smell of islands was in the air.

"Okay," Ollie said. "Action stations, boys, moon or no moon."

The gunners went into the turrets and to the 20-mm. Oerlikon aft. Everybody put on steel helmets and life jackets as the mufflers came on, choking the engines' roar down to a soft mumble.

"Even with the moon," Ollie said, "you can run up on a barge, and float Zeros—Zeros with twin floats instead of wheels—can turn up any time. Always be ready for action, Charlie, just as soon as you clear the entrance."

"Right."

"You know the chart? Good. Lunga Point is twenty miles from Tulagi; we've got a little naval base there, and Henderson is behind it. Fourteen miles northwest is Doma Reef—looks like a whale's back at low water. That is enemy-held territory; be careful you don't run up on that reef—plenty of coral around and it's only about fifty yards from the beach."

"I'll be careful."

"Okay. Six and a half miles further along is Cape Esperance. The Cape is where the Japs make most of their landings. Watch close in there; you might get fired on from the beach by anything from rifles to mortars."

By now the moon was above the water; it climbed swiftly and the sea was black and silver, with the dark islands riding high. Visibility increased minute by minute.

"Jesus," said the quartermaster. "Ain't that moon beeyoo-diful?"

"Yeah," the radioman agreed. "A moon like that useta

make me think about girls, but now all I think is that I'll get back with my ass in one piece."

"A man would think you guys were scared." Ollie grinned.

"We are," the quartermaster said. "We're not like you, Commander. We don't wanta get kilt."

"Oh, crap."

"Mister Noble, this guy's nuts," the radioman protested. "He ain't scared of *nothin'!*"

"That's all *you* know." Ollie laughed. "Now, Charlie, look over there." Noble followed Ollie's finger and saw the dark, high bulk of a mountained island; it had a sawtoothed peak, and the glint of surf was visible at its base. "That's Savo Island, friendly territory. Get ashore there and the natives will take care of you until we pick you up. If you get sunk fifty yards off Esperance, you swim away from the beach! Don't get captured, Charlie. They've found marines tied to trees with their feet burned away, and all cut up. The sharks are kinder."

God, the things men do to other men! Noble thought. This was no joke. No chivalrous enemy here, and no mercy if captured.

Guadalcanal drew closer, its mountains climbing steadily over the few stars, sawtoothed against the dark blue of the sky. Here and there white flashes blossomed; now and again a flare held above the jungle a moment, then died.

"Quiet tonight," Ollie said.

"Quiet?" Noble thought in silent protest. Over there, a mile or so in the dank jungle, men were in foxholes watching the flare and the returning dark, listening for the rustle of leaves. Quiet? What of the dozen or so marines who would die tonight? For them was it quiet?

Noble saw the black whale's back of Doma Reef; close beyond its white beach was the jungle, black and quiet. No doubt, right now, a Jap soldier lay within a hundred yards of him, watching the boat and fingering his rifle. Esperance, dotted with broken transports and landing craft. Savo to the right, beyond the haunted waters of Ironbottomed Bay. Ships in their dozens, men in their tens of thousands lay beneath the black and silver surface; Noble shuddered as he looked across it. He was afraid of this place.

Once the hum of an airplane's engines sent the PT men into a tense watchfulness. A bright light broke from the darkness a mile ahead, swaying, floating.

"A goddamned flare," Ollie said harshly. "Sonofabitch thought he saw something."

"To all ships and stations!" the radio crackled. "The condition is red, the condition is red. Over."

"He's telling us?" Ollie grunted sourly. "Watch close, boys."

A squall blew up and the sea grew rough. Waves slopped into the cockpit, and lightning flashed across the sky as thunder rolled. Once the sea leaped and roared near Savo as a bomb exploded. It wasn't close to Ollie's boat, but it made every man cringe.

"Pressure is building up again," Ollie said quietly. "They'll be coming down again soon. I can feel it."

The PT patrolled the silent sea and her crew saw nothing, but they had lost nearly two hours during the squall, and barges might have come in from the Jap-held Russell Islands. Toward morning, the weather cleared.

"You'll be going out again tonight, Charlie," Ollie said. "Why don't you take a caulk?"

The deck by the forward torpedo tubes was sheltered from wind and spray, and Noble's kapok life jacket cushioned his shoulders, while the helmet, crown to the boards, made an oddly comfortable pillow. Worn out by the preceding week and this night, glad to forget the harsh, evil facts of death that surrounded him, Noble went to sleep, soothed by the gentle rolling of the boat.

He was shaken awake to find the gunner's mate kneeling beside him in full daylight. Almost directly overhead, palm branches were outlined against blue sky, and a white beach was only fifty yards off the bow. The gunner extended a loaded submachine gun to Noble.

"We're running an inshore patrol of the enemy coast, sir," he said tensely. "That's Esperance Beach. We might run into Japs any minute."

Taking the Tommy gun, Noble put on his steel helmet and ducked low against the torpedo tube. The shore looked peaceful where the waves crisped up the beach in crescents of white. This part of Guadalcanal was beautiful: tall, grass-covered mountains rose like velvet above the jungle. But the beach, which had once been beautiful, was so no longer. Every twenty or thirty feet lay the blackened wreck of a landing boat or barge. They were there in hundreds and hundreds. At intervals, the red-rusted hulls of Jap transports lay half in, half out of the water.

The PT moved slowly along. The coral bottom, plainly visible, sliding beneath the boat like an aviator's strip map, seemed to reach up for the hull as it passed over, then drop away behind. Noble clicked off the safety of the machine gun and slid lower behind the tube, watching the sliding sea floor with intent fascination; the very idea of being stranded on a reef fifty yards from the beach gave him the shivers. Ollie was pointing ashore; yes, there beneath a dead palmetto was the vague outline of something covered with branches. The two barrels of the forward turret swung around, leveled at the object under the trees, and poured fire and smoke from their muzzles, drawing red hot tracer-lines from the guns to the target, awakening the morning from calm and quiet with an ear-splitting roll of sound. The heap moved and leaped, blowing up with a crash that sent flames twenty feet into the air while a puff of black smoke rose among the palm trees. An ammunition cache. Noble looked uneasily around, feeling the defenseless vitals of the boat, the gas tanks a waiting torch, all lying naked before the menace awakened by their clangour. His stomach felt shriveled.

Almost at once the PT came upon a landing boat, hauled

166

well up from the water and partially hidden with branches. The 20-mm. aft started purring its rhythmic groups of five or six, and the landing boat quickly disappeared under a haze of explosions, capped by the final leap of flame from ignited tanks. The Prep Tares watched the beach narrowly. The Japs wouldn't stand for this quietly. The trees waved in the morning wind, and only an occasional bird called as the shore slid past. The PT reached the end of Esperance Beach, a point where tangled underbrush came down to the water's edge.

"There, under those bushes! Aren't those ammunition cans?" Noble cried.

"Right. Good eye, Charlie. Open fire."

As Wakefield spoke, a dozen puffs of white smoke blossomed out of the jungle in a confused clatter of sharp rifle fire; bullets thudded into the PT; one spanged and screamed from the tube only inches from Noble's head, and another drilled through the canopy behind him. The heavy machine guns drummed back an answer. Tracer bounced from the tree trunks, knocking off chunks of wood, and ricocheted from stones; 20-mm. shells exploded with their flat wham and flash-bulb flicker. Noble saw that several rifles were firing from low, thick brush close by the water. He leveled the submachine gun over the tube, looked down the short barrel, lined it up, and squeezed the trigger. The beautiful little animal purred. Slim streaks of flame poured into the bushes where leaves and branches flew and dirt puffed. The bushes thrashed. The rifle fire stopped. Noble thumbed the catch, letting the empty thirty-round clip clatter to the deck as he slipped in a fresh one. The forward machine guns shifted fire into the piled ammunition and it exploded noisily.

The PT turned away from the beach in a growing ripple of rifle fire and ran for it. Noble looked up at Ollie in the cockpit. He was laughing as though at some great joke, and his laugh grew as he caught Noble's eye. Charlie didn't feel like laughing—he was too scared and shaking badly—but Ollie's amusement was contagious; and soon he felt an idiotic grin take control of his face, as the green island with its hidden enemy dropped away behind them.

Print was waiting at the dock when Wakefield's boat got back. The other three PTs, each with a captain of one of the new boats aboard for instruction, had been back for over an hour, and he was beginning to be worried.

"Here they come, sir," McLeod said, scratching his bare and hairy chest. Print knew McLeod as the best chief machinist's mate in the Flotilla. "The old man is always the last one back."

"I don't see Charlie," Print said nervously.

"Ah, Mister Wakefield is grinning; he don't grin when he's lost a man. You seem to like Mister Noble, sir; reckon he's a good skipper."

"He suits me."

"Ike Sterns said the same," McLeod agreed. "Well, I don't blame you for being anxious; good skippers don't grow on trees. Though I will say we've got our share in this outfit."

"There he is!" Print exclaimed. He was glad to see Charlie grinning palely from across the narrowing distance. He liked the guy, sure; but there was more to it than that. Without Charlie, he'd be in command of the Ninety-Seven, and he wasn't ready for that, not yet. He had come to like the boys too much to be responsible for maybe getting them killed. He knew that thought bothered the skipper, too.

Noble looked worn out when he came ashore; his eyes had black smudges under them and he was pale under his tan.

"You better hit the hay," Print told him. "You look pooped."

"I can use some sleep," the skipper agreed. He grinned. "Getting the hell scared out of you is exhausting work."

168

17

PRINT AND THE BOYS set out for the Ninety-Seven, stripped and forlorn-looking in the bushes. They took her over to Mocambo, where the torpedo crew shifted fish, putting in four that had just been adjusted and set. The crew then went over the engines and guns, and Ike tried the smoke generator, nearly causing an air-raid alarm in the process. By noon chow the boat was ready.

Print ate and went to the village to rest up for the night's patrol. As he lay on the cot he admitted to himself he was spooked as a calving cow with a wolf howling over the rise. He wished he could sleep like Charlie there, snoring away in the next cot.

Warder had been thinking about Clara and the children. The tent was pretty hot, in spite of the lifted sides and the fact that it was in the shade. He heard Benton squirming and whispering to Floyd. The kids were really excited, he thought with amusement. Thinking then of Pearl Harbor and Midway, he realized that he could be killed, and here he was getting into another fight. Well, hell, he thought. I've had a good life, a good woman, children, plenty of loving, enough living to know that it's the living counts, the day-to-day getting along. He knew that a man in health, with his gut filled, a boy to look up to him, and a woman to sleep with, was pretty well off. He could think of old drooling men he'd seen, long past love or caring. If he got killed tonight, he'd be spared that, anyway. He reckoned that if he got it, he would have pretty well skimmed the cream. Hell with it. Still he kept remembering things. Pretty soon Mr. Print and the skipper stuck their heads in the tent and said, "Reveille, you railroad men. Let's go take a swim."

So many men were eating aboard the *Marlboro* that the Ninety-Seven's crew had to sit at mess tables out on the covered deck, but that was a lot cooler than the messroom inside. Something was bothering Benton's throat and stomach so that the meal of Spam, dehydrated potatoes, and coffee was giving him trouble. When he'd listen to the guys talking, the lump would leave his throat and he could swallow again; then he'd remember that he was going out to fight that night, that he might be shot at, maybe killed, and the lump came back worse than ever. He didn't get much eaten before it was time to go aboard the waiting boat and go down to Sesapi.

The sun was setting and the breeze off the bay was almost cool as the Higgins boat came alongside the Ninety-Seven. As he climbed onto the fantail, Mr. Noble slapped his back and said, "Raring to go, Benton?" Benton told him he was, and went to the ammunition locker by the 20-mm. He was loader for it at battle stations, and if Ike had to be busy with torpedoes or smoke, then he'd be firing it. Benton checked carefully to see that all the magazines were filled and ready. He knew they were, but he had to be sure again. It was nearly dark under the thick mangrove trees, but after the boat moved out into the channel it was in daylight again.

As the Ninety-Seven came in under the high hill of Tulagi and tied up with the other eight boats of the duty section, Everard looked briefly at the shattered palm trees and shell holes on the hill. The duty section was ready to go. The Professionals, this half of the Flotilla called itself. He smiled at the thought. The other section was titled The Varsity. Then as the boat lay by the dock waiting for Noble to return with the patrol orders, Everard thought of how he'd wanted the life of action. Well, here it was at last. The jungle was nearly black, and its high-hummed voice, broken by an occasional guttural cry, reached all across the bay. A pallid light still lay over the dock and the boats, where men moved quietly and spoke in low voices, except for an occasional ring of laughter. Everard's radio set was warm and on frequency, tested out five by five. The forty-five was heavy on his hip; he shifted the canvas belt, checking its load with trembling hands. The shark knife, worked into the pistol holster, the canvas clip-holder with its two extra clips, and the cloth-covered canteen. His steel helmet and life jacket were on the chart table.

"There's the moon," Josiah Hill said with satisfaction. "They tell me that the Japs aren't around much when the moon's bright."

"So I hear." Everard agreed.

"I calculate I can stand that." Hill sounded comfortable. "I wa'n't ever in a hurry to . . . What's that?"

"What?" Then Everard caught it, a far-off low rumble. He held his breath as the sound grew, then died away. He saw other men turn and look to the northwest. "That was thunder," he said.

"Oh, oh," Hill said, not comfortable now. Print came up from the chartroom.

"All set for the initiation, boys?" he asked, smiling.

"Yes, sir," Everard answered, and just then the thunder sounded again. Print swung to face the northwest, but he said nothing.

Darkness was thick over the bay but the moon was beginning to glimmer above Gavatu, where the Japs still lay rotting in their cave-tombs, when Everard saw the flicker of light from the curtained door of the radio shack, followed by the red points of cigarettes and cigars as the captains came down to the boats.

"Individual patrol," Noble said cheerfully to the waiting crew as he came aboard. "Four boats going out, including ours. I drew low card."

"Let me go along next time, Skipper," Jim Print said. "I know how to talk to a card deck."

"I'm glad somebody here does. Anyway, we act independently, patrolling close inshore from Doma Reef all the way around to Visale, about a mile beyond Esperance. Cactus says a minor front is closing in, so there may be some barges running in from the Russells. We're supposed to intercept them. Anything we see that's not a PT we can blast."

"By God," Johnson said eagerly. "You mean I'll get me a shot at a barge?"

"Maybe. But no shooting without orders. Everard, here's the code. The enemy is Scotch."

"Scotch?"

"Yes, sure, Scotch whisky. Doma Reef to Esperance is soda, Esperance Beach is water. Beyond Esperance, ginger ale; Esperance to Savo, Coca-Cola. Get it?"

"Yes, sir."

"Boat calls are by captains' first names. We're Prep Charlie. The others are Prep Jake, Prep Howard, and Prep Bill. Now if somebody says, 'Scotch in ginger ale,' what do they mean?"

"Enemy ships beyond Esperance, sir."

"Right. Okay, Warder, wind 'em up. Well, boys, this is what we came for. Keep cool, don't fire without orders, and keep your eyes open."

The Ninety-Seven's lines came in and she followed Prep Jake down the bay, with the moon patch showing the course. But behind the boat, clouds were mounting bit by bit into the sky, and thunder sounded again, still far off. When the dim-purple range lights came into line to port, the boat turned hard starboard and followed their invisible line out through reefs and close by a small island to Sealark Channel.

"Come to course 247 degrees, Hill," Noble said. He rang the engine-room buzzer three times, and when the mufflers

172

were closed, the relative silence seemed louder than the motors had been. "All hands put on helmets and life jackets. Man your battle stations."

Always before, the heavy steel helmet had felt uncomfortable and somehow false and silly to Everard. Now he suffered its weight gladly, pleased to have even the slight protection of the curved steel against the unfriendly night sky.

Larry Floyd was an engineer, but his battle station was on deck, since Noble had decided that two men were enough in the engine room during action. Floyd was assigned to assist with the depth charges and torpedoes. Now he stood with Ike Sterns and Bill Benton at the 20-mm., glad that he could see what was going on. The moonlight was reassuringly bright, but over on the starboard bow he could see clouds masking the stars, one by one. He had heard that in the bad weather coming up they might find some barges. He was excited, and he guessed he was scared too, though he wasn't going to tell anybody that. The more he thought about shooting at people the more scared he got. Then he remembered Jane, and it seemed as if her bed, with her in it, was the best place he'd ever been.

Noble spotted Doma Reef in the moonlight easily enough, and went in west of it until he was so close to the beach that he could hear his crew muttering and shifting around. About sixty or seventy yards off, he turned right to parallel the shore. He knew that along here he could have touched the sand with the bow without running aground.

Jim said, "Charlie, I'm sure as hell glad you turned. I was figuring you were going ashore to rope the Japs."

"That's an idea. Would you like to put your brand on some of them?"

Jim looked at Noble intently, then smiled.

"Well," he said slowly, "I've branded some pretty surprising things in my life."

Print wondered what Charlie would have said if he had told him about Di. He had been thinking about her for the last hour; especially her creamy smooth skin with the red Split T's on it. He felt a tremor run through his body at the thought. Then all of a sudden he couldn't see Charlie. It was as if someone had turned off a light.

"What happened?" Print said.

"The moon's behind the clouds," Charlie said quietly. Print looked up. Sure enough, the edge of the clouds had reached the moon. Then thunder sounded again, much closer now, and a wind was blowing from the northwest. Two or three big drops of rain came down.

The Ninety-Seven was off the western end of Esperance Beach when Noble saw the dark splotch in the water on the starboard bow. He put the glasses on it and saw the square front and back of a barge, and a touch of white wake. The rain had stopped, and Noble could see the enemy fairly well.

"Jap barge on the starboard bow, Johnson," he said. "Open fire when you see it." He picked up the radio mike, keeping a tight control on his voice: "All Preps from Prep Charlie. Small Scotch in water, small Scotch in water. Over."

Noble took the wheel. Johnson yelled, "I see him!" Noble called, "Open fire, open fire!" swinging farther to port to give Johnson a clear field. He heard Jim curse and Joe Hill mutter something. Then the guns started rolling, the flashes blinding in the dark, and the red tracers slashed away, bouncing first from the water, then training, moving, then splattering against the sides of the barge. The boys were yelling, the guns flaming away. Noble buzzed once long, the mufflers came off, and he shoved the throttles forward, pushed back on his heels by the sudden acceleration. The PT shot in on the barge until she was fifty feet on its quarter and Johnson was making every shot a hit. Noble noticed with pleasure that he was firing bursts with enough of a pause between to avoid melting the barrel. Noble swung parallel to the barge and the after turret and 20-mm. opened up. The noise was astounding in the hitherto silent night.

With the fans of fire converging on it, the barge was slowing,

174

listing; the PT passed within twenty feet of it. Josiah Hill sprayed it with a Tommy gun; Jim ducked below and came back with a riot gun. Flashes flickered aft on the barge and red streaks glimmered before Noble's eyes. Something whapped into the cockpit armor and screamed away; wood splintered. Everything was firing now. Noble came hard right, circling around the barge's bow, out of her heavy fire. The heavy machine-gun bullets were smashing the length of the barge, the 20-mm. shells bursting continuously inside her. She slowed, stopped, heeling over, her fire silenced. The Ninety-Seven raced down her other side, pounding her. Even above the gunfire, Noble heard a scream. This barge was done, but he saw other dark shapes with the bow waves before them. The Ninety-Seven was between them and the beach. Noble swung for the first.

To Johnson it was almost like quail hunting, when a fellow sees the bird go up and aims his gun without knowing he's doing it, leading right without figuring it, and then pulls the trigger and sees the feathers puff and the bird go down. By God, hadn't neither one of the guns jammed on that first barge, and he'd had it under his sights for a long time. The bottom of the turret was covered with cartridge cases and links. Johnson saw the other barges now; the Ninety-Seven was heading toward them. He stood up high in the turret and pulled the double handles of the guns up with him. He lined them up as close as he could to the white water under the dark blob and pressed the trigger. The guns bucked some, not much, on the good, solid mounts; the worst thing was the muzzle blast that blinded him. He saw the tracers bounce off the water to one side and he brought them onto the barge. It was like pointing a hose: twelve hundred shots a minute, ball, tracer, and explosive. God damn! They made a light when they hit, and the barge starting shooting back. Johnson could see pieces of her go flying around where his big bullets were smashing into her. How that powder smoke did smell! He kept pouring it on, pouring it on, cursing to himself and having a hell of a time. The Ninety-Seven came alongside, and all the other guys started shooting, and that barge just sort of went to pieces and started burning and sinking.

Noble was drunk with speed and fire. He circled barges, battering and piercing them with his guns. Ten seconds to one, twenty to another. They seemed everywhere. Red balls of tracer floated toward Noble, seeming to veer away just before striking his eyes. Others hit the boat, but none of her crew was down so far. Roaring, spitting fire, circling like Indians around a wagon train, now slowing alongside the biggest of the barges, the Ninety-Seven continued the slaughter. Small-arms fire flickered along the barge's sides. Jim was pumping the twelve-gauge sawed-off, spraying the barges with buckshot. Noble heard the roar of another PT's engines; no place for an accident! He fired the Very pistol toward the nearest barge. The star burst, the flare swung in its parachute, and light poured over the scene, revealing two sinking barges, others disappearing toward the shore, and yet others still coming on. The other PT turned its guns on a barge alongside and the Ninety-Seven picked another victim, with Noble too excited for fear or mercy, feeling only a slight shame at the unequal fight. In the light of the flare he saw Johnson's dead-calm face with the carved grin, as his guns thrrumped, thrrumped, thrrumped. In fire lulls, Noble heard a forty-five cracking from aft. Still another PT roared up and set to the vicious work. Then suddenly the remaining barges were past, with the PTs following them in to the beach, forward guns raking and tearing them, but unable to stop them. From the dark trees beyond the dimly-seen white sand, red points burned; a pair of flame hoses showed where machine guns were firing at the PTs from shore. In the gun flare, Noble saw the spaced splashes of a machine-gun burst rip past his bows. He swung hard to starboard, raced around with his deck leaning, banking, and out again.

Suddenly all the firing stopped. Everything was over. Noble was wet, and shaking hard. He eased back the engines, slowing

176

to move with the nearest PT. He realized that he saw it easily and well. He looked up to see that the clouds had broken and the moon was shining through. Behind him, the dark island seemed to grow and expand in the light, and the sea was black and silver, with Savo riding high like a ship before him. Noble rang for mufflers and closed in on the other PT. Someone waved from her cockpit.

"Nice going, Charlie!" came Jake Hughes' voice. Noble shouted in reply. He was very tired. The worst was over; the moon was out. He could smell the hot metal of the guns, hear the excited babble of his crew. God, he was tired!

Radelewski sat limply on the edge of the engine-room hatch, feeling the wind on his face and seeing the way the moon lit up the water and the islands. He was still holding his forty-five, its barrel hot from firing. He had used up three clips on the last barge; why, the PT had been so close that the paint was scraping! He remembered that he had been scared crapless when the shooting started, and Warder had said, "Go on up, Ski, if you want to; I'll handle the engines. You'll feel better if you can see what's happening." When Radelewski had hoisted himself to the hatch, there had been a barge right alongside and in the light from a flare dangling in the sky he saw men in the barge. He had hauled out the forty-five and started shooting, and right away he wasn't scared any more.

Now Warder stuck his head up and said, "Okay, Ski; the shooting is over. Come on back down."

Radelewski didn't want to move. He felt as though he had worked hard all day and then screwed all night, but he stuck the pistol back in its holster and dropped back down into the engine room, which was hot, noisy, and stuffy after the breeze blowing across the deck from the sea.

Benton was glad when at about two o'clock in the morning Noble put the crew on watch and watch, with the section off-watch allowed to sleep on deck. For an hour and a half Benton was alone at the twenty, knowing that if a barge

177

came in sight suddenly, or an airplane dove on them, he'd
be the one to shoot back. But nothing happened, as the
Ninety-Seven kept going back and forth near the shore, which
was bright in the moonlight. Then Ike relieved Benton and
he went to sleep in his life jacket. When he woke up, it
was daylight and the boat was nearly home.

Benton was happy to get in. People were standing on the
dock pointing to the bullet holes in the boat; she had taken
a dozen hits, and looking at them, Benton realized how
lucky they had been that nobody was hurt. He and Larry
Floyd walked over onto the dock together, and the chief
petty officers, the ones who kept the boats running, looked
at the two boys with strange expressions on their faces. They
didn't treat Benton and Floyd like kids any more.

The Ninety-Seven's next patrol was a quiet one, for the
moon rose full and red at about eight o'clock, climbed and
turned silver, making the waters around Guadalcanal bright
as daylight. Over on the big island, shells flashed at intervals, and sometime after midnight there was an air raid. The
planes were high, because of the flak, and the Ninety-Seven's
crew didn't see anything of them coming in.

"Goddlemighty!" Sterns exclaimed. "They're really catching
it over there."

The distant rumble of bombs and shellfire was continuous.
Searchlight beams were probing around the sky over Henderson, with the red, quick flashes of AA fire jetting among
them, like Fourth of July fireworks at this distance. Now
and again the beams of light would catch a little silver object, and others would come swinging across until the plane
was the center of a fan of searchlight beams, with the red
flowers of flak grouping close around. Twice a trapped plane
went down, leaving a red streak against the sky. The night
was very calm, and the red glare of the air raid flickered in
the water, turning it black and red. When it was all over,

the PT men heard the noise of planes, high up, going home.

The twenty-fifth gave the Ninety-Seven another easy night, but it was after ten when the waning moon came up.

"I don't like to see that," Noble said quietly to Print. "They'll be sending surface ships down before long."

"The boys are pretty anxious for action, Charlie."

"I know. Getting a whack at those barges to take the first edge off was good luck. But you know the barges can't really do much fighting back. When it comes to destroyers, we'll be the ones with the dirty end of the stick."

On the twenty-seventh Noble cut a high card, and his boat spent that night alongside the dock. Somewhat uneasily, Print saw that the moon didn't rise until 11:25, and he remembered what Charlie had said. The dark nights were upon them, and Print could feel the growing tension at the PT base.

Noble noticed at once that Ollie wasn't smiling as the boat captains filed into the radio shack on the twenty-ninth. Noble had been feeling pretty good after two full nights of sleep, and with the Old Ninety-Seven running well, her bottom newly scraped and painted while she was dry-docked for bullet-hole repair. Now, looking at Ollie's stone face, he felt nervous and unsure.

"Here it is, boys," Wakefield said. "The coast watchers have radioed that the Tokyo Express was ready to sail at sunset; they'll be here by midnight. That gives them one hour off Esperance to unload troops and supplies before moonrise. We want to stop them."

The boat captains moved uneasily, and some among them murmured. Bill Shagg took his cigar out of his mouth and muttered, "Well, we've done it before."

The Ninety-Seven drew Soda patrol area—Doma Reef to Esperance—with Harris Brocker's boat as running mate. The PTs got under way in darkness so thick that Noble had to follow the phosphorescent gleam of the leading boat's wake in going out of the harbor. Ollie, who with Dave Poker's boat, had the night's hotspot, led the column. These two boats would patrol from Savo to Esperance, where they might easily find themselves pinned against the beach by enemy destroyers.

Midnight, and not even the stars were showing. Noble was balancing on the little seat above the armor plate, his eyes tired from constant searching through the seven-fifty binoculars. Above the soft murmur of the motors he caught an occasional fragment of conversation from the boys in the cockpit. Noble watched the sky, and the dark, bitter island with its occasional shellflash; most of all, he watched the sea to the northwest, unable even to see Savo in the sullen blackness. The Ninety-Seven was heading east, and the sight of Doma Reef, outlined with pale-green flame from the breaking swell, was the signal to come about.

"Bring her around, Hill," he ordered. Gently the boat came to port, swung, and steadied on the reciprocal course. Noble's mouth was dry. The time was getting close. He looked over to the right, where Prep Harris moved along like a ghost, fifty yards away.

"This is when it starts, boys," Noble told his crew. "Remember to roll your sleeves down to prevent flash burns, keep your helmets on, see that your life-jacket ties are tight."

"I wa'n't scared before," Hill said half indignantly. "But I am now, after you said that."

"Good. That gives me company."

A couple of the men laughed nervously. Noble was scared, but he knew what he had to do, and that by past averages the boat had a very good chance of coming through unhurt. The Ninety-Seven rolled slightly as she muttered along. The air was heavy, seeming to exert a palpable pressure; the darkness felt like black cloth against Noble's eyes. The engines purred, the island moved by the Ninety-Seven. . . .

Some distance ahead furnace doors opened on red hell. A string of red balls arched through the sky, moving very slowly. The slam of the closed doors reached Noble, interlaced with the rattle of machine-gun fire.

"There they are," he said through his dry lips as he brought the glasses to his eyes.

"From Prep Ollie. Scotch in Soda, Scotch in Soda! Six of . . . Scotch in Soda!"

Static and gunfire marred the message, but the meaning was plain enough. More red beads spread across the sky, more doors opened on flame and slammed shut, echoing across the water. A searchlight crashed on silently from a dark shape, and Noble saw its beam touch a grey, elongated shadow that whirled across its path. A PT boat! More tracer floated with the rattle of machine guns, and the light went out.

"Look out! Look out! Sleeper by Savo!" the radio squawked.

Noble, nervous and shaking, was at the wheel and throttles. Jim stood behind the simple torpedo-director. "We're going in," Noble said. "Stand by torpedoes."

He eased the throttles along to the upper limit of speed possible with the mufflers on. Ahead, the crescendo-diminuendo roars of wide open motors were sharing the night with the slam and crackle of gunfire. The Ninety-Seven reached the beginning of Esperance Beach and, even without his night glasses, Noble saw the dark shapes of destroyers made more evident by the quick flash and glimmer of their guns. Close by, a white column of water rose gleaming into the night, then settled again.

"Jesus Christ!" Noble heard somebody say. He was all right; he was going to come through. He was scared, he wanted to take a leak, he wanted to run, to go home, to be safe, wanted these things so much that nothing else mattered but one thing—but that was an unchanging wall. He had to get a good shot with his torpedoes. He hated them, goddamned stinking fish anchoring him to this scene, to this place, by their presence in his tubes. Get 'em off, get 'em off; then he could break mufflers and go home at forty knots —five minutes to safety; but first he had to get his torpedoes away with a shot that had a chance of hitting.

181

"They're getting close, Skipper, they're getting close!"

They were indeed. Noble saw the leading destroyer change course to the east, heading now directly for the Ninety-Seven. The enemy was going to parallel the beach, maybe go on down to Lunga and shell Henderson Field. The Ninety-Seven was going to be pinned between the white beach and the line of destroyers! Noble thought in half-panic: got to get out of here! His fingers shook on the button as he blew the signal. The mufflers came off, but the motors' roar was unnoticeable in the general clang and slam of battle. Noble grabbed the throttles, advancing them, pushing them; the roaring grew and the Ninety-Seven began to slash through the water, gaining speed. Noble turned the bow hard right, getting away from the trap of the beach. He would circle around, get the Japs between himself and the island, and have a dead-cinch bow shot. Prep Harris was already clear, out of the enemy's path. Noble shoved the throttles forward a little more, and the engines suddenly, damnably, spluttered, caught, and died.

"Holy Christ!" somebody screamed. Jim Print slammed against Noble and out of the cockpit, running aft to the engine room. Noble heard starters whine and fail, whine and fail. The bow was at right angles to the Japanese column which was headed directly for the boat, less than a mile away now. Thirty-five knots—in three minutes or less they would be onto the Ninety-Seven, she would be smashed, he and his crew dead! There was nothing he could do but hang to the dead wheel and glare at death approaching. He couldn't fire torpedoes, couldn't do anything. Blind terror captured him fully, and he grabbed the radio mike.

"From Prep Charlie, Prep Charlie," he screamed. "Prep Harris, anybody, come help. Engines stalled ahead of enemy; come alongside and take off my crew. Prep Harris, Prep Harris. Come in, come in. For God's sake!"

The radio was a mélange of messages, cries, admonitions, warnings. An exultant shout, "Got him, got him, got him!"

Had Prep Harris heard him? What good would it do if he had? He couldn't take the crew off now, the enemy was too close! The rubber boat? Take to the water? The starters whined and failed, whined and failed.

Then an engine coughed, spluttered, roared; another, another! The throttles moved as the engineers gunned the motors from the engine room. The Ninety-Seven began moving! Hope came back to Noble; the PT was moving perpendicularly to the enemy course, across their bows. Tracer like red baseballs floated her way. Guns crashed, and Noble smelled the acrid stink of gunfire and smoke screens. Surely the Japs saw him, surely they did! Now the PT was at full speed, the white wake and rooster tail flags in the night. Noble held his breath and gripped the wheel, expecting destruction momentarily.

Then the Ninety-Seven was away, out of the enemy's line, she was in the lovely dark, and the glare of firing was getting farther away. A black shape drew up alongside, a PT boat moving with the Ninety-Seven.

"Prep Charlie from Prep Harris, are you all right now? Are your engines all right now? Over."

Print came into the cockpit and Noble grabbed his arm. "Are the engines all right?" he yelled, hoping in his belly and guts that Print would say no.

"I think so!" Jim shouted. "Feed lines clogged; got them free with the wobble pump."

So Noble had to do it. He picked up the mike again.

"Prep Harris from Prep Charlie. My engines are okay now, repeat, okay. We're going in again. Over."

"Good, from Prep Harris. Over."

Noble looked at the fight, seeing it dissolving, falling back toward the western end of the island. The enemy had countermarched, they were running! Only an occasional glare of gunfire showed now, and a final string of tracer arched in the distance. The Ninety-Seven was at full speed, heading close to Savo, with Prep Harris alongside. Maybe they could catch the Japs coming out, Noble thought. He was wet all over, shaking, listening to the engines with a terrible intensity. They roared full-voiced and strong. The boat cleared Savo. The firing had stopped completely. Clear of land, the Ninety-Seven began to meet the heavier swells with swoop up, crash down, swoop, crash, with sheets of water falling over the cockpit. Nothing was visible in the black sea. Noble was sick. He didn't want to catch them: that was him, Noble; he wanted to catch them: that was the perversity of man, the shame at failure, the half-felt coward's brand he wanted to avoid. He wanted to redeem himself. He had to!

"Prep Charlie from Prep Harris. We can't catch them. It's no use. Over."

Noble knew that Harris was right, and he half rejoiced, half mourned. Even if the two boats could come up on the fast destroyers the old, tired torpedoes were too slow to make a stern shot possible. Noble eased the throttles down and swung the wheel. He was going back, giving up. Noble was glad that spray had been flying: his face was so wet from salt water that no one could tell he was crying.

18

Everard awoke in the stifling tent, naked on his cot. Groggily he saw Radelewski sitting on a box, his hair slick and wet, looking glum.

"Morning," Everard said. "Do I feel awful!"

"You and the rest of this boat crew."

"What do you mean?"

"I been up at the pool taking a swim. Lot of the base guys were there, and man did I take a razzberry when they found I was offa the Ninety-Seven. Said they heard our skipper screamed over the radio when the engines crapped out last night. I was about to cream one bastard when they pulled us apart."

"That's unfair!" Everard said angrily. "If you and Warder hadn't gotten those engines started when you did, we certainly would have been sunk. I think Mr. Noble was right in calling for help."

"Johnson says Noble was scared crapless."

Everard considered that. True enough, the captain *had* appeared to be badly frightened when the engines died; but good Lord, what was wrong with that? Noble had been remarkably calm when the Ninety-Seven started her run on the enemy. But the other fellows were waking up now, so he didn't say anything.

Jim Print realized Charlie really felt bad about calling for help. Print could tell that the skipper hated to go near the other officers; he knew Noble felt he'd cracked up in a pinch, the first real pinch the Ninety-Seven had had. The skipper was mighty quiet as the two of them walked up to the pool for a swim.

"I wish to hell there was a bar around here," Noble said as they sat in the shallow water, soaking in the coolness. "I'd like to drown my troubles."

"Ah, forget it. Harris Brocker says we were really in a squeeze; he said that anybody who wouldn't be scared then would be weak in the head."

Charlie closed his fist over the surface of the pool, squirting little jets of water. He looked over at Print.

"That's better than being weak in the guts. Well, hell. We'll show them next time."

That's what Print was afraid of. He didn't want Charlie daring himself, trying to make up for things the next time they had somebody shooting at them. Print kept remembering the sound of those guns; it wasn't all just *sound,* for he had felt them in his guts, all the way down, as well as hearing them. It was like your belly was a drum and somebody was beating it from inside. He shifted a little on the gravel bottom and sat down on a three-horned periwinkle; he jumped and shouted with a good deal of enthusiasm. Noble laughed for the first time that day.

Since this was to be a night in for them, the Ninety-Seven's officers and men went down to the base after lunch and worked on the boats that were to go out on patrol. The air was like the steam room of a Turkish bath. Print's shirt was wet through, front and back, and his face was never dry. The sun's heat felt like a weight on his head. Usually Sesapi was quiet at this time of day, with everyone who could do so staying in the shade. Now men were grouped around outside the radio shack; over in the big, wall-less mess building, others were hanging about. Print found out at once that a

186

large enemy force was reported under way for Guadalcanal and was due to arrive some time before moonrise that night.

"I reckon the Varsity is going to get it in the neck this time," George Shagg said. "I'm glad I don't have to be out there tonight." George was a stocky, quiet officer who had been at Guadalcanal from the first PT arrival.

"Guess again," Harris Brocker said. "We've got a cruiser force coming in; the Varsity will probably spend the night right here."

"That blamed Varsity," Bill Shagg grumbled, caressing his pirate-sized black beard. "They get all the luck. Well, at least we can watch the show from the top of the hill."

Just then the yeoman mail orderly came over to the officers.

"Are you getting Commander Daggs' mail off to him by air?" Noble asked him.

"Yes, sir. They gave me an argument over at Cactus, but I told them we had the commander's orders, and it went through. He won't have to wait for his mail, sir."

"Good." Print wondered why Charlie's face was set so hard. Things were really riding the skipper these days.

"Say, what gives with this commander of yours staying down at Nouméa?" Bill Shagg wanted to know.

"Why, he wants to make sure all the squadron gets off in good shape," Noble said.

"I think I'll put in to be his assistant." Bill grinned.

"They tell me," Harris Brocker said, "that if he was stationed at Espiritu you could hear him talking clear up here."

"He's got plenty of balls," Noble agreed.

"And knows how to knock 'em together, huh?"

"Speaking of your squadron, Charlie," Harris Brocker put in, "Ollie says there are four new PTs over at Lunga Point. We've got some transports unloading marines over there, and I guess the PTs came up with them. SOPA is keeping the boats to help screen the transports until they're unloaded. They'll be over sometime tonight."

"Joy, joy," Noble exulted. "Somebody greener than me.

Say, if you guys tell them about my burning out three radio tubes shrieking for help I'll take away your atabrine ration."

"Radio? Radio? Did you use a radio? Hell, I heard you three miles off and I didn't even have my radio turned on."

Print noticed the way the captains grinned at Charlie, and he knew that they didn't blame the skipper in the least. People who knew what it was like out there were tolerant. It was base force men, new ones, men who had never been out, who were talking and laughing about the Ninety-Seven. Print saw with relief Charlie's face lighten at the tone of this ribbing he was getting now.

Soon after dark the officers and men of the Ninety-Seven started up the hill behind the base. All members of the base force not on watch, as well as most of the Professionals, were strung along the hill in the dark. Noble bumped into somebody. It was Ollie.

"You're going to see the show too?" Noble said.

"You don't get many chances like this, and we ought to really clobber them tonight. We've got five cruisers and about six destroyers. Coast-watcher reports say that about a dozen Jap destroyers are heading down."

"Those are the odds I like," Noble said.

The crews gathered in a flat spot on the hilltop where there was an uninterrupted view of Guadalcanal, Savo, and Ironbottomed Bay. The sea was like black glass; not a breath of air stirred and only a few stars shone dimly through the high haze. The islands were vague black bulks. Influenced by the still, oppressive night, the watching men were very quiet.

An hour passed and part of another. As the PT men sat comfortably on the grass, airplane engines roared behind them, back and forth from one end of Tulagi Harbor to the other. This puzzled Noble until Ollie explained that the taxiing aircraft were the cruiser float planes, which had landed in the afternoon, trying to take off to drop flares on their mission of illumination. "Look at that water!" he said.

"Smooth as a virgin's belly—no wind at all. They can't lift 'em off the water without a little wind, or at least a few small waves."

Through his night glasses, Noble now saw what seemed a blob of darkness in the water between him and Lunga Point. He swept the glasses left—another, another, yet another. More ships followed. He could make out the light flicker of their bow waves, phosphorescent in the still water. The shapes hauled off to the right.

"There's our side," Ollie said.

Other glasses were trained that way, and Noble heard men muttering. He said no more, gripped by the strongest feelings. He knew so well what was now taking place aboard those dim shapes. The bridges, dark and quiet, with eyes straining into the night; CICs with radarscopes shining weirdly; brightly lighted engine rooms that were hot foci of power, quiet even with the high, medium, and bass drones of the turbines; the turrets where men crouched, sat, and stood, wedged in with steel and explosive; and the handling rooms below, refrigerated, aseptic as operating rooms, ammonia-scented with the explosive charges waiting in scoops and trays, ready for hoisting. Thousands of Americans were there, most of them as blind to what might follow as moles beneath the earth, but all awaiting the word that should come soon.

"Ah, we'll bust hell out of them," Radelewski muttered confidently. Noble felt Jim Print stir, but he said nothing. Noble trained the glasses over toward Cape Esperance.

"I hope you're right." It was Ollie, in a low voice. "I see the Japs off Esperance now."

To Noble it seemed that everyone stopped breathing. Through the glasses he could barely make out the lean dark shapes—destroyers, the report said—moving swiftly between him and the light beach of Esperance. His hair prickled at the sight and the belly-clutching fear of last night came back.

"Hell, Ollie," Bill Shagg said. "We've got five cruisers

189

and half a dozen destroyers. The Japs won't have a chance."

"Those Nips are good with a torpedo, Bill. They're in torpedo range now. Thank the Lord they haven't got radar."

Tension grew. Noble choked, now hot, now cold, in spite of the sultry night. If the fleet wiped out the Japs, it was possible that he might have no more bad nights out on Iron-bottomed Bay. If the Navy lost, if it lost . . .

Red light puffed far out in the black water and red balls soared into the air. More red glares broke out in a long line as ship after ship commenced firing. Within seconds, all the American ships were spouting shells like bundles of Roman candles lit off at once. For a moment all was silent except for the hoarse breathing of the transfixed men around Noble; then the thunder reached him, unending, savage, making the ground tremble beneath him. The shellfire increased to an unbelievable torrent.

Then, from over by Esperance came the high-reaching flame of an explosion that showed beneath it the long, lean hull of a Jap destroyer. Wham! Wham! Wham! Wham! Shell after shell hit her, fire soared high, she was a torch being blown to fragments. The men around Noble were yelling. Then, from one of the dark shapes behind the seething fire of the American guns, two great white columns rose high into the air and a cruiser exploded, wallowed, settled, halted, while from her forecastle great torrents of flame soared higher than her mastheads.

"God Almighty!" Jim's voice was shaking. "Those poor bastards!"

The men were silent now, with no more cheering. Noble heard Ollie cursing quietly. He started to speak when a tremendous explosion smashed from the bow of a second American cruiser, seemingly tearing her into two pieces; he saw her stagger on with her severed bow, a turret still aboard, floating off and back to one side, the truncated nose of the ship itself spouting fire.

"We're getting licked!" Ike roared. "Oh, goddammit, come on boys; hit those bastards! Hit 'em!"

The spectators stood in horror, seeing a third American cruiser smashed, then a fourth. Each explosion was worse than the last, and the steel ships with their loads of oil, gas, and explosive burned like torches on the water, lighting the scene—Guadalcanal's shores, the mountains beyond, Savo—crimsoning the sea.

"Come on," Ollie said, taking Noble's arm. "Pass the word for all operating personnel to report back to base. We'll want every possible boat for rescue work. Let's go."

In a few moments most of the crowd were streaming back down the hill, stumbling in the dark, dazed by what they had seen. Defeat, this was defeat! Noble thought. The Japs might come on in, might shell Tulagi; there must be dozens of them to have done all that. A thought hit him: the Ninety-Seven's engines were torn down for a fifty-hour check. She wouldn't be able to run before the next afternoon. But he had to try to help somehow.

On the dock, where motors were beginning to roar and men slipped on gear as they piled aboard the boats, Noble saw Jake Hughes' PT just pulling away and hastily boarded it. The boat took him to a scene that was beyond his full comprehension—the smoke-streaked night and the voices of men crying out plaintively from far, near, everywhere. The fires were burning low and the night was totally dark, making it hard to find the swimming, floating men; but by dawn Jakes Hughes' boat was covered with more than a hundred survivors. Blood made the decks slippery, and the stench of burned flesh sickened Noble. But he marveled at the tough spirits of these men, for even the seriously hurt made little complaint.

In the end, three of the four cruisers were saved. The sun was just fully coming up when Hughes' boat returned to Tulagi, after depositing her survivors at Lunga Point, and she passed the *Minneapolis*, the first cruiser hit, inching her way painfully into sheltered waters with the aid of the tug *Bobolink*. Noble looked at her dully. He was filthy with blood and fuel oil, frightened as well, and utterly exhausted by the terrible night. He had to rest; he remembered with a shock that when night came again he must go out on patrol, out *there* where all this had happened. The boat tied up. Noble climbed wearily to the dock and the first man he saw was Pat Bunch.

"Come aboard my boat," Pat said, grabbing his hand, "I've got a bottle of whiskey, and you need it. Come on!"

Noble did need it, but not even the warming liquor succeeded in bringing him to life again the way just having Pat Bunch around did. It was like waking up in the bright morning after a nightmare.

Noble took Pat with him that night for an indoctrination patrol. Pat came aboard the boat at Sesapi in the dusk, complaining bitterly about having to ride in such filth and squalor.

"A disorganized garbage scow," he said, peering around at the Ninety-Seven. "Half-wrecked, in addition. You guys come over to the Ninety-One and I'll show you a real PT boat."

"Sir, can we give him a razzberry?" Sterns asked.

"He's just a poor unfortunate out of the first division, Ike. Treat him gently."

"Gently, sir. Aye, aye."

As soon as the Ninety-Seven pulled away from the dock, Sterns and Ding Hau came up from below with a mattress. They placed it on the deck forward of the canopy, put a pitcher of lemonade beside it, and then escorted Pat gently but firmly to it.

"Here you are, sir. Rest yourself, sir. Take it easy, sir. Shall we have some music, sir?"

Bunch reclined grandly on the mattress and clapped his hands languidly.

"Bring on the dancing girls; in the first division we always have dancing girls."

"I heard that said, sir," Sterns agreed. Noble was surprised to see Johnson come up with his guitar, for ordinarily he kept it ashore. All the crew but the duty engineer and the quartermaster gathered around and struck up "Old Ninety-Seven." Noble came in with the air horn, as usual, laughing to himself as he saw the men on Ollie's boat, just ahead, stare back open-mouthed. "Captain of the Pinafore" followed next, and Noble took his part vigorously, glad to forget his thoughts of the dark night ahead. The boats hit the range, passed just to port of Kokumbona, perfect replica of a Hollywood South Sea island, and came out into Sealark Channel. The crew was in the middle of "Bless 'em All," uncensored, when Noble regretfully sent them to battle stations. Mattress and music disappeared, and in three minutes all hands were equipped and silent at their stations, with the motors muttering under mufflers.

"How does it strike you, Pat?" Noble broke the silence.

"Dig me Momma, I want to go home. They play *rough* out here; look at what they did to those cruisers."

"Yeah, but this isn't a cruiser."

"That's what worries me."

Noble showed his friend the works, as it had been shown to him; all the landmarks that now were engraved in his mind like acid etchings on a metal plate. The Ninety-Seven had the bitch patrol tonight, Charlie told him.

"Bitch patrol?" Pat asked.

"Yeah, that's what we call the run beyond the Visale River to Kamimbo and Morovovo. Not only are there reefs everywhere, but you have the mountains between you and the base so you're cut off from radio communications."

Just then Everard announced he could no longer reach any of the other boats or the base, and tension grew heavy. Reefs were everywhere, and each dark shadow on the water turned itself into an enemy. Coming back around to Esperance, Noble spotted two landing barges, broke mufflers, and roared in with all guns firing. The Ninety-Seven sank one barge and chased the other in to the beach, raking it with machine-gun fire.

"Wow!" was Pat's only comment after the firing had stopped.

"A few more corpses for Ironbottomed Bay," Noble said wearily, feeling his usual sickness at this incessant killing, "although I guess another dozen or so won't make much difference."

At 2:30 in the morning, the three-quarter moon came up, tired and red with waning, and minute by minute tension lessened with its growing light. By four the sea was luminous, and the boat went into watch and watch. The sun of a new day was barely up when the PT came to the dock again.

"I'll tell you what I'll do," Pat said loudly, so all could hear. "If we ever have a vacancy in the first division, I'll try to persuade the boys to let this boat have it. It's a pretty good boat considering its station in life."

Noble's crew grinned and gave a united razzberry.

The mail came in that afternoon, and while waiting for it to be sorted Everard wandered into a little hut by the water's edge, in which several of the base engineers had set up their cots. Opposite the door—in the lightest spot on the walls—was a large photograph of a handsome and quite nude young woman. Everard looked at the picture with approval. Unmarked by the obscenity of the censoring airbrush, the photo escaped the furtiveness of legally tolerated pin-up girls. Quite simply and honestly, Everard compared the picture to his memory of his wife.

Martha was fully as beautiful as the pictured woman, in fact, more so. Yet Everard could no longer remember when she had stood before him as this pictured woman stood. There had been a time, of course, but the accustomedness of years had removed some of the excitement of going to bed together. Everard still admired Martha's body as she walked across a room without clothes, or stepped fresh and cool from the shower, but he hadn't looked at her for a long time as men looked at this shadow girl, this key to their dreams. If ever he got back to his wife, Everard resolved, never again would he let habit dull him to the glory of married life.

Everard's thoughts were shattered by the shouted, "Mail Call!" and he left the hut quickly. A stack of letters from Martha was waiting for him, and he seized upon them eagerly. Yet when he had read the last one, he was almost sorry he had gotten them. He had never felt such an intensity of emotion as he did then, such a terrible physical and spiritual wanting. Scrawls from the children were enclosed, and he was glad that he had found privacy before opening his mail. "I love you, Daddy. Come home soon . . ." Oh, God, what am I doing here? Everard groaned. Why do ten thousand miles lie between me and the people I love best in the world? Quit calling on God, he said to himself; you rejected what He gave you. No! I valued what He gave me so highly that I had to leave it before I could deserve it. That voice was stilled, but others came back. Martha's whispering in the dark: "Oh, John, that was lovely. Let's do it again. You're just lazy, darling." Everard buried his head in his hands.

Noble and Pat Bunch walked down behind the mangrove swamp, to the right of the base at Tulagi, where the marine foxholes, abandoned now, lay just as their occupants had left them: messy holes in the ground with crude bunks built into them, and littered with a few torn letters or candy-bar wrappers.

"How was Gerry when you left?" Noble asked.

"Fine," Bunch said. Noble looked up in surprise at the hopeless note in Pat's voice. "She sent you her love."

"That was nice of her."

"She's a nice girl. Nice! What a weak word for Gerry. I never guessed how the whole world could be wrapped up in one woman; when I left her, everything went down the drain.

It scares me, Charlie; hell, without her I'm incomplete. Leaving her was like taking a knife and cutting myself in two."

"I know, Pat."

"I heard you had a girl somewhere around Archer's. She wasn't just fun, then?"

"What you just said about leaving Gerry is exactly the way it was with me and . . . my girl. Only worse."

"Worse?"

"Yes. My girl is married."

"What a tough break."

"Never mind. It was worth it. I'll make her divorce him and marry me—if I get out of this."

"Doesn't she want you to come back to her?"

"No. She has a daughter, and it would mean losing her."

"You poor bastard. No wonder you look older and sorrier these days."

That night Noble lay sleepless on his cot under the stifling mosquito netting. Oscar the Rat rummaged in the thatch overhead, dislodging bits of mud and straw that dropped to the floor or the top of the mosquito netting. From outside came the tenor hum of insects, the occasional grating squawk of a bird, and once or twice a high, sweet, shrill song. Jim was snoring slightly; Ernie Swiss, a *Hornet* survivor, was muttering and groaning in his sleep. He had dengue fever, and an attack was coming on. Noble moved on the worn sheet, hand-washed by natives at a nickel a throw. Kathleen. The memories started coming back, memories he had tried to repress. Kathleen walking about the house unconcernedly naked, her low-pitched, clear voice calling to him tenderly. He writhed on the cot. Oh, Western wind, when will you blow? Christ, that my love were in my arms, and I in my bed again.

On December seventh, Jim Print waited in the dark by the boat. He smoked one cigarette after another. The courier boat was in and the envelope with the dope lay in the radio shack with the captains. Print fretted with the waiting, but at last he caught sight of the little group of officers walking toward him. There was no joking or laughing among them; that was bad. But then he already was sure the Express would run this night.

"Jim?" Noble said. "There you are. Okay, we've got ten of them on the way down. The airedales hit them but didn't do much good. We're all that's left, and we'll have to take them on."

He sounded serene, almost pleased, Print thought. This bird is glad about it!

The lines came in. Print had the wheel. "Take her away, Jim," Charlie said pleasantly, and the Ninety-Seven, one of eight PTs going out to fight ten destroyers, was on her way down the harbor.

The sky held no moon and when the Ninety-Seven reached Savo Island the Bay was pitch black, and rough as well, with occasional whitecaps driving into the cockpit, and thunder sounding from the northwest. The Ninety-Seven's patrol was from the southeast corner of Savo to Cape Esperance. It was, as Charlie cheerfully told the crew, the hotspot of the evening, and they should be the first to find the enemy. At midnight, the Ninety-Seven was on a leg of the patrol course from Savo to Guadal, a half mile out from the smaller island. Noble was standing beside Print, binoculars at his eyes. The engines were purring away; no one was speaking. Not a star was showing, but the rain had stopped and there was a slight transparency to the night.

"Jim," Noble said excitedly. "I see them. They're just coming into the Bay, and we're on a good course for a shot."

"Where are they?" Print tried to match the skipper's voice.

"Just follow my glasses." Print did so, and on the dark line of the ocean he saw the fleeting, nearly invisible shapes of the invaders.

"Okay," Jim said hoarsely. "I've got them. Seven, maybe eight. All destroyers, I guess."

"Keep your glasses on them. Hill! Stay on our present course, and set the throttles for 1250 RPM, twenty knots."

"Present course, 1250 RPM, aye, aye, sir."

"Everard, broadcast this warning: 'All Preps from Prep Charlie; Scotch in water, eight of them, riding the rails. Over.' "

Print heard Everard repeating the words into the mike. Christ Almighty! he thought; what's got into Charlie? He sounds like this was some game.

"In about five minutes we'll be in position for a good bow shot," Noble said quietly.

Sonofabitch! Print thought. Maybe you're not scared, but by God I am! I don't want to go in that close on eight destroyers. Noble's calm and easy manner was infuriating when he, Print, was shaking and scared to hell and gone.

All right, Noble whispered to himself; I got that sentence out. My voice sounded strange to me but at least I kept it steady. Wish I could say the same for my hands and my gut. Feel like I'd swallowed a tray of ice cubes and half of them stuck in my throat. He knew perfectly well that the Japs might already have seen the boat, that at any second the shells might start coming over; he knew, further, that he had to wait five minutes before arriving at a range that would give the old World War I torpedoes a chance to hit. Death was over there in those dark shapes; almost worse, mutilation was there as well. A leg torn off; arms gone; face gone; your testicles shot off. It happened more often than people liked to admit. He remembered men they had picked up from the *Northhampton* who had been gone from the waist down, just shreds of flesh and white bone below the life jackets. That was Noble's nightmare, and beside it almost nothing in the world mattered. Coward—hell yes, I'm a coward. Court martial? Stuff it; the worst you can do is shoot me cleanly dead. Medals and pretty ribbons? Hell with them. But something he couldn't understand kept him standing there with his glasses at his eyes, watching the

Japs; kept him from changing course, from speeding up to get in quicker, from slowing down to reduce the wake. He was pushing on each foot to keep his knees from shaking. He didn't know what it was that kept him fast. Maybe it was the memory of his terror when the motors failed; maybe it was, far behind him, the warm bed with the soft flesh and the love he had to be worthy of. Maybe even it was Jim Print, who stood there like a rock, glasses to his eyes, his voice steady and quiet. Christ! Noble thought; I envy Jim his courage.

Noble didn't change the course; he set the torpedo director for a range of 600 yards and kept going. He had the sights lined up, and as soon as the bow of the first destroyer came into view over the notch he would fire torpedoes, put the rudder hard right, and try to sneak away. It was impossible that the Japs didn't see them, they were getting so close. Noble closed his hands on the grab rail until they hurt; he bit his lips, he held in physically the cold and growing turmoil in his belly. Print, right beside him, was softly whistling "The Old Chisholm Trail." That lucky sonofabitch, to be born without nerves! Noble was getting sick. He was going to vomit. . . . Wait! There. Coming close.

"Stand by!" Noble said, and Print unlocked the firing circuit.

Notch, foresight, and destroyer lined up; Noble held on to composure and ordered:

"Fire one! Fire two!"

The boat jolted; a heavy whoosh sounded from starboard and port, and with a clang and rasp of metal the two long, dark shapes shot out of the tubes and splashed heavily into the water. Powder-smoke and the stench of hot oil blew over Noble.

"Fire three! Fire four!"

One torpedo splashed into the water, but there was no sign of the other.

"Percussion!" Noble rasped and heard the thwock of Stern's

mallet on the firing-pin again and again. Hell with that fish!

"Hard left rudder!" Noble grated, still hanging on. He heard the exhaled breaths of everyone around him. Still the Jap line came on, dark and silent. The Ninety-Seven was forever turning; now she was parallel to the enemy, now and at last heading away from them at right angles. Jim pointed and Noble saw another PT, a hundred yards away, also coming around in a turn. So two sets of fish must be under way toward the enemy. Now the Ninety-Seven was all the way around. How Noble yearned to take a chance and throw off mufflers, shove the throttles forward as far as they would go, build up speed, and get away. He couldn't stand this much longer. . . .

An orange light glowed alongside the leading Jap destroyer. Noble stared back at her, open-mouthed with suspense. The orange glow grew, expanded, climbed, and with it a high column of black and white water. Orange glow became vivid flash, then flame, and the volcanic upsurge illuminated the long grey vessel beneath it, and briefly, the careening shapes of the others astern. The white column of water fell back into the sea but the flames still climbed. The sound of the explosion was low and rumbling and Noble could feel it in his body, quivering up from the disturbed ocean. He gazed stupidly around his boat; he expected the crew to be shouting with joy, yet in each face that he could see by the light of the burning ship he found only the stunned apprehension that small boys might feel, on finding that their camp fire had spread all over the vacant lot. The Ninety-Seven was close, too damned close; the second destroyer in line sparkled redly, viciously, fore and aft; elevated trains rushed toward Noble and shell spouts were flung from the water halfway between the two retreating PTs.

Noble signaled the mufflers off; then gently but steadily he shoved the throttles forward. Lightened of her torpedoes, and as if weary of muffled creeping, the Ninety-Seven stuck her nose up and tore through the water as Noble ordered

Hill to turn hard right toward the shell spouts. The other boat had done the same, and the two PTs came within ten yards of each other for a brief instant. The next shell struck to port, so close that Noble could hear the sharp crack of the splitting air, and something smacked viciously into the bow of his boat. He pushed Hill from the wheel and started zigzagging. With his free hand he drew his forty-five and fired two shots into the air—the signal for smoke. Behind the Ninety-Seven guns were thundering all along the Japanese column, and Noble felt each crash in his belly; but it was better now that he was running at full speed, doing something. . . . Where the hell was the smoke? Hadn't Sterns heard his signal? Noble looked aft again and cried out with relief at sight of the funnel of white smoke boiling up from the wake.

The moment of greatest danger came as Noble swung hard left, running perpendicular to the previous course, with the boat's location made perfectly evident by the moving, forward end of the rising wall of smoke. But at this speed he didn't need to hold the course long. One shell came close as he swung right again, reversing course, going behind the smoke screen, holding this reversed course until the boat reached the center of it. Then he turned away from the enemy and streaked it for the southernmost end of Savo. Behind him, the wall of smoke billowed slowly upward, illuminated by enemy searchlights. They could not see the PT at all, and no shells were even close any more.

"Thank God for that smoke!" Print gasped.

Noble didn't answer; he had to devote all his energies to keeping his knees stiff. The boys were yelling now, and he heard snatches of exultant chatter. He should throttle down now, put on mufflers, and creep, but he wanted so damned badly to be out of the action area. Savo was just off the port bow, and the Ninety-Seven was beginning to swing around the point to safety.

"*Watch out!*" Print screamed. "Charlie, LOOK!"

Dead ahead, 300 yards away, just rounding the southern end of Savo, was a Jap destroyer. The enemy had sent a sleeper south of Savo in hopes of doing just what had been done. Noble spun the wheel madly, the boat careened and skidded through the water, dragging her long tail of wake and smoke around in a 180-degree turn.

Whrramm! went the destroyer's bow gun, and a white splash climbed into the air, so close that the concussion jarred Noble's feet from the deck of the boat. The PT was still making smoke, and Noble had the throttles wedged against the forward end of their quadrants, praying for more speed. Back the PT streaked, heading northwest now, only a hundred yards from Savo's beaches, with the destroyer after her like a hawk. The smoke was billowing up and blinding the Jap gun crew forward; otherwise the Ninety-Seven would have been finished, for the enemy kept up a heavy fire through the smoke. Tracers swept forward through the smoke, passing over and around the Ninety-Seven, making spaced rows of white in the water.

"Depth charges!" Noble shouted, and Jim lunged out of the cockpit. As he did so, the Jap searchlight came on, and she was so close that the light seemed high in the sky, as if coming from a two-story building from across a street. From its high position the light beam just skimmed the top of the smoke and settled on the PT. Christ! Noble could have counted the individual hairs on the backs of his hands; the light seemed to burn, he was so exposed. He glanced back and in the light saw Print and Sterns kick a depth charge over the side, just as the gunners commenced firing at the light. It all happened at once: the bath of light, the splashing depth charges, and the roll and spaced rattle of the twin fifties and the 20-mm. The destroyer's bow gun fired again through the smoke, the PT's tracers found the bridge, and the light went out. Then, even in the new dark, Noble saw the heaven-reaching pillars of white water from the two depth charges rising just off the destroyer's bow, and felt the concussion of the water's turmoil.

"I'll bet that shook up his saki for him!" Hill shouted. The destroyer fell farther behind now, still wrapped in smoke, but Noble's relief was brief. From out in the bay, the still-moving column of the enemy, now well past the burning hulk of their leader, opened fire on the Ninety-Seven. Marked by the spreading smoke behind and outlined against the dark island, with her tracers fanning backward toward the destroyer, the PT made a good target. Spouts rose before her bows, shells slammed into the wake, once, Noble was sure, hitting alongside and bouncing over his head. Shells exploded in the surf and among the palm trees ashore. The long enemy line was a winking, snapping stream of fire. The Ninety-Seven needed four minutes to run the length of Savo and gain relative safety, but in that moment Noble lost all hope of making it.

Jim was back in the cockpit clutching Noble's arm; he could hear his exec cursing; anyway, no more whistling, Noble thought savagely. Noble was cutting the land close, terribly close, for he wasn't going to waste any distance. At forty-five knots the land streamed past; the boat's wake lay in the outer surf, she was so close. The mountain echoed back the sound of the engines and the crack of gunfire. The boat rocked violently in the ridged white surf that caught her abeam. Noble held his breath, wondering wildly what it was like to have a shell explode beneath your feet; surely at any second they would get it. The air was a rushing wall; white spray streamed over him, blinding him. Which would it be? A coral rock tearing out the bottom, or a bursting shell?

A point of land jutted out ahead; Noble swung left to increase clearance, slamming by the point so close that for a moment he thought he was lost, and whirled around the point, fishtailing inward. Another point ahead; the Ninety-Seven tore around it, with the trees and rocks a blur of motion as from a railway window at night, and, unbelievably, the boat was around the end of the island and safe! The firing died away, noise cut off suddenly by the shoulder of the mountain.

"We made it!" Print gasped. Noble was beyond speech or feeling in that moment, drowned in a vast relief. He kept the engines at full speed, and pulled himself together.

"Keep a close watch on that point," he ordered. "He may still be after us." He dragged out the forty-five and signaled to Sterns to stop making smoke. For an endlessly long space of time the boat roared on through the black waters toward the northeast.

"Guess he didn't follow us, Charlie," Print said at last. "No sign of him."

Print's relief was plain in his voice, and the skipper was sure that his own showed equally clearly.

"Good. Now watch the other end of the island. They might send another sleeper around."

For another three minutes Noble maintained speed, taking the boat well clear of the battleground before dropping the engines down to 1200 RPM and ringing for the mufflers. Silence blessedly flowed over the Ninety-Seven. Noble's knees were so weak that he gave the wheel to Hill and climbed to his under-way seat, remaining there nerveless and limp, his head rolling on his shoulders with the motion of the boat. The crew was very quiet. "Jesus Christ!" Noble heard Johnson say in a pained voice. Hill took out a handkerchief and mopped his face, keeping one hand on the wheel. Print turned around and looked up at Noble, his face a blur in the darkness.

"Charlie," he said. "Skipper, I guess we got us a destroyer."

It was only then that the cheering started. Noble brought his attention back to the radio; he had been barely conscious of its constant uproar and interchange while the Ninety-Seven was being chased around the island; now it was relatively quiet, perhaps because of Savo's blanketing influence. Then he heard Ollie reporting to base that the Japs had pulled out without landing troops, leaving one destroyer behind and taking a cripple with them. Noble slid down to the deck and picked up the mike.

"Prep Ollie from Prep Charlie," he said. "I have Bakered, I have Bakered. Request permission to take a drink of rye whiskey. Over."

"Prep Charlie from Prep Ollie. Affirmative, boy, and I do mean affirmative. You can paint a scalp on your cockpit, bud. Over."

"Okay, boys." Noble had to speak loudly to break through their cheering. "We've got no boats down and no survivors to worry about, so let's go home."

The bow swung, and the Ninety-Seven went over the rippled, clutching waters, going home to safety and rest.

19

THE DIFFERENT ATMOSPHERE at the base was quite evident to Everard after the Ninety-Seven, along with Dave Poker's boat, was credited with torpedoing a destroyer. When they returned to Sesapi, even before going to the village to sleep, Noble's crew stood by on the dock while a yeoman painted a Japanese naval flag and the silhouette of a destroyer on the cockpit. In that moment, Everard knew why Indians took scalps from their opponents. Men who had made remarks about Noble before, went out of their way now to speak to him. Everard was glad to see that the skipper showed no change at all, except to grow more cheerful than he had been for some time; actually the radioman attributed this more to the presence of Pat Bunch than to their military success.

Bunch was quite the most amazing individual Everard had ever met; he had never seen the lieutenant's spontaneous cheerfulness and humor matched. In addition, his manner was precisely the same toward base force seamen as it was toward the squadron commanders—friendly, cheerful, helpful. He and Noble were together constantly ashore. Everard saw them, both on line now, in the shifting crowd of officers and men outside the radio shack, waiting for mail to be delivered.

Charles Noble received letters from his parents, as well as

from a classmate in Washington. He didn't pay much attention to the typed letter in the business envelope with the insurance company return address. Only after he had read his other mail did he open it, grinning wryly at the thought of life insurance at Guadalcanal. Inside the envelope was a hand-written letter, and at sight of the writing a physical shock rammed through him. Kathleen! He stuffed the letter back and shoved it in his pocket. This letter he must read alone. Pat had already gone off to read his mail from Gerry. Down the trail to the mangrove swamp, Noble passed the final wandering reader and sat down on the rotting wooden frame of some long-gone marine's bunk. Through the odor of mold and dampness he could smell gardenias and lavender. . . .

My love. This is the thing I swore I wouldn't do. Oh Charles, my for-six-weeks darling, nothing has changed, not my mind, not anything; you can't come back to me for the reason you know. But since I said good-by to you from the door of our cottage (you waved so forlornly, and you looked so *old*) I have been empty with such a terrible emptiness. I thought that it would go away, that my daughter would fill it. She filled another emptiness, but this one remains. I love you, Charles. I could not go on without writing you. I tried but I could not successfully pretend that you never were.

Will you write me just once—maybe twice—at the address on this letterhead? A friend of mine works at this company and she will get your letter to me. Oh, I am shameless, but I must know that you are alive and well. If anything happened to you I might never know! Do be careful, my love; don't be a hero; save yourself for the girl whom I envy and hate already, who will never be good enough for you.

Remember the little waves under our window . . . the way the birds woke us . . .

I love you.

207

A wave of memory, dulled in the past weeks of action and fear, rushed over Noble with a scalding fever of desire. But he could write her now, he could speak to her as her letter had spoken to him. . . .

On the ninth of December, the sliver of moon set at eight in the evening, leaving the waters black around Guadalcanal. That night the Ninety-Seven was strafed by a Jap float Zero that missed its pass and went on to Pat Bunch's boat. The Ninety-One's guns caught it, and red blossomed out from its blue exhaust-points as it went swooping up and down, exploding as it hit the water. Afterward, barges came in, and the Ninety-Seven sank one of them. The Ninety-One got two. But in the Flotilla, two men were killed and three wounded by machine-gun fire. The PT corner of the Tulagi cemetery was growing, and each death was felt by the men of the Flotilla.

The next morning's half-day of sleep revived the crew of the Ninety-Seven. Print blessed Charlie's thoughtfulness in buying the phonograph. How much the simple tunes meant to all of them, foolish words that turned to magic. The men sat under the palms in the late afternoon, soothed by the knowledge that this was their night in, and listened to the records. Savo Bill, one of the local chiefs, came by. He listened with delight to "Paper Doll."

"Fellow music bokkis," he said to Noble. "I give you for him two wives, one canoe. You sell? Good canoe!"

Print didn't dare look at Charlie's face, and he heard one or two members of the crew choking down their laughter. They all knew what Charlie was thinking. The women, loving God, the women. Coal black, pipe-smoking, betel-nut-stained; they were old women before they were out of their teens.

"No, Chief," Noble said gravely. "Music bokkis god belong us. No sell him."

Savo Bill nodded, impressed. The look in his eyes said that he knew a good bargainer when he saw one.

"Three wives?" he said hopefully. "Three Mary? One new; only twelve year belong along her."

Print saw Charlie's lip twitch, but the skipper remained calm and dignified, even managing to look regretful as he shook his head.

"My tambo," he said with dignity. "I keep music bokkis."

The chief gave up.

On the night of December 11, Pat Bunch woke Noble; they smiled at each other and got aboard their respective boats. Noble was assigned as a part of the three-boat striking force, along with Dave Poker and George Shagg. That night, the PTs didn't have long to wait, for the enemy came in at 2300. Wakefield spotted them first; he fired torpedoes and missed, cursing violently over the air. The striking force went in abreast, with Noble disgusted and ashamed that all the old fears came back: nausea, coldness, and the extreme physical effort required to remain calm as his boat muttered in slowly against the alerted column. The striking force got to within a thousand yards undiscovered; it celebrated this feat by firing twelve torpedoes, wheeling as one boat and starting out of there. Shellfire winked; the PTs broke mufflers and retired at full speed as a destroyer exploded and settled back burning into the water behind them.

Noble saw it all: the lone PT swooping in at full speed, lighted and silhouetted by the burning destroyer. It wove and tore, dashing, zigzagging, the evasive course so time-wasting that when it got in close enough the column had advanced so far that the lousy World War I fish were too slow to reach the target. The PT roared out again. Noble couldn't breathe or speak; he knew it was Pat, it had to be Pat because of the spot from which it had started in. The PT escaped into darkness in a welter of shell spouts, still carrying torpedoes; and the Jap column still came on.

"Oh, Jesus!" Noble gasped in relief. "I'm going to kick your ass, Pat."

What was that? The whirling roar of a racing boat! Pat was turning, going in again on the bow, having gained distance ahead on the slowing column.

"Prep Pat from Prep Ollie!" the radio crackled. "You crazy bastard, get out of there, get out of there! They can see you! Withdraw, withdraw! This is an order!"

"Dig me, Momma!" came Pat's voice. "I got 'em this time. I'm going in!"

The Ninety-One made her second run. Incredibly, she dodged among the shell splashes, made position and slowed; and Noble saw, in the light of the burning ship and the flashing searchlights, the splashes her torpedoes made hitting the water. The Ninety-One gathered speed, turned, started out.

Noble felt the hit, felt the red explosion that engulfed the boat. For a moment the PT was quiet and dark on the water, slowing, dying. Then it exploded with a great white flash, like a monstrous flash bulb going off.

Noble was crying. He couldn't help it. There was nothing he could do, nothing at all. And it was all for nothing, all wasted, for Pat's torpedoes missed. Yet not quite for nothing; the Japs must have been impressed by the American *Banzai* charge, for they countermarched and got out of there.

The rest of that night Noble searched the dark water for a splash, listened for a cry. Back and forth he took his boat, not caring about anything now. Let the Japs come back; he would stay here until he snatched Pat from the sharks of Ironbottomed Bay. As the PTs searched, the stars disappeared and rain began coming down. Noble couldn't even see the bow of his own boat. He listened above the purr of motors for a shout, a pistol shot. He kept at it through all the night that remained and into the grey dawn. He didn't speak. He seldom removed the glasses from his eyes, and his crew was silent and searching with him.

In the hard light of dawn Noble saw the splashing and heard the distant crack-crack-crack! of a forty-five. He spun the wheel and rammed the throttles as far forward as they would go. In a moment, the Ninety-Seven arrived at the little group in the water.

"Take her, Jim," Noble said. He went out on the deck, looking down. Two men were holding a third between them, dreadfully still in his life jacket, floating in the clear water face upward like a cork. It was Pat. Noble saw his face, the staring eyes, the motionlessness. The men were Bertram Pollock, the cook, and Raven the torpedoman, whom Pat had once threatened to paint dungaree-blue from the navel up.

Noble jumped into the water feet first. Lines came down and he passed them under Pat. Unbelievingly Noble saw his friend being lifted into the air and swung aboard above him. Raven was too weak to climb, so Noble stuck his feet into the loop of another line and he was hauled to safety. Then Bertram. Noble saw a dull-yellow gleam in the water below and knew it was a shark turning and wheeling; but Johnson was alert, and the two forward machine guns hammered at the water until the shark went away. Then without knowing how he got there, Noble was back on deck, looking down at Pat.

He was dead, the laughing eyes were dull brown marbles. His chin hung slack. Noble tried not to see the white gleam of his leg bone where the sharks had torn him.

"We wasn't . . . " Bertram was muttering, crouched on the deck by Pat. "We wasn't going to let them goddamned sharks get the skipper. We stuck with him. Mister Noble, is he dead?"

Tears were rolling down his cheeks.

"Yes," Noble said. "He's dead."

Noble carried Pat onto the dock at Sesapi, keeping him covered with the flag they had placed across him. The men standing around murmured softly; the waves also murmured softly; Noble understood one as well as the other. The morning sun cast the shadow of the flagstaff and flag across the dock. Noble carried Pat through the shadow and placed him gently in the shade, still under the flag. Noble stood up and caught Jake Hughes' eye.

"Did they find any of the others?"

"No, Charlie," Jake said sadly.

"I'll go report," Noble said. Jake nodded; Noble heard the subdued voices of his crew behind him and felt Jim Print's hand on his shoulder as he stumbled through the morning sunshine to the radio shack.

It was dim in there and it took his eyes a minute to adjust. "Ollie," he said. "Ollie, I . . . "

Then Noble could see the man sitting by Ollie at the desk, still sitting though Ollie was standing up and coming toward Noble.

"Sit down, Charlie," Ollie said. Then Noble's eyes cleared and he saw that the man at the table was Lt. Commander Morton Daggs.

20

NOBLE WALKED out of the radio shack still numb and uncaring. His report was made and he had talked with Daggs. It had been an effort to try and remember who the commander was; every moment or so Noble's mind would ask, who is this? Why are you talking to him about unimportant things when Pat is dead? But he had gone on talking. When he had first seen Daggs, Noble had expected him to do his worst; however, it was borne in upon his weary, numbed mind that the only change in Daggs' attitude toward him was for the better. Bluff, loud, even friendly, he had congratulated Noble on his destroyer and had sworn profanely that it was only the beginning for the squadron.

"I'll take over now, Charlie," Daggs had said at the last. "You done a grand job, but we'll go out and do a better one together, hey?"

Noble was too tired to think, but he could only assume that Daggs hadn't received the picture from the detective outfit yet. Then what the hell had brought him up from Nouméa? Let it ride, let it ride. Noble knew what he needed. When the Higgins boat took him to the village dock, he climbed out and walked quickly shoreward, his shoes clanging on the metal surface. He crossed the village to the sick bay, a large hut, set on stilts on a grassy and breezy point. Inside the building he found Dr. LaSalle sitting at an improvised desk doing his paper work.

"Hello, Charlie." LaSalle's stubby, Groucho Marx mustache twitched with his smile. Doc's eyes, which could be frosty at times, now were warmly sympathetic.

"I feel like hell," Noble told him.

"I heard about Pat Bunch. I'm sorry. You were good friends, weren't you."

"Yes. We were roommates at the Academy."

"That so? Well, here's your medicine." LaSalle brought out a bottle of medicinal rye and poured a glass half full. Noble drank half of it down. He gagged for a moment, so tired that he felt sick. The sickness passed, the warm glow grew, and Noble drank more. Doc leaned back in the chair and clasped his hands behind his head.

"Shame to drink it this way," Noble commented. "I'd sure like a tall glass and some ice cubes."

"I know. Here, have another. It will help you sleep; you'll feel better when you wake up."

"I won't feel any better." Noble shook his head slowly. "But maybe I'll be able to keep from showing it."

Doc nodded. "It's a hard thing, losing a friend. It will dull down fast though, out here. I've seen it before. So much happens that a week is like a year of ordinary living. Damned good thing that it's so."

"Poor old Pat. He had the most beautiful girl for a wife that I ever saw. He didn't seem to mind so much the idea of being killed, but he was terribly worried that he might come back blind, or without legs, or without his . . . " Memory returned, and even in his grief Noble smiled, remembering what Pat had said. Well, at least Pat didn't have to worry about that. And Gerry was young. She had loved Pat, but she could get over it.

Noble drank nearly a full glass of the whisky, and when he started back to the hut his legs were like those of a rag doll.

The hut was dim and breezy, cool after the sun. He undressed and climbed under the mosquito netting. Almost at once he was asleep.

After its morning rest, the crew went over to the cemetery on Tulagi to pay its last respects to Bunch. As Print walked along the dock he met Commander Daggs. "Good afternoon, sir," Print said, saluting. Daggs did not return his salute; he didn't even look at Print, but kept right on going. Print turned and looked after him, puzzled. They'd always gotten along well enough. What the blazing hell? There was no chance the commander hadn't seen him; hell, he'd looked right *through* Print. A thought struck him. Delilah! He began to sweat even more than usual. Had Daggs found out about him and Delilah? If so, it could be bad as hell—being in a combat zone with your commanding officer out to get your hide. Print felt disturbed enough and miserable enough without this too.

A half-dozen bodies were to be buried that day. Ghost-eyed men with green-touched faces stood around, not solemn exactly, Print thought; they were without the feeling, which is so strong at civilian funerals, that one is separated from the deceased by an immense, uncrossable chasm. Rather, each man realized that he might be one of the dead tonight, or in an hour, or perhaps tomorrow. The next waiting cross might be his. The bugle blew and the tired marines fired a ragged volley. Print saw that Charlie's face was set and pale. The skipper was very quiet as they went back to Sesapi along the muddy path.

Print had hoped that the first meeting with Daggs was a fluke, an encounter when the commander was preoccupied or worried, maybe even scared: Print would be the last man, God knew, to blame anyone for letting the atmosphere of this place get under his skin. But even though Daggs attached himself to the Ninety-Seven, he avoided speaking to Print, even giving him orders indirectly through Charlie. Once or twice this had not been possible; then Daggs' commands were

215

blunt and cold, couched in the fewest possible words. The crew noticed it; even Noble, still lost in grief, came out of his apathy and looked at Print in a puzzled manner.

On the day after Bunch's funeral, Daggs had all the members of his squadron assemble before the radio shack. There he let them know unequivocally that he was assuming command.

"I haven't got anything to say against the way things have been run up here," he rumbled. "All I know is that *this* outfit is going to run my way. We'll go on patrolling with the other squadrons, like we been doing, only when I find anything that I don't like, then by God, with no ifs or ands or buts, that thing is going to be changed. Got it?"

He stared around at the officers and men, his face red, his little eyes bloodshot. His flush wasn't a healthy red, and it faded away soon. He licked his lips.

"I hear some of you officers have been getting away with it, staying behind that armor in the cockpits while the men are in the cardboard turrets under fire." Daggs glared around. "Me, I won't ask any man to take a bigger risk than I'm taking. I'm going out on patrol tonight, and I'll have my eyes open. Tomorrow I expect you'll find a few changes around here. All right. That's all."

To Everard it seemed that the reappearance of Commander Daggs had brought an added strain to the men of the squadron. For the previous weeks, the working of the outfit had dovetailed so well with that of the other groups that they had thought themselves one. Officers and men had lived together so closely and well that discipline had ceased to be necessary, all members of the Flotilla considering themselves simply a group of men struggling with a common, complex problem. The only difference had been that some men wore khakis, others dungarees; the first ate in one stuffy room, the others in a second room, or out on the deck passageways. In all other ways, officers and men had lived the same life, as one unit. This closeness had been a thing the crews had valued, and

Everard knew that the officers liked it too. They had depended on each other without thought or worry; now the men wondered. A few found food for thought in the commander's words about enlisted men in exposed gun positions.

"Yeah," Radelewski said. "Print and Noble do stay behind the armor plate, don't they?"

"Crap," Warder said in disgust. "That armor plate won't stop anything bigger than a twenty-five caliber rifle bullet. And when Ding Hau had a stoppage the other night, under fire, Mr. Print was back helping him mighty quick, wasn't he?"

"That's right," Ding Hau agreed. "Ain't nobody safer than anybody else on these boats."

When the boat next went out on patrol, Johnson saw the commander was good as his word. Daggs was in the cockpit. But as soon as the moon went down, around midnight, it seemed to Johnson that the commander talked mighty quiet for him. Along toward morning the boat found some barges and chased them in to the land. Johnson was all right as soon as he got to shooting. The Old Ninety-Seven tore two or three of the barges all to pieces. It was quiet after that, and as soon as it was full light the boat went in close to run up and down the beach and shoot up any supplies the gunners could see. Johnson didn't like these inshore patrols very much; it gave him the fidgets to sit there in plain sight, close to all the trees and bushes. The boat had just got in close, and Johnson was scroonched down as far as he could get and still see the beach when he heard old Daggs say, "Print, get up in that forward turret awhile. Let's see how your shooting is."

Print came up right away, looking kind of funny, but he grinned at Johnson and hopped down into the turret. Johnson didn't much like Print shooting his guns, but he climbed out and went aft, over on the side away from the land. If it hadn't been for Daggs he would have gone into the cockpit, but it looked mighty crowded with him in there. The boat went along, and now and then Daggs or Noble would point out a landing barge that looked like it might run, or maybe a pile of cans and boxes in the brush, and the guns would start going. Pretty soon, just as Johnson expected, the boat found some Japs and they started shooting back. Johnson heard old Daggs holler, "Get out of here, Noble! Goddammit, don't take all day!" and just then one of the boys stationed at the 20-mm. gun went down, kicking like a shot rabbit. Johnson got there quick, Ike right with him, and it was the kid Benton, shot square through the throat. He had both hands at his neck and the blood was spurting through his fingers, and he was trying to talk, and choking, and he looked scared to death. When Johnson grabbed Benton he could feel his heart pounding, like a crippled bird when you pick it up and you can feel it living in your hand, and then you knock its head against the gun barrel and it's gone. Benton was gone like the bird, too; all of a sudden, he wasn't kicking or choking any more.

Everybody looked pretty sick, and Johnson thought the commander seemed the sickest of all. Johnson had blood all over him, and so did Ike. Nobody said much all the way back to the base. Daggs jumped out onto the dock and went away, while the rest of the crew took care of Benton. Ike took him off the skipper's mattress on the canopy, with the flag over him, and carried him onto the dock as carefully as if he were still alive. Noble looked on, his face sad and angry at the same time. Nobody said much but Ike, and all he said, over and over again, was, "Them sonsabitches. Oh, them sonsabitches!"

Noble had thought that the loss of Pat had dulled him for lesser griefs, but Benton's death showed him that he still had untapped sorrow. It was soon blunted though; already Pat was fading, and this last was just another burden to add to fear, exhaustion, Dagg's presence with its daily reminder of guilt, and a suspense that grew through the hours. After Benton was buried he had a talk with Jim Print.

"Charlie," Jim said. "Am I nuts or is the commander gunning for me?"

"I don't know." Noble *didn't* know; Daggs barely spoke to Print, and there was hate on his face whenever he looked at him. But why? Noble had expected this of the commander, but directed at him, not Jim. "Why would he have his knife out for you?"

"It's crazy, but all I can think of is Delilah. She, well, she was pretty mad at me once. Maybe she told Daggs about us."

"I don't think Delilah would do that. She seemed like a pretty square shooter to me."

"That's what's so screwy about the whole deal. Hell, I didn't, well, rape her, you know. We were good friends, too; that's not always the way but it was this time. I can't imagine her telling Daggs anything, but I can't imagine what else it could be. He's sore as hell at me over something. Did you see the way he looked when he ordered me into the turret this morning?"

"I did."

"He was hoping I was going to get knocked off. Goddamn it, Charlie, this about throws me. That's why he went so close to the beach and hung around until we got fired on. He damned near got his druthers, too," Jim added grimly. "A bullet went through that turret within three inches of me."

There wasn't much that Noble could say to comfort Jim, other than to tell him that he, Noble, was going to be in the same fix any day now, just as soon as Daggs got that letter from the detective agency. And that he wouldn't do, feeling a reluctance to burden Jim with his troubles.

Sometimes it seemed to Noble it would be better to have it over with Daggs. He no longer feared the commander, but a deferred emergency grows larger in the mind and he was tempted to tell Daggs everything. But what good could it do? To hell with it, he thought; when he finds out, he finds out. Noble half-grinned to himself. Poor Daggs; he'd have Noble in the forward turret and Jim on the 20-mm. and climb right up the beach with the Old Ninety-Seven. Then Benton weltering in his blood came back to Noble and he lost the grin.

The next morning Bertram Pollock, Pat's cook, came to Noble where he was working in Manson's office on personnel records.

"Mr. Noble, I hear you lost a man the other night."

"That's right."

"Sir, I'd like to ride your boat."

"I've already got a cook, Pollock, I'm sorry."

"I don't give a damn about that. I just want to get onto one of them guns. You was the skipper's friend, Mr. Noble, and I want to ride with you."

Noble thought swiftly. After all, he was squadron exec, and this was part of his job. Still, a cook to replace a seaman. He was about to say no when he saw Pollock's anxiousness.

"Okay," he said. "Move in with the boys over at the village."

"Thanks, Cap. I've already talked to Sterns. I'm glad to be on your boat, Mr. Noble."

Spanish fly, Cap? You gettin' any lately? Lord, Noble thought; I'm getting lonely. Still Bertram—Pat had warned him never to call him Bertie—was like having part of Pat on board, and he felt a little better as he turned back to the records of dead men and the lists of personal effects.

The PT Flotilla moved gratefully into the moonlight time, and men tired from weeks of tension relaxed a little. While the moon grew and was full, and commenced to wane, they could expect to live. For ten or twelve light nights, until after Christmas, they could be reasonably sure of a quiet time. The Ninety-Seven had a further reason for relief: Daggs had announced that he was taking over the Flotilla base work, and would no longer ride the boats regularly. No Daggs, no darkness. Noble heard Jim whistling a song other than "The Old Chisholm Trail," and even found himself laughing one morning at one of Bertram's outrageous jokes.

Dinner, such as it was, tasted pretty good to Noble on the evening of December 18. He had the patrol duty, but the moon was already in the sky and wouldn't set until nearly four; moreover, the forecast was for good weather. With some luck the Ninety-Seven might even spend the night alongside the dock. Noble finished a plateful of vienna sausage stewed with tomatoes, gulped some water, and went out on deck with his coffee cup. Shortly, most of the duty officers joined him, smoking, drinking coffee, and watching the sunset. It was unusually beautiful, Noble thought, with purples, yellows, light greens and reds. High, thin cirrus clouds made a red hatching against the blue sky. The creek was like a mirror.

"If I said this was pretty, would anybody here throw me overboard?" Bill Shagg looked about him, grinning.

"I could maybe look at it if my crotch would quit itching," Harris Brocker said.

"Hell, haven't you tried any of the Doc's blue paint?"

"Blue paint, my red and rosy! That's sulphuric acid with ink in it. I'd rather itch than burn alive."

"Hell, yes," Rich Davis agreed. "I let him paint me the other day and I can show you the scorched places on my pants. No bull."

Noble lit a cigar and tried a smoke ring; it drifted whole and tangible in the calm air. "Doc tried it out on Savo Bill yesterday," he said.

"What happened?"

"Savo Bill offered to go out and catch a Jap if the Doc would let him paint the bastard with it."

"Duty boat!" someone shouted. "Come on, you lounge lizards. I want to get those cards drawn. I'm sleepy."

"Charlie, I wish you'd let me draw tonight," Jim said wistfully. "You must be lucky as all get-out at love, the way you draw cards."

"Oh, no you don't!" George Shagg was very positive about it. "Boat captains do the drawing." He grinned. "Charlie

221

here is the only man in the Flotilla I can beat every time."

"It's just that I'm honest," Noble explained as he stepped aboard the waiting PT. "I'm going to insist that these card-sharps roll their sleeves up."

It didn't do any good. He drew the lowest card turned over. Not only the patrol, while four luckier captains slept, but the bitch patrol.

"You be careful, Charlie," Ollie warned him. "Remember all the reefs; you'll be out of radio communication too."

"I'll be careful."

"Okay," Ollie said with his slow grin. "I don't think you'll find anything bigger than a barge."

Noble went down to the boat, throwing an appreciative glance at the beautiful, beautiful moon. "Wind 'em up, boys," he said to his assembled crew. They groaned.

"What was it this time, Skipper?" Sterns wanted to know.

"Three of clubs."

"We've got to change Charlie's luck somehow," Jim said thoughtfully. "I'll see Savo Bill tomorrow."

"Go to hell. Take her away. I *like* spending the night on the water. I *love* it."

"Selfish bastard. Okay; bow line in. Stern line there. Watch the fenders, Floyd."

Even in the moonlight levity turned off abruptly as the crew put on life jackets and steel helmets and manned battle stations.

By midnight the moonlight was so bright that there was blue in the sky, and the whitecaps looked blue; there were few stars, and Print could make out individual trees over on Guadalcanal. He was glad there were waves enough to make the shoals break.

"Spooky over here, isn't it?" he murmured to Charlie, who nodded.

"Everard, try the radio again," the skipper said. "See if you can pick up anybody."

"Aye, aye." Everard picked up the microphone. "From Prep

Charlie. Testing. To any Prep, to Villa D'Amour, to Cactus Control. This is Prep Charlie. How do you hear me? Come in, please. Over."

They stood silent with the speaker frying gently, broken occasionally by bursts of static. Everard tried again.

"No use," Charlie said. "We've got too many mountains between us and home. Come around to starboard, Hill."

Print looked on down to the southeast along Guadalcanal. The island lay between them and any help, dark and brooding above the silver sea. A mile down the coast a long low rock was visible. Like Doma Reef, only . . . Wait a minute! It was moving. Print brought up the glasses, trying to keep the quiver from his hands. In the glasses he saw the long, low form of a submarine.

"Submarine!" Print squeaked, his voice uncontrolled. He could feel the shock his words carried. Charlie spun around, his face white in the moonlight, and followed the direction of the glasses.

"Christ!" he exclaimed. "You're right. Unlock firing circuits. Ike! Fish ready? Good. Stand by depth charges. We'll go in slow. On your toes, boys."

Print hated him again for a moment, hated himself. Why had he seen the damned thing? It was unfair; this should have been a quiet and uneventful night, one which could pass without this choking fear that always rose in him when the boat made an attack. But, hell, what was the matter with him? This wasn't a line of destroyers, this was a submarine, and if it saw the PT, it would crash dive and that would be that, unless the Ninety-Seven could drop a depth charge close enough to smash him.

"He'll see us," Josiah Hill muttered. "He'll see us for sure."

"He's heading in to shore," Charlie said. "Set up the torpedo director, Jim."

Once Print got started, he felt better; it was an easy problem to set up, but a poor shot from the sub's quarter. No

223

chance at all from the present bearing, for the PT was too far abaft the beam of the sub.

Print was not conscious of his breathing. The motors purred and the boat moved uneasily in the cross swell. She wasn't closing fast; the sub probably was making twenty knots; twenty-five was about the Ninety-Seven's top with mufflers on. Still, two thousand yards. They have to see us!

Livid red blossomed from the center of the black shape and a high-pitched scream tore by the PT, ending in white water leaping into the moonlight fifty yards astern. Charlie hit the buzzers, the mufflers came off, and Print moved the throttles forward; the boat roared ahead.

"What the hell!" Charlie cried. "He's not diving!"

The sub fired again and the shell hit off the starboard side. Chasing the salvo, Charlie swung over toward the spout, and a third shot hit along the boat's wake. Now the sub was heading directly out to sea, white water curling along her. Print looked at Charlie, wondering what the skipper would do now.

What the hell can I do now? Noble was thinking. What the hell can I do? The approach had been bad enough, now this. Why didn't the sonsofbitches act like they were supposed to? Go on, submerge, you bastard, submerge! No radio, no help. Noble had to take this submarine alone. He couldn't go back without getting him or driving him under. Under? He *couldn't* go under! That was it. Damaged by a depth-charge attack, or maybe a bomb, so he couldn't submerge. Heading in for one of the deep coves, or a river mouth, where he could tie up and camouflage until he could repair the damage. Judas! Noble muttered. We're both caught! He couldn't let go and the sub had a four-inch gun and machine guns. Noble grabbed the wheel and swung right, paralleling the sub's course, now 1500 yards away. If he could pull up on the enemy bow, he could fire a spread with a good chance of a hit. A shell screamed by so close overhead that Noble ducked. Red balls of tracer floated out toward the PT.

"Hold fire!" Noble shouted. He swung the wheel right and left, jinking around, zigzagging, 200 yards in, 200 out, 50 in, 50 out. The sub kept shooting, but she had no fire control other than local pointer, and the PT was hard to hit. Once Noble held the wheel over to make a complete circle, and then tore straight ahead at forty-five knots. The evasive action was slowing the PT, but little by little she drew up on the sub. Five minutes more and Noble could fire that spread.

Then the submarine turned dead away, leaving Noble looking down his stern, and the next shell hit squarely in the PT's wake. Noble whipped right, left, and settled back directly astern of the enemy.

"Fire two!" he shouted.

Puff of smoke, slither, rasp of metal, and splash as the long torpedo slid from the tube and hit the water. Noble jinked again. Firing one fish would leave the boat off trim, but to hell with that. He couldn't waste more than one. The damned old Mark Eight clunker could still do about five knots more than the Jap; it was barely possible that the fish might catch him, particularly if he turned out of course at the right time. Thousand yards at five knots—six minutes it would take. Hopeless.

He couldn't depend on the miracle of that fish hitting. Again he started in to overhaul the sub. This could keep up all night! He didn't dare cut the sub closer; that would take the PT into machine-gun range and between the mgs and the four-inch, the Ninety-Seven would be blown out of the water before she could get close enough. And if she did escape and close in, the sub could simply turn away again. Blam! Blam! Blam! That was a fast gun crew. Noble was wet with sweat, cursing to himself, but he worked that wheel. He jinked and wove his way to the enemy beam again.

Noble looked at his watch. Five minutes. One more; maybe the first fish would hit.

But it didn't. The last minute went by, and Noble knew that the shoot had missed. God damn these fish, he groaned.

Why don't we have the new ones? The boat jarred and leaped; something splattered against the cockpit, the boat shook, a shell spout rose from the water alongside the bow, away from the enemy. What the . . . ?

"Charlie!" Jim yelled. "That shell went through the bow; the planking wasn't heavy enough to explode it."

Too much, too much to stand. Noble held his breath and tried the wheel, but he could feel no change in the boat. Jim ducked below; he was back again in seconds, his face pale.

"Moonlight showing through both sides!" he shouted. "Both holes are out of the water. Jeeesus!"

Noble grabbed Jim with his free hand. "I'm going in; tell Johnson to smother that damn gun with machine-gun fire. Go stand behind him, be ready to take his place if he gets hit. We've got to do it, Jim. We can't quit."

"Aye, aye—Charlie."

Noble saw him by the turret shouting to Johnson; then he turned and waved. "Here we go!" Noble shouted and turned the bow dead for the submarine, boring in. The first shot missed cleanly; Noble zigged for it and swung back; at forty-five knots, one minute would take the PT right in on the enemy. Johnson's guns started drumming. The tracers went to the right of the sub, swung left, and fell on the gun just aft of the conning tower. When the next shell should have come, it did not; three seconds later the gun exploded again and the shell screamed close above the cockpit. Johnson's guns were a steady roll. Tracers floated toward the PT and she shook under hits; something slammed off from the cockpit armor, screaming away. Somebody cried out. Four hundred yards! Three hundred!

"Fire one!"

The fish hit the water, heading straight for the sub. Noble swung right, going out on the sub's quarter. The swing unmasked the other turret and the 20-mm., and in seconds three streams of tracer were flashing into the Jap gun, exploding there, glancing redly away into the sky, drumming at the conning tower with its spitting machine guns. On the beam, Noble swung dead for the sub, yanked back the throttles, and fired the last two fish as the pancaking bow slowed the boat down for the shot. Noble turned away at once, jamming the throttles forward, and ran for the sub's bow, his guns an unbroken, drumming roar. The Ninety-Seven was flashing across the sub's bow; the sub was turning to try to avoid the fish, and then one of them hit. Red, submerged flash rising into the air, dull roar, climbing white water. The submarine seemed to break in two; bow and stern took high angles. Within seconds the sub was gone, and in the moonlight Noble could see the black oil dimming and smoothing the white maelstrom of its sinking.

21

FLOYD STOOD IN the sunshine trying not to move, even with the tickling sweat rolling down his face. The admiral had finished reading the citations, and now he was pinning the medals on Mr. Noble, the Silver Star and the Purple Heart. Mr. Noble still had the bandages on his cheek where the wood splinter had hit—he hadn't even known about it until Everard had told him his face was bleeding. Four more of the crew had been hit with wooden splinters; Floyd had one in the arm, and Radelewski had caught one in his tail as he was heading down the engine-room hatch. The kapok life jackets and steel helmets had turned most of the splinters, and none of the wounds amounted to anything; still Doc LaSalle had growled that he had to treat 'em, and by God that meant wounded in action. It sounded pretty good to Floyd, but it didn't feel good. That splinter in his arm could have been bigger; or it could have hit his stomach. He didn't want any more Purple Hearts.

He felt shaky when the Admiral pinned the Bronze Star and the Purple Heart on his chest, and shook hands with him. Then it was all over and the crew went back to the tents to stow the medals away and put on their working clothes. The boat was all repaired, and they were going to spend the rest of the morning working on it.

Floyd remembered with pleasure the fuss at the PT base that morning when the Ninety-Seven came back with the shell holes in the bow, the canopy and crew's dayroom smacked full of bullet holes, and with three prisoners and a lot of stuff picked up out of the water. Everybody was waiting at the dock, and to Floyd it felt like the time his high school team beat Wilbur Cross at football. He was pretty proud to be on the Old Ninety-Seven. Now she had a destroyer, a submarine, and seven barges painted on the side of the cockpit.

"See this stuff?" Radelewski said, taking off the medals. "I'll swap 'em all for a piece of tail on Sand Street."

"You'd better hang on to the medals," Everard said. "You're going to find it rather difficult to show the ladies your wound scars."

Radelewski ignored the radioman and looked the best medal over carefully. Bronze Star. Hot damn! His old man was going to be tickled.

"Bronze Star," he said scornfully. "Noble got the Silver Star, you'll notice."

"Why not?" Sterns demanded. "He was the one took us in. I couldn't a done it."

"Bull. I'd have took us in right away instead of hanging around getting shot at. Just lucky we didn't get blowed to hell and gone."

Heroes or no heroes, the Ninety-Seven had the patrol that night. At least there was moonlight, and the run was quiet, as was the next and the next, for the weather stayed clear until after Christmas.

Not much of a Christmas, Radelewski thought to himself afterward. Two lousy cans of beer for each man, and all the torpedo alcohol was under lock and key over on Mocambo. That same movie they had seen in Efate was shown down at the village, and he grudgingly joined in on the Christmas carols sung by the assembly. A lot of the natives were there, and they sang fine, though you couldn't recognize the words.

Worst of all, the moon didn't come up until after the show, maybe ten-thirty, and Ski knew that the dark nights were on them again. His belly tightened up and he hastily regretted some of the blasphemy he had muttered that day. Maybe he'd better run over to Guadal on the courier boat pretty soon; he hadn't been to confession and Mass in a long time, and there was a Father over at Lunga Point. You'd think the goddamn brass would have a priest on Tulagi, but that was the Navy for you.

Larry Floyd stayed inside the native church, which usually did duty as a movie theater, until the last carol was sung. There was a curious feeling of lightness in him, and the sickness that had come over him at seeing Benton die had gone away. It had done so during the interdenominational service held in the village that morning. At first Floyd had been uneasy, but he remembered the Father in Norfolk had told him that when no Catholic chaplain was available, he should go to a Protestant one. The lightness persisted as long as he was in the church that night, singing with the others; when he came out into the breezy, almost cool, village and saw the moon, the lightness gave way to stabbing fear. An intense homesickness overcame him; nostalgia for home, family, and the merry Christmases of other years shook him hard, leaving him spent and miserable. "I've gotta get out of this!" he murmured to himself in the darkness. "I've gotta get out, I've got to!"

Jim Print almost welcomed the return of the dark nights. Shortly before Christmas, Daggs had taken to riding the boat again, and his hostility to Print had become unmistakable. Print knew that the men were commenting on it among themselves. But now, with the dark nights ahead, he felt quite sure that Daggs would stay at home.

He was right; when the Ninety-Seven went out on the twenty-seventh, Daggs was not along. Print was almost gay, in spite of the recurring fear that stayed with him until the moon began silvering the water just before midnight.

"Glad to see that moon," Noble commented with a sigh.
"*Love* the moon. Say, do you remember how it looked through trees when you'd park on a moonlight night with a girl?"

"Don't!" Noble grinned. "You want to make me cry? And what's eating you tonight, Wild Bill Hiccup? You act like you've had a shot of whiskey."

"Better than that, you blanking smokepipe. The cockpit is so nice and roomy."

"I get you." Print thought the skipper sounded worried. "Look, Jim, if there's anything I can do."

"I've thought plenty about it, but there's no way out. Hell, maybe he'll get over it. If he doesn't, I guess I'll have to apply for transfer to another squadron."

"I'd hate to lose you."

"You can't do that, Mister Print." Josiah Hill spoke up from the wheel. "Don't you go bustin' up the boat."

"You'd be damned glad to get rid of me, Josiah; don't grease me. The skipper here is the one who can give you that rating."

Noble could tell by his tone that Jim was pleased. He knew that he himself got along well with his men and had their loyalty, but they all seemed to have a genuine affection for Jim. Well, Noble thought, so do I.

Even though the nights were dark, the Express didn't run. Air raids hit regularly at Henderson Field, and float Zeros hunted over Ironbottomed Bay. The PTs had almost nightly engagements with landing boats coming in from the Russells, but no destroyers appeared. The PT men became tense.

"She's going to be a bitch when she hits," George Shagg declared, hitching up his pants, a characteristic gesture. "They're piling up something big to throw at us."

Noble was sure Shagg was right.

Then on January third, in a blinding rain squall, the Express ran. Caught, with no chance to fire fish, the Ninety-Seven was chased clear across the Bay, past Savo, and all the way to Sandfly Passage before the persistent destroyer behind her would give up. This experience shook Noble and his crew; they were a jumpy group when the Ninety-Seven nosed cautiously out of the narrow channel and sneaked back toward Esperance.

The build-up continued. One night float planes raided Tulagi, roaring up the creek only feet above its surface, strafing and bombing blindly. Half awake, Noble fled across the village in shorts and unlaced boots, Tommy gun in hand, to plunge behind the gullied banks of the brook. His speed had been increased by arching tracers from a strafing plane. For Christ's sake, he demanded bitterly, can't a man even sleep on his night in? He went back to bed, and just before morning a tense sentry shot and killed a PT crewman who had wandered out of a nearby shack.

"I seen somebody move!" the stunned sentry cried. "I thought he was a Jap."

A glum lot of PT officers gathered on the *Marlboro* for breakfast. Those who had had the night in looked as weary as the returning patrol men. No one laughed, and the table talk was short and uneasy. Noble was sickened by the Spam on his plate.

"They're putting the pressure on," Ollie Wakefield said. "The barges have been getting some troops through, and God knows how many the Express landed last night. Things point to a big push ashore, and that means more trouble for us."

"The boys are getting jittery," Noble said. "What do I mean 'boys'? Hell, I'm jittery myself."

"Me, too." Ollie didn't grin. "Nothing else is available right now, Charlie. We've got to stop them."

The Professionals were on patrol the night of the eleventh. As the boat captains assembled in the radio shack, Charlie Noble, chewing nervously on his smoldering cigar, knew that this was going to be a bad night.

"Nothing sighted," Ollie told the captains. They stirred uneasily, and Noble bit down on his cigar. He knew damned well the Japs would be down. "We're going out full strength," Wakefield continued. "The coast watchers might have slipped up in this kind of weather. Moonset is at twenty-three fifteen. Patrol at very low speeds and don't fire at the float planes. We're after destroyers. All right, let's roll."

Ding Hau shifted his weight, settling his back more comfortably against the side of the turret. The Ninety-Seven was pitching and rolling, and he had the guns locked into position; he kept one hand on the release, even though the moon still gave some light. Ding was scared, but he had been scared plenty times before and he reckoned he could stand it. All in all, the Navy had been good to him; he was satisfied in the work he did; he knew that he was a good cook and that cooking was important. He had seen a lot of places and things, and had made love to many pretty women. When he had gotten tired of one place, the Navy had always taken him to another. He patted the guns and touched the ready ammunition cans, each with 250 rounds of fifty-caliber coiled down in it. Ding liked the guns. He was pretty sure he'd be shooting them before morning.

Noble reached up and shifted the heavy steel helmet on his head, cursing the float Zeros that made wearing it advisable. The PT was working along at twelve knots, and the wind whistled over the deck, moaning in the whip antenna and guns. Out here, four miles northwest of Savo, there was nothing to break the waves, and conditions were wet and rough. Salt water sloshed continually over the cockpit; to have salt in your eyes was bad enough any time, but when your life depended on what you could see it was plain crap-filled hell. Thunder sounded off to the northwest.

"Hear that?" Jim said unhappily.

"Yes. With this wind we had to expect it. Sure as hell the Japs will be down in this."

Noble cursed again as a wave took him unaware from the

blackness and drenched him. He looked up and saw the quarter moon just touching the water.

"There she goes," he said. Thunder sounded again, closer, and in the last light of the moon, Noble saw black clouds boiling up in the northwest, where the squalls and Japs came from. "Okay, Ninety-Seven," he called. "Stand by."

God, it's dark, Jim Print thought. The few stars left were fading rapidly. Guadalcanal was only a dark blur, Savo little better. He could barely see the other PT a hundred yards over on the beam. Salt water poured on him in buckets, and he yearned for his bed with Di beside him. A drop of water pelted his face, rolling down to his lips. He licked it into his mouth. Fresh. What a climate. Rain starting; it came pelting down like it was going to fill the cockpit; you couldn't see twenty feet in this. The wind was getting stronger, too. White flickered eerily over the world of tossing, uneasy waves. Print felt sick. Damned lightning; it lit up the blanking place just long enough for a man to think he saw something, then it was gone, leaving him to sweat blood until it flashed again.

Charlie Noble was thinking about a bed too; Kathleen's warm, perfumed bed with rain pattering on a roof above. God, why do men ever leave it? he thought. So they can have it, the answer came. All through history, men have had to fight to keep what they loved. Pray God, Noble thought, that after this war the world will be able to get along without fighting. But he knew he wouldn't bet on it. More thunder. Damn this blanking squall.

"All Preps," the radio said suddenly through the static. "All Preps stand by for code message."

Noble froze as Everard opened the charthouse door, the faint blue light touching his cheekbones, making his wet face and eyes shine. He ducked down and came back with code pad and pencil, to stand wedged in the charthouse door. The message began its gibberish. Everard looked up the words and read them out one by one, writing unsteadily in the chop and roll.

"Seven enemy vessels." Everard's voice had a somber pitch to it. A wave broke over the bow, and he ducked below as the wind howled derisively. "One cruiser." A vivid flash of lightning sheeted the water world. "Six destroyers." No one else spoke. "Course one two five." Jim Print coughed. "Speed twenty-five, distance twenty-five. 2300."

"Twenty-three hundred!" Noble cried. "An hour ago! They must be here now! Watch it, boys, watch it. We can't let 'em slip by!"

What good? Noble thought desperately. A man couldn't see beyond the bow. Everywhere he looked he saw dark shapes in the water, then spray and rain flailed his eyes and he saw nothing. Glasses were made useless by the spray. Then some freak of wind and wave gave respite, and Noble saw irregular notches of black in the water. He looked above the place, keeping only a corner of his eye on the spot. Several dark shapes were stealing rapidly through the tossing sea, already beyond the Ninety-Seven, already inside the line.

"There they are!" Noble said, just as the radio shouted: "Scotch in Water, Scotch in Water. They're right on top of us!"

Noble cursed; part of the attack group had slipped by earlier; that was Ollie's voice, and destroyers must have pinned him against the beach. He swung the bow left and opened the throttles. The Jap vessels had disappeared in the murk. To hell with them; he would push in and try to get a whack at the ones close to Ollie and Howard Warren. Ollie's voice came again, strong with excitement but still cool.

"Deploy to starboard, Howard. Attack, attack!"

Choking silence filled the men in the cockpit. Sterns and Floyd clung to the forward tubes, mallets ready in case the impulse charges didn't ignite. Noble felt a terrible fear. Ollie was in a hell of a bad spot; if he went under, Daggs would be senior officer in the Flotilla. In place of a magnificent leader, calm, soft-voiced, and fearless, there would be Windbag Daggs. These thoughts occupied a part of his mind, but mostly it was just fear for Ollie. To lose him as well as Pat would finish Noble. He advanced the throttles as far as mufflers would allow and headed the boat directly for Esperance. Ollie's voice came again.

"Good going, Howard, we got one. Swing starboard now and we'll go through. Come on, boys, let's get the . . ." A crash filled the speaker, a scrap of word was heard ". . . hit . . ." and then silence. Howard's voice, "They got Ollie, they got Ollie; he's down over off Esperance! Send every . . ." That message was cut off as though by a knife. The squall lifted momentarily, and over toward Esperance, Noble saw a red glow and the blink of tracer. The rumble of gunfire drowned the thunder. Then the rain shut down again.

"Dig me, Momma!" Noble yelled, remembering Pat. "I'm going in!"

He took off the mufflers and went tearing through the murk at full speed.

"This is Prep Bill, they're pulling out. Look out! One's frying off Esperance!"

Noble caught the glow of flames; another glare burned to the left, and as he watched there came the flash and impact of an explosion. Then dead ahead he saw a white V with a dark shape above it, and his mind registered.

"Look out!" Jim shouted. A Jap destroyer was coming directly for the Ninety-Seven and was only a hundred yards away.

"Open fire, drop depth charges!" Noble screamed. He headed the boat just to the side of the white V; Jim was out of the cockpit, then the boat was speeding alongside the grey high bulk of the enemy ship, not thirty feet away, too close to be hit by Jap fire. Noble's gunners opened fire, their guns raving, three streams of tracer slamming through thin steel sides only feet away. Then they were past, the destroyer was lost behind in the murk, and the PT leaped and pounded over her wake, the cockpit flooded anew with green water, blinding everyone. Noble spotted another dark shape before him to starboard; he hit the throttles, the bow dropped, and he fired all fish in a quick snap shot. Almost immediately a PT roared past the Ninety-Seven, white wake high, smoke pouring from her generator, guns blazing at a searchlight that loomed through the rain. The searchlight went out; Noble buzzed for mufflers, turned hard, and headed for Savo. His torpedoes fired, all he could do was wait to pick up survivors. Slowing, silent, the Ninety-Seven eased toward the island. Noble spotted the surf, crept as close to shallow water as he dared, and stayed there, using only enough engine to stay clear of the shore. Complete silence, except for the drum of surf and the endless roar and rustle of wind and rain, fell over the boat.

"Sorry, Skipper," Jim muttered huskily to Noble. "I didn't have time to drop depth charges."

"Too quick," Noble agreed shakily.

"I could have touched her with a swab," Print said in awe. "I don't want to get that close any more, Charlie."

"All Preps, this is Prep Bill," the radio blared. "We've picked up a rubber boat with Ollie and Mitch and all but one of their crew. They're okay."

"Thank God!" Noble exclaimed. Ollie was a cliff to hold to; he couldn't imagine going out without Ollie's calm presence somewhere at the other end of the radio circuit.

"Jesus, I'm glad," Jim sighed. "How about poor Howard and Les and their boys? Let's go search, Skipper."

"You bet." Noble advanced the throttles and the boat began to move away from the shelter of the island.

When morning came, clear and calm, the PTs had picked up seven more men, three alive, four shark-torn. But of Howard Warren not a trace. High above in the bright sky, the fluffy clouds were cream-gold in the morning sun, as, carrying their dead, the PTs returned to their base.

22

JOHN EVERARD SAT on a ration box in front of the tent and looked glumly about the village. He was tired. He had gotten to the point where he'd wake up in the morning tired, even on the rare occasions when he'd slept all night. Partly it was the heat; his skin was never dry, day or night. Rain fell half of every day and his spare shoes grew whiskers of mold overnight. Fungus had attacked his body as well, so that his arms and crotch itched miserably. So far he had escaped dengue and malaria, though over on Sesapi the rate was close to eighty-five per cent.

But Everard knew that mostly the weariness came from fear and tension. The strain of the past weeks had increased to a point where he was never wholly calm and relaxed. Meals eaten in haste, heat, and fear brought hot waves of indigestion. Formerly laughing and pleasant men had become surly; the spirit had nearly gone out of them.

Everard knew that fear, especially if too long continued, was a poison. First it had been bad, then it had gotten better; now it had become much worse. The onset of fear had been marked by the night Wakefield's boat had been sunk, and the loss of Warren's boat with the men who had been his companions and friends during the weeks on the *Gasper*. Two nights later the Express had run again, and as the Ninety-Seven crept through the dark against the enemy line, one shell had clipped the radio antenna, and another had fallen within feet of the fantail. They had been lucky to get home. But luck could not last forever.

After one more action the moonlight had returned, but still float planes and barges came through every night; on nearly every patrol someone in the Flotilla was killed or wounded. All through the moonlight time this skirmishing had continued. Now even this interval of relative peace was over, and the dark nights were returning. Everard felt totally unable to face the prospect before him. Tonight, the Ninety-Seven was going out, and the moon would not rise until ten o'clock. That was all right so long as a float plane didn't find their boat with a bomb. But on the next patrol, darkness would last until nearly eleven, and after that the Express would start running again. Everard looked down at his trembling hands.

Ike Sterns came out of the tent. He was unshaven, and haggardly green with dengue fever.

"How is it today, Ike?"

"All right, only I'm shaky as an old man's dong. I'll be pretty good for a while now. Say, there's the commander. What's he doing over here at this time of day?"

"I couldn't say, Ike. Looks as though he were going to the skipper's hut. Yes, so he is."

Charlie was sleepily surprised to see Commander Daggs step through the doorway of his hut. The guilt he always felt at sight of him came strongly, and he stood up. Jim rolled out of his bunk and came to attention in skivvy pants. Had this been Ollie, Noble mused, he would have sunk deeper into his cot and it would have taken a shoe to rouse him.

"Good morning, sir," Noble said, echoed by Jim.

239

"Morning, Charlie. Carry on, hell, don't get off your tail for me. Nice place you got here. Lot cooler than that stateroom of mine on the *Marlboro*."

"Home sweet home," Noble said. This was the first time the commander had been in the hut. Now that he was out of the strong light of the doorway, Noble saw that Daggs was wearing clean, pressed khakis from the tender's laundry and was clean-shaven. He looked better than he had for some time.

"Is the boat all set, Charlie?" Daggs asked, sinking into a chair.

"Yes, sir. We have the patrol tonight."

"Good. How about you, Print?"

"Why . . . what do you mean, sir?"

"How are you feeling? You all bright-eyed and bushy-tailed?"

"Well, I'm as ready as anybody else, sir." Noble could hear the surprise in Jim's voice.

"Good. Good. We've got a special job tonight, men. I've just been talking to Wakefield and Hughes. It seems like the big brass wants to know what's going on in the Russells."

"Oh?"

"We're going to go see."

"How's that?"

"The Ninety-Seven will go to the Russells. I'm coming along. We'll get under way as soon as it's dark, about nineteen hundred, and be there at about twenty-one hundred. Right?"

"We'll have only an hour before moonrise, sir."

"Just you leave that to me. Charlie, if there's anything you want for this patrol, just tell me. Now, I'd kind of like to talk to Mister Print here, alone."

"Yes, sir," Noble said. Jim was in pants and shirt now, and his eyes met Noble's, their glances reflecting mutual puzzlement.

"I'll be down at the dock," Noble said. He walked out of the hut, hesitated, and went over to the crew's tents.

Inside the hut Jim Print felt cold fear rise in his throat, then sink down to his belly. His watch ticked loudly in the silence.

"Charlie's a good man," Daggs said conversationally. "I thought at first he was going to be a little stiff—hell, you know how the regular Navy is—but I reckon I squared him away that first day. Yes sir, he's got to be a good man. I'm proud of Charlie."

"He's a swell boat captain, sir."

"Glad to hear you say it, Print. Now, about you. I don't want anybody to hear about this, Print, not until the time comes."

"Yes, sir."

"You're a good outdoor man; I hear tell you've done a lot of hunting and fishing out there in Wyoming."

"Why, yes, I've been outdoors a good deal."

"Fine. You're the man for the job, all right."

"What job?"

"The job of going ashore in the Russells and scouting them." The shock was physical; for a moment Jim couldn't speak.

"But . . . I'll only have an hour, sir. There are float planes based in the Russells, and you won't want . . . "

"I know what I'm doing, Print. We'll put you ashore in a rubber boat at twenty-one hundred, and then come back here. Tomorrow night we'll pick you up at the same time, same place. Simple, isn't it?"

Simple! Good holy Christ, suicide rather! Jim tried to control his shaking hands, and anger came to help him.

"Suppose I don't want to do it?" he demanded.

"What's that? Look, Print, I'm not asking you to do this, I'm ordering you. Get that? Do you know the penalty for refusing your commanding officer's direct orders in the presence of the enemy? You get shot. You're going with us—you've already said you feel all right—and when we get there, if you don't get into that boat and go ashore, I'll shoot you myself."

Loving God, he was really caught. Daggs was his squadron commander, not in any way officially subject to Wakefield's orders. Oh, that sonofabitch. Delilah, Delilah! He noticed that Daggs was watching his face and grinning, and Print tried to make it expressionless.

"All right," he said. Despair flowed over him. Oh, the hell. He'd long ago decided he wasn't going to get out of this war alive.

"Good," Daggs said, grinning more broadly. "I'll see you get the Navy Cross when you get back. Of course, you may not get back, but we all got to die sometime, haven't we?"

"I guess so."

"Now when we get down to Sesapi you take anything you want from supply; if I was you I'd get a few grenades and maybe a Tommy gun. Trench knife too. You might have to kill somebody without making a racket."

"Yes, sir." Jim sat looking down at the floor. This was the end, then. A thought struck him. Maybe not. Perhaps he could get ashore unnoticed by the Japs, find a hiding place, and just stick there. He felt a little better. He might get back yet. Daggs stretched his legs out before him comfortably and sat back. He lit a cigarette without offering one to Print.

"A good woman is mighty nice, isn't she, Print?" he demanded slowly. He seemed amused.

God damn the medieval sonofabitch! Jim thought. Avenging his sister's honor.

"Well," said Daggs. "Isn't she?"

"I can't remember." Jim's forty-five was over on the cot, and for a moment he considered grabbing it and shooting Daggs. The commander roared with laughter at his answer.

"I know what you mean, Print. Look, I'll let you in on a little secret. The big boys think that the Japs will give up if this next push fails. Soon as Guadalcanal is secure, this whole outfit is going to be piled aboard a transport and run down to New Zealand. A guy I know says you have to fight the women off down there, beautiful women. I reckon we'll all find out what it's like again. Think about it, Print. You're a man who likes his loving."

Print said nothing but glared at Daggs with mounting hatred.

"Of course," Daggs said reflectively, "that's only for them that gets through alive. Them that don't, they don't have to worry about women any more, do they, Print?"

"No." Jim was proud that his voice was even. God. Poor Pat Bunch, and Benton, and Howard Warren; all the others lying in Ironbottomed Bay or over in the cemetery, and this bastard could talk like that.

"Let's go down to the dock," Daggs said, standing up. "About time for the boat." He hesitated, then grinned at Print again. "You're not the first man to follow his gristle into a lot of trouble, Print."

Tulagi Bay was a pool of red from the sunset. To the west a strip of pale-green sky showed over the jungled hill, then came gold and pink with a layer of strange, pale yellow. The rest of the sky was red, and in the east, night was black on the clouds. No wind blew, and the long ripples from the Ninety-Seven's wake looked like colored oil. A flock of cockatoos flapped across the cliff of green, seemingly themselves colored by the vivid light. Charles Noble spared the sunset one long glance, then came back to the cockpit. Daggs sat morosely still on the bench. Jim was below; this was unusual, but then Jim had acted unusual all afternoon, having disappeared until nearly time for early supper. When he had shown up, he was glum and almost surly, quite uncommunicative. Noble himself was far from happy with the night's mission. True, it would be better than meeting the Express, but it seemed a large risk for a very small gain. He shook his head and gave it up. He'd heard Ollie trying to argue Daggs out of the expedition, but the commander had just walked off. Well, here we go, Noble thought, then almost smiled at the trite expression, trite because it crossed everyone's mind, and usually his lips, at the moment of departure on a mission. Or another phrase that men used on the brink of action: This is it. It, the great unknown, the moment, feared, dreaded—It.

Coming off the range beyond the shoals, Noble set a course for the northern end of Savo Island and nursed the engines up to 1900 RPM, thirty-five knots. Beyond Savo they would probably run with mufflers on. Noble considered it always a good idea to allow as much margin as possible, and he most certainly did want to get away from the Russells before the moon came up. Strange, he thought, to have the shoe on the other foot. No doubt this was the way the Japs felt coming into Guadalcanal.

Halfway to Savo, with full darkness now closed in, Jim came up into the cockpit. In the brief, blue light from the charthouse door Noble saw that his face was set hard. Almost immediately Daggs went below.

"It seemed funny without you up here." Noble said. "How you doing, boy?"

"Lousy," Jim said. Noble was struck by the timbre of Jim's voice.

"I'll probably keep Hill on the wheel," Noble continued, "so I want you to handle the chart work, particularly coming back. We'll doubtless be in something of a hurry then, old chap, and I want to be sure we won't try to ram a blanking reef right out of the ocean."

"I won't be coming back with you." Jim's voice was lifeless.

"Oh, cut out the crap." Noble was strangely annoyed. "This ought to be duck soup." The devil. It wasn't like Jim to talk this way.

"No, no, I mean it," Jim said. "I'm going ashore on the Russells. You're coming back after me tomorrow night."

"What?" Noble felt dazed. "You're kidding me."

"Nope. All Daggs' bright little idea."

"He can't mean it—what the hell, Hill, you're twenty degrees off course! Watch it, man."

"I wasn't thinking about the goddamned course!" Hill said,

swinging back. Noble looked at him sharply. Hill seldom swore.

"You ain't bullin' us, Mister Print?" Johnson asked furiously from the turret.

"No," Print said. "What the hell; I'm just going to do a little scout and get a pretty medal."

"Yeah. Look, Mister Noble, when he comes back up you get him forward theah by the hatch, tell him you see something in the water. I'll blow his guts out with the machine guns, and we'll all say the Japs done it—one of them goddamn float planes."

"Don't be a fool, Johnson!" Print said, but the tone of his voice showed he was touched.

"I'll push him overboard," Everard said, and Noble believed the Ninety-Seven's gentleman and scholar meant it.

"Look, boys," Noble said quietly. "We all think the same of Jim, but this kind of talk doesn't help any. If the commander heard it he could have us all locked up, or shot. I'll go down and talk to him; I'm sure he doesn't realize what he's doing."

"Talk to him good, Mister Noble," Sterns said quietly. "He's the commanding officer, and we'll do what he says, by God. Even if he gets us all killed we'll follow orders; he's still a naval officer. But for God's sake, Skipper, make him change his mind."

"I'll try," Noble said. "You've got the deck, Jim. I'll be back topside in a little while."

"There's no use, Charlie," Jim said hopelessly.

"We'll see."

Noble went through the hatch and closed the door behind him. The chart was on the table with the dim blue light focused on it. Down the ladder to the red linoleum deck and the galley and wardroom—he hadn't sat in that wardroom for weeks—and Noble was at the door of his cabin. He knocked. He heard movement inside and knocked again.

"Yeah?"

"It's me, sir, Noble. I'd like to talk to you."

"Okay. Come on in."

Daggs was lying back on Noble's bare bunk. Light glinted on glass beyond him, nearly hidden on the mattress. It was a bottle, and Noble smelled whiskey in the air.

"Well, Charlie?"

"Commander, I want you to change your mind about putting Jim ashore in the Russells."

"Goddammit, Charlie!" Daggs bellowed, sitting upright. "What the hell do you mean by that? I'm the commander of this blanking squadron, ain't I? I'm your superior officer, ain't I? Well, knock off the crap. Print's going ashore; hell, many a man before him has had some dangerous duty. Is he any blanking better than anybody else? You're just wasting your time, Charlie. If that's all you wanted to say, just turn around and get your ass out of here!"

The crawling evil that had threatened Noble all day, all week, indeed ever since Daggs had come to Tulagi, descended on him. He knew he was not the bystander he seemed to be here. He had to know.

"Commander," he said, "why are you doing it?"

"What?"

"Why are you sending Jim ashore? You know he'll be killed; there's not much cover on the Russells and we know they're full of Japs."

"It's a scout, Noble, that's all. Now shut up."

"Commander, why do you hate Jim?"

Daggs reared back on the bed, put his feet on the deck, and stood erect.

"Hate him? Why shouldn't I hate him after what he's done to me?" Noble caught the whiskey-laden breath, and he saw that Daggs was half drunk. "Look, Noble, I'm gonna tell you, and then I want you to get back up there and keep your goddamn mouth shut and tend to your goddamn business. 'Member what I told you in Nouméa? 'Bout the detectives and the picture?" Daggs fumbled in his pocket and brought out a stained envelope. "Here, look at this and then you shut up!"

246

Noble took the envelope with stiff and icy-cold hands. He opened it and took out a glossy photograph. He could not believe what he saw.

In pitiless plainness, the picture showed Jim Print standing on the little terrace of the beloved house, with Kathleen in his arms. The shock was devastating. In a flash, Noble saw what had happened; the afternoon when Jim had come by returned to him. Noble had left for Archer's, and later, in bed, Kathleen had told him of Jim's idiotic kiss, the yell, the rest of it. And all the while someone had been on the steps to the beach, someone with a camera, the detective sent by Daggs' agency. Oh, my God! Noble thought, it isn't Daggs killing Jim, it's me!

He could shut up, return to the cockpit, and no one would ever know the difference. Jim would think it was his relationship with Delilah; Daggs would be satisfied and search no more for his wife's lover. No one would know.

No one but Charles Noble.

He knew what he had to do. It was the hardest struggle of his life, but he realized that to live under some circumstances is worse than dying. Here he was, face to face with a moment he had dreaded, finding it worse than he had ever imagined.

"Commander," he said, handing the picture back to Daggs, "you're wrong."

"Wrong? Hell's fire, that's Print kissing my wife, ain't it?"

"Yes. But Jim was only visiting. He was trying to keep Kathleen from crying when that picture was taken."

"What's that? Visiting? How do you know?"

"Because . . . because I was living with your wife, Commander. Jim was there visiting me."

Daggs sat on the edge of the bunk, wagging his head back and forth. His red face was that of a man who has received a dreadful blow.

"You? *You,* Charlie Noble, *my friend?* You were living with my wife?"

Noble flinched at the word. Friend; could the man actually have thought of him as a friend? Poor bastard; suddenly it

247

poured over Noble in waves. Noble, with his politeness, his pretense at liking automatically given a commanding officer, had been taken for a friend. Now the revelation Daggs had made at Nouméa about Kathleen was explained. This poor, defeated bastard had fallen so far short, all his life, that he mistook as a friend a man who disliked him.

"Yes, Commander," he said, strangely calm.

"Well, by God . . . " Daggs breathed heavily. "I don't believe it. You're just trying to cover up for Print."

"Commander." Noble looked Daggs squarely in the eye. "I could tell you things about Kathleen, things that would convince you I have been her lover. Must I do it?"

For a long moment, Daggs stared back at him.

"No," he whispered.

Noble stood waiting. He deeply pitied the big, gross man hunched on the bunk.

"All the time," Daggs whispered—the first time Noble had heard him speak so softly—"all the time you were the one? You lived with my wife? You?"

"Yes, Commander."

"All right." Daggs' voice was dull and drained of life. "Go back up and tell Print he's not going ashore. You are."

"Aye, aye, sir." Noble stood at attention and saluted. Daggs didn't look up. Noble turned and went to the door. He looked back once more and Daggs was raising the bottle to his lips. Noble went out of the door and back topside in a strange new world. In a way he felt better than he had in a long time, for uncertainty and fear were gone. On deck he took Jim aside in the darkness and told him. Jim was speechless.

"No, Charlie," he said, recovering at last. "No; I'm not going to let you do it."

"You can't help yourself, Jim. I've told him everything, and I have my orders. I'm going to carry them out."

Speaking the words made the fact quite clear to Noble. He really had to do this. This was the payment for love, for ecstasy. This was the debt he owed. To whom? Daggs? Partly, poor bastard. To himself? Yes, that too, in part. To God? He had done wrong; his love for Kathleen, so sweet, so right in so many ways, had been unsanctified. Was Noble's predicament, his certain death, after all the punishment for sin with Kathleen? Was God a grim God who marked each transgression in the Book, as some Christians said?

Or was it not retribution at all? Had love been payment in advance, a gift, a lovely recompense for one fated to end his life young, never knowing wife, children, happiness? Had it been marked in the Book that Pat Bunch too must die, and so, in balance, had love been given to Pat? And to Charlie Noble? Was the perfection of love's gift atonement for early death?

I'll take the second explanation. And as he came to this conclusion, Charlie Noble knew it to be true. He had been rewarded early; he must pay.

He came back clearly, almost at ease, to a world where the engines muttered astern and white water, reflecting gently in the starlight, peeled away from the bows.

Charlie Noble was deeply moved at the crew's reactions to the news, their protests and exclamations.

"You can't do it, Mister Noble!" Everard cried out. "We can't do without *you*, sir."

But he convinced them. He made them know that it had to be either Jim or himself. They took it. Noble smiled sadly to himself. He knew that his crew really liked him. But they loved Jim.

Once he thought fate had intervened. The engines died halfway from Savo to the Russells. He went to the engine room at once.

"You've got to fix it, boys," he said.

Warder looked at him a long moment. "All right, Skipper," he said. "We'll fix it."

They did so but it took an hour and a half; by the time the Russell Islands appeared as dark, low blurs on the rim of the sea, the moon was coming up. Daggs was standing alone at one side of the cockpit.

"Commander," Jim said, realizing that Noble wasn't going to speak. "The moon is up. We can't go in, sir. We'll be spotted. And sunk, sir. All of us."

"We're going on," Daggs said hoarsely.

"Stay on course, Hill," Noble ordered. "I'll go below and get ready."

Noble put his wallet and papers in the desk and blacked his face. He strapped on the trench knife and put on his belt with the forty-five and shark knife. No helmet; it might bother him in undergrowth. The Tommy gun and the clip sling. Three grenades. Three K rations. The canteen. He looked about the room. He touched a bulkhead lightly and went out.

When he came back on deck, the largest of the Russells was barely half a mile away. The night was bright, the rubber boat ready.

"Go in slow," Daggs said. "Don't make any wake."

Noble felt Jim's hand on his. He squeezed it. The equipment felt heavy on him, and the knowledge of what was to come was even heavier. This made it complete and utter suicide; there could be no doubt that the Japs had spotted the PT, and even a rubber raft would be an unmistakable mark on the silver sea. Had Noble expected to live, he would have refused the mission, but he knew that the balancing of that Book was at hand.

The PT lay to a quarter of a mile from the land. Sterns and Floyd dropped the rubber boat from the fantail. Noble paused for a moment. He would have said good-by to Daggs, but the commander was forward in the cockpit and every second was precious—not for him, for the boat and his men.

"Good-by, Jim. Good-by, boys." He summoned cheerfulness. "See you tomorrow night, right here."

"We'll be here, Skipper," Sterns declared. "By God, we'll be here. See that you are."

Noble stepped down into the boat and picked up the paddle. A deep sadness at what he was leaving lay over him. He should have been filled with terror, but he wasn't.

He paddled slowly away. The Ninety-Seven's engines murmured more strongly, and white water ridged at her stern as she moved off. As she went by Noble, he saw Jim's uplifted hand in the cockpit, and he knew that his men were watching him. Slowly the PT swept by, heading home. Noble looked after her just once, then paddled for the shore.

He covered fifty yards. Then—it was inevitable—came the sound of a float Zero's engines. He saw the slim wings in the sky against the moon. The plane was diving on him! He saw the nose line up, the thin wings, heard the whine of wind and the roar of the engine. Prepared for dying, he yet fought to live. He stood up and went off the raft head first, swimming and diving deep. He felt the multiple concussions of machine-gun bullets, and stayed under as long as he could. He came back into moonlight to see the raft a deflated patch of fabric, floating on top of the gentle swell. From seaward came the rattle of guns.

Noble whirled around in the water and looked toward the sound, forgetful of the depths beneath him, of sharks, and the Jap-filled islands ahead. The plane was diving on the Ninety-Seven, the red necklaces of tracer dangling from her wings, plain in the blue moonlight. Red fountains gushed up to meet her from the PT, and Noble heard the unleashed roar of the engines whose every tone he knew so well. Salt water splashed into his face and he blinked. The plane swooped up and around with a banshee wail of wind and propeller pitch, climbed, and came down again. Again, tracer and splashes seemed to engulf the PT but she fired on still. Noble, in terror, saw splashes on each side of the boat. She must have been hit!

A third attack. The float Zero swooped down, pitiless sprays of tracer flying. Noble heard in his heart the thrumming rattle of the Old Ninety-Seven's fifties and the twenty. White light flashed from the plane's wing, again, again; it swooped up, halted, and nosed down. Red flames were pouring along the plane, tracers were criss-crossing around it; it swooped flaming and fell into the water with a vaulting flash.

251

"They got it, they got it!" Noble shouted

Water splashed by him in spaced, small geysers. He looked ashore to see a winking red light from a point of land, and other smaller winking points on the dark line. Rifles and machine guns! He was done; the Japs, fully alerted by the battle at sea and the plane's attack on the raft, had seen the dark spot of his head on the moon-bright waters. Still, he would fight. He dove, swam as far under water as he could, and came up to the throaty roar of engines, as the bulk of the Ninety-Seven slashed between himself and the shore. All her guns were firing, with tracers arching toward the island. The slick wood of her sides brushed against him; he saw the figures above, heard Jim's voice, "Come on, Charlie, come on!" The rope splashed in the water, he found a loop and put his foot in it, waved a hand, and felt the PT move to seaward, still firing. The rope pulled him from the buffeting water, strong hands grabbed his arms and lifted him aboard and into the clutching arms of his crew. He felt the beloved decks and sank to them nerveless, hearing only the babble of voices, and the pounding guns that were abruptly shut off. Then the world was filled with the wonderful roar of the great engines carrying him back to life.

Jim was in the cockpit, and when Noble's legs would work again he went there and felt Jim's arms around him.

"Charlie, are you all right?" Already Noble had said "Yes" a dozen times. Other hands were on him, his crew was around him, slapping his back, cursing happily.

"I'm all right," Noble said again. "What happened? Did the commander change his mind?"

His foot touched something soft. He moved it and looked down at a dark mound in the corner of the cockpit.

"That plane," Jim said in a strange voice, "got a burst into the cockpit. Nobody was even touched, but . . . him."

Noble looked down at the figure sprawled in the corner of the cockpit.

It was Commander Morton Daggs. And he was quite dead.

23

THE LAST DAYS of January passed in continuous rain. Dog fights rattled in the skies overhead; planes strafed and bombed and were shot down. Two New Zealand corvettes attacked and rammed a Jap submarine off Kamimbo. On Guadalcanal, soldiers and marines squeezed the enemy into tighter spring-compression back of Esperance. Prowling afar, major naval forces of both sides awaited the next strike. On the last day of January, Jap planes sank the heavy cruiser, *Chicago,* and coast watchers sent hurried messages that a big Express was collecting up The Slot.

Jim Print awoke slowly, his head aching and dull. He groped from under the mosquito netting and went to the door; the rain had stopped, the sky was clear. Seven o'clock, and he and Charlie had had nearly nine hours sleep. He shook Noble awake. The skipper groaned and sat up.

"It's not raining," Print said. "Let's go take a quick dip before the boat gets here."

Wearing only skivvy pants and shoes, carrying towels, soap and forty-fives, the two officers walked up the jungle trail. A bird was singing off somewhere, and the insect chorus was stilled for day. There were some clouds, and the just-rising sun made a pattern of red in the eastern sky. They came to the pool, undressed, and waded in.

"Man, that feels good," Noble said.

"It sure does," said Print, sitting neck-deep in coolness; I almost feel good, he said to himself, and found himself whistling. Well, why not? He had had two full nights' sleep; the nightmare he had lived through with Daggs was over. Thinking of Daggs, he stopped whistling. He felt sorry for Daggs, but so many better men had died that he could not sincerely mourn. Charlie had told him of the picture. What a strange thing. That funny, innocent-looking little man with the camera a detective.

What made him happiest was the realization that Delilah didn't hate him, that she hadn't gone in pain and anger to her brother. Print hadn't hurt her as he feared he had. Maybe yet these war years might work a change in Di, leave her capable of happiness, and then . . .

His thoughts blurred, and he reached out and splashed water on Noble. "Know what day this is? First of February. Lord, wasn't that a hell of a January? Hope I don't see any more like it."

"You and me both. But February one also means we've got the patrol tonight. Guess we'd better get rolling."

Jim and the crew spent the morning on the Old Ninety-Seven, making the accustomed checks and adjustments, while Noble went to the squadron office; now that he was squadron commander, paper work filled most of his daylight duty hours. Lunch on the *Marlboro* was uneasy. Through the open ports of the steamy wardroom drifted the pulsing sound of gunfire. Even though he knew the rumble was being made by U. S. destroyers shelling the island in support of the marine-army push, Noble was uncomfortable. Every bit of information received during the morning had pointed to a large-scale enemy attack that night. Heavy Jap forces were at sea, even battleships and carriers. These would not come to Guadalcanal; they were seeking American carriers. But dozens of destroyers also were gathering; destroyers and cruisers would be the

PT Flotilla's night visitors. The devil with it, Noble muttered. I'm going to forget it for now.

Lunch over, Jim yawned. "I'm sleepy again," he said lazily. "even after last night."

"It's the heat."

"Yeah, and all the sleep we've missed. Let's hit the hay."

"I guess we'd better. We'll need everything we've got tonight."

"It's going to be tough?"

"Plenty tough. We don't know exactly how bad yet."

"Oh, God," Jim muttered, lightness gone.

Lying naked under the netting back in the hut, Noble heard Jim's breathing go deep and regular; at intervals he groaned in his sleep, but at least he had left the stinking Solomons for awhile. Noble envied Jim his ability to go to sleep within minutes, almost anywhere or anytime. Noble lay sleepless, his belly, heavy with Spam and dehydrated potatoes, knotted up in tension. He sighed. Long ago he had thought he had reached his limit, yet time after time he had managed to summon strength from some hidden reserve. He knew the reserve was nearly gone, maybe all gone; he might crack tonight. At the moment he felt like it. Only the knowledge that the campaign for Guadalcanal was nearing its end made him able to face the patrol ahead.

Ahead. At the thought, an enormous sadness overcame him. He remembered how conscious of the future he had been that morning, weeks back, when he'd had to write the letter to Kathleen, as Daggs' wife. Two hours before, Commander Daggs, the big man who had hidden his insecurity under loudness and who, perhaps, had never known what friendship was, had been buried. And Noble, one whom Daggs had thought a friend, had to write a love letter to the dead man's wife. Noble had grimaced at the thought. Love letter? No, he couldn't write of love to Kathleen, though no man stood any longer between them. That would have to wait. He knew she loved him; when he got home again they could get married, and

255

then they could know forever the happiness of their six weeks. That had been when the sadness hit him—a sadness caused by a total inability to believe in the future. Life's tenure was too frail in this time and this place. Noble continually told himself that if he survived this crisis, then almost certainly respite would come. He could go to New Zealand and have an excellent chance of being returned to the United States to form a new squadron and become its commander. Of course, after a few months with Kathleen, it would be out again to more dark islands and fiery nights. But he would have had time with her. That would be something. That would be everything.

New Zealand, home, Kathleen, marriage. A wonderful prospect! If only he could have believed in it.

Noble had looked down at the paper and wondered if he should write at all? Yet when Kathleen received the sparse telegram from the Navy Department she would want to know more. The shock would be bad enough without her having to wonder if he, Noble, had been killed as well. Yes, he had decided, he would write; he had taken up the pen.

. . . My Kathleen. Before you read this you will know that Morton is dead. He died well; I was with him and he died in a way that can make his daughter—and his wife—proud of him. I am well and we should soon be relieved. I don't say the things that I want to say, for this is not our time. I can only say that I have not changed and will never change. God bless you. Faithfully and forever—Charles.

Now, lying on the cot, he closed his eyes, trying to relax; but the darkness became the darkness of Ironbottomed Bay, and he could not shut out the flecks of tracers and the red glare of guns. Suddenly he was shaking so hard that the cot quivered beneath him. Sweat poured out on his forehead. As he reached out to save himself, he found the image of Kathleen coming through to him. All right, he said to himself, now I know where that reserve has come from—memory, I guess, and love. Okay, I've held off drawing from it, but no more. I'll use it up now; then I'm through.

He forced his mind back as, through streaks of redness, he once again saw Kathleen and himself on that moonlit night after they had returned from dancing. Once again he heard her soft voice welcome him: "Come into our house, my love," on the night they had both known they would be lovers. . . .

In the moonlight, the brown door of the cottage looked grey. He unlocked it with shaking hands and gave the key to Kathleen. The moon was a glory in the night. Peepers were calling, a bird chirped drowsily above; salt waters sighed below.

Inside, he kissed her; she responded, then danced out of his arms, twirling in the center of the room, the white dress with its bright figures swirling about her.

"It has been such a lovely evening! Let's have a nightcap."

Noble followed her down the steps; he went into the kitchen and mixed the drinks. When he came out, Kathleen was lying on the wicker chaise longue. He handed her one of the glasses; he put his on the floor and knelt beside her. He kissed her, feeling the soft lips move beneath his, and her body lift on the chaise. From the corner of his eye he saw her grope for the floor and place her glass there too, then both her arms were around him. He kissed her lips, her eyes, her ears; he buried his face in her hair while she murmured against him. He kissed the hollow of her throat and her dress where it swelled over her breasts; and then, almost without his willing it, the white dress was huddled around her waist, and her breasts were bare.

Seeing them now for the first time clearly, Noble marveled at their beauty, at the unbelievable purity and wonder of their curves, the roundness, the small pink nipples.

He rested his face on her breasts. She caressed his hair

and face with her hands, then lifted his head from her, kissing his cheeks and mouth and eyes. He smiled at her. "Dearest?" Eyes bright, she nodded; she drew up her dress and rose.

He made the rounds, washing the glasses, locking the doors, and then he stepped out onto the terrace to look at the stars. In that moment, his happiness was so great it seemed uncontainable.

He heard her call to him and he came in. Kathleen, dressed in a sheer blue negligee, walked across the room to the bed, which was turned down. Its bedside lights made the only illumination in the room. She sat on its edge and looked gravely at him.

There was no holding back in her kiss when he went to her. She was trembling, smiling again, her eyes shining and never moving from his face. He reached down and undid the negligee. He kissed her throat, lost in her faint perfume, a blend of soap, lavender, and clean flesh. He drew her gown over her head; her breasts were gardenia: petal white, curved with the curves of the flowers, silk to his touch.

She settled back on the white sheets, watching him. Awkwardly, even bashfully, he undressed in the light with her eyes upon him. Her face was so serene that it seemed lighted from within.

"You're handsome like that," she said. "I'm so glad you're not bowlegged or hairy!"

Even in that moment he laughed at this. He reached over and kissed her, then sat beside her as she lay down, studying her, memorizing her with eyes and hands, getting the feel of her body so mingled with his that he could never lose it.

"You're so sweet, Charles. You'll never know how much your tenderness means," she said.

Slowly, with love, he came to her. War and worry faded away, sin vanished, death was gone; especially death, for a man who truly has love need never fear death.

They lay quietly together afterward, touching coolly, shoulder, hip, and thigh. Noble felt like a cloud, buoyed up, relaxed, happy and warm. Her breath was gentle again. He leaned over to kiss her breasts and her lips. Her eyes opened and she smiled drowsily, happily.

"Let's sleep for a bit now," she said.

"No," he said. "We might sleep through the night; I don't want it to pass so quickly."

Her eyes were on his. She moved slightly on the sheets. "Never fear," she said softly.

"I love you."

"And I, you. You'll never know how much, or how gratefully."

Her hand was in his as he fell asleep, and he still held her hand when he woke up later. . . .

Noble opened his eyes from sleep, warm and content; he thrust out his hand, reaching for Kathleen, finding netting instead, then emptiness; instead of perfume and cool sheets there was a hot, dank stench. Eyes opened wide, he looked above him at the mosquito netting, then around at the crowded little space with ration boxes, cots, the lanterns, the two bureaus from the boat, clothes lying about.

"Oh, Christ!" he said, and lay back on the moldy pillow. Staring straight above him, he felt, to his shame and horror, tears trickling from his eyes. He breathed deeply. Dream? That hadn't been a dream—it had been the night itself relived, love experienced again. A warm gratefulness suffused him. What a wonderful gift! The west wind of home had blown in his sleep. He wiped his eyes and face and lay back. His hands were steady now; he felt weak but calm. He wouldn't break; he knew he was ready to face whatever was coming.

Only then, with the regaining of serenity, did he notice the sound of battle from far away: gunfire and the thud of bombs. Men were dying over by Savo.

He looked at his watch. It was time. He swung from the sweaty cot, woke Jim and went with him to the pool. They found their crew already there, together with others of the boats going out that night. The community bath was noisy and crowded, but still refreshing. Noble, not yet free of the wonderful experience of his dream-memory, left early and went back to the hut.

Strangeness lay over the room as he walked in. He changed into low black shoes that would come off easily in the water, and black socks, for white attracts sharks. Morphine syrettes, canteen, knife, forty-five, cigars and matches. Steel helmet. Life jacket. He hesitated, then took his wallet from his pocket and placed it in his suitcase, together with a wrist watch. He looked about the hut and down at the nude South Sea girl who lay on his bureau. He reached down to pat her black head. Then he went down to the dock to wait for the Higgins boat.

The early meal for the duty section was a tense affair, with jokes and laughter vainly trying to hide the mounting uneasiness that had grown in the men with the lowering of the sun.

"Poor old *DeHaven*," Ollie commented gravely. "Jap planes smacked hell out of her over by Savo this afternoon."

"Sunk?" Bill Shagg asked.

"Yes. Two hundred men lost. Keep an eye open tonight; it's possible you' might find a survivor."

"The poor guys," Shagg said quietly. "How about tonight, Ollie?"

Silence dropped over the table, the officers arresting any motion to listen.

"Coast watchers and air patrol say they are on the way. The Express will run, all right. I thought it might come last night, but I guess the Japs are waiting for the Professionals."

"That blamed Varsity. Wish one of those birds would swap with me—I've had enough of being a hero."

When the duty boat pulled away from the *Marlboro,* Jim

was standing close by Noble, but neither said anything. The sun was setting among clouds and the horizon was scarlet, with a black and purple rim. The entire sky overhead was red, shading to pink in the east. The creek was red. The waters were still, and the PT moved through a red pathway, with palm trees making black designs on a red mirror.

During the session in the radio shack Noble was stiff with fear. He could feel his face muscles ache with the effort of keeping his face unmoved as the dope was read out.

"Seventeen destroyers, three cruisers. They should arrive at about twenty-three hundred, eleven o'clock. Usual place—Esperance—usual course and speed." Ollie stopped and looked down at the papers he held. "This is the big night, boys," he went on. "We don't know what they're up to, but if we lick 'em this time, we've got Guadalcanal sewed up. Without reinforcements, the Japs on the island will be wiped out within forty-eight hours. We've got to keep them from getting troops ashore if we want this thing to end now." He paused. The spaced exhalations of the boat captains' breaths could be heard. God, Noble thought. I wish it were morning and this night over.

"We'll have no help from any ships," Ollie went on. "There'll be two SOCs and three Catalinas equipped for night work. The Black Cats will hit them first, well out. Then it's up to us. The SOCs will try to spot for us. Any questions?"

"Sure," said George Shagg. "My seasickness is coming on again. Can I stay home?"

"Of course; all you have to do is get one of the Varsity to take your place. Now, any *questions?*"

"You sadist," Shagg grinned.

"Okay, ninety-day blunder. We'll have eleven boats out —that's only two ships apiece for us, so it'll be a breeze. The barroom code—you remember it. Enemy ships are Josephine, friendly ships are Sally. Savo Island to Esperance is Kelly's Bar."

Wakefield went on to give out patrol stations. The Ninety-

261

Seven had a hot spot between the southeast tip of Savo and Esperance beach. The main orders were to stay slow and quiet, get the fish away, make hits, and then try to ease out. Stand by in safe waters to go back and search for survivors. That was it. The officers searched deep for some joke as the meeting broke up. One or two succeeded.

The crew was grouped with Jim on the forward deck and Noble heard their talk cut sharply off as he stepped aboard.

"What's the dope, Skipper?" Jim asked.

There was no lightness in Noble's voice as he told them. No one spoke for a minute or two, and the roar of a nearby engine was startling in the silence. Eleven PTs against twenty warships. Noble didn't wonder that each man was wishing he were somewhere else.

"Well," Jim said at last. "Shouldn't be any trouble finding a target. Wind 'em up, Warder. Let's go, gang."

The men slowly went to their stations, Noble took the wheel and throttles, and his patrol mate, Dave Poker, grinned across at him in the light from the chartroom door as the Ninety-Seven's lines came in.

"Good luck, Charlie."

"Same to you, Dave."

The starboard engine churned and the stern moved out. Noble slipped the port engine into gear, and the Ninety-Seven glided astern. She came slowly about and headed down the bay.

24

No HURRY, TAKE it easy, Noble thought. He moved about the boat with a word for each member of the crew. He checked the smoke generator with Ike standing beside him. He rubbed the barrels of the forward machine guns and swapped a word with Johnson, who always seemed happy to be under way. Ding Hau was snuggled down in the after turret, and Bertram was on the 20-mm. Noble poked his head into the engine room hatch and made the circled "perfect" gesture at Warder and Radelewski. Good boys all, Noble thought.

"Skipper," Everard called to him from the cockpit. "Cactus says the condition is red."

"As usual. Hear that, boys? Watch out for planes."

Everard settled back against the corner of the cockpit after replacing the mike. He was quite calm. He felt that they would come through this night—by now he had complete confidence in Noble and Print. And afterwards—Mr. Noble, now squadron commander, had already sent in a recommendation that he be enrolled in the officers' school at Quonset. Everard knew that his qualifications, enhanced by this tour of sea duty, would make acceptance almost certain. He would move Martha and the children up to Newport and resume his old life, partially at least, and serve a proper part in the war, no doubt in Washington. More important, he could know that all his life had been enriched and given meaning by this interlude. He felt vastly more mature; he knew men now; he had lived with them and found solid goodness in them, values quite apart from social standing, education, or wealth. He warmed at the thought. The friendship he had for the men of this crew would always have a special meaning no other friendships would equal. Even Ski concealed beneath his cynical coarseness a strangely solid integrity. When the war was over, then Everard would be fully ready to return to the world of the mind, having known both worlds. He was almost happy now.

Within an hour, the boat was on station. To the northwest the stars blinked slowly out as clouds rose into the sky, and the usual night-thunder was barely heard above the engines. Lightning flickered behind the clouds. The Ninety-Seven took up the patrol. The light breeze drifted spray back to the cockpit, and to starboard Prep Dave was barely visible as she moved in company. Back and forth the Ninety-Seven went, between Savo and the scarred white beach of Esperance. In this little stretch of water, Noble knew, perhaps fifty thousand men had died in less than six months.

At 10:30 a fragment of voice broke through the continual static on the radio.

". . . Black Cats . . . there they are . . . Flock of 'em. Going in."

Everard leaped for the radio and turned it high. Silence, except for the frying of static.

Then: "All ships and stations. Enemy sighted. About twenty ships. Speed thirty, course one two five. Have attacked. Position twenty-five miles northwest of Savo."

"Well," Noble said, his voice strained. "That puts the lid on it. They'll be here by eleven-thirty. Jim, watch speed so that we'll be just off Savo at that time."

Josiah Hill spoke up suddenly.

"Look over there above Esperance. High up on the mountain."

In the blackness, three steady lights were shining, sending a message. At the sound of airplane engines, Noble brought the propellers to a stop, while two planes droned low overhead, searching. Noble could see the double floats that marked them as Jap Zeros, not SOCs. The phosphorescence was unusually bright tonight; even with hardly any way on, the boat's wake was still dimly visible. The men at the guns followed the planes across the sky. No one spoke. A low mutter of thunder rolled down from the northwest.

As if at a signal, every man looked that way. Savo was a blur; stars were gone. No one spoke as thunder muttered again. Double storm was about to break. Not even starlight pierced the waters of Ironbottomed Bay.

Josiah Hill touched Noble's shoulder.

"There they are, Skipper."

Noble looked to see a number of shadows moving over the dim line between sea and sky on the starboard bow.

"Come right," Noble said calmly. "Jim, you fire them." The bow came to starboard as he picked up the mike and spoke into it. "From Prep Charlie. Josephine in Kelly's Bar. About ten of them." He hesitated. "Luck, boys. Over."

He had scarcely finished speaking when another voice broke in. "Josephine! Coming around the north side of Savo; two destroyers!"

Ding Hau's strained voice: "Skipper. Behind us, this side of Savo. Some more of 'em!"

"Jesus Christ!" whispered Jim Print, prayerfully. The Ninety-Seven was completely surrounded, but she moved steadily on toward the middle column, doubtless the troop carriers heading for Esperance. The world seemed suspended in eternity as the range closed. Noble's knees were weak and his stomach was heavy and cold, his hands so wet that the heavy glasses nearly slipped from them. He fought to keep his voice steady.

265

"Speed up a little, Jim. We want a good bow position; we've got to make them good."

The pulse of the engines stepped up slightly. The range narrowed. Seven hundred yards . . . Six hundred yards. . . . The greenish-white wave at the bow of the leading destroyer was plainly visible. Noble sat stiffly on his little seat high on the cockpit bulkhead, above the armor. His legs shook. Five hundred yards. Johnson sighed in the forward turret, plainly heard in the silence.

"Fire torpedoes when you're on, Jim," Noble said. Four hundred yards was plenty close enough.

"Three and four—Fire!" The boat lurched as the torpedoes flung up spray and vanished, trailing green, underwater wakes. "One and two—Fire!" The other two fish hit the water. Some excess oil in the starboard tube flared up like a torch. Noble groaned at the sudden illumination. The boat turned abruptly about, the engines moved up the scale, and the wake rose and spread. Red flares mushroomed from the leading enemy ships and shells rumbled overhead. Searchlights came on. The engineers opened the mufflers, Jim shoved the throttles forward, and the Ninety-Seven tore through the exploding water at full speed. The bow climbed and wet spray shot back on Noble. He noticed his sleeves were still rolled up and thought of the hell Ollie would raise about that. Looking back he saw the leading Jap ship explode in a tower of fire.

Shells landed near the bow, and the PT pitched. Noble whipped out his forty-five and fired two shots—the smoke signal. Ike had been waiting and the smoke arose instantly in a billowing jet. The boat turned and leaped. Shells burst on the starboard bow, cracking fragments through the air and dazzling Noble.

"Left! Left!" Noble shouted. The world turned to glaring flame. It was hot, and the sulphur was thick. The bow dropped, flame and fragments flew, and Noble heard himself crying, "Oh, Jesus Christ! We're hit!" And then it was black fog, and piercing the black came a terrible scream, "Oh, my God! I'm hurt! Help! Help!" Blackness - - - - - - -

Print pushed himself from the cockpit bulkhead. The boat was burning. In the light of the flames he saw Charlie Noble lying on his back, motionless, his face relaxed; the flames leaking through the deck planking licked at his bare right arm. Josiah Hill lay across his legs; the top of Hill's head was gone. Another body—the cook Bertram Pollock—was lying by the 20-mm. A groan pierced Print; he saw Everard sitting and holding onto a leg that ended at the ankle.

"We've got to get out of here," Print tried to tell himself. There was a cry astern, "Skipper! Skipper!"

Dark forms and pale faces came to him in the firelight. He didn't try to identify them; at any second the tanks would explode. Weeping, Sterns stooped and rolled Hill off the Skipper's legs and moved the bare arm out of the narrow flames.

"They're done," Jim said, hurry tearing at him. "Let's go. Grab Everard."

Holding the radioman among them, the little group of men staggered across the deck and plunged into the water.

- - - - - - - the black fog lifted. Noble opened his eyes to find himself alone in the cockpit, flames leaping about him. He was standing. He tried to walk, his one thought to escape this terrible heat that was devouring him. He couldn't walk; his knees buckled and he crawled on hands and knees through a wall of flame and over a deck where fire oozed through the seams. He thought of the thousand gallons of hundred-octane gas beneath him. It might let go at any moment. At last he was at the edge of the deck. With his last strength, he heaved himself over and down into welcoming blackness.

The cool, cool water, delicious, unbelievable in its coolness, closed over him. He thought crazily—that's my last ride in a PT boat.

His life jacket dragged him to the surface. His hands and face were numb, but he felt no pain. The Ninety-Seven was a hundred yards away, barely moving now. Her stern was toward Noble, with the generator still smoking, and it looked so solid and undamaged that he felt foolish for having leaped off, and thought of swimming after her. Then the PT swung around, and he saw the length of the deck covered with flames, and the shattered side.

The steel helmet was heavy on his head. He reached up his hands to unbuckle the strap, but to his amazement his fingers wouldn't work, and agony shot through them when they touched the rough canvas of the strap. He vainly tried to take the heavy seven-fifty binoculars from around his neck. He tried to unbuckle the pistol belt, but pain forced him to stop. Light from the burning boat was all around him, and he held his hands above the water. They were swollen and dark; and long strips, white in the firelight, hung from his hands and arms; the air started to burn, and he slid his hands back beneath the surface.

"I'm burned," Noble told himself. "I'm burned bad as hell!"

His face, too, was burning. He dipped it into the water and the burning lessened. He was numbed by shock; he felt no great pain now, and at that moment fear seemed a muffled and useless thing.

A shape drew near; red flashes burst from it and Noble heard the sharp rattle of machine-gun fire. A flurry of splashes rose from the water a few feet away. More flashes and more little spouts. He was mildly interested. He heard Jim shout somewhere.

"Get the hell outa here, boys. They're shooting at us!"

A dulled panic filled Noble. He tried to swim. No use. He could barely move his arms. Resignation overtook him again. The firing continued spasmodically for a while, then stopped, as the shape vanished into the night. The flames from the

Ninety-Seven were dying down, but as Noble looked about the bay, he could see five other fires glowing.

His helmet was growing heavier. With an effort, Noble could stay on his back with his face clear of the water; then he'd roll over frontward and water would close over his mouth and nose. He would lie gathering strength and then thrust his head back. Soon the unceasing weight would push it slowly beneath the surface. This seemed to go on forever.

Noble heard Jim crying out the names of the crew, and he listened to the answers. At last Jim shouted, "That you, Skipper?" and he summoned strength to answer.

"I'm all right. A little scorched, but still kicking. Everybody accounted for?"

"Everybody except Hill and Pollock. The shell got them. Christ, Charlie, we thought you were gone. Everard is hurt awful bad. I've got a tourniquet on him, and I've given him morphine so he's out now. Some of the other boys are cut up a little. Nobody else seems bad."

Weariness flooded over Noble; waves slapped at his face. He rolled over on his back again and achieved some sort of stability. Then the fierce scene of burning ships faded away.

John Everard opened his eyes. The salt water was cool on his face. Swimming in Long Island Sound at night was fun but where was the moon? It had been shining over Westport when he and Martha had gone down to the beach, undressed and waded out naked. God, Martha was beautiful in the moonlight, her blonde hair glowing but seeming darker than in daylight. . . . Pain shot through him, a terrible weight seemed to be hanging from his right leg. But he was still in the water.

"What?" he faltered, unable to say more. This weakness; why was he unable to move his arms and legs?

"John," Print said, hand on his shoulder. "It's all right, you're going to be all right."

"Ahhh," Everard sighed. He remembered, he remembered. The PT going in after the enemy, the red-hot flash, and then . . . nothing until now. But why did his right foot hurt so badly?

"My foot," he said. "My right foot. It hurts."

"All right, John. We'll fix it. Warder, hold his arm up. I'll give him another syrette."

Something pricked Everard's arm. In a little while his foot stopped hurting and he went to sleep. He was smiling. He'd heard Ski's voice and Ike's, Floyd's, Ding Hau's. They were with him, all around him. His friends were with him. Thank you, God, he said. It is wonderful to have friends like this.

Jim Print was scared. Christ, he was scared. He'd gotten his belt around Everard's leg and twisted it tight, but now the damned sharks were about, drawn by the blood. Print's legs were dangling in the dark water—at any minute a shark might take one from his body. But Print could not leave Everard to be eaten alive by sharks. He could not.

Everard groaned and flinched. Print forced his hand to the radioman's leg and followed it down. With a horrible shock he touched something rough, slick, cold. A shark! Print shouted and kicked, felt his foot come into contact with something. He dragged out his forty-five, held it above the surface long enough for the water to drain from the barrel, and fired into the water three times. The shark went away, but phosphorescent circles in the water showed it hadn't gone far. The PT men were in a closed, arm-locked circle about Everard. A shark coming in to him must encounter them. So they would stay. They had to stay.

Noble came to again, choking. He was very low in his life jacket; the ties had loosened and he was slipping out of it. His eyes were hard to open, they were swelling so badly. He

270

saw a gleam of cold light making a circle in the water beneath him. A shark! He choked back a panic and raised his voice; he was surprised at its strength:

"Oh, boys. Where are you?"

A hail came back. "Over here, Skipper. Are you all right?"

"I'm afraid not. My hands are burned and I can't get my helmet off, or tighten my life-jacket ties. I'll be out of it pretty soon. Can a couple of you swim over here and lend me a hand?"

"Hang on, Skipper. We'll be with you. Keep yelling so we'll be able to find you."

Noble continued to yell and the friendly, anxious voices came closer. Just when he thought he couldn't hold up his head another minute, two men came out of the darkness and grabbed his life jacket. They tore off the helmet, unbuckled the belt, and let it and the glasses sink into the water. As someone pulled at Noble, the belt fell away. Morphine gone. The hands retied Noble's life jacket, turned him on his back, and started towing him toward Savo. From their voices, Noble knew they were Sterns and Ding Hau.

"That was just in time, boys," he said.

"You shoulda yelled sooner, Skipper. How are you?"

"Not so hot, boys. You haven't got something you can hit me over the head with, have you? I guess we let the morphine go with the belt."

"God, I'm sorry, Skipper. I never thought. Mr. Print used up all of his on Everard."

"It's all right."

"We've got a little water. Have a drink?"

Noble hadn't fully realized his thirst until he had emptied the light canteen. It brought new life, but still his eyes were hard to open. He could only force the lids apart for a moment, then a heavy weight forced them shut again. He heard concussions in his ears. Sterns was firing his forty-five into the water to scare away sharks. Noble was burning up. Thirst grew unbearable. But there was no water. That was mockery.

271

No water to drink, but cool water lapped his chin. He had to struggle hard to refrain from opening his burning lips and letting the coolness pour down his throat.

He must have blacked out; Sterns was shaking him gently. "Skipper, we've found a floating coconut and I've got it open. Here, open your mouth."

Gasping, Noble threw back his head and felt the rough bark of the nut on his lips. He drank deep of nectar. He opened his eyes and murmured broken thanks.

Hours crawled by. A thin sliver of moon rose above the waters. Then one of the PTs searching for survivors came close enough for Noble to hear its engines. Sterns and Ding Hau shouted wildly, cursing their empty forty-fives, but the boat moved on into the dark. He passed out.

Noble forced his eyes open. Dawn covered Ironbottomed Bay. It was like waking from nightmare—to find nightmare. But it was wonderful to be able to see again through the narrow slits of his lids. Now nothing hurt much, and nothing seemed worth worrying about. Kathleen was in quite another world; he sank into a half stupor. The water was cold, but it soothed his burns and made them bearable. He longed for water to drink. Even more he longed for something solid beneath his body, something to lie down on, to go to sleep on, something between him and the waiting sharks.

"Where are we, boys?"

"Just about where we were, Skipper. This tide is pretty strong, and we haven't made much headway."

Even in his lassitude Noble could realize something of the devotion and unselfishness these two men had displayed. They could have let him go hours ago, and perhaps have been ashore on Savo by now. But they had fought on all through the dark hours of the night to give him a chance for life. He only hoped that someday he could tell them how he felt about it.

The sun had turned the water to gold when Ding Hau cried, "Here comes a PT. She's heading our way. Everybody splash and yell."

Ike and Ding Hau yelled and kicked. Noble threshed his feet in the water, surprised at the strength hope had given him. There were a few moments of unbearable suspense, then Ike said, "They see us, Skipper. They're heading for us. You don't have to splash any more, Charlie. We'll be out of this in a few minutes."

This was too much for Noble. When he opened his eyes again, the side of a PT towered above him. Its height above the water was surprising. Noble could have kissed the hull. He felt lines beneath his shoulders and knees, and he was lifted slowly into the air, out of the water that seemed to hold on with clutching fingers. And then the blessed dryness, the solidness of the sun-warmed deck that was so protectingly beneath him. He sighed, and carefully relaxed the control which he had held through all the dark hours, lest he scream and cry and grow mad with fear. He opened his eyes. A ring of familiar faces hung over him, Ollie's among them. Noble managed a smile with lips that felt huge and stiff.

"Good morning, boys. Thanks a lot. Got any water?"

A canteen was held gently to his lips, and he forgot everything as the wonderful water poured down his throat. He didn't stop drinking until he had emptied the canteen.

"How are you, Charlie? Somebody get some morphine. God, I'm sorry this happened to you."

The emotion in Ollie's voice made Noble want to cry. He thought with longing of the morphine and sleep. But two of his boys had been killed. He didn't know whether anyone else had seen that Jap explode, and he wanted Hill and Pollock at least to have the credit of having taken some Japs with them.

"Wait until I report," Noble said with an effort. The air was making his burned body hurt now. "I don't feel too

273

bad," he said. "It's just as if somebody heavy as hell was sitting on top of me."

"Okay, Charlie, take it easy. Here's Jake's boat now; he's got Doc LaSalle aboard, and you can make your report while he's fixing you up."

Noble's next impression was of the kind face of Doc LaSalle bending over him, lips grim under the Groucho mustache, and Doc saying, "Hello, Charlie old boy. How're you feeling?"

Noble remembered giving his report to someone, slowly and painfully, while someone else worked over him, putting cooling things on his arms and hands and face.

Ike Sterns knelt over Noble. He paid no attention to the people around as he looked down at his skipper with compassion and horror. Noble's face was big and round as a balloon, his burned lips, like large, half-risen red rolls around his mouth, moved feebly as he spoke. The arms were flat on the deck; the doc was snipping off the skin strips.

"Christ!" somebody muttered. "How can he do it?"

Ike could have told him that anyone who survived a night in the water of Ironbottomed Bay could do anything he had to. Ike was crying as he looked down at Noble. One of the skipper's hands moved on the deck.

"Where's Ike?" Noble whispered. Doc LaSalle got the needle ready. "Where's Ding Hau?"

"Right here, Skipper," Ike said. "We're right here."

"Thanks, Ike. Say hello to Jim and the boys for me." The needle sank home. The voice wavered. "Old Ninety-Seven . . . good boat."

The caricatures of eyes closed, and the skipper sighed and relaxed.

Noble awoke again to darkness. Someone was pulling at his left hand, hurting it like hell.

'What?" he said, not making more than a whisper.

"It's your Academy ring, Lieutenant," a strange voice said.

"We've got to cut it off or you'll get gangrene in that hand. Just a minute now. We've nearly got it sawed in two."

"Ah, give me the pieces," he murmured. ". . . want to keep it with me."

"We'll hang it around your neck, Lieutenant."

Memorial Hall and the ring dance; the famous orchestra moaning from the dais, water from the seven seas in compass binnacles, and Judy—God, wonder where Judy is now—dipping the ring in the water on a blue-and-gold ribbon. Then dancing through the six-foot ring, pausing under it to have Judy slip the red and gold on his finger, and then to kiss under the ring.

"Okay," he murmured.

Consciousness again. He jerked on the cot. Bombs were falling close by. Their concussions ripped through him, shook him, reduced him to jellied fear. This wasn't fair! Kings X, Kings X, he cried out mentally. Then he become conscious of other things. He was above ground in a tent—he could hear the canvas flapping and shaking in the blasts. From his side came voices. "Little joe . . . Crap out you sonofabitch. Snake eyes, Mac, snake eyes. Gimme them bones." A crap game. Then Noble knew. Air raid on Guadalcanal and the seriously wonded couldn't be carried underground. The crap shooters beside him were hospital corpsmen who would not leave the wounded to die alone. Noble knew that these men couldn't help him if a bomb hit the tent, they could only die with him. But they would not let him die alone.

"Hit them a lick for me," he murmured.

"This guy's awake. How you coming, Mac?"

"Fine. How about a drink?"

The end of a glass tube eased gently through the small part of Noble's lips he could open. He drank. Darkness came back.

Someone was near him. Greyness dissolved and he felt hot pain in his arm.

"The doctor," a voice said. "Lie still, Lieutenant. Through in a jiffy here."

275

"Doc," Noble said weakly. "How soon will I go back to the . . . squadron?"

"Not for a long time. You're going back to the States. The war's over for you for a while, son. You're leaving here on a plane in an hour."

Rising and falling. Cool air. Roar of motors that vibrated inside Noble. "Wind 'em up, Warder. . . . Oh, hell, gang, let's roll. Wind 'em up, Ski."

Again someone was beside him.

"PT?" Noble muttered. "Get . . . under . . . way . . ."

"You're on a plane, Lieutenant," a voice said. It shot thrills through him, for it was a woman's voice.

"A girl!" Noble said in the roaring darkness.

"Yes. I'm a Navy nurse."

He was more awake now. "What color's your hair?" he asked.

"Black," the voice answered. "Shh. You're weak. Don't talk."

"Hold my hand," Noble said, wanting to touch her, to knew she was real.

"Oh . . . Lieutenant—I can't. They're all bandaged. So is your face."

"What color are your eyes?"

"Green. Now, hush."

"You've got a wonderful voice."

"We'll be in Efate in an hour, and they'll make you good as new there."

"Yes . . . I . . . I've got a girl, Miss. . . . She's waiting for me." Yes. Waiting for him. Kathleen with brown hair and hazel eyes; she had a wonderful voice, too.

"I'm glad, Lieutenant. Now why don't you go to sleep?"

Sleep, Noble thought. Yes. Sleep. Home soon, Kathleen would still love him, no matter if his hands and face were scarred and twisted. Her sweetness, her kindness. Kathleen was waiting for him. He was going to her. In one night that had lasted an eternity he had gone through hell, and surely God didn't demand that sinners suffer two hells. He had expiated his sins; he had gone through fire. Poor Daggs, gone and finished. Long ago Noble had felt only compassion for the big, really sad man. Now Noble had paid, he had had his hell. Kathleen was waiting. He could make her happy. They would buy the little cottage . . . they would be together forever.

"Yes," Noble said. "I'll go to sleep."

He no longer fought the gathering darkness. The dark was like velvet; and it came slowly down and lifted him up, and as it did so he wondered why the voice beside him was sobbing.

25

Jim Print was sitting on the steps of the hut in which he and Charlie Noble had lived. Beside him, and on the steps below, sat the remnants of the Old Ninety-Seven's crew—Johnson, Floyd, Sterns, Ski, Ding Hau, and Warder. They were still waiting for the final dissolution of an entity that had been their whole existence. Print knew they felt lost. They were no longer the Ninety-Seven boat—just survivors.

"I reckon it's over," Sterns said, looking up at the blue sky and the bright sun.

This was February 4. The Japs had finished evacuating what was left of their army on Guadalcanal, and Ironbottomed Bay was silent and peaceful, glinting in the sun.

"Yes," Jim Print said.

They were silent. Jim was remembering the morning they had come back, two days before. The flag over Sesapi had been at half mast, and a solemn silence had hung over the base. Three boats lost and twenty men dead. Even the thought of relief and New Zealand could not, at that moment, bring much pleasure. Jim, who had been on Dave Poker's boat, stumbled ashore and found Sterns on the dock. "God, the skipper's bad hurt," Ike had said. "They've already evacuated him. He's burned all to hell."

Jim had made his report, and then, feeling a need to be with the men who had accompanied him into Ironbottomed Bay the night before, he had hunted them up. Their eyes had brightened at sight of him. Doc LaSalle, furious and bitter, had come ashore with his khaki sleeves rust-brown with dried blood. He had broken out the whiskey; dazed and numb, the men drank it, afterward dropping off into a heavy sleep. The next day they had said nothing, done little. Now they sat here, feeling the first slight return of life.

"Look," Radelewski said. "There's the Doc." A note of adoration had crept into Ski's voice. "Where's he going to?"

Dr. LaSalle's stocky figure came toward them from the dock. Jim watched him. He turned right, toward the sick bay. In a moment he reappeared, carrying a quart bottle in each hand. This time he came straight toward the hut.

"The hell," Ike said wonderingly. "Haven't we had our nerve medicine?"

"Don't say nothing!" Radelewski hissed quickly. "Maybe he's forgot."

Dr. LaSalle came up to the waiting group.

"Boys," he said, "I brought you a present. And your boy Everard is going to be all right. Hell, a foot is nothing; you can even play tennis with an artificial foot."

"Jeez!" Radelewski said, reaching for a bottle. "That's swell, Doc!"

He hastily opened it and took a deep drink. Floyd handed Print the other bottle, and the latter opened it. The doc sat tiredly on the steps.

"I'm mighty glad about Everard," Jim said. "You look beat, Doc. Care to join us?"

"Don't mind if I do," Doc said. He drank, and started to hand the bottle to Print, but the latter gestured to Warder.

"Are we still under treatment, Doc?" Jim asked.

"For that little swimming party of yours the other night —no. This is for something else."

"What's that?" Jim asked.

"Well . . . I don't know how to tell you this. But your skipper—Charlie Noble—died on the way to Efate. I just got the word."

Jim Print sat stunned on the steps. The sun was blinding his eyes.

"Charlie?" he said quietly.

"Yes. On the hospital plane." Doc's slow anger broke. "Goddammit to hell! I hoped they could save that boy." He got up and walked furiously away.

Not a man moved his eyes from the doc until he was out of sight. Then Jim looked down at the crew. Ike Sterns had placed a bottle on the step beside him.

"Hell," Sterns said gently. "Oh, hell!" He picked up the bottle and drank.

"He was a good skipper," Ding Hau said solemnly. "There ain't so many."

Radelewski spoke up harshly. "Hell, just another Academy bastard. They're plenty of 'em left."

Ike Sterns half rose; Jim did too. Then he saw Sterns sit down again, heavily. Radelewski had turned his face away from Sterns, and Print saw the tears on his cheeks. Radelewski blew his nose.

"How about the goddamn bottle?" he said fiercely. "You blanking hogs!"

Over on Sesapi a PT motor roared to life. It purred, then advanced with testing throttles to a piercing, shaking roar. The wind blew in from the west. The shadows of the palm fronds moved on the ground. Another PT engine joined in with the first; they roared together in unison. Beyond Sesapi and the roaring PTs, Savo stood in the blue water, looking over to the white mark of Cape Esperance across the sparkling surface of Ironbottomed Bay.

Author's Note

The participant in historical action who wishes to write a novel based on such action faces a special problem. Most characters in fiction are images of reality—tags and bits of people the author has known, encountered. Officers and men who were with me at Guadalcanal may find their own accomplishments here attributed to my fictional characters. They must not be deceived. The men who move and talk in THE SLOT *are purely creatures of my imagination. The officers and men of my own boat, the PT 111, must not imagine that they find themselves portrayed as the men of the Ninety-Seven.*

One character may require special mention. Commander Daggs is purely a result of the novelist's need to have an opposition, a source of conflict, more personalized than the enemy met in darkness. Daggs carries no part of any man I have ever met. The PT officers and men with whom I served were good men, and I number all of them among my friends today.

For me this book has been the reliving of an experience. My hope is that in reading it, PT men will find themselves living those days again, and that readers who were not in the boats may get some faint idea of what it was like to ride in, live in, fight in, and come to disaster in the motor torpedo boats of World War II. These days are dead. We hated them then, we would not have them come again; but after fifteen years may we not look back at them for a few hours and say —Those were days that counted in our lives.

Middlebury, Vermont.

Made in the USA
Middletown, DE
24 September 2023

39254612R00175